Can't Fight This
Feeling

Kelly
Hunter

Kat
Cantrell

Jules
Bennett

MILLS & BOON

CONTENTS

Return Of The
Outback Billionaire
Kelly Hunter

Kelly Hunter has always had a weakness for fairy tales, fantasy worlds and losing herself in a good book. She has two children, avoids cooking and cleaning and, despite the best efforts of her family, is no sports fan. Kelly is, however, a keen gardener and has a fondness for roses. Kelly was born in Australia and has traveled extensively. Although she enjoys living and working in different parts of the world, she still calls Australia home.

Books by Kelly Hunter

Harlequin Modern

Claimed by a King

Shock Heir for the Crown Prince
Convenient Bride for the King
Untouched Queen by Royal Command
Pregnant in the King's Palace

Visit the Author Profile page
at millsandboon.com.au for more titles.

Some rise by sin, and some by virtue fall.

—William Shakespeare, *Measure for Measure*

PROLOGUE

THE RED RIVER GUM floorboards in the ballroom gleamed with the shine of fresh beeswax polish and the soft glow cast by dozens of antique wall sconces. Every set of doors along the generous expanse of wall to the west stood open to the veranda beyond, even if doing so would provide scant protection from the night moths drawn towards the light. The rest of the homestead at the heart of Jeddah Creek station had been dusted, buffed and made to look like the expensive Victorian-era folly it was. Whoever had thought to bring white wrought-iron features and open verandas into the middle of a red desert landscape bloated with dust, drought and a fiercely relentless sun had been quite mad. That or English and dreaming of the world they'd left behind.

Judah Blake often wondered how long it had taken his English ancestors to realise people dreamed so very differently here.

He'd been back a little over a week, and if he still found going through an open door or eating whatever he felt like whenever he felt like it a challenge, he liked to think he kept those challenges to himself. He'd been born and raised on Jeddah Creek station; he knew this harsh land and all its wonders. He'd conquer being back here soon enough.

His eighteen-year-old brother, Reid, had been the one to suggest some kind of party to celebrate Judah's return. Judah had been the one to turn his brother's modest suggestion into a society ball. He'd needed to know just how much damage his imprisonment had done to his family's standing, and what better way than to send out invitations to a big charity ball and see who showed up?

He'd spared no expense—no one would ever complain of his hospitality. Whatever a guest wanted to drink, they would find it here. The food had been flown in alongside catering staff and musicians. A small army of cleaners, tradesmen and a couple of event co-ordinators had spent the week preparing the homestead to receive guests. Stock hands had spent days setting out a parking area for all the private planes and helicopters those guests would arrive in. Not all the guests would be wealthy. Some would arrive in little outback helicopters more suited to mustering cattle than providing luxury transport. Some would bring the family Cessna, the outback equivalent of a family car. Jeddah Creek station ran straight across the border between Queensland and the Northern Territory and was a nightmare to get to by road.

And yet, out of the several hundred invitations he'd sent out at short notice, only a handful had been declined.

He could blame some of that willingness to accommodate him on his family name. His father had been a member of the English aristocracy—a lowly baron who had married the daughter of a viscount and fled to Australia to escape the sanctimonious superiority of her relatives. But his parents were dead, one after the other, these past six months, and Judah was *the* Blake now, with all the fealty it entailed.

He could blame some of the attendance on the fact that he'd been blessed with a handsome face, wasn't yet thirty, and wasn't yet married. And he was rich—Old Money rich, even if his recently deceased father had burned through most of it. He also had thirty billion dollars' worth of New Money, courtesy of two cryptocurrency investments he'd made at just the right time.

He'd tried to keep that windfall quiet, but in the rarefied world of one-percenters there were always some who made it their business to know which way the money flowed.

And that, above all, was why so many people had chosen to show their faces here tonight. With thirty billion dollars sitting in his back pocket, it apparently really *was* going to be that easy for the same people who'd ignored him for more than seven years to step up now, forgive him his sins and welcome him back into the fold.

Amazing how many of them had already been in contact on account of investment possibilities that might be of interest to him. Good causes, all. Could only help him restore his tarnished reputation, they'd implied, and he'd smiled fierce and flat and told them he looked forward to catching up with them soon.

They had no idea what kind of man he'd become. *He* had no idea what kind of man he would be now that he was out and blessed with more wealth than he knew what to do with and so many open doors.

All he knew was that he wanted everything back the way it was. His parents alive. His soul not yet stained by what it took to get along in a cage, but it was too late for that. Nor was he ever likely to will his parents back to life.

Retrieving the parts of Jeddah Creek station his father had sold off, though…that was something he *could* set right. His birthright and his solace. *His* land, not Bridie Starr's.

'Don't do anything rash once you get out,' the visiting psych expert had said in the days before his release.

As if Judah hadn't spent the past seven years and then some learning to control his every thought and feeling.

'Avoid split-second decisions.'

Guess the doc had never had an inmate with a shiv heading towards him, fast and furtive.

'Give yourself time to adjust.'

This sounded like halfway good advice.

'Your reading of people will be off. Give others the benefit of the doubt.'

Like hell he would.

Bridie Starr had taken temporary possession of land that belonged to him and the fix was very simple—nothing rash about it.

He wanted it back.

CHAPTER ONE

'DO YOU KNOW what you're going to wear?'

'I haven't decided yet.' Bridie Starr stared despondently at the lemon meringue pie Gert had whipped up seemingly out of nowhere and wondered, not for the first time, where the other woman had learned to cook. Not around here, that was for sure. Here being the channel country of central Australia, and far, far away from any kind of crowd. Bridie had been born and raised here on Devil's Kiss station. Gert hailed from Barcoo, a few hundred kilometres to the south. Neither place tended to grow master chefs.

Gert arrived at Bridie's homestead for three days every fortnight and made the place bright with beeswax, laughter, shared cooking and conversation, before heading next door to Jeddah Creek station to do the same for the Blakes. A two-day stint with the Conrads to the north, and then Gert would return to her home and set up to make the trip all over again.

Gert was the glue that kept people around here connected.

'I'm not sure I even want to go to the Blakes' ball,' Bridie confessed.

'Can't say I'm surprised.'

And why should she be? Bridie's shut-in tendencies weren't exactly a secret.

'But you have to go,' the older woman continued briskly. 'People will be looking to you to see what you'll do now that Judah's back. It'd be cruel to act as if you're scared of him.'

'I'm not scared of him.' And she didn't want to be cruel. 'It's just…why did he have to go and throw a society ball, of all things? Out here?'

Gert's thin lips stretched into a smile. 'Used to be a time when fancy balls were all the rage at Jeddah Creek station, you're just too young to remember them. They put on at least one a season and all the fancy types would be there. The things we got up to…' The older woman sounded positively wistful. 'Your mother loved them. She and your father used to dance all night long, and they were good at it.'

Bridie's mother had left the world not long after Bridie had set foot in it. Gert was the only person who ever talked freely about her.

Her father never spoke of his wife at all.

Okay, so her mother had loved dancing and balls. Maybe Bridie could learn to love them too. She'd already RSVP'd that she and her father would be there. No way could they stay away after everything Judah had done for her. And she had to be presentable, which wouldn't be hard, what with a closet full of rarely worn designer clothes at her fingertips, all of them tailored just for her. Granted, they were half a dozen years out of date, but haute couture never really dated. All the age of a piece did was show other people for how long someone had been obscenely wealthy.

Bridie didn't consider her wealth obscene, but once upon a time she'd modelled such clothes and sometimes she'd been allowed to keep them. She'd been a rising star with the face of an angel and a body on the cusp of womanhood. She'd had absolutely no clue about the predators roaming the glittering, crazy world of high-fashion modelling.

Her awakening had been a hard one.

'What did people used to wear to these balls? Full formal?'
'Absolutely.'

'Breast medals and sashes and things? Gloves for the women?'

'No to the medals and sashes, yes to the family rings and jewels, sometimes gloves,' answered Gert. 'Landed gentry and all that. Sometimes it's subtle, but it does show.'

Bridie blew out a frustrated breath as she tried to mentally turn Judah next door into Lord Judah Blake, peer of the realm, bona fide English aristocracy. 'Right, then. Gown time. She pushed a hand through the thick waves of summer-wheat-coloured hair, liberally sprinkled with darker shades of brown, and vowed yet again to get a proper haircut before the ball.

'He phoned this morning wanting to speak to you.'

'Judah?' She'd been dodging his calls all week.

'So ring him back.'

She nodded, knowing full well that returning his call would take more guts than she had. At least at the ball they'd be surrounded by people and the conversation wouldn't get too personal too fast. Ease into things slowly was her motto.

'You're not going to call him back, are you?' stated Gert flatly.

'No. But I will be at the ball, dressed to impress, and I *will* speak with him then and welcome him home and shower him with gratitude and whatever else I need to do. Trust me, Gert, I have a plan.'

'Good girl,' soothed the older woman. 'Have some pie.'

Something was up. Gert never let anyone at the lemon meringue pie before it was cool, but she cut Bridie a slice and watched with barely contained disapproval as the warm filling oozed all over the plate.

'Now.' The older woman's steely gaze could have skewered a razorback at a hundred paces. 'Let's get this sorted, sweet petal.'

Sweet petal... Oh, this was bad. Worse than when Bridie

had used the giant Limoges vase that used to sit at the end of the hallway as a frisbee target...and nailed it.

'What are you going to wear?'

Judah watched from his vantage point at one end of the ground-floor veranda as his guests spilled out of the crowded ballroom and into the night to speak in glowing terms of the landscape they'd flown over to get here and the beauty of the old two-storey Victorian house in the middle of nowhere.

Jeddah Creek station, what a magnificent place.'

'Judah, you're looking so well.'

And for the truly brave, *'I miss your parents and I'm sorry for your loss.'*

His brother was somewhere inside, ten years younger and almost a stranger. Reid had been running Jeddah Creek in the four-month gap between their father passing and Judah getting home, and he'd done a good job.

The boy—man—had a strong network of school friends, all freshly graduated and most of them taking a break year before stepping into whatever their families had planned for them. Plenty of Reid's friends were here tonight and he hoped to hell they could hold their liquor because he wasn't exactly polic-ing them. Maybe he should have a word with the exorbitantly priced bar staff the event co-ordinators had insisted on hiring. Let them know that monitoring the alcohol intake of his guests, young and old, was their job, not his.

And then Reid stepped into place at his side, his blue eyes bright and searching.

'She's not here yet. She promised she'd come,' said Reid by way of greeting.

'Who?'

'Bridie.'

There was only one Bridie in Judah's universe and he'd been trying to set up a meeting with her for days. So far, she hadn't even had the courtesy to return his calls. 'Maybe she had a pressing engagement elsewhere.'

'Not Bridie. She's practically a shut-in. Wouldn't leave Devil's Kiss station for years after the incident, and even now she has to work her way up to going out.'

'Then perhaps she's working her way up to it.' The thought of Bridie not making the most of her freedom didn't sit well with him. Stubborn tendrils of anger flickered to life inside him. He'd sacrificed his freedom in service to her. The least she could have done was make the most of her opportunities.

'I know she was worried about how everyone might gossip about her and you,' continued Reid. 'She wasn't looking forward to that part.'

Boo-hoo.

'She's a photographer now,' Reid said next.

He knew.

'Landscapes mostly, of around here. I took her up in the mustering helicopter a month or so back. We ended up taking the door off and rigging up a harness so she could lean out and take aerial shots. I haven't seen them yet, but she said they turned out real good.'

They had.

Resentment curled, a low buzz in the pit of his stomach, and all because his teenage brother was what? Friends with Bridie Starr? Her confidant?

Why hadn't she returned any of his calls?

Bridie was in between him and his brother in age. Twenty-three now, no clueless girl. Would he even recognise her? Of all the photos sent to him these past seven plus years, not one had been of her.

'See that your friends don't drink too much tonight. The last thing we need is an incident.'

'I know. They know. There won't be one.'

How could his teenage brother be so very sure?

Reid seemed to read his mind, and smiled, fierce and swift

and just that little bit familiar. 'Your reputation precedes you, man. They'll behave.'

'Does it cause you trouble? My reputation?'

Reid shrugged. 'Not out here.'

'What about when you were at school?'

Another shrug. 'Saved me the trouble of being friends with fair-weather people. That's what Dad used to say.' He squinted towards the east. 'This could be them. Dunno why I expected them to come in the long way around when it's so much quicker to cut across country.'

Judah waited as the thin spiral of dust on the horizon turned into a plume, and a dusty once-white ute came into view. Hard to know what he was feeling, with his emotions locked down so tight, but now was not the time to lose the iron control he'd spent so many years developing.

So what if curiosity was killing him?

So what if the thought of her being a hermit made him seethe?

He could still use that information against her if she didn't bend to his will and sell him back his land. And why wouldn't she sell? She'd done nothing with the land she now owned. It was just sitting there waiting to be reclaimed.

By him.

After all. She owed him.

It took fifteen more minutes before Tom Starr and his daughter walked up the front steps of the homestead and stopped in front of him, and if Judah had thought Bridie astonishingly beautiful before, it was nothing compared to the looks she possessed now. She had a mouth made for crushing, wide-set eyes the colour of cognac, and hair every colour of brown he could imagine— from sun-bleached streaks of honey-gold to burnished bronze shot through with the deepest mahogany. Natural colours, all of them; her hair had been the same wild woodland riot when she was a child.

She still possessed the body of a dancer, all fine bones and elegance, and she carried herself like one too. Her slip of a dress covered her from neck to knee and was a deep twilight blue. No sleeves, no jewellery. Her only accessory was a little black purse that she clutched in front of her body with both hands, her knuckles almost white.

She could barely even look at him.

'Thank you for coming.' His rusty manners had been getting such a workout tonight.

She glanced up, startled, and he found himself enmeshed. Falling into memories he didn't want in his head, and as for allowing them to surface, no. Just no.

'Wouldn't—' She had to stop to clear her throat. 'Wouldn't have missed it. Thank you for inviting us.'

Such pretty lies.

He wanted to reach for the tension knots in his neck. He wanted to reach out and see if her hair felt as silky as it looked.

He wanted to possess this woman who had never been his, who he barely knew but for the fantasies about her that he'd woven in his head. He wanted his father back, an explanation for all the photos she'd sent him month after month, and above all he wanted to know why she'd bought into his birthright. Did she honestly believe he wouldn't be back to claim it?

But what he really wanted—needed—was time out away from her so he could claw back the composure he'd lost the moment she'd locked eyes with him. 'Reid, why don't you show Bridie where she can freshen up and then get her a drink and a plate of food?' Babysit, he might as well have said, but Reid seemed up for the role and Bridie looked grateful.

He watched them go, remembering that at sixteen she'd walked the catwalks of Paris and graced the cover of *Vogue* magazine.

It still showed.

And then he dragged his gaze away from her retreating figure and prepared to greet her father. 'Tomas.'

'Welcome home,' offered the older man. 'I'm sorry your parents aren't here to greet you.'

'So am I.' He'd never once imagined when he went away that they'd be dead before he returned. 'Maybe you can tell me what happened to my father's business acumen and why he died practically bankrupt.' And why no one had told Judah, and why Tomas had been helping Reid out on the farm in every way he could.

'You sure you want to talk about this here?' Tom Starr didn't look as if he wanted to discuss much at all. 'We could set up a meeting.'

'Been trying to set up a meeting with your daughter all week, Tom. No one's answering and I'm all out of patience.'

The older man looked puzzled. 'Why call Bridie? She doesn't know anything about your father's business dealings.'

But it hadn't been Tom Starr's name on those property deeds, it had been Bridie's. 'What happened to my father?' At least he could get some information from the older man. 'Before he died he let go of things he'd treasured all his life. Cattle bloodlines. Family jewels. *Land.*'

Judah watched as the older man seemed to age another decade before his eyes.

'Grief.' The older man swallowed hard. 'Grief and anger at the way you were treated swallowed your father whole. After you were convicted, your father drank more. So did I and more often than not we drank together. I had plenty of shame to drown and he had a son who'd protected the defenceless and paid an unfair price for it. Your father kept telling me his fancy lawyers would find grounds for appeal, and I just kept on praying it'd happen, but it never did.'

Grounds for appeal. What a joke. As for parole, that concept hadn't worked for him either.

Maybe it had something to do with his swagger.

'A couple of years back I made the mistake of telling your father I was the one who pulled the trigger,' Tom offered gruffly.

Judah stiffened. 'We had a deal. We *swore* that would stay between you and me. No one else.' They'd done it to protect Bridie. So a child would have her only parent at her side to help pick up the pieces of her life. 'You *swore*.'

A man was only as good as his word.

'I thought it would help if he knew you were a hero twice over.'

Some hero. More like a fool. 'Did it?'

'No. He turned even more bitter and twice as uncaring.'

'So who else did you tell? Does Bridie know you pulled that trigger?'

'No one. No one else knows what happened that night. I— after that I thought about it, but—no.'

Why not? He was itching for a fight and he didn't know why. Why did his father get burdened with the truth and not Bridie as well? She was an adult now, wasn't she? No longer that terrified broken child.

'Protect Bridie,' the older man offered weakly. 'She'd take it hard if she knew.'

Protect Bridie. It was the reason he'd shouldered the blame in the first place, all the way to lockup. He'd arrogantly thought his sentence wouldn't be a long one. He'd had the best lawyers money could buy and virtue on his side. He'd never dreamed he'd spend years imprisoned for his supposed sins or that both his parents would be dead before he got out. More fool him.

Protect the innocent children.

How could that be *wrong*?

'My father had hardly any money left when he died. He'd sold off land. You were his friend—or tried to be. What happened?'

'He started playing poker. It was something to do other than stew, I guess. He tried to get me interested, but I'm a lousy poker player and the buy-in was out of my league. Turns out your father wasn't much of a poker player either. I bailed him out of debt a couple of times. I took out a mortgage, but in the end I didn't have any more to give without losing Devil's Kiss. I know he got more money from somewhere, but it wasn't from me.'

There was a ring of truth to the older man's words. 'How much did you give him?'

'None of your business, lad. Give means give. I'm not asking for it back.'

'And you have no idea why your daughter's name is on some of the title deeds for Jeddah Creek station?'

Silence greeted him. A depth of shock that couldn't be feigned. 'I don't know anything about that.'

Interesting.

'Look, I can't say how Bridie got her name on those deeds,' said Tom. 'But at a guess, I'd say she bought them off your father because he had gambling debts to pay that he didn't want your mother to know about. Bridie's not worldly. She doesn't crave power or money or fame, but she does—or did—have money saved from her modelling days and inheritance money from her mother. She doesn't have friends, but she has a good heart, and she owes you, we both do, so please, when you ask her why she holds those deeds hear her out.'

'I would if she'd return my calls.' Hard to believe Tom didn't know about those.

'I know you've left messages for her. I urged her to answer you, but Bridie can take a while to commit to doing things. Fear can paralyse her. And I know people think I mollycoddle her, and maybe I do, but she didn't come back from that night ride whole, Judah, none of us did, and it's been a long road back to even halfway normal for her. She's doing her best here tonight, and she's doing it for you, so don't—'

'Don't what? Turn on her? Take my anger out on her? Why would I do that when I've spent more than seven years *helping you protect her*?'

'I was going to say judge,' the older man said wearily. 'You're angry because helping us—protecting her—has cost you too much, and I get that. God knows I can never repay you. But don't judge my daughter the way you have every right to judge me.' The other man met his gaze dead on. 'She doesn't have a deceitful bone in her body. You'll see.'

Bridie couldn't seem to stop her hands from shaking. She'd clasped them behind her back in an effort to stop the tremors, but that move exposed the boyish contours of her chest to the gaze of others and she didn't like that either. She'd tried folding her arms in front of her and wrapping her fingers around her upper arms, but that came off as utterly defensive, she knew, and that simply wouldn't do. Holding a drink of any kind was out of the question. Holding someone else's hand might have grounded her but she hadn't done that since her early childhood when she'd held her father's hand or her aunt's hand, or Gert's.

The couple standing next to her started up a conversation about the country they'd flown over to get here, and Bridie joined in, sharing a little local knowledge, and learning in turn that they were from Sydney and the parents of one of Reid's friends. She was then able to talk about Reid's flying lessons and pilot's licence and how they occasionally mustered stock these days using drones rather than helicopters. Reid could fly those too, and so could she.

In ten minutes, she made more small talk than she'd made in six months, but her hands had stopped shaking and her stance didn't feel quite so rigid. She felt almost relaxed. As if she really could mix in with an unknown group of people and do it well.

And then the string group started up and Judah took to the dance floor with a woman old enough to be his grandmother and wealthy enough to wear rings on every finger and pearls at her neck and not give a toss about whether it looked overdone.

The couple beside her took their leave and headed for the dance floor too, such courtly manners for the middle of no-where, and she wondered whether Reid was up for making a welcome home speech to his brother and whether she'd be called on to say something too. Was that the kind of welcome home she should be considering? Some grand public gesture to cement her allegiance to the man who'd saved her life?

There was no water on the drinks tray a waiter dangled in front of her so she took a champagne and wet her lips and tried not to look like a wallflower in her Givenchy dress and Jimmy Choo shoes, both of them dragged from the bowels of her wardrobe. She'd worn her hair long and had cut bangs into it just before she'd come. Bangs to frame her face and shield her eyes. Eyes she could feel widening as Judah returned his dance partner to the side of an elderly gentleman and locked gazes with her.

His lips tilted into a half-smile as he headed towards her and there was nowhere to run. He didn't ask to take the glass from her hand, he just took it and set it on a nearby table and held out his hand.

'Dance with me.'

It wasn't a question.

She took his hand, hers cold, his warm, and pretended she was back on the catwalks of Paris with all eyes upon her, assessing the clothes and the vision of a celebrated designer. She'd liked modelling beautiful clothes once upon a time. She'd loved strutting her stuff on the catwalk, fluid and assured, pretending she was a dancer or Audrey Hepburn or Coco Chanel. Pretending she was someone special. That particular flight of fantasy got her to the dance floor, small mercies, only now she had another problem as Judah turned towards her and put his palm to her waist.

'I can't waltz,' she whispered, panicked. For all that Gert said her father had been quite the dancer in his day, he'd certainly never taken the time to teach his daughter that particular skill. 'I never learned.'

'Then we'll sway from side to side like half the other couples on the floor. I don't care.' He drew her in and the scent of eucalyptus and something altogether masculine drifted with him. 'Put your hand on my upper arm.' He kept gentle hold of her other hand and she did as suggested, and his arm was warm too, beneath the fine fabric of his suit.

She squeezed just a little bit and he raised a wicked eyebrow in return. She was used to wiry men with plenty of muscle and not a lot of fat to be going on with, but Judah was built to a whole different level. 'What have they been feeding you?'

'Slop.'

He probably wasn't joking. 'Sorry, I—stupid comment. The food tonight is excellent.'

'You haven't eaten any.'

How did he know? 'Well, it looks good.'

'So do you.' Words that made his lips curl in a whole different way from before, and if that was a smile, heaven help him. 'But you already know that.'

'I do know that. I dressed up in my best because I wanted to make sure I honoured your welcome home party by looking as put together as I can.' She followed his dance lead, stepping slowly side to side, and fixed her gaze over his shoulder.

He added a slow turn to their swaying. 'I liked the photos you sent.'

One a month, every month, since he'd gone away. She felt his gaze on her face but refused to look at him. 'The first ones weren't very good.'

She could feel his shrug. 'They were to me.'

'I almost stopped sending them. You never wrote back.'

'What would you have had me say?'

And there was another question she had no answer to, but the music kept playing and their feet kept moving and maybe they didn't need to say anything. She'd shown her face and accepted his command to dance—as if she'd had a choice—and she felt as if she held lightning and thunder in her arms. Why wouldn't she feel that way? He was her ultimate protector and he'd paid mightily for taking on that role, sacrificing his freedom so she could survive hers.

'You haven't answered any of my calls,' he said.

'I…know.'

'Too busy or too afraid of me?'

Another question she didn't know how to answer without throwing every vulnerability she owned at his feet for him to tread on. She spared him a glance. Those eyes…some kind of mossy green, ringed with such a dark navy-grey around the edges. She'd always thought him fierce on account of those eyes. A force to be reckoned with and a perfect match for wild Jeddah Creek station.

He'd killed a man who'd been stalking her. Pulled her bound and shaking from the cramped, pitch-black car boot she'd been trapped in and delivered her safely into the arms of her father. He'd been locked away because of it, and she owed him her truth.

'At first I was afraid of everything and everyone. Shadows made me jump. Other people made me cringe. I could barely leave my room. And then one day my father yelled at me from the other side of my bedroom door. He said, "Judah's the one sitting in a prison room staring at the walls, Bridie, not you. How do you think he'd feel about squandering his freedom on someone who's refusing to live?"'

'Smart man, your father.'

She couldn't look away from him. 'A week later I went to the kitchen for breakfast. A few weeks after that I made it to the back door and stepped out onto the veranda. I took a picture and sent it to you.' She'd kept right on sending them. 'For seven years, six months and two days I've thought of you sacrificing your freedom for my life. It made me step out of my comfort zone and keep on walking. So, am I afraid of you? No. But I have been using you for years as a cattle prod to help me face my fears. My feelings for you are complicated.'

'I'll say,' he muttered, after a very long stretch of silence.

She had nothing more to say. Nothing to do except fidget beneath that watchful, wary gaze.

'What are you going to do now you've lost your cattle prod?'

'Do you always ask such difficult questions?'

He shrugged. 'I don't usually ask personal questions at all. Like you said, whatever is between us is complicated.'

She looked around the glittering ballroom filled with Australia's beautiful and wealthy and wondered if any of them walked with fear as a constant companion, like her. Or which of them had broken the law and paid the price, like Judah, and how hard they'd had to fight to come back from that. 'I'm glad you're back. I didn't answer your calls because I wanted to tell you in person. *Thank you* in person for saving me.'

She felt the tension in him rather than saw it. A simmering waiting quality that burned. A heavy-lidded gaze that banked hard, but not before she'd seen the sudden flame of sexual interest in his eyes. Oh, she'd seen that before, but not from him, never from him.

And she might not be afraid of him, but she *was* afraid of what could happen to a man with too much pent-up desire and not nearly enough self-control. They lost their minds and let fantasy rule. They saw only what they wanted to.

And then Judah loosened his hold and stepped back, and suddenly she could breathe again, even if her hands were too clammy and her body too hot.

'My father sold you land in the last year of his life. Yes or no?'

'Yes.' She'd been dreading this part of the conversation. 'It's complicated. The money didn't always go directly to him. Sometimes I paid bills for him instead.'

'You mean gambling debts.'

'I didn't ask. But, yes, probably.'

'I want that land back. Whatever you paid, I'll pay it. More, if that's what you want.'

'No, you don't understand.'

'Double the price you paid. I want it back.'

'Judah, you don't understand. It's not for sale. You can—'

'Everyone, if I may have your attention.' His voice rang out across the ballroom, stopping music and movement and turning all eyes towards them. His arm at her waist was a band of steel, keeping her in place, but why? What was he doing?

'First, I'd like to welcome you all here tonight. I appreciate the time and trouble so many of you have taken to get here. Welcome to Jeddah Creek station. I hope you find the hospitality and the connections you make here tonight to your liking.'

A waiter approached them with a tray full of drinks and he took one and passed it to her before collecting another for himself. 'Secondly, I'd like to introduce one particular woman to you all. A woman whose name you will have no doubt heard in connection with mine even if you haven't met her personally. A woman of rare compassion and resilience. Someone who has seen the darkest actions mankind has to offer and yet somehow manages to retain her sanity and goodness.'

He couldn't possibly be talking about her.

'Someone who inspired me to look outward rather than in, at a time when all I could see were concrete walls and prison bars. A pioneering soul, with a vision for merging two great farming families and two iconic properties to allow for more conservation projects and forward management of the land we hold so dear. Ladies and gentlemen, please raise your glasses to Bridie Starr.' He smiled down at her, all shark. 'My future wife.'

Say *what*, now?

Wife? What wife? Had he lost his mind while in prison? A little bit of insanity to accompany that very impressive, very fine physique?

'Smile,' he ordered softly, as the guests applauded, and showed her how to do it. 'People will take one look at you and think we're not serious.' He touched the rim of his glass to hers. Just that little bit lower than the rim of her glass, to be precise, and wasn't that supposed to indicate some measure of respect? 'To us.'

'What us?' she hissed behind the cover of golden bubbles. 'What exactly do you think you're doing?'

'Getting my land back.'

'By *marrying* me?' She laughed. She couldn't help it. She was still laughing as she lifted the glass to her lips and proceeded to drain it. Moments later a waiter had whisked it away and they were dancing again, her mind a whirl and her body following along behind. 'Can you be *any* more insulting?'

'You refused to sell. What did you think I would do?'

'Oh, I don't know. You could have waited two more seconds and *listened* to what I had to say. You could have easily done that, but no, straight to blackmail and coercion and *marriage*? Are you *nuts*?' She stepped in close, super aware of all the people beginning to move around them as she raised her lips to his ear. 'The only reason I bought the land in the first place was because I didn't want your father selling it to anyone else. I kept it safe from harm so I could return it to you, because I *owe* you.' She took a deep breath and let the true depth of her anger show. 'I was two seconds away from *giving it to you*. You utter *idiot*.'

CHAPTER TWO

IF JUDAH HAD learned anything in lockup it was to never back down, even if you had just picked the wrong fight. That mindset had got him through more than seven years of prison politics alive and relatively unscathed. Whether it would get him through the rest of this dance remained to be seen.

'We don't have to stay engaged for long,' he tried, and she trod on his toe with the point of a scissor-tipped stiletto. 'Ow.'

'You're absolutely right.' Her eyes glowed like cognac. 'Five minutes should do it.'

But he couldn't break their engagement five minutes after announcing it. He had a reputation to protect. Status that relied on money, hype and his willingness to kill to protect the innocent. Foolishness could never be part of that mix. 'One month, and I'll make it worth your while. Diamonds. A carat a day.'

'And now he thinks I can be bought...'

Everyone has a price.

'I'll pay triple whatever you paid for my land in the first place.'

'Really not motivated by money...'

What was she motivated by? Had she mentioned anything he could use? Anything at all? 'Ah, but think of the privacy you can buy with it. I hear the Conrad place might be coming on the market soon.' The Conrads were their current neighbours to her north.

She eyed him sharply. 'Who told you that?'

'The Conrads. Look, the only reason I went with the marriage plan in the first place was because I never dreamed you'd be so stup—'

'*Do* keep going,' she murmured dulcetly. 'Dig that hole deep.'

'I never dreamed you'd be so *generous* as to *give* the land back.' Where was the grift in that? The jockeying for every tiny advantage? 'You realise all this could have been avoided if you'd taken my calls?' Ouch. Ow! So much for fancy butter-soft-leather dress shoes. 'Do you know how sharp your shoes are?'

Although not as sharp as her tongue.

In prison, he'd been Mr No Feelings at All.

Ten minutes after clapping eyes on Bridie and a tsunami of emotions was threatening to overwhelm him. Anger, desire, yearning, embarrassment, frustration and more desire—all of it itching to escape him no matter how many other people here tonight would see and use his weakness against him.

For years and years and far too many *years* he'd been waiting for the day when he could come home to Jeddah Creek and put his life back together and build on the legacy his family had left him. He'd make his parents and his brother proud. He'd restore the family name he'd dragged through the dust. He'd become a philanthropic force to be reckoned with.

Instead, here he was, ten days out and about and making an utter fool of himself.

'Don't do anything rash. Avoid split-second decisions.'

Too late for that.

'Give others the benefit of the doubt.'

Missed that one too, even with Tom Starr's blatant plea to do just that.

All he'd sensed was her resistance to selling the land that should have been his and he'd been back in the prison yard, fighting to win.

How could he be so stupid as to let her get under his skin?

It was too hot in this ballroom full of expensively dressed predators.

And what was this wave of cold sweeping over him like nothing he'd felt before? Not when he'd stood before the court, waiting for his sentence to be handed down. Not when he'd tried to stem a dead man's wounds and bathed his hands in blood.

He didn't realise he'd stopped moving until Bridie stepped from his arm and tugged at his hand.

'Come on,' she muttered. 'We've danced enough.'

And then they were leaving the dance floor and heading for the nearest exit, and he did not have control—couldn't even breathe for the iron band around his chest. All he could do was hold on and hope she knew where she was going.

'Blake.'

Devlin Conrad stood in their way, his wife Judith at his side, and both of them were beaming.

'Please, may we be the first to congratulate you on your engagement?' said Judith. 'What a wonderful union. It makes so much sense. And your land-care initiative is music to our ears.' She glanced towards her husband. 'If you added our property into that mix, just imagine what you could do.'

Devlin Conrad nodded. 'We should talk about that.'

He could only nod.

'Are you looking to sell?' asked Bridie.

'Yes, but not to just anyone. To you both. To make our run part of your vision.'

'Done.' How he squeezed the word out he'd never know. But it took the last of his air.

'Yes,' said Bridie quickly. 'We'll be in touch. So sorry, excuse us, we forgot the ring.'

She led him to the veranda and then to the left, around the corner, trying the handle on every door. He'd never noticed before how evenly spaced they were and how much they reminded him of institutional corridors.

At last she found an unlocked door and pulled him in, shutting the door behind them and pushing him against the wall with a surprisingly firm hand. They were in the old stone laundry and the only light came from the slatted shutters high above the door, and with the dark, enclosed space came a fresh panic that had nothing and everything to do with being a fool.

'Breathe,' she demanded, and he would. Soon.

Just as soon as he got out of this cell.

'You're having a panic attack.'

This time it was his turn to lead her through an interior door and into a long lit hallway. Was he blue yet from all the breathing he wasn't doing?

He needed space.

Space and quiet and no people tracking his weakness and waiting for a chance to come at him.

The formal sitting room was at the end of the hall, with its dark jarrah wainscoting and parquetry floor, its pressed tin ceiling and deep blue walls and expanse enough to swing a cow. It also housed several of the most uncomfortable Jacobean needlepoint armchairs in the world, a couple of ancestral portraits and a dusty collection of stuffed hawks.

It was still better than the little concrete laundry.

This time Bridie had the forethought to switch on the light beside the door. Her action lit a naked globe hanging from a long cord in the far corner of the room. There were other switches, other light sources in the room. That one had been left in place to please historians.

'Shall I shut the door or leave it open?' she asked.

'Leave it.' He didn't close doors these days, not one in all the time he'd been home.

'Still not breathing,' she reminded him, and he vowed to get right on that. Might as well hang onto the back of a chair while he was at it, in the interest of staying upright.

Breathe, you scum.

Can't you even do that right?

Breathe.

Bridie walked around the edges of the room, turning table lamps and feature lights on until it was lit up like some kind of mad night at the museum, and he tracked her every step.

There'd been no stuffed birds in prison. Heaven knew it was an odd thought to be having, but he held to it and somehow it reassured him. Breathing resumed. Bridie kept paying him no attention.

'Who's the stuffed hawk collector?' she wanted to know.

'My great-grandfather. The one in the portrait over the fire-place.' The one who'd come to Australia but had never ever managed to call Jeddah Creek station home. A failure, they'd called him. Too pampered for the outback. Soft in the head.

But he *had* stayed the course and built the family wealth for the next generation of Blakes to inherit. Only with his burial back in England had he finally returned home.

Bridie continued her leisurely lap of the room and stopped in front of the portrait. 'It says here his name was Edward. Very noble.'

'It wasn't a panic attack.'

She stood there looking like an angel in the glow of a butter-yellow lamp as she turned to study a John Constable painting of the English countryside. 'I used to get them a lot,' she said quietly. 'Panic attacks. I thought I recognised the signs. Not that it matters—I needed to get away from the crowd before I had a meltdown too.'

'It wasn't a meltdown.'

''Course not.' She slanted him a look from beneath impossibly long lashes and he promptly lost what little breath he'd managed to scrape together. 'I needed to leave the ballroom. I thought I was serving your needs as well.'

His need was blindingly clear.

This wasn't a prison yard. Bridie hadn't been looking to screw him over. She'd had no beef with him at all, although she probably did *now*. He needed to apologise.

'I'm sorry.' Those words came easier than expected. 'I over-reacted when you said you weren't selling the land. I didn't let you finish. I didn't listen and I put you in a bad position.'

He shoved his hands in his pockets and stared at a stuffed goshawk, with its delicately striped breast feathers and sharp yellow eyes.

How a dead bird's glare could shame him into wanting to be a better man he did not know, but that was exactly what it was doing. Or maybe it was the undeniable goodness of the woman who stood quietly in the shadows. Giving him space. Doing her level best to see to his needs.

'I can make another public statement later this evening and break the engagement,' he offered. 'You don't have to be there. People can think what they want.'

Another rash, split-second decision.

Just what he needed.

Bridie trailed her fingers lightly across the carvings on the back of a chair. 'What about the Conrads' offer?'

He'd barely registered that. But he did want their land and he hoped to hell they'd still be interested in selling it to him once he'd called the engagement off.

'I mean, it's not as if you don't have the money,' she continued quietly. 'But they mostly seemed interested in selling it not just to you but to *us*.'

There was that.

'I'd like to hear about your conservation plans too,' she murmured.

He stared.

'And I'm thinking that if we stayed engaged for a while we could both save some face. You could buy the Conrad place, and I could have a fiancé for when I'm in Sydney next. That'd be good.'

She was doing a better job than he was of planning their way out of this mess. 'What's in Sydney?'

'A gallery exhibition of some of my landscape photographs.

Part of the agreement is that I be there in person on opening night. You could come too and be my...' Her words tailed off as if she didn't know how to finish that sentence.

'Cattle prod?' he offered.

'That too. You can be my notorious muse if you like. I'm sure the gallery's publicist would be thrilled.'

'When's it on?' He hadn't left Jeddah Station since leaving the correctional centre. Given tonight's performance in public, that was probably a good thing. Was he ready for Sydney? He didn't know. But if he didn't go he'd never know. 'When's your exhibition?'

'Two weeks this coming Thursday. The gallery is at The Rocks and I'm staying at the Ocean View, near the bridge. I'll book another room for you; we wouldn't have to share.'

The thought of sharing a room with her brought forth a whole new set of problems he didn't want to admit to. 'I can do that.' His need to negotiate and control what was happening took hold. 'In return we commit to one month's fake engagement.'

'There's more.'

'More gallery openings?'

'More that I want from you in return for committing to this fake engagement.'

He spread his hands and waited.

She took a deep breath. 'Reid's been talking about building some eco lodges up on the ridges between Jeddah Creek and Devil's Kiss. He wants to bring tourists in. Give them a taste of red dirt and endless skies. Helicopter rides. Quad bike tours. I hate the idea but if it's going to happen, I want to be part of it. Financial investment, a voice when it comes to what type of tourists to target, the lot. It's not that I don't trust Reid, but he's young—'

'And you're not?'

'And enthusiastic,' she continued doggedly. 'And you're talking about putting strangers on my doorstep, and privacy and safety is a huge concern for me. I want a say in how it's done.'

He had no idea what she was talking about. His little brother hadn't yet seen fit to mention those plans. 'I can't promise anything without Reid's input.'

'He looks up to you. He'll follow your lead.'

Judah sincerely hoped not. 'If he does agree to involve you, we can announce the deal when we break our engagement. Better as business partners and so on. And for that I want three months' worth of fake engagement to you.' Having a temporary fiancée might even help bring others on board with his not-for-profit conservation trust plans. Investors loved a settled man.

'Agreed.'

For someone so seemingly fragile, she certainly knew how to combat coercion, intimidation and fake engagement announcements. She was making him feel like an amateur.

'Breathing back to normal now? That band around your chest loosening up? Chills gone?'

How did she—? Goddamn panic attack symptoms. 'Yes.'

'Great, because Reid and my father are standing in the doorway and I think they want a word with us.'

Great. Just great. How much had they heard?

He turned, squared his shoulders, and prepared for the worst.

'Interesting announcement,' said Reid. 'A little warning would have been good.'

'Spur of the moment,' he offered. *Give* him his land back after buying it fair and square. Who *did* that?

'We'd been talking about land mergers and conservation options and business deals and when the Conrads started talking about selling we might have got a little carried away,' said Bridie.

Reid ran a hand across the back of his neck as if working out the kinks. 'So is your engagement like a fake one to get people on board, or some kind of business merger, or are we talking the real thing?'

'It's real enough,' said Judah and stared his brother and her father down. 'Any objections?'

'I'm good.' Reid shared a glance with Tom. 'I'm also going to go find sane people to drink with now. And, uh, good luck.'

Reid left. Tom stayed. The older man looked from one of them to the other and back again, finally settling his shuttered gaze on Judah. 'She'll forgive you anything. You should know this.'

'No, Dad, not anything,' corrected Bridie. 'But I don't think Judah's beyond repair. You don't think he's beyond repair either—you've praised him often enough over the years, remember?'

And why shouldn't he have Tom Starr's approval? Judah wanted to roar.

That night…that crazy, bloated clusterfest of a night that had branded Judah a killer and Tom a grateful father still haunted them all. Would they ever be free of it?

Until this moment he hadn't truly understood that the answer was *no*. The lie at the heart of it would never let him and Tom Starr go. 'Good to know I'm not *beyond repair*.'

'Hey, no, wait. Repair was my word,' Bridie said hurriedly. 'And definitely the wrong word. Dad, I know the engagement announcement surprised you and you want answers. And I'm not going to insult your intelligence by claiming it wasn't a bit spur of the moment. It's probably not going to last, but while we're on a roll why not explore what we might be able to do conservation-wise if we were to combine Jeddah Creek, Devil's Kiss and Talulah Sky? Think about it.'

'If he hurts you—'

'Dad, I'm not sixteen any more. I'm not so naive I can't see the make of a person or whether they're out to harm me. I'm not being taken advantage of. I'm not doing anything I don't want to do, and Judah's not out to harm me.'

Judah and her father locked gazes.

They both knew what happened to people who chose to harm Bridie.

'Let me know when you want to leave,' said Tom. 'I'm ready whenever you are.'

'Half an hour,' she said.

'Half an hour,' echoed her father and left, as if he couldn't stand watching them a moment longer.

'How are you tracking?' she asked when they were alone again, and the honest answer was not well. He kept waiting for retaliation and instead he got fragile little Bridie doing her best to soothe him, humour him and, heaven help them all, *protect* him.

This was not how his world should be.

'Getting there,' he muttered. What else could he say? *Take me back to lockup where I know how the world works?*

He crossed to a painting of wolfhounds racing across a field of green and lifted the painting from its hook to reveal a safe—one of several in the house, but this one housed some of the family's older, finer jewels. Or, given his father's gambling habit, maybe it now held the paste equivalent.

'You need a ring. Come and look.' He gestured her over and opened velvet box after velvet box of jewellery. The diamond and emerald tennis bracelet looked sparkly enough and he opened the clasp. 'Give me your wrist.'

Bridie held out her wrist and he fastened it and thought of the zip ties they used on prisoners and hoped to hell she didn't feel similarly tied down. At least her wrists weren't bound together. 'My grandmother had a diamond and emerald ring that should be in here somewhere. The emerald is the centre stone with two diamonds either side and she had slender hands like you.'

A dozen different rings of various shapes and sizes later, he found the one he was looking for and eased it from its snowy velvet cradle.

There was something timeless about it. The emerald a rich and vivid green that held its own against the diamonds that flanked it, all of it set in filigree white gold.

'Oh, wow,' she said. 'Art deco.'

'Yes or no?'

'Oh, yes.'

She held out her hand. He slid the ring on her finger and it fit as if it had been made for her.

She watched it sparkle for a time and then nodded. 'Beautiful. I'll give it back when we're done.'

'Keep it. When we finish up you should keep it.'

She looked startled. 'I couldn't. It's a family ring, isn't it?'

Why was she so surprised by his generosity when hers had humbled and shamed him? 'And now it's yours.'

Their re-entry into the ballroom brought on a torrent of congratulations and well wishes.

What would he do next, people with bright smiles wanted to know, and then didn't know what to do when he said give back to his community, restore his family name and preserve the land in his care.

Congratulations on your engagement, they said. What a fairytale ending for you both.

Let me know when you want to do business, they said, as if he were a goose fat with golden eggs.

Bridie too had to weather a swollen river of effusive comments.

'Look at you, all grown up and so beautiful.' That seemed to be the general verdict and she wore the comment awkwardly.

'I can't help the way I look,' she murmured to him after one such comment. 'It's not exactly a skill.'

'What a catch you've made,' others said to her in his presence. 'A lord of the realm, fiercely protective and money to burn. Lucky *you*.'

Her hands had begun to shake again.

Maybe it was his turn to rescue her. 'Time's up,' he told her. 'Let's find your father and get you out of here.'

She didn't protest. She did lean over and press her lips to the edge of his mouth in farewell, and it would have taken only the tiniest turn of his head to light a fire he'd have no hope of ever putting out.

'Talk soon,' she said, and he gave the tiniest nod because her scent was in the air and words were beyond him again. 'I want to know which photos of mine you liked best. Make me a pile and once all your visitors have gone I'll show you where I took every one of them. A welcome home trip.'

'You'd do that?'

'Of course I will.' She stood too close. It had been so long since he'd held a woman in his arms, any woman, let alone one who could make his head swim. His control was stretched so very thin. 'It's just kindness.'

Judah returned to his guests and followed his original plan for the evening to make himself available. He drank sparingly and listened to business plans and politicking. He took note of relationships and the levers that sustained them. He filed away every last sniff of information he collected and made no promises whatsoever when it came to what he intended to do with his money. He was back in touch with the movers and shakers of this world and he fully intended to carve out his place in it, but it would be on his terms, not theirs. By the end of the evening the smarter ones had figured as much, and the rest…they'd learn.

When the party wound down and people went back to their luxury planes and had their pilots take them away, or slept in their planes, or stayed on in his guest rooms, Judah took a farm ute and headed north, away from all the people, until he reached a stand of old red river gums with their distinctive bark peeling back to a smooth and ghostly white.

He spread out his swag in the bed of the ute, with the tailgate down and the vast sky above. Thin mattress, canvas cover, and a pillow so soft he could hardly bear the comparison to the prison lump he was used to. He wondered if his brother would suggest he get therapy if he made this his bed for the foreseeable future.

No walls. Just stars.

No other people breathing, snoring or weeping. He'd swapped those sounds for the thrumming of riverbank insects going about their business.

This place. Photo number sixty-two of the eighty-eight photos Bridie had sent to him over the years—he'd memorised each one before carefully handing them back across the desk to be put with the rest of the belongings he'd been stripped of.

She had no idea how much her photos had meant to him, those monthly reminders of who he was and where he belonged.

He'd had no idea how closely they might have documented her steps these past years. From the safety of her back door to the edge of the veranda. From the old Hills Hoist hung with freshly washed clothes to the edge of the house paddock and the windmill and water trough. Such familiar things, each one set just that little bit further from her homestead.

He wasn't the only one to have lost years of freedom because of the actions of a thwarted madman—he knew that now.

In his absence, she'd built him up to be someone he wasn't, but he'd done exactly the same to her. They needed to move past that if they wanted to be business and land conservation partners. He'd agreed to that, heaven help him. Same way he'd agreed to be her fiancé for the next three months. He who had no business whatsoever being around someone so delicate and beautiful. Someone who could unravel him just by looking in his direction. Someone who could make him forget where he was with the touch of her hand.

He missed intimacy so much and she was right there... ready to forgive him anything. Thinking of him as some kind of hero—and what a joke that was, even if thinking of himself as a hero had made his incarceration that much easier to bear. Protector of the innocent, no matter the cost. Honourable to the end. A man of his word.

A *good* man.

Until tonight, when he'd ripped that myth apart.

Forcing an unwanted engagement on Bridie. Lying about it

to his brother and her father and everyone else in order to save face and belatedly offer Bridie what protection he could. Pledging to buy Conrad land under false pretences. Wanting to take Bridie's sweet, parting kiss and turn it into an inferno.

Not exactly a good man any more, was he?

'Don't do anything rash. Avoid split-second decisions.'

'Give yourself time to adjust.'

'Give others the benefit of the doubt.'

He'd done *none* of that and Bridie had paid the price with an engagement she couldn't possibly want. He'd allowed Bridie to protect *him* when he'd fallen apart, and that couldn't happen again. He needed to undo all the tics he'd learned in prison and figure out who he was and who he wanted to be, and above all keep his desire for Bridie's touch to himself and *not* take advantage of her goodwill and sweet nature and sense of obligation.

Pull yourself together, Judah, don't be a disgrace.

Be a better man.

Rather than be ashamed.

CHAPTER THREE

'WHERE'VE YOU BEEN?'

Judah halted at the question his brother threw at him from his position behind the kitchen counter. A large cooktop and a couple of ovens lined the wall behind his brother, with a cool room at one end and a regular fridge at the other. Odd, how such a seemingly innocent question might grate on a man who'd been forced to account for every minute of his day for such a long time. Or maybe not so odd at all.

'Because I made a heap of breakfast for the guys before they left and I saved you some. So what'll it be?' his brother continued, oblivious to Judah's scowl. 'The works? Bacon, sausages, tomato, scrambled eggs, toast. Or there's the veggo option of bruschetta. I didn't make that one. Nico's training to be a chef.'

'And Nico is…?'

'A friend from school. Trent Nicholson. Good man.'

He should probably stop thinking of his brother and all his friends as boys. He should also stop being so quick to take offence. Soon would be good. Making some kind of decision about what to eat for breakfast would be good too. *Any time now, slowpoke, you can do it.* He doubted the prison psych's advice to take his time when making decisions applied to something as simple as food choice. 'I'll take the second one.'

'Coffee too?'

'You're speaking my language.'

Reid beamed and set about getting the fancy machine to produce liquid heaven, and Judah finally forgave him that very first 'where've you been?'. 'You said your friends have already gone?' The city caterers were still around, he'd seen them on his way in, but they too were scheduled to leave by lunchtime. Solitude again.

'Yeah. Couple of them could have stayed on, but I didn't know how you'd feel about that. You were pretty clear about wanting everyone gone by this morning.'

'That didn't include your school friends. This is your home too.' Clearly, they had some work to do when it came to communicating wants and needs.

Reid slung food and coffee in front of him and Judah pulled up a stool and tucked in, still silently marvelling at the taste of good food. Not to mention he now had unlimited access to all kinds of kitchen utensils that could so easily be shaped into shivs. Not that he needed to shape anything into a shiv, given that a row of kitchen knives was right there behind his brother, stuck to a magnetic strip on the wall.

His brother followed Judah's gaze. 'You keep looking at them. Why?'

Probably not a good idea to mention that he was counting them. Again. And that he counted them every time he walked into the room to make sure they were all still there.

'They can go in a drawer if you like.'

'Then I'd have to open the drawer to count them and that'd be worse.'

Reid had his mouth open and his fork loaded but everything stopped at Judah's gravelly confession.

'I see,' he offered quietly, and then slowly filled his mouth with food.

Judah tried to see any trace of his freckle-faced eleven-year-old brother in the quiet eighteen-year-old stranger sitting across from him and could find none. Reid was whipcord lean, tanned and a recent haircut had gone some way towards taming his thick, wavy brown hair. His blue eyes were still as bright as Judah remembered, except laughter had been replaced by a wariness usually reserved for freshwater crocs.

'I expect it'll take a while for you to adapt,' his little brother said carefully. 'I had some calls from a social worker before you got out. She gave me a bit of a rundown on what to expect.'

'What did she tell you?'

'Are you feeling angry, frustrated and depressed yet?'

'Not yet.'

'Good start.' Reid nodded encouragingly, and for some reason Judah wanted to laugh. 'Anything changed so much you barely recognise it?'

'Apart from you? No.'

'Do you feel overwhelmed?'

Last night didn't count. 'No.'

'Any negative influences I should know about?'

'I had a run-in with a horsefly yesterday and won. I'll try not to hang around them too often.'

'Good luck with that out here. Any addictions?'

'Not yet. And I doubt I'm going to become addicted to your breakfast conversation.'

'Har har. I'm checking in with you like they told me to. Guess you pass the test.' Reid nodded his approval. 'You want to come flying with me today? I can show you the new access road and set of yards we put in up near Pepper Tree Ridge.'

'You could.'

'We could pick Bridie up on the way. She likes it up there.'

Why wouldn't Reid and Bridie get together every now and then and have formed a friendship born of common ground and neighbourliness? Why did he scowl at the thought of it? 'I'd rather we didn't include Bridie. Not today.'

'Trouble in engagement land already?'

'No.' How much should he confess? But the thought of looking like a weakling idiot in front of his brother didn't sit well with him. He was the *older* brother, dammit. 'But it's not exactly a traditional engagement and I like a bit of distance.'

'I'll say,' muttered Reid and narrowed his gaze. 'Do you blame her?'

'For what?'

'For getting kidnapped and you having to sully your soul and kill a man in order to get her back?' Reid had a frown on his face.

'Do I blame Bridie for my sullied soul? No.' He didn't *have* a sullied soul. Not yet, and he aimed to keep it that way.

For the first five years of his incarceration he'd stuck steadfastly to the idea that it was nothing more than his *duty* to protect the weakest link in his world. Damn right he could still look at himself in the mirror and know he'd done the right thing.

His resolve had faltered somewhere around the seven-year mark when his mother died.

When his father had followed not two months later, passing so swiftly they hadn't even been able to arrange prison leave for Judah to say goodbye, Judah's resolve had faltered some more.

He'd missed so much. Left his parents alone out here, then left Reid to fend for himself. Reid, who for these past six months had been in charge of thirty-odd thousand square kilometres of some of the most dangerous and inhospitable grazing land in Australia. A property Reid didn't even have a claim to because Judah as firstborn son had inherited the lot. But not one scrap of that was Bridie's doing or Bridie's fault. 'I don't blame Bridie for any of that. My actions, my responsibility.'

'Hero.'

'In your dreams.'

'Yep. Big hero.'

'You keep thinking like that and I'll only disappoint you. I don't want to disappoint you, Reid. I want to get to know you and for you to know me.'

A sentiment that silenced his brother completely.

'Bridie mentioned last night about you wanting to build tourist lodges up on the ridges,' Judah continued carefully. 'Care to share?'

His brother nodded, his eyes brightening. 'I want to build a couple of luxury eco-tourism lodges up above river bend. Fly-in fly-out, a minimum five-day package, with fishing, sunset cookouts, stargazing, sunrise wellness yoga or something, I don't know, and day trips out to Carper's Ridge. This is my home and I love it, but it's lonely, and that won't change unless we change it, you know?'

'Or you could move to where the people are.'

Reid held his gaze. 'Is that what you want me to do? Go? Firstborn takes all when it comes to land, I know that. And I can set down elsewhere if you want me gone. But you asked me what I want, so I'm telling you. I want to stay here. I want to fly interesting people around and find out how this place inspires them. I want a home of my own, one day, on Jeddah Creek land or nearby, and if you buy the Conrad place, maybe I could go there. Eventually or something.'

'Definitely.'

'Yes!' Reid flung his arms in the air and did a lap of the kitchen island, every inch the teenager. 'Yes! My hero.' Reid came at him from behind, wrapping his long arms around him and kissing him on the side of the head. Whatever discomfort with physical contact Judah had with people, Reid clearly hadn't inherited it.

'Don't make me lunge for the kitchen knives, man,' Judah protested. 'Get off me.'

'I love you.' Hug. 'My brother the land baron.' Kiss.

'Okay, that's enough.'

'Mate, we need to work on your people skills,' said Reid, returning to his side of the counter, thank God. He was like an overgrown puppy. 'But apart from you buying all the land, and me wanting in on that deal in any way I can, what do you think of my eco-tourism idea?'

'Would you like a silent, cashed-up brother for a partner?'

'Hell, yes.'

'What about a concerned neighbour for a partner? One who wants a say in how things will be run?'

'Tom?'

'Bridie.'

Reid frowned and scratched his head. 'Bridie wouldn't be silent.'

His take as well. 'Correct. But if we're going to have a tourist area we need a development plan. Set limits that won't be crossed and have happy neighbours, Bridie in particular, and make sure she doesn't feel threatened by you bringing strangers onto their land.'

'You're protecting her,' said Reid with a sigh.

'Would you prefer I didn't?'

'No.' Reid scratched his hair and left a peacock's ruffle in the dark mess. 'Or yes. Maybe I want her to push on more than she does.' He shrugged. 'Maybe we can do three lodges. One for your use, one for mine, one for Bridie and her photography. She could run courses. Teach.'

'Or maybe she won't be into that at all,' Judah warned. 'But you could ask.'

Reid nodded. 'Or you could.'

'Silent partner, remember?'

'Not so silent now though, are you?'

'Set a business up to serve a need and it'll grow. And, yeah.' He'd been thinking about conservation management plans for years and he liked where his brother's head was at. 'Maybe not so silent after all.'

Bridie couldn't quite comprehend what her father was saying. Possibly because he was saying very little.

'I'm heading off for a while.' That had been his first sentence, swiftly followed by, 'Don't expect me back any time soon.'

'But where are you going?' She followed him out to his twin

cab as he tossed an old-fashioned suitcase in the back. The vehicle was old enough to need new shock absorbers and back brakes and probably a couple of tyres. Serviceable enough when driving around the ten thousand or so square miles they called Devil's Kiss, but beyond that he was pushing his luck.

'But where are you going?' she asked again when he didn't respond.

'Might go and see your aunt for a while.'

'In the Kimberleys?' Because that was where Aunt Beth lived, and as well as needing a reliable vehicle to get there, even a one-way trip was likely to take days. Her father had never once left her here alone for days. 'Is she sick?'

He shrugged, squirrelly and unable to meet her gaze.

'Are *you* sick?' Although, if he was, surely he'd be heading east for medical care rather than west.

'No. I just need to get away from here for a while. Maybe a long while.'

And then he pulled her close, kissed her cheek, muttered, 'Take care of yourself, love,' and was gone in a cloud of dust that would linger for half an hour before settling.

She stood alone, hands on hips, in front of the white wooden homestead, a few carefully tended gum trees flanking it, and watched him go with a sinking feeling she hadn't felt in years.

Not as if he were leaving her unprotected.

She was a perfectly healthy twenty-three-year-old, born and raised on Devil's Kiss remote cattle station and perfectly comfortable around spiders, snakes, reptiles, feral pigs and uncivilised bulls. She knew every bit of this land and the people on it.

Curtis and his elderly partner, Maria, lived in the station-hand house—retired now and living rent free in exchange for the safety of their company and a few odd jobs here and there.

Jake and Cobb were salaried cattlemen and they and their wives and children lived in newer cottages further north and closer to town. She could call on them at any time if anything that she couldn't do needed doing.

She had Gert for three days every fortnight, and Gert even had a room in the house. It wasn't as if Bridie was being abandoned in the middle of nowhere.

Shucking her boots at the door—because why undo all of Gert's hard work?—she stepped into the kitchen area of the grand old homestead that glittered like a shimmery jewel in a desert of burnt umber. It was a one-storey house, not nearly as big as the Blake place, but similarly Victorian flavoured. It had a corrugated-iron roof and wraparound verandas framed by elaborate wrought-iron lacework. Stone walls kept the inside of the house reasonably cool and the windows and abundance of French doors leading onto the verandas let in light, but not sunshine, and that too helped to keep the scorching heat at bay. Nothing ever kept the dust out.

Gert looked up as Bridie entered, the screen door clicking shut behind her. 'All good?'

'Hard to say. Dad just lit out for parts unknown like his tail was on fire. And I don't know when he'll return. I don't understand. He seemed fine last night. Even after the engagement announcement.'

'About that...' Gert had been at the ball. 'Bit of a surprise.'

'Mm. More of a business arrangement than anything else.'

'Will we be seeing him here today?'

'Judah?' She had no idea when she'd be seeing him again. 'Er...not that I know of. Deals to cut, guests to farewell, that kind of thing.' She assumed...

'You should see if he wants to come over. I'm making ginger snaps.'

'I don't share your ginger snaps with just anyone.'

'Not even your fiancé?'

'Maybe if he asks nicely. Anyway, I'm heading for the darkroom. If anyone phones, come and get me.'

'You mean if your fiancé phones?'

'Or Reid.' Reid might want to talk with her about the way she was trying to shoehorn in on his tourism plans. 'Or Dad.' Just in case he saw fit to tell her what was wrong. 'But if anyone from the gallery calls, I'm not here. I'm out getting that final shot and it absolutely will be with them before opening night.'

Gert snorted and flapped her hand in Bridie's direction. 'Go.'

Bridie usually found developing film and pictures the old-fashioned way cathartic, but not today. Today her spacious darkroom reminded her of the lengths to which her father had gone to make it not remind her of the car boot she'd been bundled into during her abduction.

They'd fitted an old sitting room out with a revolving no-light no-lock door, and red LED strip lights. They'd covered windows and built benches and hung clothes lines for photos to hang from. These days her set-up was as good as any commercial darkroom in the city. Not that there were many of those left, given the advances in digital photography and automatic printing.

Thing was, she loved watching an image appear, ghostly at first, and then more certain, except today she wasn't feeling very certain about anything.

Why had her father left Devil's Kiss so suddenly? Had Judah's reappearance dredged up too many ugly memories for him? He'd never say that, of course. Keep going, move on, no need to obsess.

She and her father had each been given ten free psych sessions after the event, courtesy of some government programme or other, and surely there was nothing left to talk about or even think about after that?

Facts were facts. Her father and Judah had been driving farm utes and between them had railroaded Laurence Levit and his zippy little sports car straight off the beaten track and into the superfine red dirt. Laurence's car, with her in the boot, had bumped over shrubbery and swerved hard before coming to a stop, bogged to the axels, and no amount of revving had done anything but dig them deeper.

Car doors had slammed. Bridie had started kicking and hadn't heard much, but she had heard the shot. Then Judah had been there, reaching for her, his face pale and shocked. A rufus red moon had hung low in the sky, silvery light glinting off the blade of the knife he'd used to cut the tape that had bound her hands and feet. She'd clung to him like a burr and his arms around her had been like bands of warm steel and he'd smelled like sweat and fear.

Her father hadn't tried to save Laurence at all, but Judah had tended the fallen man once he'd handed her off to her father. His efforts after the fact had earned him a charge of manslaughter rather than murder. He'd been just twenty, younger than she was now. Twenty and imprisoned on her account, and she'd always had a hard time finding the justice in that, but there was no point dwelling on it.

Move on, said her father, who'd been wholly uncomfortable in Judah's presence last night, and who'd taken off this morning for places unknown.

Bridie's big, beautifully appointed darkroom, which she usually took so much pleasure in, wasn't working for her today. Not when memories held sway. Better to be out and about, searching for that elusive final photograph for her exhibition—the one that would link all the rest of them. She already knew what needed to be in that shot. Fear. Foreboding. Freedom. Wonder.

All she had to do was look through the lens and find them.

'Change of plans, Gert. I'm heading out to take some shots and I'll be back before you leave.' Bridie sailed through the kitchen and ducked into the wet room for her boots and hat. 'Wish me luck.'

Two days later, with the weather radar promising late-afternoon thunderstorms if they were lucky, Judah finally paid her a visit. Gert was at Judah's now and her father still hadn't called, and if the sight of Judah strong and stern and unmistakably present made her unaccountably happy, probably best not to mention it.

'Greetings, fiancé of mine. How's it going?' she asked, aiming for breezy and doing a fair job of it if his almost smile was any indication.

'Not bad.'

She loved the rumble in his voice and the way he stood at the bottom of the steps, boots planted firmly in the dirt and his jeans clinging to strong legs. His cotton shirt had seen better days and the sleeves had been rolled up to expose corded forearms and prominent veins. He wore a black felt hat that dipped at the front, pinched at the top and sat level at the sides. He looked so quintessentially of the outback that it put her at ease. No matter where life had taken him, he'd grown up here, he knew this place the same way she did and there was comfort in that, and security. 'If only your wheeling, dealing billionaire buddies could see you now. What brings you by?'

'Gert said your father was away.'

'Yup.'

'For how long?'

'He didn't say.'

'I've been trying to get hold of him.' Judah studied her from beneath the brim of his hat and she wished she could see his eyes a little more clearly.

'Join the club. But if he's heading for Broome, he's likely well out of range.'

'What's in Broome?'

'My aunt.' The same aunt who'd travelled with Bridie to Paris all those years ago, both of them so totally out of their league they'd been easy pickings for a predator like Laurence. He'd been Bridie's modelling agent, and her aunt Bethany had never stood a chance against his calculated seduction. It had made his obsessive control over Bridie's career all the more insidious. His growing need to possess Bridie in every way possible had kicked in some time after that.

'How is Beth?'

'She blames herself for bringing Laurence into our lives and not realising how dangerous he was. She went into exile after the kidnapping. My father says she's too ashamed to show her face here.'

Judah frowned. 'That's cracked.'

'I know. I miss her hugs.' But he wasn't here to get the low-down on her dysfunctional family. 'Have you asked Reid about me joining you guys in the eco-tourism business?'

He nodded.

'And?'

'You're in.'

'Yes!'

'But it's growing as we put together a mission statement and growth goals.'

Say what now? 'Meaning?'

'I want to roll Reid's project into some broader, strategic land preservation plans I have for the area. Buy the Conrad place. See if your father will turn over some of Devil's Kiss land to the project.'

Mr Moneybags and clever along with it. How many times would she have to shift her take on this man, now that he was home? 'I'm about to head out and try and get some shots of the storm front coming in. Want to fill me in while I'm doing that?'

He looked towards the darkening sky. 'You want to be out in that?'

She so did. 'By my calculations it's going to break over the eastern channel plain. I aim to be just east of Pike's river crossing when it does.'

'And your father's not here to know if you'll return. I'll come.'

A blessing for protective neighbours. 'I'll drive.'

Five minutes later they were on their way, heading out in her Land Rover, and she tried not to obsess too much about how good Judah smelled. Some kind of body wash or soap with a hint of woody musk. Expensive. Totally wasted on cattle, but definitely not wasted on her.

'Can I photograph you today?' And before he could say no or ask why: 'From a distance and for dramatic impact and perspective. You against the storm.' A fitting end to a set of photos that had always been about him, whether he knew it or not. 'A visual reminder for me that you're back where you belong and maybe now we can all move on.'

He looked out of the window and didn't answer, and she didn't push. He hadn't said no, and that meant he was thinking about it. If he at some point put himself in her camera's way she'd have her answer and they wouldn't need to talk about it ever again.

'Tell me about this exhibition of yours,' he said, and she had no problem at all with that request. 'Twenty of my best photos, printed and framed and about to be hung by professional curators in a light-filled gallery in fancy-pants Sydney. I need one more, and I'm fretting because I don't have it. The home run. The closer.'

'And this storm's going to give it to you?'

'Maybe.'

Already the sky was darkening to the west, the red dirt beginning to glow with that peculiar Armageddon light. Every contrast more vivid for not being bleached away by a relentless sun. Oncoming clouds, light at the edges and deepest grey in the middle, heavy with the promise of life-giving rain and the not-so-subtle threat of utter carnage.

Best not to get caught out in these fast-moving cloudbursts or they could be bogged for days, but she'd checked the wind direction earlier and figured they'd be able to stay just south of it.

Assuming the wind didn't change.

She headed off track and they cut across the loose dirt and scrub until she reached a shallow river crossing that the vehicle made short work of. She pulled up on a wave of dirt not long afterwards. From here the ground undulated to the north and west and flattened to the east and, with the right light and the right lens, subtle panorama contrasts could be found.

Set-up only took a few minutes. Tripod and cameras, lenses and light meter and Judah watching in silence, his very fine butt planted on the bonnet of her ride, knees bent and his boot heels hooked over the bottom rung of the bull bar.

'Storm's that way,' he rumbled when she snuck one too many glances in his direction.

'There's a food basket in the back if you're hungry.' She'd hit the fridge hard after he'd said he would join her. Double brie, quince paste and fancy crackers, she had 'em. Anzacs with wattle seed. Dark chocolate with raisins. Leftover ham sandwiches with real butter and Gert's magic relish. She had it all. A honeymoon basket, she'd thought with horror as she packed it, and had thrown in a couple of tins of baked beans and a round of salami in case they got stuck and also so that it wouldn't be a honeymoon basket any more. 'Drinks are in the esky.'

'Are you practising for when the lodges are built and you're bringing city photographers out here?'

'Yes. That's what I'm doing.'

Not trying to honeymoon him at all.

She'd made him grin and wasn't that a pretty sight? Her fingers itched for a camera even as she turned her back on him and bent to put her eye to the nearest camera and tripod. She wanted to play around with the zoom on this one. Heading back to her kit, she fished out a thin wire presser that would allow her to take a shot without pressing any buttons on the camera itself and creating movement she didn't want.

'You have a lot of gear.'

More than she needed, true. She'd once thought that taking the perfect shot was all about the gear, but experience had taught her differently. 'I don't need half of it. I have my favourite cameras and lenses and I know how to get the best out of them. Live and learn.'

She could feel him looking at her. The weight of his gaze

skittered down her spine, but she refused to turn around. 'I kind of do better if I think of life as a learning curve. Mistakes are part of it.'

She took a few shots, fine-tuned the set-up, and then hauled the picnic basket onto the bonnet next to him, fished out a ham sandwich and waited for the storm. It might not pass this way. She might have misjudged it.

But she didn't think so.

Several minutes later Judah dug into the picnic basket too and she waited for some snide remark about her food choices.

Instead, he looked utterly lost for a split second before muttering, 'All right, I am here for this,' and digging in.

He ate as if he'd been underfed for years and she ate up that vulnerability in him because it made him less perfect in her eyes, more human.

And then the world turned amber and the storm clouds rolled in.

She got to work as he packed away the picnic, always aware of him but focused on capturing the landscape in front of her.

When he sauntered out in it, welcoming the rain that raced across the plain towards them, she photographed him. The strength in his silhouette and the acceptance of the storm as he stretched out his arms and received the opening lash of stinging rain. Violence. Renewal. Nothing was fixed, least of all him, but he was her focus. Judah Blake, killer and saviour, his hat in hand and his face tilted skywards. Vulnerable and mighty.

Back in this place that had built him.

It was a spur-of-the-moment thought that made her set her cameras to take continuous shots so she could join him, taking his hand and drawing him into a dance more elemental by far than the one they'd shared at the ball. They spun and they stomped and tears filled her eyes and she let them because they'd mingle with raindrops and wash away and who would know the difference?

'You're here,' she yelled, as lightning lit the sky and thunder rumbled and the rain pelted against them. 'I'm so glad you're here.'

And then he pulled her towards him, kissed her, and Bridie's careful, considered world exploded. When the debris cleared there was only rain and Judah, bringing her to life in ways she'd only ever dared to imagine.

Whatever he had to give, she could take it and it wasn't because of some nebulous sense of obligation for all that he had done. She wanted him.

He was back where he belonged, and she wanted him and that was all.

With a ruthlessness born of necessity, she drew him in.

CHAPTER FOUR

JUDAH HAD NEVER spun out of control so fast or slaked his need with such ruthlessness as he did now. Any gentleness he'd ever owned was gone, washed clear away as he framed her face with his hands, the better to devour her.

Bridie's hands were restless, trapped little fluttering sparrows at his chest, his waist, restless until she burrowed beneath his shirt and found skin.

He pulled her closer, his hardness impossible to conceal against her softness. His hands slid lower, lifting, positioning, unable to stop himself from thrusting against her.

Let me in.

She stilled. She tried to speak, or sigh, or maybe it was a protest, and that last thought was enough to douse him more thoroughly than any storm ever could. She didn't want this.

She didn't want him.

He wrenched his lips from hers and buried his face against her neck, nowhere near ready to let go of her and back away, but he had to.

'I'm sorry,' he grated.

'Hm?' She wove her fingers through his hair, keeping him there as she burrowed in closer.

He had no finesse. To rut against her much longer and that

would be him gone, spent and sticky in his jeans—worse if he managed to get her out of her jeans because then there'd be nothing to halt his reckless, greedy descent into animal behaviour. Judah cursed and put his hands to Bridie's hips, put some air between them, the better to get his brain to start functioning.

Her gaze met his, glazed, confused. 'Why are we stopping? This is perfect. You're perfect.'

What a thing to say to a man like him. 'You don't even know me.'

She stepped back, eyes narrowing, and her hands went to her hips. 'I could get to know you. We could get to know each other and then maybe we could do more of the kissing.'

'It wouldn't stop at kissing.'

'So? I wouldn't want it to.'

'You don't know me.'

'But I'd like to.'

He tried again to make her see reason. To understand his position. 'You won't like what you find.'

'How do you know?'

'After what I did to you at the ball, how could you *not* know?'

She looked at him a good long while, mindless of the pelting rain, and then took a careful step back. 'You're too hard on yourself, Judah. But if you don't want what I'm offering, I can't make you take it. We can just call it a spur-of-the-moment kiss. Forget it ever happened.'

'Let's do that.' He'd spent too many years thinking of this woman as fragile and terrified and young. And maybe she'd grown in years but she had no experience with someone as greedy for touch as him. As unstable as him. Seven long years and counting, and he didn't trust himself to be the kind of lover she needed. 'Trust me, it's for the best.'

He tilted his face to the sky and let the stinging rain pellets wash him clean of his burning desire to get naked and dirty with a woman too pure for him to sully. 'Please. We're not doing this.'

Had she touched him again his resolve might have broken,

but she turned away and trudged back to her cameras, and he could only hope those canvas covers she'd set up over the camera bodies had done enough to protect them from the downpour.

By the time he came back in and Bridie had packed up, the storm had passed and red mud caked his boots. She passed him a towel in silence, not quite meeting his gaze, and he gruffly thanked her.

He couldn't have felt any worse.

'Are you ready to leave?' she asked quietly.

Note to self: never reject a woman's advances without having your own ride home.

The drive back took three times as long on account of the rain, but they didn't get bogged and eventually they pulled up alongside his truck. Bridie's hair had started to dry in loose curls to frame her face. Such a perfect profile to go with her long lashes and flawless skin. No wonder the modelling world had gone all in for her. No wonder the predators had come circling.

He made a hasty exit and then turned back towards her— simultaneously glad to be out of the car and shamed by his mishandling of the afternoon. 'Look, Bridie, you're very beautiful.'

She had a fierce glare. 'Tell me something I don't know.'

'I haven't had sex in nearly eight years and my self-control is hanging by a thread. I don't want your gratitude, your pity or to hurt you, so it's best I stay away from you. See out this farce of an engagement and then leave you be. Do no harm. Savvy?'

'Got it. You're too big, bad and dangerous for innocent little me.' She stomped towards her homestead and he figured that was it, but then she turned and fixed him with a soggy kitten glare. 'Does anyone actually believe that's who you are?'

'You'd better believe it,' he yelled, because seriously. 'Shouldn't you be *thanking* me?'

'For being a tool? Why does that need praise?'

'For my restraint!'

For stopping when he did, so as not to overwhelm her? For *protecting* her? Again, because apparently it was his lot in life to get screwed over for love of protecting Miss Bridie Starr, bane of his existence.

I'm not depressed, he could tell Reid when he got back to the house.

I'm peeling out of my skin for want of a woman I dare not touch.

Apparently, I'm also an idiot.

Bridie spent the rest of the day seething, developing film, and coming to the bald realisation that she'd somehow just taken some of the best photos of her life. Danger. Foreboding. Homecoming. Pleasure.

The cameras she'd set up to take a shot every thirty seconds had caught those moments of them together and they were more beautiful than she could ever have imagined, and she couldn't ever show them to Judah, or anyone else, because he'd turned her down.

For reasons that made no sense.

'Complete and utter idiot,' she muttered the following morning as she dumped a tea bag into a huge mug and switched the jug on to boil some water. Because she'd had glorious love-soaked dreams all last night and she most certainly had not let the memory of yesterday's kisses go. *Hell, no.*

'Are you talking about my brother?' a voice wanted to know, from somewhere over near the doorway, and there stood Reid, hat in hand and hair unruly. 'Because he's also a surly bastard.'

'What are you doing here?'

'I came to talk business. I'm also here to check up on you and see if your father's home yet.'

And that was another reason for her foul mood. 'I haven't heard from him.'

'Have you spoken to your aunt?'

'Not since the trial,' she muttered darkly. 'And before you ask, I never cut her off. I love my aunt, even if she's *another* complete and utter moron. She blames herself for being taken in by a monster who courted her to get to me, and she's too ashamed to speak to me. I phoned. I wrote. I *begged* her to come see me. To forgive herself because I sure as hell didn't hold her responsible for someone else's insanity. Fat lot of good it did.'

'Er...right.'

'How come I didn't hear your helicopter?'

'I came on the dirt bike.'

She hadn't heard that either. Existing in a world of her own, her father would have said had he been around. Which he wasn't. *Stubborn old goat.* 'And you're also here on business, you said?'

'Yep. Tourist lodge business. What are your thoughts on retractable roofs and floor-to-ceiling glass windows?'

Bridie blinked.

'So that someone who, say, doesn't like feeling hemmed in and doesn't like sleeping indoors, doesn't have to sleep in a swag in the back of his ute every night.'

Reid sent her a beseeching look, inviting her to buy into his problems, but she didn't want to because she knew exactly where Reid's problems led. 'Judah?'

'Yep.'

Right.

'I just want to make it easier for him to get his life back, you know?' Reid continued. 'He's not always...coping. And it's the little stuff.'

Judah didn't exactly appear to be coping all that well with the big stuff either—if impromptu wanton kisses followed by a hasty retreat could be classified as such. Or maybe she was the only needy wanton person around here. 'What's not to love about disappearing ceilings and walls? Turn all the lights on and bring every insect for six kilometres around for a feed.'

'Okay, so my plans might need work,' Reid conceded. 'Wanna help?'

Two hours passed as they sketched cabin design after cabin design and talked about how best to accommodate eccentric guests with all sorts of needs. Reid's enthusiasm was contagious, and Bridie's interest in putting lodges on the ridges became real. She *wanted* this project to succeed. Two hours and three arguments later, they had a cabin layout they both liked. Bridie sat back, pleased with their progress. 'I'm on board with this.'

'Don't sound so shocked.'

'But I *am* shocked. I want these eco-tourism plans to work. I want to bring people here.'

Reid grinned and punched a fist in the air. 'I knew it! And you're going to be a world-famous photographer soon. That's a given.'

She put her palms to her face and rubbed as butterflies found a home in her stomach at the thought of the final picture she'd chosen for the exhibition. 'I'm going to try.' The words came out muffled. 'What if the media fixates on my past, instead of my work? Drags me through the mud, and Judah too? And by extension, you.' She lowered her hands. Her fears came from a place of experience. 'You were probably too young to remember the way the press treated the story.'

'I was at boarding school. Believe me, I remember.'

Oh. 'Sorry.'

'Not your fault, but you're right when it comes to not wanting to stir up that hornet's nest.' Reid picked up a pencil and began to number the cabin plans. 'I want to protect my big mean-dog brother. He's not nearly as tough and indestructible as he thinks he is. I thought your father would be here to help me.'

But her father wasn't here. 'How can I help?'

'Judah wants to talk about putting some Jeddah Creek, Conrad's and Devil's Kiss land into a conservation trust. Get your father to give him a call so he can get moving on that.'

'What else? And by that I mean something that's vaguely within my control.'

'Maybe invite him around for breakfast or call him once a day or something, so he knows you're okay over here. Same way you and Tom used to tag-team me after Dad died. Just...

check in once a day. He worries about you over here on your own, and so do I.'

'I'll group-text you both a photo every day.' Problem solved.

'He could use a friend.'

'Reid—' She shook her head, hoping he'd understand without her having to explain. 'My feelings for your brother are complicated. Friendship's a stretch. There's so much in the way of it.'

Physical attraction. Saviour status. Rejection...

'What if you try befriending him in Sydney? Do stuff together. Sightsee and all that. That could work.' Reid sounded so hopeful. 'But don't be surprised if he stays out all night. He does that. I think it's because he can't stand sleeping inside four walls.'

Maybe she could order a roll-out bed to put on a balcony. Or she could just walk with him through the city all night long, befriending him. Which would make her the grumpiest emerging landscape photographer ever. 'I will be a sphinx in the face of your brother's strange sleeping habits. No comment.'

'Thanks.'

She enjoyed watching Reid striding past his teen years and turning into a truly caring and responsible young man. 'That's if he decides to come to Sydney with me at all. He might not.'

'He said he would, didn't he? My brother keeps his word.'

'Yes, but maybe I shouldn't have pressed him to come with me in the first place.' She'd been thinking of her own challenges when it came to stepping out of her comfort zone. 'It honestly never occurred to me that Judah might have issues with those surroundings, and frankly it should have.' She needed to stop clinging to her Judah-as-Superman fantasy. It was self-indulgent at best and had the potential to be downright destructive.

'I'll go alone.' Gulp. 'That's fine. I'll give your brother a call and let him know I've had a change of plans. I can invent a girlfriend who's joining me or something. Give the man an out.'

'I didn't say to sideline him,' objected Reid. 'A change of

scenery might do him good. What's wrong with sticking to the current plan and being there for him, if he needs a friend?'

'Yeah, but...' Reid didn't know about the kissing.

'Don't make me pull the *You owe him compassion and understanding* card.' Reid looked utterly serious. 'Because I will.'

'Oh, that's harsh.'

Reid glared.

'Can we agree that I need to at least give him the option of not going with me to Sydney seeing as, by your own admission, he's not coping with the little things?'

Reluctantly, Reid agreed.

Bridie did phone Judah later that afternoon. Not much of a phone conversationalist, Judah, and Bridie was little better.

They did 'hey' and 'hope this isn't a bad time to call' before she got down to the business of giving him an out when it came to him joining her in Sydney. 'Hey, so I'm thinking of heading to Sydney a day earlier than planned, and that's probably not going to work for you, so maybe you might want to rethink joining me at all?'

'Is this about the kissing?'

'Ah, no? Not entirely. As in, I'm aware there'll be no kissing if you do come.'

'It's for your own good.'

Did he seriously believe what he was saying? She had a feeling he did. How did such a good man develop a mindset that he was no good at all? Had his years in prison damaged him beyond repair? 'Yes, well. Not sure I agree with you there, but moving on. You don't have to come.'

'Is your father meeting you there?'

'Er...' She still hadn't heard from him. 'I'm going to go with no.'

'He still hasn't been in touch,' he guessed flatly.

'No, and I'm worried about him, but that's a different conversation.'

'I can come to Sydney a day earlier with you. Not a problem.'

Oh. 'Even if it's awkward between us?'

'When is it not?'

The man had a point. 'Okay, well, thank you. Wednesday departure, then, and a Saturday return.' How had she managed to add another day to the trip rather than cutting him loose? *Good job, dimwit. Really good job.* 'It's really not a problem if I go alone. You saw me at the ball, navigating people with ease.' Slight stretch of the truth there. 'I am all prepped.'

'Good to hear, but I'm still coming with you.' She could hear the iron in his voice. 'I gave you my word.'

CHAPTER FIVE

SYDNEY HARBOUR GLITTERED like the jewel it was as the plane banked hard, allowing Bridie a bird's eye view of the bridge, the Opera House, the skyscrapers and the roofscapes of the suburbs beyond. She and Judah had flown first-class commercial from Cairns, picking up the final leg of an inbound plane's international flight, and from the moment she'd boarded, Bridie had been having a champagne experience.

And her pleasure might just be contagious, given Judah's wry grin every time food or beverages were offered.

She'd opted for an easy-travel fabric—synthetic, lightweight, no crush—and the draping neckline of her shirt likely plunged a little too low, and her shoes were once again sky-high, but she'd added a scarf in every imaginable shade of blue and draped it just so, and she was surviving the nakedly admiring glances strangers kept giving her with surprising nonchalance.

Pretty woman. She'd owned that label once and made a career of it. It had brought Laurence into her life, but it had also opened her up to the world beyond Devil's Kiss, and that world had once been her oyster. Maybe it could be again.

All she needed was confidence enough to seize it. Blazing confidence.

Except for those moments when she kept fiddling with the

bracelet Judah had given her, or twisting her engagement ring around and rubbing at the stones with the pad of her thumb and hoping to hell those pretty stones didn't fall out on her watch. Maybe if she sat on her hands…that might help, but then Judah would probably ask if she was scared of flying and she would have to either nod and lie or confess to their 'engagement' bothering her more than she wanted to admit.

He was all easy control, with a coiled energy simmering beneath that mighty fine skin, and if she could just duplicate that combination, borrow some of his armour for the weekend, that would be great. Shake off the nervous tension that not even two glasses of very fine champagne could dim.

There would be a car and a driver waiting to take them to the hotel once they landed. She'd brought two pictures with her for delivery to the gallery, all bubble-wrapped and boxed, so as to stay undamaged during the trip. The curator had seen the images already and immediately wanted to hang both—a move Bridie had yet to give the go-ahead. Judah hadn't seen them, and if she wanted to use them in the exhibition, he needed to.

Not that he was truly recognisable. More of an outline bitten by rain, but it was him.

There was such a thing as permission, and she didn't have it and that was a problem.

Just ask him.

'Judah?'

He looked up from the newspaper he'd been reading, eyes like flint.

She chickened out at the last moment. 'Would you like to swap seats? The view's really good.'

'Keep looking,' he murmured. 'You're the landscape photographer.'

And there was her cue. 'Sometimes I take pictures of people. People in landscapes. Sometimes they turn out really good. Good enough to exhibit.'

He knew exactly what she was talking about, she'd stake her

life on it. But he made no comment at all as he turned his attention back to the newspaper.

'If art is a journey, then you're part of my journey and your freedom is the finish line when it comes to my current body of work,' she continued doggedly.

'Do what you want with the photos you took,' he muttered, without looking up.

'I'd like you to see the one I have in mind for the exhibition,' she pressed. 'You're in it. You're facing away from the camera, but it's you.'

'If you think it's good enough for the exhibition then it is. I don't need to see it.'

'Do I have your permission to show it?'

He nodded curtly.

'Can I get that in writing? Not that I don't trust you to keep your word, but the gallery needs the surety.'

'I'll sign their form.'

'Thank you. Would you like to see the photo?' She had it on her phone. 'There's another one too, but I'm not as sure about that one. I'd really like you to look.'

'I'll see it on the night, won't I?'

'Yes, but...' He looked up, pinning her with his gaze. 'Okay, right. It'll be a happy surprise.'

Stop fussing, Bridie. He's said yes. What more do you want?

Apart from everything he was willing to give.

The hotel was everything a majestically placed five-star branded establishment should be, with the manager, a majestic example of understated yet reverential welcome, greeting them himself. 'Mr Blake, of course. And Miss Starr. You'll be occupying the Bridge Suite.'

This was news to Bridie, and she glanced at Judah for confirmation.

'It's bigger,' he said.

'Yes, indeed,' said the manager. 'Four hundred square metres of premium living space, with two bedrooms, living and dining areas, spa, stunning harbour views from floor-to-ceiling windows, a substantial terrace area and twenty-four-hour concierge.'

'Looking forward to it,' she said faintly. Guess being a gazillionaire opened up all sorts of doors, walls, windows and so on.

'Is there somewhere your artwork needs to go?' the fellow asked, and yes, yes, there was.

'I'm expecting someone from the Bridge West Gallery to collect it this afternoon.'

'But of course, Miss Starr. And will you be keeping it with you until then?'

'Thank you, yes.'

'I shall inform you when they arrive. We have the work of some of their artists here in the hotel, although the Bridge Suite, from memory, currently houses a small Olsen and a Noonan.'

She knew one of those names. 'Lovely.'

'They are of course available for purchase.'

'Of course.'

A porter materialised beside them. 'Andrew, please see Mr Blake, Miss Starr and their belongings to the Bridge Suite,' the manager said.

Andrew nodded and a few minutes later saw them settled into the most luxurious apartment Bridie had ever been in. 'How much is all this costing?'

'No idea,' said Judah from the terrace area. 'But it's on me.'

'But I said *I'd* pay. I was the one who invited you here.'

He shrugged, smiled, and suddenly looked inexplicably amused. 'What's a Noonan?'

'No idea.' But suddenly the amazing view of one of the most famous harbours in the world glittered that little bit brighter. There was so much movement out on the water, what with all the ferries and the boats motoring along and a deep rolling swell beneath them. So many people over near the Opera House, walking, eating at the restaurants that dotted the quay. That stunning view, and the utter indulgence of the spa room and the rest of the suite, almost drew her attention away from Judah, who'd ditched his business blazer and tie but kept the immaculate white shirt beneath. He was busy rolling up his sleeves, and, sure, the harbour view was amazing but nothing could compete with corded forearms, broad palms and long, strong fingers at work.

Maybe his bare chest could compete.

The muscles of his back.

What if he had a bath and then stood up to sluice down, facing the window? She could be watching from the doorway. Voyeurism had never been so appealing.

'Something wrong with my arms?'

Was that a rumble in his voice or a purr?

'Not that I can see.' Nope, all good. She refused to be embarrassed because she'd been caught ogling him. Time to check out the other view. White sails, blue skies, the play of light reflecting off skyscraper walls and windows. So busy. Was she ready for all that?

There was no rush, was there? She had time to catch the breath Judah had stolen.

They settled in while a maid unpacked their clothes into separate wardrobes in different rooms. The person from the gallery came to collect her work, and left her with the promise that the collection would be hanging in the gallery from midday tomorrow, and if she wanted to drop by earlier and introduce herself to the staff she was most welcome to. Mr Blake was also most welcome, and had needed no introduction. The gallery guy knew who he was and stood ready to fawn all over him at the slightest encouragement.

Judah didn't give it.

She had the unsettling feeling he was almost as uncomfortable with their fancy hotel suite as she was.

'Okay, famous person,' she said when they left. 'I'm for walking across the bridge and past Luna Park and ending up at Wendy Whiteley's secret garden. It's been years since I was a proper shut-in. I'm willing to find out just how far I've come. Want to join me?'

She turned from that beautiful view to find him watching her through narrowed eyes.

'Okay, make that please come with me. Yes, I'd be using you as a crutch. You're spectacular in that role, by the way. I've never felt so safe. But if you walk with me today, what's to say that tomorrow I won't walk to the gallery on my own? And back? With a detour through the shopping area at The Rocks. I could stop for a snack all by myself in the most crowded coffee shop I can find.'

'You could do that today,' he said drily.

'I could.' She tried to inject a little surety into that statement. 'I might need to work my way up to "I will", hence my invitation. I'm crowd-challenged, not stupid.'

He smiled as if he couldn't help it, and it was a wondrous thing, watching this man relax into his skin.

'I guess I could be of use,' he said, and there was that purr again. Did he know he could send goosebumps dancing beneath her skin at the sound of it? Or that he was making her want to offer herself up to him all over again and to hell with being a virgin? She could go out and get rid of that here in the city and be right back in time to accommodate him. In her dreams this was entirely possible.

In reality, she'd never do such a thing, so if anything was going to change in order for them to get together it would have to be him. Not that she was trying to pressure him, because she wasn't. Kisses were out, friendship was in. Their fake engagement was nothing more than her being willing to wear a pretty ring.

They walked the bridge. They found Wendy's garden with its towering fig trees and magical view of the bridge. They caught a water taxi back and it took them beneath the bridge and deposited them at Circular Quay just as dusk turned the light that particular shade of purple. She itched for her camera, but she'd made a conscious decision not to bring it with her, the better to simply observe.

Not once had she felt threatened by her surroundings or other people.

Judah too seemed to take the city in his stride. He didn't have a lot to say, or maybe his body language spoke for him. Walking relaxed him, or being out in the open did. He hadn't like being cooped up, no matter how enormous the hotel suite. The restaurant they ended up at had an outdoor eating and bar area with a mighty harbour view. One drink turned into two as he asked her what a successful exhibition could do for her. What else she wanted to photograph. Where else in the world she wanted to go.

'Baby steps,' she replied. 'I'm all about getting this exhibition squared away, never mind what might come next.'

'Think big,' he urged. 'Go hard. Figure out your next steps now, before you need to take them.'

'Yet there I was offering myself to you in the rain and you were all no, no, I'm far too much for you to handle. You thought I should start small.'

His fingers stilled on the glassware in front of him. His gaze met hers, fierce fire banked by shadows.

'You give contradictory advice,' she continued. 'Just saying.'

No argument followed, just silence, tense and heavy.

'But I'm not dwelling on that. Much. Maybe a little bit. But I am willing to move on. Maybe we should give friendship a go.' Subtlety be damned.

'We could start by telling each other something only a friend would know.'

'Never eat from my plate,' he offered.

'Former model here. I barely eat from my plate, let alone someone else's. Thank you for sharing, though. Not your food, obviously, but your thoughts on sharing food.' Befriending a billionaire ex-con who had rejected you was hard. 'We're sharing a bottle of wine, though. Hurrah.'

'Now you,' he murmured. 'Spill.'

What was something about her only a friend would know? She barely had any friends beyond Gert. 'I have a night light in my bedroom. It's cunningly disguised as a power socket plug-in that shows where the door is, but it's a night light. I can't sleep without one.'

He didn't make fun of her. She gave him points for that.

'If I'm in a room I like to face the door,' he offered.

'What if there's more than one door? Like here?' The balcony eating area had several ways in and out.

'Then it's my back to the wall.'

Good thing they'd been able to accommodate him. 'None of the vehicles we own have boots. It's tray tops, twin cabs or Land Rovers. I'm very indulged.'

'That's all we have. They're practical.'

Something in common at last! 'Does this mean we're best buds now?'

'No.'

'But worth a try, right?' Was his sense of humour really that dry? Did he even have a sense of humour? Who would know?

He caught the eye of a hovering waiter and nodded for the bill before returning his attention to her. It settled on her like a weight she wanted to carry with her always. 'Definitely worth a try.' He waited a beat. 'I was angry with you when I heard you were a shut-in for a lot of years. I wanted you to soar so that my sacrifice was worth something.'

She didn't know what to say.

'I understand trauma a lot better now. Taking your time. Finding your way. Figuring out how to fit in. That's where I am right now. Inside.'

'I know.'

'That's why it's not a good idea for you to get too invested in me. I'll only let you down.'

'I know that's what you think.' She'd been there. She'd spent years in that place he was now. And she wept for him.

The bill came and they were out of there a couple of minutes later. The walk back to the hotel was downright romantic, given the artistry of the city lights and the lingering warmth of the day.

Silence helped.

The way they fell into step, shoulder to shoulder.

He didn't talk. Not even when they reached the hotel and the lift doors opened and she stepped inside and he didn't.

'You're staying out for a while?' May as well make it easy for him.

'Yes.'

He didn't even try to come up with an excuse for not wanting to return to the rooms. This beautiful, broken man who refused to admit he was having a hard time fitting back into a world without bars. His dignity, pride, or even just his strongly developed sense of survival, wouldn't allow him to show weakness at all. And Bridie, forewarned, projected sphinx-like serenity. 'See you in the morning. I'm aiming for breakfast at eight in the suite. I'll save you a seat.'

'You do that.'

Not exactly a commitment to join her, was it? The lift doors began to close.

He stayed facing her even as he took a step back. 'Sleep well, Bridie. Give Noonan my regards.'

And then there was nothing but her reflection in mirrored metal doors.

CHAPTER SIX

IT WAS AFTER one in the morning, and Judah was heavy eyed and dreaming of sleep as the Manly ferry docked at Circular Quay and someone on the intercom told him and the cuddling young couple at the back of the ferry, and the old woman sitting inside the well-lit interior, to please alight and have a good night and that the next service would leave at five-thirty a.m.

Shame about the service stopping for the night, because he'd have ridden that ferry until dawn if he could have, and if that made him odd then so be it. Being out on the harbour soothed him. He'd missed the movement that came of travelling somewhere. That and horizons—he'd missed them too. After growing up in the outback, not being able to see a horizon every time he looked up or looked out had nearly broken him.

But he'd done it. Made it out, still young and fit and wealthy enough to live a life of riches and privilege others could only dream of. Viscount Blake, with a brother who worried about him and a beautiful woman who wanted his kisses, and, failing that, wanted to be his friend.

All told, he was a very lucky man.

He let the fifty-dollar note in his pocket drift to the floor as he passed the old woman on his way to the exit ramp. She had a trolley with her—one of those two-wheeled contraptions with a handle and a little seat—and a backpack as well. For reasons he couldn't quite pinpoint he figured she had nowhere to go. Ride the ferry, kill some time. Try not to give in to quiet desperation.

'Young man?'

He paused.

'You dropped your money.'

She had a look of steadfast honesty about her. As if it was all she had left and she wasn't giving it up without a fight. It was the same way he felt about his integrity. Other people could think what they liked about him, but *he* knew he was a man of principle.

'No, I didn't.' He picked it up and handed it to her, and helped her with her trolley as she tottered down the ferry ramp ahead of him.

'You're not from around here, are you?' she asked.

'No. And you? Where are you from?'

'Long story.' She had kind eyes and a twin suit with pearl buttons, this elderly woman with no home.

'Buy you a coffee over there if you have the time.' He nodded towards an all-night coffee house. 'I have time.'

By the time they parted, Mary—her name was Mary—had a room in a nearby hotel for a week, breakfast included, all the money he had on him, and his phone number. She'd worked as her late husband's bookkeeper all her life. Her husband had been a gambler, but she'd always had a roof over her head. Until he died and the creditors came calling.

'My accountant is looking for a bookkeeper,' he told her. 'You'd have to relocate to a small town in western Queensland and you might not like either the place or the work, but I can vouch for the people. If you're ever interested in taking a look, give me a call. I'll get you a plane ticket there and back so you can have an interview.'

'Sweet man, don't waste your money. I'm sixty-seven years old. Who's going to employ me?'

'Well, the accountant's seventy, so you still have a few years on him.'

She laughed and it was a hearty sound. He liked that. Other people's indifference to her plight hadn't yet broken her. 'I'll give it some thought. Thing is, I've lived in this city all my life. I don't know if I can change.'

'I understand.'

'You're a good man.'

'I want to be.'

By the time he reached his hotel on the harbour it was three a.m. and his hyper watchfulness had dimmed to a casual interest in his surroundings, made all the more possible by the lack of people.

He nodded to the night staff. Clocked their features and the names on their badges and headed for the suite. His room had a wall full of windows and a sliding door out onto the terrace, and maybe this was the moment he'd finally bed down inside a building rather than out.

The bed on offer looked softer than a cloud, all fluffy whites and soft greys with some navy stripes thrown in for variety. There was a feather and down quilt. Or maybe an even flasher just down model. Definitely no shortage of pillows. This was bedmaking at its finest, complete with turn-down service, slippers and a chocolate on his pillow, which he ate because it was there.

If this much bed wooing didn't fix him, nothing would.

He thought of homeless bookkeeper Mary and her fear of the unknown.

He thought about Bridie the shut-in and how far she'd come.

And shucked down to his boxer briefs and gave the bed a try.

Bridie woke early enough to catch the sunrise and this time she reached for her camera. She loved this time of day when the light still glowed softly and magic stirred the land. Judah lay sleeping on a recliner on the terrace. She didn't mean to wake him—she thought she was being stealthy and quiet—but when she turned back after getting her shots his eyes were open, even if shadowed by the forearm he'd flung across his face.

'I couldn't help myself. Look at that view.'

'What time is it?'

'Quarter to six.' Give or take.

He didn't groan, but it was close. A proper fiancée might have asked him what time he got in. A proper fiancée might have stayed out all night with him, but she was neither of those, although she did know full well that it had been after three before he got in. 'I ordered coffee from room service. Shall I order one for you? How do you take it?'

'However it comes.' Suddenly he was on his feet and stretching, and it was impossible not to look. He wore only boxers and there was not an inch of the man's body that hadn't been sculpted and honed to perfection.

'Let's try that again,' he rasped. 'Strong and black, no sugar and cream on the side.'

'I'm on it.' She left him on the terrace and called his order in, and if she snapped a couple of stealth photos of him out there enjoying the view for her own private collection, well, she would wrestle with her conscience later.

She so rarely got to photograph people—that part was true.

The novelty of it was making her take stealth photos of this man—a rationalisation so blatantly false she rolled her eyes and vowed to stop lying to herself.

He was beautiful.

Beautiful and dangerous and so utterly compelling that whenever she saw him she itched to capture a little piece of him to keep. A glance. The cut of his jaw. His stance. She wanted to memorise them.

Oh, hell. That was stalking behaviour.

Nausea crawled down her throat and threatened to return with bile. She found the shots and deleted them, conscience cleared, but the bitter aftertaste of obsessive behaviour still lingered. No one deserved to be the unwilling focus of someone else's obsession. She knew that better than anyone.

So when the coffees came and Judah entered the kitchen to get his, she studied him with a detached eye for detail and a determination to treat him with respect. 'I took a look at the clothes I packed last night—bear with me because I am going somewhere with this story...'

Maybe he hid a smile behind the rim of his coffee cup, and maybe he didn't, but somehow she could sense him unwinding into the space she'd left for him.

'And I'm heading out this morning to find new clothes to wear tonight. And because I wish to be friends with you, I'm not asking you to come with me and endure hours of boredom. You do you, I'll do me, and I'll be back after I've been to the gallery. I'm aiming for a late lunch up here in the suite, because I'll have had enough of people by then and I'll need to recharge before the exhibition opening.'

'Sounds like a plan.'

'I really would like for you to be there for me this evening,' she continued doggedly. 'I'm going to be nervous.' She was *already* nervous. 'But you don't need to be there if it's really not your thing.'

'In the eyes of the world you're my fiancée. It's your first show. I'll be there.'

'If I take your hand and squeeze, it'll mean I need to get out of there before I have a meltdown. And I know artists are known for being temperamental, fragile, or all ego, but I'd rather not be seen as any of those things.'

'Even if you are?'

She sipped her coffee and took strength from it. 'Yes, even if I am those things underneath. I don't want to show that vulnerability to the world. I think that's something you might understand and I'm asking for your help.'

'You'll get it.'

'Thank you.' She could ask for nothing more. 'Coffee's good.'

'Very.'

'I took pictures of you this morning when you were out on the terrace.'

'I know.'

'I deleted them.'

He said nothing.

'You dazzle me. You have such presence. All that coiled strength and power. I want to see how it works, break it down into understandable pieces, but I'm not a stalker and the thought that I'm beginning to act like one horrifies me. I won't ever take pictures of you again without asking your permission. I think that's important for both of us to understand. You have my word.'

'Okay.'

She could see his chest rise and fall beneath the thin cotton of the T-shirt he'd thrown on, along with sweatpants. 'You do realise I'm sharing a full basket of vulnerabilities with you here?'

'They weren't exactly hidden.'

Ouch, Judah. Ouch. 'You could reciprocate by revealing one of your many flaws. You might be scared of emus.' She loved it when he smiled, no matter how small. 'No?'

'No.'

'Razorbacks?' Those huge wild pigs were mean mothers.

'No.'

'Ghosts?'

'I'll give those their due,' he offered. 'I have a few.'

But he didn't name them and she didn't press. Why on earth had she mentioned ghosts to a man who had killed to protect her? And then lost both his parents less than a year ago, while in prison for his sin? 'They can dance with mine,' she muttered. 'They might even be the same ghosts. I bet you're afraid of mice.'

'In plague proportions? You betcha.'

See? They could have a meaningful, getting-to-know-you conversation if they tried. It took great patience and good coffee. And now she needed to retreat and leave him be, because she wasn't pushy or needy or utterly infatuated with him. She was Bridie Starr of Devil's Kiss station and life was full of joy and pain and growth and heartache and that was all just part of living. And dammit she wanted to live. 'So, I'll see you this evening?'

He nodded.

She turned away.

'Hey.' He'd waited until she was almost to her room. 'For what it's worth, you dazzle me too.'

By six o'clock that evening, Bridie's bravado seemed to have fled. Judah watched with growing concern as she refused a bite to eat and started pacing instead, pausing every now and then to look at the paintings on the wall and in doing so somehow make her silhouette look even smaller.

'How many people need to be at this opening for it to be a success?' he asked, and she wrapped her arms around her middle and looked blankly towards him.

He tried again. 'How many pictures do you need to sell for the exhibition to be a success?'

'I'm sure the gallery has a percentage in mind, but I don't know it. Sell-out show sounds good, though.'

He could help with her sell-out-show wish. He'd already secured one picture by calling through to the gallery this afternoon. He'd agreed that whatever picture of him she'd chosen to display could be part of her exhibition but hell if he was going to let it end up on someone else's wall. The gallery director had initially told him it wasn't for sale. Money had taken care of that objection. She'd promised not to sell the picture to anyone but him.

'Does this outfit look arty enough?'

She looked to him for an answer, but how would he know what arty looked like? Didn't arty people slink around in black trousers and turtlenecks? Or was that look owned by success-ful tech titans these days?

Bridie wore a vivid blue silk top streaked with grey and the burnt orangey brown of the channel country she called home. Sleeves to her elbows, the neckline as high and tight as one of his shirts. The top angled in towards her impossibly tiny waist and with it she wore severe grey trousers that flared at the bottom and didn't go anywhere near to covering lace-up black boots. It was a fashion look, as far as he could tell, and she wore it very well. 'Yes. You look fantastic.'

'Fantastically arty though?'

'Yes.' And he looked like a suit, because he only had a few looks and one of them was outback scruffy and another was prison rough and neither would do here. 'How did you get into modelling in the first place? Was it something you wanted?'

'Oh.' She looked momentarily surprised by his question. 'No. I didn't think about my looks at all much when I was growing up. I was just me and there was no one around much to see me anyway.'

'So how did you start?'

'I was in Melbourne with Aunt Beth for my fifteenth birthday and we'd gone to David Jones department store because she was going to buy me some make-up. That was her gift to me. It was the first time I'd ever seen those little make-up booths with women just standing around looking beautiful and waiting to make other people look beautiful too.' She smiled at the memory. 'Everything was so *glossy*. So there we were and this make-up lady had just given me smoky eyes and cheekbones and then this beautifully dressed power woman rushed past and then backed right up and pointed at me and said, "*You*, come with me." It was fashion week. An hour later I was walking down the catwalk, filling in for a model who hadn't turned up. And that was that. Hello, modelling career, with my aunt as my manager.'

'Did you like it?'

'I loved the clothes, the make-up artists and hair stylists fussing over me, and the way I could sometimes barely recognise myself after they were done. Yeah. And then they took me off the catwalk and turned the camera on me and I got to see what great photographers could do with light and colour and settings and perspective and I was hooked. I wanted *that*, photography, only by that time Laurence was my manager and my aunt's lover and he didn't want that for me at all. He got more controlling. Started coming to every shoot. It only got creepier from there. I think he wanted a dress-up doll.'

Even after sitting at trial and hearing that Bridie had been beaten and kidnapped but not sexually abused, he hated thinking about what might have happened had Laurence not been stopped.

'Anyway. It cured me of wanting to be anyone's fantasy image ever again.' She crossed her arms in front of her and cupped her elbows.

He tilted his head, digesting her words. 'So how are you going to manage your public image and keep the crazies away this time around?'

'I'm kind of hoping that being engaged to Australia's most dangerous ex-con billionaire is going to do the trick. And I know it's wrong of me to put you in the position of having to protect me again but...' She looked away. 'You're the best there is.'

That right there was the reason there could never be anything between them. Her expectations were totally at odds with the screwed-up, shut-down mess of a man he was beneath all that protective saviour gloss she kept painting on him.

'Would you like a drink?' she asked next and gestured towards the mini bar. 'Something to help settle my nerves. Not champagne, that'd go straight to my head.'

'There's beer.'

'Perfect.'

'Okay.'

He fetched one for each of them and put music on. He

watched her take the tiniest sip, not nearly enough to settle her nerves so he held out his hand and said, 'Dance with me,' because holding her in his arms and not putting any moves on her was clearly his torture method of choice and he figured it would keep her mind off the exhibition for a while.

His dancing hadn't improved since the ball and neither had hers, but they made do, in the shadow of one of the most famous bridges in the world and with a light show spinning across the Opera House sails.

'People are going to love your art,' he told her. 'You're going to charm them with your arty-looking self and talent until they beg for more.'

A dimple dotted her cheek when she smiled. 'I'll hold that thought close.'

'No problem. Seriously. Your photos are amazing. You've got this.'

They made it to the gallery with ten minutes to spare. The owner, Sara, greeted them with a relieved smile, plied them with alcohol and introduced them to the rest of the gallery staff. The gallery floor was grey concrete and the walls a severe kind of white that only gallery spaces could pull off. It pushed people's attention towards the art, he supposed, as, drink in hand, he turned his attention towards the photographs on the walls.

He recognised some of them because they were ones Bridie had sent him over the years, only the ones she'd sent him had been schoolbook size. These ones were larger, some of them much larger. The two panoramas on display, one below the other, ran the length of the wall.

Sara drew Bridie away, talking business Judah didn't need to know, so he planted himself in front of a red river gum tree he knew of old and studied the people who came through the door. Bridie would find him when she wanted to, and meanwhile the room began to fill. A wealthy couple to start with, a tourist, a student with a date he wanted to impress and maybe they were only there for the free food and drinks, but not all of them had free food in mind.

When one of the gallery staff discreetly enquired whether he was interested in purchasing the red river gum, because another guest was interested in buying it, he said no, and moved to plant himself in front of the next picture.

Bridie played the shy emerging artist to perfection as gallery owner, Sara, introduced her to various guests. Judah left them to it, watching from a distance and trying not to look too menacing. He'd just turned to study the pair of panoramas again when someone backed into him.

He turned. She turned, and flushed beet red to match her hair. Not a threat—though he checked his pockets to make sure that his wallet was still there. It was.

'I'm so sorry,' she began. 'I need a rear-vision mirror—oh!' Her eyes widened as her gaze reached his face. 'It's you.'

'Do I know you?' He didn't recognise her.

'No?' Now was the time for her to introduce herself, but she didn't. 'I mean, no, you don't know me and I don't know you, but you're the one in the picture.' She gestured towards a wide doorway leading towards another part of the gallery. 'In there.'

Judah raised his eyebrows. 'Ah.'

'It's very compelling.'

'Is it, now?' If he could get away without looking at it this evening, he would. Put simply, he didn't want to have to look at his mug in a photo and pretend he thought of it as art.

'My friends were joking that you couldn't possibly be real, but here you are.'

'Here I am.' *Save me. Save me now.*

'Such a shame it's already sold.'

To him, yes. It had better be. He looked for more red dots below the paintings in the room. Three sales out of nine paintings in the first half-hour. Clearly it was time to add more purchasing weight to the show. 'If you'll excuse me.'

He caught the eye of a gallery assistant who was at his side in an instant.

'May I help you, sir?'

'I want to buy the two panoramas over there.'

'Certainly.' Moments later, they too had red dots underneath them.

'How do I pay?'

'Ms Starr's instructions are that you don't pay. Whatever you want from the collection is yours.'

That wouldn't do at all. 'Do you know who I am?'

'Of course, Mr Blake, sir.' The man was unflappable. Judah swung between being righteously annoyed and reluctantly impressed by the man's intransigence. 'Whatever pieces you want here tonight are yours. Ms Starr's orders and already cleared with management.'

How generous. He didn't want any part of it. 'In that case, I believe you misunderstood my intentions. I'm buying the panoramas on behalf of Sirius Corp, not in a personal capacity, therefore Ms Starr's offer cannot apply.' Sirius Corp was the name of the company he'd formed with Reid and Bridie to build the eco retreats. 'If there's a third panorama on offer, I want that too.'

The man beamed with bright enthusiasm. 'There is one other, and of course your purchase on behalf of another entity is a different matter altogether. If you'll excuse me, I'll see to the paperwork.'

Money. His family had always had it. Never before had he wielded it with such cynical understanding that success could be bought. Or at the very least, the impression of success could be bought.

He helped himself to a canapé—some kind of smoked salmon, cheese and chives in pastry option—and headed towards the wide doorway that would lead him deeper into the gallery.

He didn't see the photo at first. Not until he walked past the floating wall in the middle of the next room, but there was no avoiding it after that.

The picture took up at least half of the wall and he could all but feel the storm bearing down on him. True to her word, you couldn't see his face, but every line in his body screamed with a primal summons for nature to have a go at him: bring it on and don't make the mistake of thinking that taking him down was ever going to be easy.

Was this how he looked whenever a prison fight had been in the offing?

'Powerful, isn't it?' said a voice from beside him, and it was the gallery owner, whose name he now couldn't recall. 'But then, you're a very powerful man these days.'

'Is she going to let me have it?'

'Buy it? No. As I mentioned on the phone, it's not for sale. But it's yours for the taking, nonetheless. No one else gets to have it. Have you seen the other one?'

'What other one?'

'Turn around.'

He turned and this time he felt the impact of the picture like a punch to the gut.

All his fierce warrior majesty had morphed into boyish delight as he and Bridie danced in the soaking rain. Hand in hand, joyous and free—he looked so happy he couldn't stand to look at it for fear of that feeling being ripped from him.

He hated it.

He couldn't stop looking at it.

At Bridie, incandescently beautiful and tuned so finely towards the storm and to him, sharing her joy with him. Two seconds later she'd been sharing her body with him, swapping kisses, greedy hands on rain-slicked skin, tasting and taking. The memory played out while he stood there and stared. No thought for his current surroundings or the image he might be presenting when faced with his unshielded self.

He hated it.

He wanted it gone. 'Take it down.'

'But, Mr Blake... May I call you Judah?'

'No.'

'Mr Blake, I have no intention of bringing ladders and staff out and taking that picture down *now*. Let's talk again tomorrow.'

'Talk about what?'

It was a measure of his preoccupation with the photograph that he hadn't sensed Bridie's approach. She spoke lightly, with an undercurrent of anxiousness in her voice. Her eyes held the same wariness, along with a plea for him to be okay with her exposing them for all to see.

'You said there was a picture of me in the exhibition. You said nothing about hanging a picture of *us*.'

'I thought—'

'Wrong, Bridie. You thought wrong. I do *not* give my permission for you to show this here. I have not given my permission, do you understand?'

'Mr Blake—'

That was his name. He turned towards the gallery owner and made his position perfectly clear. 'Cover it up or take it down. Those are your choices.'

'Judah—'

'Bridie.' One word, with a world of warning behind it. 'I'm offering you a very simple solution, because I like to think I'm a very reasonable man.'

Her jaw firmed, as if she wanted to disagree with him. 'It's dust and rain and life and growth. It's joy. It's the best photo here.'

'It's *personal*.' Couldn't she see how vulnerable he looked? Didn't she realise how private that moment of welcome and renewal had been to him? How he'd let his guard down just once and let her—and only her—see his weakness? 'There is no other place on this earth that I can be me, except for out there. And you want me to share that with strangers?'

He couldn't.

She was asking too much.

'Mr Blake, Bridie, much as I love a good scandal, I really do recommend you set your differences aside for the next hour or two and concentrate on selling art. Red dot on the wall here, see? We can take this picture down tomorrow and when asked, I can say it's at the request of the buyer that it no longer be shown and that this is why collectors should come along to see new works on opening night. This particular piece is *not* part of any marketing material. It's not catalogued online. One night and gone, and for anyone here tonight it will be nothing but a faint memory. Unless we make a production out of removing it, and then it'll be a story.'

He hated it when other people sounded entirely reasonable and he still didn't want to agree with them.

'I'm taking silence as consent.' Gallery owner Sara smiled encouragingly at them both. 'Drinks all round. For this, I'll even break into my private stash. Anyone for a whisky?'

'Okay,' said Bridie swiftly, and come to think of it her face did look kind of pale beneath all her skilfully applied make-up.

He wondered if he looked thunderous. More like a storm about to break than the smiling man in the pictures.

Bridie turned to him. 'Judah, I'm sorry. I am. I never dreamed you'd react this way to a picture of us in the rain. I had no idea.'

Neither had he.

'Don't do anything rash.'

'Avoid split-second decisions.'

'Give yourself time to adjust.'

Once again he'd done none of that and Bridie had paid the price. 'I'm sorry.' He was. 'I'm not a hero. I can't be that exposed.'

She glanced at the photograph and shook her head as if to clear it. 'I wish I could see what you see when you look at that photo. To me, it's everything I want home and happiness to be, and it's beautiful. You're beautiful like that. You're free.'

'Are there any more like it? From that day?'

'Many, many. The cameras took a photo every thirty seconds. It caught everything.' Her chest rose with the strength of the breath she took. 'You're welcome to see them. I can destroy them. I did ask.' Her eyes pleaded with him to agree with her. 'You *knew* you were standing in the frame.

'I'd never show them,' she added. 'And some of them crossed a line and became way too personal, I know that. I just—I didn't think this one did. I did offer to show it to you on the plane. I *knew* I should have made you look.'

'My bad.' She was right. He'd agreed without knowing what he was agreeing to, and that was on him. 'Spur-of-the-moment reaction.' God knew he'd been warned about *them*. 'I'm coming good.'

He still couldn't bring himself to look at the photo again.

'And here we are.' Sara spared him an answer by way of shoving a silver tray with three crystal tumblers full of Scotch under their noses. 'All but one of the works have sold, and the night is still young. A toast.' She raised the last glass. 'To a remarkable new talent and a sell-out exhibition, I'm sure.'

'Really? All but one? Which one?'

Astonishment looked good on Bridie. Not quite as good as... what did she call it? His gaze skittered over the photo on the wall—the part with Bridie in it, whirling against the storm.

'Boots 'n Dust,' answered Sara. 'Bridie, darling, I'm being asked if you take commissions. Come and meet this wonderful couple from South Australia. I believe they own a grazing property down that way. Can you spare her, Mr Blake?'

'I can spare her.'

'You won't leave without me?' asked Bridie.

Why she still wanted him anywhere near her spoke volumes about her lack of alternatives. 'I won't leave without you. I might step outside though.' Let the lack of walls calm him. 'Text me when you want me to come back in.'

'I will.' She leaned up, her lips to his ear. 'I'm really sorry you don't like the photos but, please, please look at them again. Your superhero photo against the storm is stunning. *You're* stunning—all your inner strength and might. As for the one of us, the you in that pic is every bit as bold and beautiful as you are in the other one, and it's exactly what I want for you, whether I'm the one to share it with you or not.

'Happiness and joy, Judah. Because you deserve it.'

CHAPTER SEVEN

IT WAS HARD to feel like a successful landscape photographer when the man walking beside her was so tense and withdrawn. She should have stuck to landscapes, or at the very least forced Judah to look at the pictures she'd added to the exhibition at the last minute. She hadn't meant to hurt him. He probably hadn't meant to hurt her either, with his emphatic objection to the portrait of the two of them, but he had.

Their tentative friendship was withering away in the silence and she had no idea how to resurrect it.

'You're not coming in?' she asked as he stopped at the entrance to the hotel foyer.

'Not yet. Figured I'd walk for a bit.'

'Want some company?' It was a long shot, because every bone in his body suggested that, no, he damn well didn't.

He looked to her boots. 'In those shoes?'

'I have walking shoes upstairs.'

He shrugged, which could mean anything, but he stayed by her side as they returned to the suite, which was still as luxurious as they had left it, only now there was a bottle of champagne, a fruit basket, and chocolates on the dining table, along with a note congratulating her on her resounding opening-night success.

'From the gallery,' she murmured. 'I'll just go change my shoes.'

'Don't bother.'

Right, so he definitely wasn't interested in enduring any more of her company this evening. 'Okay, no. Didn't mean to intrude on the rest of your evening.'

'I meant that tiredness hit me like a hammer on the way up to the suite and what's not to like about the thought of opening a bottle of celebratory champagne and kicking back now that we're here?'

'Oh. Okay.' Four seasons in one day, that was him.

He reached for the bottle of champagne and made short work of opening it. 'Congratulations. You did it. Sold every painting.'

'And managed to hurt you in the process.' Might as well say it.

'I overreacted. Lashed out.'

'Again.' Because he'd done similar at the ball.

'Again.' He poured the champagne and left plenty of room for the bubbles to rise before topping off the glasses and handing one to her. 'I'm not proud of my behaviour.'

'Do you know why you do it?'

'I have a fair idea.'

She waited, and waited some more, and finally he spoke.

'I don't like being vulnerable. In prison…' He set his glass down on the table and looked her in the eye. 'In prison that's not on. You lock down hard and try to become as emotionless as you can. Nothing gets to you. No fear, no anger, no laughter. Nothing. Emotions are private. And now they're all coming out, all those feelings I don't know what to do with any more, and I feel exposed and it's dangerous. *I'm* dangerous when cornered. I need more control.'

She'd wanted him to reveal a few flaws, hadn't she?

Well, he'd just revealed a few monsters. 'And soon you *will* have more control, because you're honest with yourself and you're working on it. It's not a permanent character flaw. You're downright inspirational.'

'You need to get out more.'

'There's nothing wrong with my judgment.'

'I'm sorry,' he said simply. 'For my behaviour at the ball. For my appalling behaviour tonight. You deserve better.'

'Apology accepted.' He was so hard on himself. 'Please. Can't we just relax? Put on some music and take this party to the patio? You can stare out over the water and brood. I can close my eyes and pretend I'm back home dancing beneath the stars where no one can see me.'

'I see you.'

She turned away, suddenly shy about all but inviting him to look at her.

'You look at me, too,' he added.

How could she not? 'I know.'

'Have you ever had a lover before? Or is that too private a question to ask?'

'I'll answer you.' Honesty was important to her. 'No, I haven't.' Twenty-three-year-old virgin, that was her. 'And it's not because I've been waiting around for you to return. I mean, you were older when we were growing up and I might have had a tiny crush on you in my teens, but it wasn't a fixation. You were the hot older boy who lived next door. I think that's normal enough.'

He made a noise that could have meant agreement and she decided to take it as such.

'After you went to prison, my thoughts ran more along the lines that you were part of my world and I wanted you back in it where you belonged. It wasn't a romantic notion. More of a guilt-induced notion.' She put her glass down. She wasn't thirsty any more.

'You were a kid and you needed protection.' Those words were enough to make her look at him again. 'I don't blame you for what happened. Never have.'

A weight she never knew she carried rolled off her shoulders. 'Really?'

'Really. I don't blame your father or your aunt either, for allowing you to come into contact with a charming sociopath hell-bent on possession. Do you blame them?'

'Of course not.'

'Good. So lose the guilt and don't expect my forgiveness. No one made me do anything I didn't want to do, so there's nothing to forgive.'

'Thank you.' She steadied her thoughts. 'I'm grateful for your actions.'

'Don't be,' he said. 'It makes me question what you'll put up with from me.'

'I'm always going to be grateful to you for rescuing me, that's a given.' She turned and leaned against the railing, her hands lightly clasping it on either side of her and her back to the harbour view as she risked locking eyes with him again. 'I'm making good headway when it comes to not thinking of you as a superhero though.'

He laughed, open and honest, and she cherished the sound.

'Do you think we could press a reset button, you and me? Ignore the past. Forget the false engagement, and the way I exposed you tonight, and start over?' she asked.

'We can try.'

She turned to him and held out her hand. 'Hello. I'm Bridie. I'm not real good around people I don't know and I've never had a man in my bed before, but you make me want to.'

He was laughing again. 'Don't lead with that.' But he took her hand in his and stole her breath away with that simple touch. 'I'm Judah. And I would love to take you to bed, but I currently don't trust my control. I can't promise to make your first time what a first time should be. I'm too…greedy.'

'For touch?' He still hadn't let go of her hand.

'For you.'

'I don't suppose you could keep me in mind and let me know when that control of yours returns?'

'I can do that.'

'Will you dance with me?' she murmured. 'I'm a terrible dancer, unless it's raining, and it's not raining, but moonlight and a beautiful harbour might improve my dancing too.'

'It would be my pleasure to see if it does.'

She held his hand as he led her to the centre of the terrace. She closed her eyes the better to feel him as he turned her into his arms. Those powerful thighs of his brushed against hers as they moved and the warmth of his palm settled in the small of her back and held her close. She dropped his hand but only in order to place both hands on his shoulders. His hands now encircled her waist. It was the school formal she'd never had.

She smiled at the innocence of it all and moments later felt his lips brush hers.

Okay, maybe she could open her eyes just a fraction, the better to see his reaction to the kissing.

He was close enough to see the thickness of his lashes and the faint frown between guarded eyes that held a question.

'There's that lack of control,' he murmured.

Oh. She wouldn't have put it like that. 'Can you do it again?' Three times now he'd smiled or laughed and meant it. She was on a roll. 'You know, if we did want to take this to the bedroom, I could always tie you up.' Would he beg her to release him? Would he strain against the ties that bound him? 'How many neck ties did you bring?'

'You want to go from virgin to dominatrix without passing go? That's nuts.' But his eyes flashed fire and the hands around her waist tightened, before deliberately, on his exhale of breath, making their way to her hips. 'Also, we've only just met.'

'I feel as if I've known you for longer,' she said. 'And I'd check in with you. A lot.' Not as if domination was her goal. 'You could direct me.'

Judah groaned.

Still not a no.

'There could be safe words. Traffic-light colours.'

'And cursing,' he muttered.

'Yes, all the curse words. Not a problem.' She smiled brightly.

'You have no idea what you're asking.'

'True.' But he kissed her again and she didn't think it was a no. She closed her eyes and surrendered to the moment as fire ripped through her veins.

'Do it.'

'What?' She hadn't *actually* been expecting a yes.

'Take my clothes off, tie me up, and use me. Let's see what you've got.'

Bridie felt her breath hitch at his gravelly challenge. 'Okay.'

'Okay.'

'Okay,' she echoed again. Now was not the time for rampant insecurity to make an appearance. She was Bridie Starr of Devil's Kiss station. A talented photographer who'd just held her first sell-out exhibition. An outback woman, bold and resilient—even if it had taken years to claw her way back to where she was today. She could do this. She could slide his jacket from his shoulders and let it fall. She could undo the buttons on his snow-white shirt. After that, she'd be covering new territory. She could improvise.

'You realise you're talking to yourself?' he asked.

'Oh. Did I say all that out loud?'

'Yeah.'

'Sorry about that. Then again…you'll be forewarned.' He smelled so good, so undeniably cologne-y and male that she couldn't resist putting her nose to the curve of his neck and breathing deeply of his scent and setting her lips to the skin below his ear. This was lovely—having free rein to indulge herself and experiment.

The shudder that ripped through him was encouraging.

'There are ties in my suitcase,' he offered.

'Show me.'

He removed his cufflinks on the way and she might have objected except that following him to his bedroom gave her the most wonderful opportunity to ogle the breadth of his back and the globes of his rear.

He found two ties and held them out to her with an air of challenge that was impossible to resist. She slid them around her neck, where they hung like a dressmaker's tape. She'd get around to using them, as promised. Soon.

First, she had a man to undress.

Bridie's thoroughness was killing him. Slowly, surely, as inevitable as sunset, she built a fire in him that threatened to become an inferno. She finished undoing the buttons of his shirt, and the brush of her fingers and knuckles almost had him coming out of his skin. She pressed a kiss to his chest as she slid the shirt to the floor, and then tilted her head up towards his.

'How am I doing?' Her voice only wobbled a little bit.

'Not bad.'

'Let me just strike *gives effusive praise* off your list of strengths.' But her hands kept exploring and her eyes shone with gentle humour and encouragement.

'Pretty good,' he offered in an effort to redeem himself.

'Funny man. May I kiss you?' Her lips brushed his, more tease than kiss. 'Please?'

'Yes.'

Her next kiss delved deeper, took longer and he couldn't help but take command of it. Showing her how to savour the sweetness, and by the time he'd done a thorough enough job, she'd opened his trousers and he was making tight little sounds of what could have been taken as protest but were far more aligned with surrender.

'Are you sure you want me to tie you? I mean…this is going pretty well.'

He stepped back, but only to take his trousers off, and she looked down and her eyes widened.

'Oh,' she murmured. 'Oh, boy.'

Virgin, his mind supplied helpfully. And he was definitely no boy.

'I should, er—or you should… I mean—' Flailing looked good on her. 'How does that even fit?'

'It fits.'

'Right. Of course. Of course it does. So if you just…lie on the bed and raise your arms and grab a couple of bars on the bedhead, I'll, wow, okay, that's a lot of muscle mass. How strong is a brass bedhead, do you think?'

He curled his hands around two rounded bedhead rails and figured them for hollow. 'I'll replace it if I have to.'

'How very reassuring.'

'Tie me up, Bridie. Do it now.' Before raging need got the better of him and he reached for her and forgot to be gentle. He wasn't even sure he knew how to be gentle these days. It was as if he had two settings: indifferent or destructive. The middle ground had deserted him.

She straddled him to do it, but instead of resting any weight on him she held herself a couple of inches above him. Suddenly his hands were on her hips, pulling her down against him before she could squeak. Silk panties, warm and slippery against his sensitised skin, meant he almost lost it.

Forget his overwhelming hunger for sex and how it might scare her. He needed in.

Needed to push aside her panties and sink into tight, willing warmth.

'No, you don't.' She reached for one of his wrists and slid a loop of fabric over his hand and pulled it tight and then raised his arm to the bedhead again. 'Co-operate,' she murmured, and he gave in to the urge to bury his face against the softness of her belly and surround himself with her scent.

'I am co-operating.' His voice was muffled but he trusted her to understand. He hadn't ripped her panties off, rolled her onto her back and buried himself inside her yet. How could she possibly think he wasn't co-operating?

She tied his other hand to the bedhead and smiled as she sat back and set the palms of her hands to his chest.

'Sit,' he urged. 'Make yourself comfortable.' He almost whimpered when she removed herself from the bed altogether, but it was only to raise her top over her head. 'Or that. Do that.'

Champagne-coloured lace underwear worked for him, no doubt, and for a moment he thought she'd get rid of that too and be as naked as him, but at the last minute she seemed to think better of it.

She was all long lines and slender curves and he wanted more.

This was torture.

'Music?' She made it happen, and then returned and knelt on the bed next to him as her gaze roved over him. 'May I touch you?'

Sometime this century would be good. 'Yes.'

She started at his fingertips, a slow, thorough investigation of every inch of him until she reached the planes and ridges of his stomach. Goosebumps followed in her wake and he closed his eyes and let his passion soar. He felt her hair brush his stomach before he felt her lips.

'Is this okay?'

'Don't stop.' *Never, ever stop.*

Eyes closed, he wasn't ready for the tentative lick she bestowed on the tip of his hard length. He should have strapped his feet to the bed too, because he'd follow that warm mouth to the ceiling if it meant he could have more of it. He clenched his hands around the ties that bound him and tried not to fill her mouth with more. Her pace, not his. Bridie in control.

By the time she'd explored every part of his erection with hands and mouth, his dignity had been shredded and the sounds coming out of him had more in common with beast than man.

'I'm not protected,' she murmured.

'Bathroom. Bottom drawer. Hotel supplies.' Bless them.

Her leaving the room gave him time to claw back slim threads of control.

'Large, Extra Large and Jumbo,' she murmured as she sank back down on the bed with a handful of condoms. 'I'm guessing now is not the time for social commentary on condom marketing?'

'So not the time.'

'Jumbo?'

'Yeah.' And even that would be a stretch. 'Roll it on me, sit on my stomach and lean towards me.' Would she do it? Take blunt direction from him?

Yes.

He tried to be gentle with her as he traced the contours of her bra with his lips. When he tongued a pebbled nipple and then closed his mouth over it and sucked gently, silk and all, she fed him more and caught her breath. *Yes.*

'More,' she whispered.

He'd have headed south, but Bridie wanted more kisses. This was why he was tied up and she was running this.

And then she dropped her panties and shed her bra and sat right back down with her soft folds caressing his length, and he dug his heels in and bucked. No need for anything to go in yet. 'Rock it, yes. Like that.'

He set up a slow rolling grind to help her find her way. He was already well on his way to insanity born of unutterable need as their kisses grew wilder and a storm rose within him. Bound, stripped bare, and aching for every little piece of her she was willing to give. So good. Beyond anything he'd ever experienced.

And then she changed the angle of her hips and he nudged her entrance and eased the very tip of him in. He all but howled his approval.

'Oh, you like that?'

Queen of understatement. She did it again, took him in hand

and tested for fit, and he stilled on an upstroke, his teeth bared and his lips tight, so close to coming he could hardly bear it.

Had his hands been free… But they weren't and he was glad of it. 'More, Bridie, please. Just…use me.'

'I— It's…' She slid him a fraction further in and he met resistance.

'Perfect?' A man could hope.

'Daunting.'

'Give me your breasts again.' Maybe it'd help. This time he wasn't quite as careful. Laving became grazing, teasing turned to sucking. Bridie took more of him in and it was all he could do to stay still and not rear up and take what she seemed so determined to give.

It wasn't enough. She was hurting, not soaring. Curses left his lips as he pleaded for her to untie him so he could see to her pleasure, and his, but she refused him. His thrusting grew wilder and she stayed with him, getting looser, he thought, or maybe he only imagined she did. Her breathing grew ragged and she broke kisses in an effort to draw breath.

He came when she dug her nails into his chest. Nothing he could do about it other than dig his heels in and take his pleasure and strain and demand that she untie him.

Not until he softened inside her did she reach for the ties at his wrists. 'You bent the bedhead,' she said, but he barely heard her as he exploded into action, rolling her onto her back and getting his mouth between her legs, ravenous and apologetic for letting his pleasure come before hers.

He found her nub and set about driving her as insane as she'd so recently driven him. Inhibition had long ago left him as he set up a rough, pulsing rhythm, using his fingers to expose her and his mouth and tongue to bring her to completion. Satisfaction savaged him as she wove her hands through his hair, her eyes half hidden between generous lashes. He slid his hands beneath her buttocks, the better to position her, and figured he could stay there for ever.

She came on his tongue moments later, flooding him with sweetness, delighting him with her responsiveness.

He who hadn't held or been held in years allowed her to lead him back up the bed. 'You okay?' she asked. It nearly broke him. He didn't deserve such tenderness.

She checked his wrists and kissed the redness, a question in her eyes.

'It's nothing,' he said.

She tucked in beside him, with her head on his shoulder and her hand to his chest as if she belonged there, and he was powerless against her expectations. 'Are you okay?' he finally asked.

'I'm brilliant,' she murmured on the edge of sleep. 'Best night ever.'

So easy to please.

She'd wanted what he had to offer. She was happy with him, demons and all.

Wasn't that something?

CHAPTER EIGHT

BRIDIE WOKE THE next morning, tucked up against the hard, warm body of a sleeping man whose chest rose and fell in a slow, even rhythm. He'd turned into her at some point during the night, and how he could even breathe with her hair in his face was a miracle, but he managed it. She turned, little spoon to his big one, step one of her exit plan, and stared out through the floor-to-ceiling window at the sky, before closing her eyes and savouring the feel of skin against skin.

Morning could wait just that little bit longer, couldn't it?

Morning would mean conversation and explanation. Justification of actions that needed no justification and everything would become awkward again.

Her body ached in places it never had before, but she welcomed the feeling.

Welcome to sex, Bridie. Any complaints?

Not a one, except maybe her partner insisting he be tied up so he didn't get too rowdy for her. He hadn't. When she'd freed his hands he'd turned all that intense passion and power on her and sent her straight to heaven.

He hadn't left her during the night to go walking the streets or sleep under the night sky or whatever it was that he usually did. He'd stayed with her.

It was a heady, welcome thought given that her desire for him hadn't faded one little bit. She could go again. Her body was still stretched and moist for him. Unless... She teased her entrance with gentle fingers and felt no pain, but it was mighty damp, and when she saw her fingers they were red, and...

Oh.

Shower. Now.

Before Judah woke up and decided he'd split her in two.

She sprang from the bed and hightailed it to the bathroom and he let her go, not a word of protest and no physical restraint, and she didn't look back to see if she'd woken him. She was too busy being embarrassed.

Not until she'd washed away all evidence of last night's lovemaking did she lift her face to the spray. Was there a way to sneak back into bed with him after her hasty exit? A casual word or two: toilet break, now, where were we? Did she have the confidence for that?

Probably not.

She dressed and called for coffee and breakfast to be delivered. Same coffee orders as yesterday, full breakfast for two, and by the time it arrived and the concierge had arranged it on the table, Judah had appeared in the doorway.

'I ordered for us. Hope you don't mind.'

'I don't mind.'

He padded forward to take his coffee, his body honed for battle and his expression guarded. 'You left.'

'The bathroom was calling. Loudly.'

He studied her over the rim of his coffee cup. 'And you didn't return.'

'But I was just about to come in and try and wake you with the smell of good coffee.' There was that.

'Did I hurt you last night?'

He just wouldn't let it go. 'Physically, no. Though I'm a little sad that I've wasted so many years not having sex, because *damn*, Judah. I loved it.'

She had the pleasure of watching a slow blush steal across his cheeks. 'Oh, really?'

'Flat-out loved it.' Where were her manners? 'Thank you for the introduction. Although I'm sure I still have so much to learn.'

No offer to tutor her was forthcoming. But he did raise an eyebrow and hold her gaze.

She was Bridie from the bush and so many of its hazards didn't faze her. Surely she could continue her line of reasoning in the face of a raised eyebrow. 'You didn't overwhelm me. You could teach me. You could use hands.' Was that a flash of amusement in his eyes? Hard to tell, it was gone so quickly, leaving careful blankness in its wake. 'I'm sensing you have regrets.'

'Don't you?' he asked.

'Not one. Haven't you been listening?'

'You're in a hotel room with a man who made you tie him to the bed before he'd have sex with you. I'm wondering why you haven't fled.'

'Because it's you, and you had…reasons.' She waved a hand around to approximate those reasons. 'And I trust you.' Surely that was a good thing?

But he didn't seem to be similarly ecstatic about her confidence in him. Matter of fact, he looked downright uncomfortable. 'But I can take no for an answer, if it wasn't that good for you and you never want to do it again. Paradise lost and all that.' And on to breakfast before she fell apart in front of him. 'We have mushroom, bean sprout and three-cheese omelettes, bacon on the side, tropical fruits, yoghurt, and everything else on the menu that we don't usually have access to at home.' She lifted domes from plates as she spoke. 'Dig in.'

Maybe she'd done something right, because that was an invitation he didn't refuse and boy could he pack it away. She was more of a grazer, not all that food-focused, whereas he went for it to the extent that she wondered if he ever got full. He caught

110 RETURN OF THE OUTBACK BILLIONAIRE

her watching, and she looked away, but not before he'd downed his utensils and pushed his plate aside with an abruptness that scraped along the tabletop and every nerve she owned.

She didn't know what to say. 'More coffee? I think it's a two-coffee kind of morning.'

His nod was enough to get her heading for the phone to order it. 'Anything else?'

'No.'

She didn't press. 'When's checkout?'

'Twelve.'

With their flight at five. They had all morning to fill in.

'Do you need to go back to the gallery this morning?' he asked.

Conversation initiated by him. She'd take it. 'Yes. Probably a good move to make sure the print you don't want on display comes home with us. Or goes home with you. Or me. Or whatever you want.' Was there any ground between them that wasn't treacherous? If there was, she hadn't found it yet. 'I do want to check out the button shop near the opal shop if I have the time.'

'Button shop,' he echoed. 'Because you need buttons?'

'No, I've just never been in a button shop before. Want to come along?'

'No.'

And why would he? He might have been sitting opposite her at the breakfast table, but every word, every look, spoke of a distance he wanted to maintain. Whatever they'd done together last night, however much his body had betrayed him, he seemed driven to regain control. And control was fine, he could have it, but did it really have to come with such distance between them?

'You're kind of remote this morning. I'm not sure what I was expecting.' But it wasn't this level of awkwardness. 'Hugs?' She was rewarded with a blank stare, but soldiered on regardless. Last night she'd asked for what she wanted and received it. The strategy bore repeating. 'Kisses?'

His gaze dropped to her fingers, her wedding-ring finger in particular, and he frowned.

Oh. The ring. Right. 'It's not as if I'm suddenly expecting our engagement to become real,' she sought to assure him. 'We still have a plan to end it, and I know it's not real and there'll come a time when…oh!' Man, she was so *stupid*. 'Last night at the gallery when we argued in public… Do you want to use it to set the scene for our break-up? Because that makes sense.' Of course it did. And here she was, begging for good-morning kisses.

The melon on her plate lost all appeal, nothing but slimy squares of food she doubted she'd be able to swallow. 'When do you want to do it? Today?' She reached for the engagement ring on her finger. Why was she even wearing it when she wasn't in public? It hadn't been genuinely given. Judah definitely didn't want to spend the rest of his days with her—he could barely manage a weekend. One night had been enough for him. A night out of time. No repeats. 'I'm sorry.' It wouldn't come off.

'Bridie—'

'It does come off, bear with. I don't want to damage it.' Her clammy hands and fumbling fingers weren't co-operating.

'Bridie.' She'd given him the perfect excuse to pull back, so why did he reach out to cover her hands and stop her from removing his ring? Why did her panic soothe him? Make him feel even more tuned into her than he had been last night? Did he feel better for knowing she was even more vulnerable than him? What kind of person did that make him?

The way out of this crazy engagement was right there in front of him. He had his land back and had paid Bridie fair market price for it. The Conrad place was his. He'd been there for her when she'd launched her new career. He'd made a mistake and had done his best to limit the fallout for them both. He could end this farce of an engagement here and now and *finish* this. Minimise the damage he was doing to her. So, why didn't he just let her take the ring off and give it back to him?

It wasn't chivalry that made him reach out and close his hand over hers. He just wanted that ring to stay right where it was. 'Stop,' he ordered gently. 'Let's not do that today. We'll get around to it eventually, and when we do we'll be ready with press statements, business goals in place and a story about how we make much better business partners than lovers.'

She stilled and searched his face as if testing his sincerity, so he gave it to her and to hell with the consequences.

'As for last night...' She bit her lip and let him continue. 'I didn't do right by you last night.'

'By all means, make it up to me.'

Her enthusiasm was so good for his ego. 'I intend to. What kind of jewellery do you like?'

'Are you going to buy your way out of a hole every time you think you don't measure up?'

Was that what he was doing? 'It's an option.'

'No, it's not.' She seemed adamant. 'Not with me. If you want to put last night behind us and never do it again, just say so. I'm tough. I can take it.'

So *not tough*. He remained terrified he would do something wrong by accident and break her. 'I do want to continue having sex with you. That's a given. But I'm also expecting you to give up on me eventually, and I don't blame you. Until then have at me.'

She sat back, eyes narrowed. What had he done now? No split-second decision-making here—he was thinking hard about how a relationship between them would eventually play out.

'No hard feelings,' he added.

'That's not the point, Judah. The point is to *have* all the feelings! You walked out here this morning and you've shut all yours back down!'

'Not all of them.' Frustration was riding him pretty hard at the moment. 'If you want an open, fun-loving guy who's in touch with his emotions, *that's not me*. It might never be me. *This* is the real me. Take a good long look.'

Who could blame her if she walked away?

She pulled her hand out from beneath his and aimed a smile at him that missed by a mile. 'You're such an ass. And if you think I'm ever going to give up on you, you don't know me. Lovers or not.'

They glared at one another across the table. Bridie was the first to break. 'I'm going button shopping.'

Buttons. This whole conversation had started with buttons. It was enough to make a zip man out of him. 'Let's meet for lunch. Fresh seafood. Outdoors.'

She stood. 'Is it a date or am I back to being your neighbour and fake fiancée again?'

'It's a date.'

'Good.'

She was almost to her bedroom door. 'Bridie—'

Make that through the bedroom door and out of sight. 'The sex was good. Better than good.' He'd damn near torn his hands from his wrists with the force of his ecstasy, and practically passed out afterwards. 'Thank you for putting up with me. For keeping us safe.'

Her head appeared from the other side of the doorframe, a riot of golden autumn curls and sparkly hoop earrings. Her eyes were guarded; he'd put that look there and that was a good thing. And then she smiled, and he could have sworn the sun came out. 'I loved it too.'

He was so screwed.

CHAPTER NINE

THE BUTTON SHOP Bridie ended up visiting supplied all the costume needs of major theatre groups in Sydney. Vintage buttons were especially amazing, Bridie had a sold-out exhibition on her hands and three landscape commission enquiries and the write-up on the show was headed for the weekend magazine of the national daily newspaper, courtesy of the 'palpable tension and dramatic history between two scions of the Australian outback community'.

'I can't control what photos will be used, but with a headline like that you can bet the story will make mention of the work Mr Blake wanted removed,' Sara had told her bluntly. 'I realise that won't go down well with him.'

'Can you ask them not to?'

'I can. You or Mr Blake might have better luck with that.'

Bridie didn't look forward to letting Judah know. 'You pulled the picture from the exhibition?'

The older woman nodded. 'Where would you like it sent. Also, framed or unframed?'

'I'll take it with me now, unframed. Thank you so much.'

'And is Mr Blake in…better spirits this morning?'

'Yes. He's quite recovered.'

'If you ever become worried for your safety, *call* me. Or

come here to the gallery. I know the drill and I know it intimately. I can help you.'

Bridie blinked, taken aback. Did worldly, sophisticated Sara honestly believe that Judah would hurt her? On the strength of his behaviour last night? It hadn't been that bad, had it? 'Oh, wow, *no*. Sara, I appreciate your offer but you have it all wrong. I trust Judah with my life and for very good reason.'

'Of course, of course you do.' Sara's words flowed like redirected water. 'But my offer still stands. Call any time, and if you start talking about an imaginary exhibition in, say, London, I'll know you need help.'

'Okay.' What else could she say? 'Is this because of Judah's past? His reputation?'

'No, it's because I'm a woman of a certain age, with a lot of experience, and I lose nothing by mentioning that I am here for you if ever you need a safe place to be.' Sara gestured for Bridie to walk with her towards the office area. 'Now. Let's talk about booking you for another show.'

Judah was waiting for her when she stepped from the gallery. Only innate grace kept Bridie from stumbling down the stairs at the sight of him. 'Are you waiting for me?'

'Yes.'

'Because of this?' She held up the art tube containing the picture of them. 'Because it's right here.' She handed it to him without any more ceremony. 'The bad news is that the write-up in this weekend's paper is likely to mention it, and they're going to rake up our past connections as well as our present ones, which… I guess I expected that. Did you?'

'Of course.' He began to walk towards the quay, same direction as the hotel. 'But apart from that the write-up is good?'

'Sara thinks it will be.'

'Good. I have a water taxi ordered for half eleven. It'll take us to a restaurant the concierge recommended.'

But when they got to the hotel and he'd handed the picture

tube over to be taken to the room, he steered her towards the tiny jewellery cubby to the left of the foyer. It had a three-strand pearl necklace and diamond and pearl earrings on a black dummy's bust in the window and was so beautifully lit that it looked like a renaissance painting. The pearls glowed with a magical lustre and the lack of anything resembling a price tag suggested that budget-conscious shoppers should keep on walking.

'C'mon in, I want your advice on something.' He opened the jewellery shop door and held it for her.

Was he buying something for himself?

'Mr Blake.' The gentleman behind the counter beamed.

Judah nodded. 'Martin. This is Miss Starr.'

'Enchanted.' The man reached below the counter and lifted up a velvet pad that contained three necklaces, clearly designed for women. Bridie looked to Judah.

'For you,' he said. 'A gift from me.'

She hadn't forgotten his earlier words about buying her jewellery because he felt he'd let her down somehow.

He hadn't.

His brutal honesty—in everything he said and did—was a gift in itself, forcing her to examine her own behaviour and immaturity. 'You don't have to. This weekend is already...' she shrugged a little helplessly '...gorgeous. Thought provoking. Revealing.'

'All the more reason for you to have something to remember it by. Take a look. I don't know your taste. You might not like any of them.'

But that wasn't the problem, because she loved all of them. The problem was the no-doubt astronomical and currently invisible price tags that accompanied the necklaces.

'I can't.' She backed up until she hit the door.

'A photo a month. A lifeline to home. You gave me that.' He nodded towards the counter. 'They don't even compare. Trinkets.'

'Beautiful, expensive trinkets,' she corrected as she met the salesman's long-suffering smile.

'Thank you, Miss Starr. Yes, yes, they are all beautiful and expensive, although I can't quite bring myself to call them trinkets—even if the customer is always right,' said Martin the despairing salesman, before regrouping. 'Take this one, for example: a triplet of perfectly graded natural white South Sea pearls with a nineteen-carat fire opal centrepiece set in platinum. A classic design.'

'Gorgeous.' She admired it from afar. 'Not exactly something you'd wear every day.'

'No indeed, Miss Starr. That one's a statement trinket.' He moved on to the next necklace, lifting it and letting it dangle from his fingers. '*This* one you could wear every day.'

Maybe if you were a queen. Or, nope, not even then. Bridie eyed the diamond and sapphire art deco pendant, before turning to look at Judah. 'Are you serious?'

'Do I not look serious?' He had a smile in his eyes that was hard to resist. 'I like the third one.'

It was a modern piece. A swirling landscape of white diamonds, black pearls, cerulean sapphires and pinky-orange-coloured stones that glowed with no less dazzle than the diamonds and sapphires. 'What are the pinkish stones?'

'Padparadscha sapphires, ethically mined, of course. Aren't they wonderful?'

'Stunning.' She leaned closer and the salesman mirrored her. 'But still not an everyday wearer.'

The man spread his hands, his expression helpless. 'Madam, we don't *do* everyday wearers.'

'She'll take that one,' said Judah, and to her, 'Today's a good day. Wear it to lunch.'

So she wore it to lunch and tossed her head and felt like a million dollars as she collected admiring gazes from nearby strangers. Maybe it was the pendant they were looking at. Maybe it was Judah, handsome sod with a watchful quality about him and a stare that encouraged people to mind their own business.

But even he couldn't resist the glitter of the harbour and a playful breeze, a cold beer at his fingertips and the freshest of seafood.

'I could do this more often,' she told him with a deep sense of satisfaction.

'Glad to hear it.'

'What about you? Enjoying yourself? Because you get all flinty eyed every so often.'

'Is that so?'

'Yeah. Seagulls giving you trouble?'

'More like some of your admirers don't know when to stop staring.'

Ah.

'Do you get that a lot?'

She nodded. 'And I've never enjoyed that kind of attention, but it's what you get with a face like mine. Beauty has its price. Or they could be trying to put a price on my absolutely stunning necklace.'

'Suits you,' he rumbled. 'Why have you stayed single when you could have any man you want?'

'Trust issues, I guess. Past trauma. Former shut-in. I might look like the prettiest doll in the shop but the hidden damage does run deep. And I live in the middle of nowhere—and like it.' She narrowed her gaze. 'I wasn't waiting for you, if that's what you're getting at. I thought I covered that last night.'

'You did.'

'And I know you're probably going to tire of me, because once you do adjust to life outside you'll shine so bright you'll leave me behind. But I'm aiming to enjoy you while I have you. I like you. I trust you. It's enough.' It had to be enough. He wasn't offering anything else and she was okay with that.

Mostly.

'Who else do you trust?' he asked.

'My father, Gert, Reid, my aunt—even though she thinks she failed me. That's five. Not bad. What about you? Who do you trust?'

He shrugged and lifted his beer to his lips.

'Anyone?' She waited for him to answer, but it was a long wait. 'Not even Reid?'

'He's young.'

'He's loyal,' she stressed. 'Give him a chance.' *And me,* she refrained from saying. *Give me a chance too. I'll do my best by you.*

But he didn't need that kind of pressure and neither did she. Maybe all they needed to do was take everything one moment at a time. 'I'm having fun. Are you having fun?'

'Maybe I am.'

'Oh, go on, say yes and make my day. I like where we're sitting, by the way. Both of us with our backs against the wall so we can see what's going on. In feng shui they call this the command position.'

'Is that so?'

'Yup. I'm a fount of useless information.'

'Good to know. How was the button shop?'

'Brilliant. Buttons have stories. I bought blue ones.'

'I can barely order from a menu, there's so much choice,' he offered after a moment. 'A button store would have blown my mind.'

From teasing to serious information in the space of a heart-beat. *Pay attention, Bridie, to what this man chooses to share.* 'Were you always like that with choices?' she asked carefully, and he shook his head.

'No. In prison they take choices away. Stay there long enough and *not* making choices becomes the norm.'

'But you're making all sorts of big business decisions. Huge, important ones with far-reaching consequences for conservation and land management. How does that fit?'

'That's something I've been thinking about since my teens

and I've had plenty of time to fine-tune those dreams. There's money there to do it and making it happen is easy. There's no oysters versus bruschetta decision on the table.'

It didn't make sense to her, but it clearly made sense to him. 'I'd be impressed by your ability to compartmentalise except that eccentric billionaires are a dime a dozen.'

'We are not!'

'Maybe not,' she conceded with a grin. 'And thank you for telling me about your button issues. I like that you did.'

He looked oddly shy for a moment. 'You wanted to get to know me.'

'I still do. And when it comes to your land conservation plans, I want to help. I literally have tens of thousands of landscape and wildlife photos you can use in marketing or promo campaigns, and I'm up for taking more specific shots if you need them.'

'Just don't make me choose which ones.'

'I won't. Those decisions can be mine all mine.'

Look at us, she thought, all smiley and compatible. Take that, weekend headlines. What palpable tension and dramatic history between them? 'If I order the orange and almond cake and you order the sticky date pudding, I can try both of my favourite desserts on this menu. Not that I'm greedy and entitled, but I may just be an opportunist. Are you in?'

His smile came swiftly and, she liked to think, appreciatively. The shaking of his head suggested no, but then, 'Yeah,' he said. 'I'm in.'

By the time they arrived home that night a new understanding had sprung up between them.

No more pretending to be strong and invulnerable for either of them. Eccentricities were welcome—between them they had a fine selection—and upon request they would take a stab at explaining where they came from.

Trust didn't come easily to Bridie, but regardless of what had happened this weekend she still trusted him.

As for Judah's trust in her, Bridie figured he'd made some small headway with that this weekend, what with all she'd learned about him. They weren't friends—sorry, Reid, not a chance in hell, what with the sexy bondage times and the jewellery fit for a princess, not to mention all the button talk.

But they were something.

CHAPTER TEN

'WHAT HAVE YOU done to my brother?'

Reid stood on her veranda, hands on his hips and the dust from his buzzbox helicopter settling into every crack and crevice and on every surface it could find. 'How many times do I have to tell you?' she muttered sternly, and tried to look mean and ornery from her spot at the kitchen door. 'No helicopters in the home paddock. And what do you mean what have I done to your brother? I am his friend. I listen when he speaks, argue with him on occasion and try to keep up with the way he thinks.'

She'd also made it abundantly clear that he was welcome in her bed at any time, but so far he hadn't taken her up on that invitation.

'He's up at five every morning for push-ups and a workout, and then there's the daily meal menu—deviate from that at your peril—and then he has meetings until one, and every day he makes a point of grabbing me to watch the sun set and to tell me what he's been doing in as few words as possible. Yesterday his exact words were "I just bought a demo salt pond power plant to our west, and now I want all the land in between as well." Millions and millions of dollars' worth of deals, just like that.'

'Really not seeing your problem. Your brother's a powerhouse who now owns a powerhouse. Embrace it.'

'He still doesn't sleep in his bed.'

'Ah.' Sometimes he came to visit Bridie and told her all sorts of things about his hopes and dreams and what he wanted to achieve. Sometimes he took a stack of her print photos and took himself out to the veranda and laid them all out and then spent a good hour or more choosing his favourite.

She'd come to learn that it didn't really matter if there was something drastically wrong with the picture he chose. Celebration lay in the fact that he'd managed to choose one.

Sometimes he spent the night on the daybed on her veranda. But he spent it alone and come morning he'd be gone, with nothing to show that he'd ever been there in the first place, except that one time when a generous handful of paper daisies had appeared outside the French doors that led from the veranda to her bedroom.

If they now took pride of place in a cut crystal vase on the top of her bedroom chest of drawers, that was her business.

'Your brother's healing. He's finding himself and making up for lost time and doing a brilliant job of it. Be proud of him.'

Reid threw his hands up in surrender. 'You are so utterly gone on him.'

'Am not.'

'Are too. Last night he stripped the house of every item of green clothing, including mine, and now I can't find my best jacket.'

And he never would. 'The jacket is gone. Sacrificed to last night's bonfire. Something to do with never wanting to wear or see prison greens ever again.'

'It was my favourite jacket!'

'Have you tried wearing more pink?' She had. 'Or yellow? Or bright florals? Because you can probably influence your brother by colour alone, but don't tell him I said that. It's my secret weapon. Oh, and if you're looking for bath towels there's more coming. I ordered them this morning. Very colourful. Lots of spots and pretty patterns.'

'We already have a million bath towels,' Reid muttered as he stomped up the steps.

'Had,' she corrected. 'Apparently they were threadbare, or white gone grey, or something.' It really had been a magnificent bonfire. Very cathartic.

'Aargh!' Unlike his brother, Reid wasn't slow to let his emotions out. 'Why are you enabling him? I'll have no clothes left! There is eccentric and then there is Judah!'

There was some slight…more than slight…truth to Reid's words. 'Want some coffee? I have freshly baked Anzac biscuits for dunking?'

'I hope they're the size of dinner plates. I'm in a mood.'

'Yes. Yes, you are.' This earned her a teenage glare.

Reid was almost as at home in her kitchen as she was. She put the biscuits in front of him and turned to sort out the coffee. He'd straddle the bald blue chair with the fence paling backrest and scratch at the paint, the way he always did. The chair sat directly opposite the wood-fire stove that only got fired up in the deepest of winter nights. It didn't matter that fire so rarely burned in it. He was ready for it.

Judah wasn't the only eccentric Blake on the planet. Maybe it was a displaced Englishman thing.

'He's hired a home office assistant bookkeeper person, sight unseen,' said Reid as she put hot coffee in an oversized mug on the counter beside him. 'She's twenty-two, been in the foster care system since her father went to prison when she was ten, and she never finished school.' He pointed his Anzac biscuit in her direction. 'Let's hope she doesn't like wearing green.'

An office assistant? This was not altogether welcome news. 'Where's she going to live?'

'Shearer's quarters.'

'For how long?'

'Ask your colour censorship partner in crime. And while you're at it, remind him that his brother is not a kid and should be part of the hiring process next time, with a voice and a vote and a *say* in who gets to live in his back yard.'

'You're right. I'll tell him all that.' She didn't know what to think about another woman living out here and working closely with Judah. What if he came to like her? What if he sought out Bridie less?

'Whatever you're planning, I like it,' said Reid, watching her closely.

'I have no idea what you're talking about.' She schooled her expression into something a little less murderous.

'You don't fool me. You're shook too.'

'What is this shook? I'm good with change these days. Change is inevitable.'

'I'm glad you think so, because I'm going to Townsville this afternoon to collect our new employee. Want me to get anything for you while I'm there?'

Now that he mentioned it... 'Fresh pearl perch, a dozen rock oysters, black caviar, two lemons and a lettuce that doesn't need resuscitation.'

He stood up and swung the chair he'd been sitting on around the right way.

'If you can have it waiting for collection at hangar two, you've got it. Tell them to leave it in the cold room,' he said.

'I adore you.'

'I'm counting on it. Tell Judah I have one very nice, very olive-green woollen jumper left. Mum knitted it. When I wear it it's like a hug from someone who's just not there any more, do you know what I mean? I can't lose it. Can you make him understand that?'

'Why can't you tell him that?'

'Every time I mention the parents he shuts me down. He's not talking about them, which means I don't get to either.'

Her heart went out to him. Shades of her father, who never ever mentioned her mother because the pain was too vast. 'I'll tell him.' That was a promise. 'And I'll make him understand.'

* * *

Judah liked to think he stood still for no one, but the sight of Bridie lit by firelight demanded he halt and commit that vision to memory. Why else did he have so many bonfires at her place? He was running out of things to burn. Tonight, though...tonight she'd met him at her kitchen door in a pink slip of a dress that made him want to reach out and stroke every bit of her with reverent hands.

Reid had brought an esky full of fresh seafood back for Bridie, at Bridie's request, and Bridie had needed someone to eat it with. Reid was busy settling the new girl in, so Judah was it.

That was how Bridie had put the invitation to him, and apart from a slight curtness in her voice that he couldn't quite pin down to anything in particular, he'd taken her invitation at face value and rocked up showered, shaved, dressed for dinner and in a good mood.

Decision-making skills were coming back to him.

He didn't expect oysters, caviar and his choice of beer or champagne to be waiting for him inside the formal dining room of Starr homestead, but it was. Candlelight too and pressed tin ceiling painted duck-egg blue, with the walls a deeper blue altogether, wooden baseboards and an open fireplace up one end. Had it been winter, it might have been lit but at the moment it was stacked with wine. Photos of her parents and a pair of tall blue vases sat on the mantel. A spectacular black-and-white photo of channel country hung on the wall. He didn't need to ask in order to know that it was one of hers.

She'd gone to a lot of trouble to feed them this evening and, even if he didn't know why, he wasn't ungrateful.

He looked to the scarred oak dining table. Lots of glassware, lots of cutlery and, given his family history and schooling, he automatically knew what to do with every bit of it, no decision making required.

It wasn't until he pulled her chair out and saw her seated that he spotted the engagement ring and bracelet he'd given her months ago winking at him from the centre of the scarred oak dining room table. He took a deep breath and let it out slowly and hopefully silently as he took a vicelike grip on his composure. Don't jump to conclusions. *Don't* make snap decisions. No one went to this much trouble in order to break a fake engagement. Not that he had any experience with that. 'What's this?'

'*This* is a reckoning.' She swept a bare hand towards the table, urging him to sit. 'Either way, we're celebrating a productive few months and your outstanding re-entry into society.'

Pretty words and possibly true, but there was a pile of his family jewels sitting on the table and he couldn't quite let that go. 'What kind of a reckoning?'

'A long overdue one, according to my libido. Sit, eat.' She leaned forward and lit a candelabra full of candles and snared him twice over with her beauty. He'd gained a lot of knowledge these past few weeks, months, plenty of it to do with his neighbour, friend and false fiancée, Bridie. She was resourceful and smart. Playful. Sneaky, even. Her father was still not home and she'd taken control of Devil's Kiss station with a sure and steady hand.

No doubt about it, Bridie Starr was an extraordinarily capable woman when on her home turf, and especially when she had a camera in her hand.

Time to pay attention.

'What do you want?' He asked more plainly. 'Because if you're looking for permission to show the pictures you took of me the other day, the answer is no. Hell no.' He'd been cleaning out a water trough for the cattle with his hat, and he'd taken his shirt off because why get that soaked too, and somehow he'd broken the water stopper while he was at it, which meant he was in there, boots and all with a fix, and by the end of it, he'd just laid back and closed his eyes and let the damn trough fill with him in it, his arms trailing over the edges and his wet hat back on his head.

'No,' he'd said when he'd heard her camera start clicking, but he hadn't really meant it and he'd been too content to move.

'But, Judah, *Man in Bath*,' she'd muttered and somehow managed to capitalise every word, and then she'd started *positioning* him.

He'd given her plenty of warning to put the camera down before dragging her in with him.

'I would *never* again put any of the pictures I take of you out in the world for public viewing. Lesson learnt.' Her hand over her heart only served to highlight the necklace snugged against the gentle swell of her breasts. *His* necklace, the one he'd pressured her into accepting. He hadn't seen it on her since they'd left Sydney. What was it the sales guy had said? Not a daily wearer.

What use was it if she couldn't wear it whenever she wanted to?

His gaze slid to the sparkling little pile on the table and then away again. He reached for the champagne and at her nod filled her glass and then his. 'So what is it you want?'

'First, you owe your brother a new coat. You neglected to tell me it was his clothes we were burning last night.'

'Spur-of-the-moment decision. I'll buy him a new one. A better one.' Not green.

'He has a green woollen jumper. Your mother knitted it. He's very attached to it. Leave it alone.'

This time shame licked at him. 'I will.'

'Reid also wasn't impressed with your solo decision to bring a complete stranger into the home paddock, so to speak.'

'He's okay with it now, though.' Bridie gave him the look, one he'd recently interpreted to mean he needed to do more explaining. 'Bubbly, outgoing, down-to-earth girl.'

'Is that why you chose her? You've met her before?'

'Once or twice.'

'Don't make me beat more information out of you, Judah. Because I will.'

Her bluffing needed so much more work. 'She's the daughter of a guy I used to bunk with. I said I'd look her up when I got out and when I found her she was chipping cotton twelve hours a day, six days a week, doing the bookwork for a childcare centre in the evenings in exchange for childcare, and two weeks behind on her rent.'

'She has a kid?'

'A boy. He's nearly two. Last I saw, he'd fallen asleep on Reid's shoulder as Reid came out of the linen cupboard with a handful of baby blankets that used to be his.'

'Judah, Reid's a baby himself, especially in the world of relationships. What are you doing?'

'I'm bringing people into our lives because we need help and they might need a break, and we're building things. There's another woman heading this way next week. She's a sixty-seven-year-old bookkeeper I met on a ferry in Sydney, and if I don't trust my instincts now I never will. You willing to trust me, Bridie? They're both women. I wouldn't invite a man out here to stay before running it by you.'

'Then why not run the bringing of women out here past me too?'

'Because they're not as much of a threat to you? Being women and all?'

'Says who? Okay, I agree, it's unlikely they'd truss me up and stick me in a car boot, but there are other ways to pose a threat. They might not even know they're being threatening.'

'Threatening how?' He truly didn't get it.

Bridie squeezed lemon over her oysters and reached for the caviar spoon. 'You are so…so…irritating! And secretive. All I'm saying is would it kill you to share your plans before they hit me and Reid like a freight train?'

'That's not *all* you're saying.' He was still trying to get to the bottom of that. 'I know it's going to take a while to warm up to new faces around here, but we have plans and goals that you fully support. People with specialised skills are going to be coming in. I'm starting with these two—three—because I figured it might ease you in gently so you *can* get used to people coming and going. I thought it would help you as well as them.'

She stared at him with stormy eyes.

'In my defence, I extended one of those offers months ago and the other one weeks ago and neither of them took me up on it at the time. I'm not hiding information from you deliberately. I'm still figuring out the decision-making process and when it's an easy one I make the call because I can.' Did he really have to remind her about the buttons?

'I'm jealous.'

'You're—' He sat back. 'Of what?'

She smiled grimly. 'Jealous of a hardworking single mum who sounds like she could use a hand and who'll have daily access to you that I don't. You met a lady in Sydney who sounds like a treasure and you never said a word. You're entitled to a life of your own and I know that. It's just… I'm coming to the conclusion that I might be a little possessive. Of you. And that's not good because you should absolutely spread yourself around, doing good things for other people. It's nice. Unlike me.' She waved towards his plate of food, and then looked down at her own plate and stabbed an oyster with her fork in a way he was pretty sure no oyster had ever been stabbed before. 'These are fresh.'

'Whoa, wait. Back up.' He kind of liked the thought of her wanting to lay claim to him. No need to beat herself up about it though. He eyed her carefully. 'Can we at least agree that I have no sexual interest in these women and that you have nothing to worry about on that front?'

'No, because then I'd have to stop arguing before I've worked my way up to making my point.'

Good old logic. Not a big player in this conversation. 'By all means make your point.'

'You seek me out, you seem to like my company, and every time I ask if you want your ring back you say *not yet*. You let me see all your eccentricities and, sod knows, they're fascinating. You're fascinating.'

He wasn't exactly sure where she was going with this but surely she would get to the reason his ring wasn't on her finger soon. 'You're not finished yet, are you?'

'No. You also consistently ignore the fact that I'm dying of lust for you.'

He hadn't touched her since returning from Sydney. He'd wanted her to know what she was getting into if she was having thoughts about being with him. He'd buried lust beneath a mountain of work and had set about showing her all the negative traits he possessed. It was important before they started anything real that she knew the real him. He cleared his throat. 'Nothing wrong with lust. Shows you didn't hate what we did last time.'

'I'd like to do it again. With you. Pretty sure I made that clear. And I get that you don't want to sully me, or overwhelm me, or whatever it is you think you're going to do, but I'm a woman of experience now—'

He snorted.

'—and I'm losing hope.'

Four little words that shattered him more effectively than a crowbar to the head.

'I can't keep giving you this much of myself if you're not interested in taking this—us—any further.'

She had a knack for honest self-reflection that terrified him. And he hadn't been giving out scraps, he'd been lowering guards so deeply nailed into his psyche that they only moved a fraction at a time. 'I'm interested.' Understatement. The thought of losing whatever it was they had made him sweat. 'At the same time, I don't want to overwhelm or disappoint you.'

'But you don't disappoint me,' she said quietly from beneath a fall of lashes. 'I want another reset of our relationship. The Conrad land is yours now. You're making waves in the business world and society thinks you're golden. There's no reason to stay engaged unless we want to. My question is: do you want to?'

'Do you?'

'You first,' she said with a smile that didn't quite meet her eyes. 'I used up all my courage putting that ring on the table.'

Was she really saying she wanted to take him on for good, flaws and all? He wasn't quite ready to admit his fierce joy at that thought, even to himself, but he wanted that ring back on her finger and, timing wise, right now wasn't nearly soon enough.

'My reputation hinges on me being a reformed man,' he offered slowly, mind racing. 'I need to be seen as settled and steady. Combining Jeddah Creek and Devil's Kiss by way of marriage is a move my aristocratic ancestors would applaud. It's good business.'

'Not quite the reset I was imagining,' she murmured.

She deserved more, no doubt, but for all that his feelings for her ran deep—*you're in love with her,* a little voice whispered—she still figured him for a hero and he knew for a fact that he wasn't. The secret he'd held to for so many years, the one that had sent him to prison, clawed at him for release so that she could see him more fully, but he'd given his word and breaking it would have far-reaching and possibly legal consequences for all of them.

Hold your tongue. Give her what truth you can and make it enough. That was what he should be doing.

'I do want to marry you. I want that a lot, but I need you to be sure you know what you're getting into with me, and I don't think you do,' he told her baldly. 'That's my concern. You could still wear my ring while you figure it out.'

Her fingers rubbed at the spot where the ring currently wasn't. 'And would there be sex while I was figuring all this out? Because we haven't... Y'know...'

Oh, he knew. 'Again, I was giving you time to reassess.' And shore up his control. 'But if you need more to go on...'

'I do need more to go on.' They locked glances and she raised an elegant eyebrow in silent question. 'Your move.'

'Rest assured I'll be making one.'

'When?'

'Tonight.'

She changed the subject after that. Spoke about the latest set of plans for the eco cabins and how the indoor-outdoor spaces could become one with the help of sliding walls of glass that could swing out over a deck and either stay there to block the wind or slide seamlessly into the adjacent wall and disappear completely. Both the north-east and south-west walls had been tagged as slide-away. It'd be like living in a box without ends, but there were a few interior walls for privacy when needed, and a roof overhead…

The entire thing could be built in Brisbane, loaded in a container and trucked to the site and then put together in a day, by four labourers. If the cabins didn't stack up as promised, Judah figured the takeaway could be just as speedy.

The oysters were fresh and the caviar topped them off to perfection.

He helped her carry their empty plates to the kitchen once they'd devoured them. Two snappers sat ready for baking, covered in herbs and spices. 'What happens with these?'

'They're for the oven and I'm supposed to spoon the sauce over them every now and again while they're cooking. Easy as.'

She'd gone to a lot of trouble for him. 'Thank you for the wonderful meal.'

'Sometimes I want to try and impress you.'

'You always do.'

She got the food started and he wondered what she'd do if he leaned against the bench and held out his hand. Would she hesitate? Did she really understand what she would be getting into if she took him on for good?

'I have a question for you,' he began. 'It's about travel, English aristocracy and an ancestral home in the UK that needs a lot of work. On the upside, the money's now there to do all the work. If you marry me there'll be travel. Society connections to strengthen, or not, depending what kind of reception a murdering, ex-convict lord from the colonies is given.'

'Sounds horrific.'

'Yes. And you don't like to travel. I'm asking you to think hard about what marriage to me would mean. What would be required of you in order for me to fulfil my ancestral responsibilities. And I do plan to fulfil them.'

Her lips tightened. 'I'm not saying you couldn't find someone better for that role, because you definitely could. But it also sounds like someone should be there to guard your back, and who better than some scrappy little nobody that people will underestimate?'

'Not for long.' At a guess.

'What would your wife even be called?'

'You'd be Lady Bridie Blake, or Lady Blake, but it's only a prefix. A courtesy title. The barony would pass to our firstborn son. The only courtesy titles any of our other children could claim would be minor ones. Reid, for example, is The Honourable Reid Blake.'

'That's...pretty brutal on the younger kids in a family,' she murmured. 'And women.'

'Welcome to the peerage.'

'So, uh, children. Do you want to be a father?' she asked next.

'Yes.'

She made a small hum of approval. 'Daughters or sons?'

'Both. It'd help if they were legitimate.'

'Well, yes. I can see that.'

He held out his hand and her smile warmed his soul as she came to him willingly. He brushed her hair away from her face as gently as he could, marvelling at its softness and the warmth of her skin. 'Did you just agree to marry me and have my babies?'

'Our babies,' she corrected. 'And no, I haven't agreed to marry you yet, because you haven't asked me yet. Not properly.'

'Marry me.' He brushed his lips against hers and her eyes fluttered closed. An invitation to delve deeper and he took it. Salt on his tongue from the caviar, the sweetness of wine, and the innocent generosity of her every action. 'Say yes.'

She hummed in pleasure and set her hands to his waist. He could feel all his muscles clench as if he were ticklish and waiting for assault. But he wasn't ticklish, and the kisses continued. He let go of her hand and pulled her against him, soft heat to unbearable hardness.

She smiled through her kisses. 'You want me in your bed.'

'Never doubt it.'

'You can have me.'

'Still coming to terms with that. You haven't said yes to marrying me yet.'

She pulled back, out of his arms to check the food. 'You haven't said you love me yet. Or is that too much to ask?'

'It's not too much to ask.' But he still didn't know how to go about saying it.

'Let me guess,' she said drily. 'Love means making yourself vulnerable and that's hard for you.'

'Good guess.'

'Then I guess we'll just have to work on that. Can you hand me the plates from the warming oven?' she asked as she spooned sauce over steaming fish. He got her the plates, grateful for the reprieve, and she smiled her thanks. 'I hope you're hungry.'

'Famished.'

The tasty baked fish and accompanying greens, and the time it took to eat them, did nothing but ratchet up his tension. Was she going to wear his ring again or not? And how would he perform in bed? Would she want to tie him up again?

'Don't tie me up in bed this time,' he blurted, with absolutely no finesse.

She looked up from the delicate dissection of her fish. 'Okay.'

'Not that I—' He started again. 'I've been working on shoring up my self-control.'

'By yourself?' she teased.

'More or less.' She could think what she wanted and it'd probably be true. 'Those first few weeks at home… There were so many foods I hadn't tasted in years and I was a glutton for them, just shovelling it in. So many things I hadn't *done* in years and the need to do them rode me hard. And there you were. Willing.' He cleared his throat and took a sip of the very fine wine she'd served with this course. 'I had so little impulse control back then. I had freedom and no one was controlling my every move, and the curse of it all was that I could barely function. I wanted you and not in a good way. I wanted to *take*.' He shook his head. 'It wasn't right. You should have been scared of me.'

But she hadn't been.

'I have more control now. Over everything.' God, let it be true. 'Even with the occasional bonfire event.'

She lifted her glass and sipped, all effortless elegance and restraint. 'I know you do.'

'There's still a way to go.'

'I know that too.'

He refused dessert and then relented when he saw that she'd gone to the trouble of making lemon tart and had whipped cream to go with fat blackberries. They abandoned the formal dining room and Bridie served dessert on the veranda, and that, more than anything, calmed him.

He didn't know if he'd ever be much of an indoor person.

'Where do you go of a night to bed down when you don't stay here?' she asked.

'All over. Mostly the top of the escarpment if it isn't windy. River bend if I'm looking for extra shelter.'

'And you sleep in a swag?'

He nodded. Couple of rolls of latex mattress and bedclothes, all of it covered in a canvas outer and he was all set. 'Unless it's hot, and then I sleep *on* the swag in the bed of the truck.'

'What about the bugs?'

'I'm outback tough. There are no bugs.'

Bridie snorted at his utter bull.

'I wouldn't demand that of you,' he murmured, the thought of her flawless skin covered in bites not at all to his liking. 'I'm working my way in.'

'My bedroom has big screen doors out onto the veranda. You can't see the sky from the bed, but you could be outside in an instant. I'm inviting you in.'

He set his empty bowl down and waited with gentlemanly patience while she finished the last of her lemon dessert. They still hadn't finished the wine, but he'd long since stopped drinking it and Bridie's glass was still mostly full. Nothing they decided to do next could be blamed on alcohol.

He stood and held out his hand again, and she flowed into his embrace as if she belonged there. 'Where's your bedroom?'

He followed her to it and stepped into a world of lamp-lit linen and soft-looking pillows. Jarrah floorboards grounded the room and floor rugs added touches of silver, pink and saltbush-green. The big old four-poster bed looked so inviting with its fluffy pillows and pale blue bedspread and ivory sheets. Bridie's bedroom was classy, feminine and soothing. He loved it.

'Is this all right?' she asked, and he could tell she was waiting for him to bolt.

'It's you.'

'If I do anything wrong, you'll tell me, right?'

He had to laugh. 'That's my line.'

'See, I thought your line might have been *strip*.'

Oh, hell, yes. 'Good line. Great line. Inspired. Do that.'

She made a meal out of removing her clothes. The outer layer first, and whoever had designed her lingerie needed a medal, because it made his brain shut down completely. Lace, and plenty of it, cut just so to accentuate precisely how different her body was from his. So perfect. Practically untouchable.

'Hey.' She sought and held his gaze. 'It's only me.'

So not helping.

She reached for him with greedy hands and he responded in kind. He could be needy and greedy and reverent and tender all at the same time, couldn't he? He wanted to please. Willpower was everything. It had seen him through more than seven years of hell. Surely he could appreciate those itty-bitty scraps of lace she'd worn just for him without losing his mind?

'Just touch me,' she whispered. 'I *want* your hands on me. Any argument that I'm pure and virginal is rubbish now. I'm a woman of vast experience.'

No, she was the woman he couldn't resist. Not when she gave him so much encouragement. He toppled her onto that cloud of a bed and followed her down, the soft warmth of her skin intoxicating.

'Take a chance on me,' she murmured. 'I'm right here and I want everything you're prepared to give.'

Bridie felt the tremble in his fingers and the ragged tenderness of his hands on her skin, as she in turn took her fill. She couldn't get enough of the hard muscle that defined him, or the aching tenderness of his kisses. If this was his version of ruining her, being too much for her to handle, she could almost understand his logic.

He was absolutely ruining her for all other men.

He took forever to prepare her, with his fingers and his lips, and this time when he entered her, she welcomed him with laughing enthusiasm. Her laughter seemed to set something free in him, and he smiled as he set up a rhythm that had her shooting past the Milky Way and out into orbit within minutes.

Self-consciousness never stood a chance as she rode every pulsing, ecstasy-ridden moment, and just when she thought she couldn't go again, he snaked his hand between her legs and drew one last ripple from her as he found his own release.

She needed to tell the silent Judah with the heaving chest

just how good that had been. Just as soon as she regained the power of speech.

It took a few minutes, but finally she had the voice for it. 'Judah?' She snugged up into him, leaving little room for daylight, and his arms came around her, the fingers of one of his hands twining through her hair to rest at the nape of her neck.

'Mmm?'

'Let's do that again.'

CHAPTER ELEVEN

TOM STARR DEFINITELY didn't want to talk to him, thought Judah grimly, as he left yet another message for the older man to call him. The couple of times Tom *had* responded to his questions, Bridie had been her father's spokesperson.

Yes, to putting a portion of Devil's Kiss station into the conservation trust Judah had set up.

Yes, to putting the payment for the land Bridie had purchased from Judah's father into the general Devil's Kiss business account.

Judah had hoped his blunt request for permission to marry Bridie would have got Tom to pick up or at least return the call, but no.

Nothing.

That was two weeks ago.

Even Reid had tried calling. Reid had a lot of time for Tom, because of how helpful Tom had been during that four months or so Reid had been alone out here—before Judah had returned.

That man—his father's friend, the one who'd helped Reid through those toughest of times, the one who'd pulled Bridie through her almost withdrawal from society—was a man Judah didn't know.

When he thought of Tom at all it was with a mixture of frustration and anger, and deeply buried resentment that he didn't dare examine. That night... It had been two against one and Judah and Tom had been on home ground. They could have tackled Laurence, restrained him, neutered him on the spot... Between them they could have done *something* that didn't require ending the man. But Laurence Levit had burst from the car and charged them, and Tom, with his twenty-two-calibre shotgun that he'd used for years on the farm, hadn't hesitated and he sure as hell hadn't missed.

Judah didn't *blame* Tom for taking the shot. Not really. They'd all been running on fear and instinct.

But more and more, Judah railed against keeping secrets from Bridie. The woman who once more wore his engagement ring and who saw more of what lived inside him every day. Hopes and dreams. Struggles and failures. Hard-won success when it came to the simplest of decisions. She did more than simply encourage him. She believed in him.

He had *Notice of Intended Marriage* paperwork burning a hole in his desk drawer, and he wanted to move on that soon. *Just do it,* he thought. *Tell her you love her and that you've never been happier and just marry her and let the past stay buried in a vow of secrecy.*

Loving her didn't have to mean confiding in her, surely.

Even if he wanted to.

These days he didn't know what exactly it was that shook him from her bed in the dark hours of most mornings, but he tried to make it up to her. He'd taken to collecting wildflowers and greenery, whatever he could find, and returning with a fistful and either leaving them on her doorstep or bringing them with him to breakfast.

Bridie had clear run out of vases but her eyes would still light up every time he handed her a posy.

'Heard anything from your father?' he asked one morning after a night that had made him forget his own name and a morning spent watching the sun rise from the top of Devil's

Peak. He was back on her veranda now with a coffee in hand, no sugar, and way too much cream.

'Yes.' Bridie sat in an old rocking chair wearing a stripy pink T-shirt and darker pink bed shorts, her hair in a messy bun and breakfast in hand; to Judah she'd never looked more beautiful. 'He bought an opal mine in Lightning Ridge, complete with underground home and a hole-in-the-wall shop front, and apparently he *does* mean hole in the wall. I don't know what's going on with him. He's too old to be having a midlife crisis and he hasn't said anything about meeting a woman, but what other reasons are there for his refusal to come home? He has no interest in the management of Devil's Kiss any more and I truly don't understand. This is his home. Why won't he come *home*?'

So Judah rang again, and this time Tom picked up.

'You're a hard man to reach.' Judah spoke first.

'And you're relentless,' grumbled the older man.

'Bridie's worried about you.'

''M fine.'

'Reid misses you too.' Might as well turn those screws.

'They have you now.'

Definitely not the answer he'd been expecting. 'You have a problem with me.' Statement, not question. 'Why? I've kept every promise I've ever made. Especially to you.'

'What do you want?' He could barely hear the older man.

'Permission to marry your daughter.'

'You don't need it.'

That wasn't the point. 'It's customary to ask for it.'

The other man said nothing.

Judah gritted his teeth before he spoke again. Bridie loved this man. Reid thought the world of him. 'You left. The minute I got home you left and I don't understand why. You have people here who love you and people contemplating big changes in their lives, and you're not here for them. Why not? What have I done wrong?'

'Nothing,' Tom rasped after long moments. 'But every time

I look at you I feel ashamed at what I've put you through. The trial. Your sentence. The impact it had on your parents and your brother. On you. I'd go back in time and do things differently if I could, but I can't, and it pains me. It pains me to look at you and know in my heart what your generosity has cost you. I don't know how to make it up to you. So I try not to look at you at all.'

'Come home.' Judah didn't want Tom Starr exiled from the life he'd once loved. 'Take a look at what we're building here. Be a part of it again. And if your conscience is troubling you, we can sit down together, with Bridie, and tell her what really happened that night.'

Silence.

'Is that a no?'

'Why?' He could barely hear the other man. 'Why on earth would you want to do that?'

'Did *you* keep secrets from *your* wife?' Judah snapped, losing what little patience he had left. 'I don't *want* to marry your daughter and have to lie to her about that night for the rest of our lives,' he said, abandoning all pretence that he gave a damn about Tomas's conscience. He wanted his own conscience clear. He wanted Bridie to know what she was getting when she chose him. 'Is that really too much to ask?'

He blundered on. 'What if we sat her down and explained everything and that we did what we did to protect her? Surely she'd understand.' And be okay with a father who'd killed to protect her and a future husband who hadn't, but at least there'd be no more lies.

Tom Starr didn't reply.

'Can you at least think about it?'

'You gave me your word.'

'I know. And I've never broken it, even though you broke yours when you told my father what you did. But you could release me from my vow.' He couldn't see the other man to read his face. He had no idea what Tom Starr was thinking. There was just this sea of silence.

'We need to think about this.' There was a world of weariness in the older man's voice. 'If word ever got out I could go to prison. You could go *back* to prison. Is that what you want?'

'Word wouldn't get out because Bridie wouldn't tell anyone.'

'Are you sure about that? Because I'm not. Do you really think we should burden her with a secret she can never share without her whole world crumbling? *And* we'd be making her an accessory after the fact. Is telling her the truth really worth all that?'

The older man was right. He was being a fool. A romantic, idiotic fool. 'You're right.'

'I'm sorry, son, but I just don't see the sense in telling Bridie what happened that night and dragging her into the pit with us. You promised to protect her.'

'I know.'

'You gave me your word.'

'I'll keep it.'

'I know you will.' There was an ache in the older man's voice that he didn't know what to do with. An ache in his own heart because there was no way around this. Tom Starr was right and that was the end of it.

Their secret had to be kept.

Gert was baking and Bridie was stacking groceries; music was blaring and the sun had yet to sap the will to move. All in all, Bridie decided, life was good and she'd never deny it.

'Have you met the new people over at Jeddah Creek yet?' asked Gert.

'Yep.' A couple of times over, plenty long enough to form some opinions. 'Mary the bookkeeper is a sweetheart, but she's kind of shocked by outback living. I don't know if she'll stay.'

'What about the young one?'

'Kaylee? She's a hoot. Big laugh, can-do attitude, tough as nails. And grateful, y'know? In that way that says she's seen a lot of rough road in her life. I have a feeling she'll stay—at least for a while. Her little guy's not even two yet. Cute kid. Judah and Reid are so protective of him. You should see them.'

Gert snorted. 'Sounds about right. They have that ruling class serve-and-protect mentality, same as their grandfather did. And their father did too, before his liking for a drink ruined him.'

'Yeah, maybe.' Bridie didn't know what bits of Gert's conversation she was agreeing with, but it probably didn't matter.

'You expecting visitors?' Gert asked next.

'Nope.'

'Because there's a line of dust heading in from the east and it's just turned into your driveway.'

The driveway was two kilometres long. Plenty of time for her and Gert to head on out to the veranda and wait. Eventually Bridie got a good enough look at the vehicle to figure out who it was. 'It's my father.'

'Huh,' huffed Gert and headed back inside. Bridie waited, and when her father pulled up and stepped from the cab, she unfolded her crossed arms and ran to greet him. His hug was as solidly comforting as it had always been. 'Hello, stranger.'

'Daughter.' He pulled back. 'You're looking bright.'

'It's all this newfound independence,' she countered drily. 'I've missed you, though.'

He looked uncomfortable. 'I needed to do a bit of thinking.'

'Finished yet?'

'Doubtful. Your aunt sent a present along for you. It's in the back.'

'You saw her? Is she well?'

He nodded. 'Got herself a good man who thinks the world of her.' His gaze didn't stray from Bridie's face. 'I hear you have one of those too.'

They headed into the kitchen, where Gert had coffee on and ginger nuts in the oven. Her father smiled. Gert didn't.

'Tomas Starr, is that you? I barely remember what you look like.'

'And a good day to you too, Gert.'

The older woman fixed him with a gimlet glare. 'Your room's not made up.'

'I can make a bed,' her father said easily.

'Are you back to stay?' Bridie asked, interrupting before war broke out.

Her father shrugged. 'For a while. Mainly to see if you need anything and whether all the changes are working out.'

'They are.' She'd missed having him around. She wanted him back and for more than just a while. 'Opal miner now, huh? I would never have guessed.'

He dug in his pocket and pulled out two good-sized stones and handed one to her and one to Gert. 'It's a bit of fun.'

'Black opal.' Gert held hers up to the light. 'Tom Starr, you canny ass.'

'Plenty more where that came from,' he offered. 'You're both welcome to join me next time I head down that way.'

'Do I get to keep this opal?' asked Gert.

'Yes, it's for you. Thanks for keeping an eye on Bridie while I was gone.'

'Next time you take off for parts unknown, check in more,' Gert scolded. 'Your daughter worries about you. Those Blake boys have been worried about you too, especially Reid. He looks up to you. You encouraged that and now you've let him down.'

'He has Judah now,' her father countered.

Gert glared at him. 'And you don't think Judah could have used your support too? Tomas Starr, I never took you for such a fool.'

'Live and learn, Gert,' her father said quietly as he hooked his leg around a kitchen stool and took a seat. 'Live and learn.'

Gert headed off to the Blakes' at noon—nothing disrupted her schedule if she could help it, not even the return of the prodigal father. Bridie welcomed the privacy; she had so much to tell her father, from the success of her exhibitions to the photography job she'd agreed to in South Australia that meant she'd be away for a week, staying on a property that had a huge wool-shed with a heritage and history she found fascinating. She wanted to tell him she'd sold the season's steers for an excellent price, but had resisted culling any of the main herd when buyers had asked for more meat of any kind. The Devil's Kiss stockmen would have known which animals to cull, no question, but it was traditionally her father's role and she hadn't wanted to overstep.

She waited until after dinner when their bellies were full of home-grown steak, jacket potatoes, asparagus and sweetcorn, and her father had settled into his favourite rocking chair on the veranda, before she broached more personal topics.

'Judah's been trying to reach you.'

'He did.' Her father's eyes were darkly shadowed. 'He asked me for your hand in marriage. He's old-fashioned that way.'

'Did you give him your blessing?'

'We talked.'

Bridie's blood ran cold. Never in a million years had she thought her father would hold Judah's past against him. 'He's a good man, Dad. The best. And I am so...so in love with him.'

'He puts me to shame.' Her father looked away, out over the home paddock and on to the horizon. He took a deep breath. 'What do you remember about the night that bastard took you?'

She shook her head. She hated remembering any of it. 'Laurence came to the door and I let him in. Offered him a coffee. He'd come all this way to clear the air between us, he said, and no one else was here.'

'After that,' her father ordered gruffly.

'I told him I wasn't going back to modelling. It wasn't what he wanted to hear. He grabbed me. I struggled. He hit me. I passed out. I remember coming to, bound and gagged in the boot of a car. I remember you and Judah rescuing me and Levit bleeding out in the dirt.'

Her father nodded. 'And on the surface that's exactly what

happened. Never forget, Bridie girl, that I love you. That I did everything in my power to protect you. And that Judah went way beyond what could be expected of any man to protect you too.'

'I know this already.'

But her father shook his head, leaned forward and brought the rocker to a halt. He stared at the weathered wooden floorboards as if they were the most fascinating things he'd ever seen. 'No, you don't. Not everything. We kept something from you.'

'What do you mean?'

'Judah didn't kill the bastard who kidnapped you, Bridie. I did.'

Don't do anything rash. Bridie used the words as a mantra during her drive to Jeddah Creek homestead. *Don't act out. Listen* to what Judah had to say. And all the while, with every red dust kilometre, the foundations of her world crumbled. Her father was a killer and a liar who'd sold his soul to protect her. And Judah...not a killer, but still a liar who'd paid a huge price for his deception. How could he have chosen to do that for her and her father? She didn't understand.

Bridie checked her speed as she approached the main house. There was a child living in the shearer's quarters these days and other new people about and it wouldn't do to run over them. She parked next to Gert's truck and took the stairs two at a time, only to almost bump into Reid, who looked to be on his way out.

'Whoa, steady Freddie.' He sidestepped her just in time.

'Judah around?'

'In his office.' Judah had turned the sitting room next to the library into his office. It had French doors leading onto the veranda and Bridie didn't bother going through the house to get there.

Judah looked up from his seat behind the desk as she entered, a smile crinkling his eyes. 'Just in time,' he said. 'The cabin plans are in.'

But she didn't want to pour over building plans with him. 'I've just been speaking with my father.'

'Gert said he was back.' He lifted an eyebrow. 'Bearing opals.'

Bridie didn't want to talk about little coloured stones. 'He said you'd asked for his permission to marry me.'

'I did.'

Judah sat back in his chair, everything about him easy and welcoming, except for those watchful, wary eyes.

'You want to know what else he told me?' She couldn't keep the rage out of her voice and it seemed useless to even try.

'That he refused to give it?'

She hadn't known *that*. Apparently she didn't know a lot of things that happened around here. 'He told me what happened that night, Judah. What really happened.'

She'd never seen a person shut down so fast. Any openness in his beautiful strong face disappeared like spilt water in a sandy desert. 'What do you mean?'

'What do you *think* I mean?' she cried. 'Did my father kill Laurence Levit, or did you? Because my father just told me he did it!'

Not by a blink did Judah betray any discomfort. 'I've said all I'm ever going to say about that. I was convicted and I've done my time. Move on.'

'But my father—'

'Is mistaken.'

'Well, one of you is lying! And I'm inclined to believe him.'

Judah shrugged.

'Judah, please. *Talk* to me.'

'And accomplish what? Shall I make you complicit in a possible cover-up that took place years ago? Should I break the oath I might have made to your father to take the details of that night to my grave? What if I didn't shoot Levit? Do you want to see me up on perjury charges and your father locked up? Is that it?'

'No, I—'

'Then *stop* asking questions. Your father is a deluded old man. Don't believe him.'

But she did believe her father's startling words. That was the problem. 'But why would you *do* such a thing? Why would a young man with *everything* going for him—money, status, a loving family, good looks and good health—why would he choose to be locked up for something he didn't do? Will you at least offer me a theoretical answer to that question?' If Judah wasn't going to confirm a damn thing, could they at least play pretend while she got to the bottom of everyone's actions? 'Can't you open up to me just a little?' she pleaded. 'Because I don't understand. I just don't get it.'

'Is he of the ruling class?' Judah steepled his fingers and held her gaze, looking every inch the aristocrat. 'Or, y'know what? Scrap that. Maybe he'd simply been raised to serve and protect those in his care—the old, the frail, the *children*.'

'But if my father was the one who took the shot, why didn't he say so at the time? They might have gone easy on him. Easier than they went on you.'

'And who would have taken you in? Who would have cared for you the way your father did? Who would have had the love and the patience to help put you back together again? Your aunt? She was already struggling with her own issues. You don't have any other family. Your father was it. Who better to love and protect you than him? What if your father and that foolish young man made a split-second decision to protect you? And then did so.'

She had no answer for him. 'I'm not a child any more.'

'I know that.'

'You can tell me the truth.'

'Good, then hear this.' He spread his hands. 'I love you. And I'll protect you with my last breath, don't ever doubt it. This is me protecting you.'

Not exactly how she'd imagined his first declaration of love for her would go.

He watched as she twisted her engagement ring around and around. 'Are you going to keep that on?'

She didn't know. She was so *angry* with him. For stepping up to take the blame for something he didn't do. For defending his action as the right thing to do, never mind what it had cost him. For protecting her still. 'I'm so sorry,' she whispered.

'You're not to blame. You owe me nothing. And if you're going to take that ring off, *for God's sake just do it*!' He looked more rattled than she'd ever seen him, and she'd seen him rattled a lot. He ran an unsteady hand through his hair. 'I can't stand to watch you playing with it. That's my heart you're holding in your hands.'

His outburst jolted her some way towards recognising how hard this conversation must be for him too. 'You have to stop protecting me,' she defended weakly, even as she clasped her hands behind her back. No fiddling with the ring. Just a vicelike grip of one hand over the tennis bracelet on her wrist.

He glared at her with stormy eyes. 'I will *never* not protect you.'

'Truth is important,' she said next. 'Especially in a marriage.'

'How important?' His gaze didn't leave hers. 'If your father says he pulled that trigger I'll call him a crazy old coot and a liar to his face. If I'm not measuring up to some ideal you have in your head about what you want in a man and truth in marriage, walk away. Run. Because this is who I am.'

'I—' If she believed her father—and she did—she also had to believe that the two most important people in her life had been lying to her all along. Judah was *still* lying to her. 'I'm so confused.'

'It's really pretty simple from where I'm standing. You either understand where I'm coming from or you don't.'

She was confused and shattered. Judah was lying about who pulled that trigger. She knew he was lying. He *knew* she knew he was lying. But he wouldn't stop. 'I need time. I don't know what to think.'

He rose from his chair and headed for the interior door that led to a hallway inside the house. 'Let me know what you decide.'

'Wait!'

He stopped.

'You said you love me.' She hadn't imagined that, had she?

'I do.' He started walking towards the door again. 'It doesn't mean you have to love me back. That's not how it works.'

Moments later he was gone.

CHAPTER TWELVE

BRIDIE DROVE HOME, half expecting her father to have taken off again, but he met her at the door, no questions on his tongue but his eyes awhirl with them. She didn't know what to say to him, she really didn't.

'Judah says you're a lying old coot,' she offered finally. Might as well start at the top. 'So let's make ourselves a cup of tea and figure out where to go from here.'

She let the motions soothe her as she filled the teapot with leaves from the little tin canister that had sat on the kitchen shelf forever. Her father took his black and strong. She took hers with milk and liked it weaker, so she made sure she took first pour. And all the time she marshalled her thoughts and arguments so that the two most important people in her life would remain in her life. 'Let's take it out to the veranda.'

He picked up his cup and she followed him out, unsurprised when he chose the northern veranda with its relentlessly bright light that reached deep into the veranda and sometimes hit the windows. It had the best views, unmarred by garden trees. It was red dirt and spinifex as far as the eye could see, with very little variation in topography. Their most brutal view, in many ways. There wasn't a scrap of civilisation in it.

She sat down beside him on the veranda ledge and nudged his shoulder with hers. They both sipped deeply of the tea.

'I've missed this,' he murmured.

'You didn't have to leave.'

'Needed to get my head on straight,' he said, and she thought about that. About what Judah's return might have done to him. Judah could reject the notion all he liked but he'd done so much for them. So much more than anyone could have asked of him. And all Judah had asked of them was to let it go and move forward.

'Thing is,' she continued doggedly, 'me, you, Aunt Beth— we can all blame ourselves for the decisions that led us to that moment.' She took her father's calloused hand, with the knuckles just starting to thicken with arthritis, and held on tight. 'I should never have chosen modelling and brought Laurence Levit into our lives. Aunt Beth should have known better than to be taken in by him, but she had barely more experience with predatory men than I did. You could have come to Paris with us and pegged him as a bad one or maybe you wouldn't have, who knows? Point is, he got hold of us and then kept on coming. The law didn't stop him. Those AVOs we had out against him meant nothing out here. Can we agree on that? That Laurence Levit wasn't stopped by ordinary means?'

Her father's hand tightened around hers, a squeeze to show he was listening. 'We can.'

'So whatever happened, happened. And one way or another we owe Judah more than we can ever say. Can we agree on that too?'

'Yes.'

She took a deep breath and exhaled noisily. 'The only payment Judah wants is for us to look forward rather than back, and I am on board with that. I can understand you not being in the same place, and that feelings of guilt or shame or the need for penance might be eating at you, but I want you to know that in my eyes you are both heroes. Laurence crossed a line when he took me. All the character witnesses they put on the stand, all those people who said he was an upstanding man, they didn't look into his eyes and see their own death staring back at them. I did, and it was me or him, Dad. Me or him. I'm glad you chose me.'

Her father squeezed her hand and then carefully let it go, but Bridie wasn't finished yet.

'Judah's adamant he did the deed and he knows I don't believe him, but he won't tell the truth. He's protecting us. Even if I'd rather he didn't this time around.'

'He's a man of his word,' her father muttered with far more complacency than Bridie thought was warranted. 'But look on the bright side, at least now you know the truth, even if he never confirms it. No more secrets between you two. A clean slate before marriage. That's a good thing, so I'm told.'

Wait. 'Did you know Judah was never going to rat you out?'

Her father shrugged. 'Might've.'

Holy—

'That's…' She had no words.

'Inspired?'

More like brutally self-serving. 'You left him to hang. Again.'

'I knew he loved you and wanted to marry you. I knew he could never tell you what really happened, no matter how much he wanted to. Not if he wanted to protect you from knowing too much. But if *I* told you, he could still deny it and we'd all be protected. And you'd know what he wanted you to know but could never tell you.'

'That's insane.'

'It worked.'

Heaven help her it had, but not without cost. She remembered Judah's stricken face and furious outburst when she'd been twisting her engagement ring around and around. When she'd been doing her damnedest to understand his position. 'You took a huge risk, playing us like that.'

'It worked.' He looked towards the horizon. To the harsh land that set a person against relying on others to fix their problems. 'No secrets between you now. Be happy. Reach out for all the happiness you can hold and never take it for granted.'

'Promise me you'll stay a part of our lives,' she pressed.

Her father offered up the ghost of a smile. 'I've got opal seams to find.'

'Then promise me you'll visit often and remember on a daily basis how much I love you and want you in my life.'

'Judah might prefer otherwise. What did he call me? A lying old coot?'

'Well, you are,' she felt compelled to point out. He was also her father. The same father who'd given her the time and space in which to heal from her ordeal. The one who'd helped her live her best life.

Bridie leaned her head against the veranda post. 'I didn't handle my confrontation with Judah very well. I got all caught up in truth-telling and couldn't see the bigger picture.' *Breathe in, breathe out and try not to panic.* 'It's possible he thinks I'm going to dump him.'

Her father lowered his cup. 'Are you?'

'No.' A world of no. 'I'm going to marry him and protect him and cherish him as best I can, and he's never going to think I don't love him for being the man he is. Not for a second. Not even a fraction of a second.'

'Best get on that.'

'I will.'

Bridie had a plan. Granted, it would take the assistance of several other people in order for her to pull it off, but the end result was going to show Judah exactly how much she cherished him and all that he was.

Her first call was to Reid, and he offered no quarter, speaking before she'd even said a word. 'What have you done to my brother? He's been working like a demon all morning to distract himself from thinking your engagement is off.'

'It's not off.'

'Mind telling him that? In person? Soon? As in, I will come and get you in the helicopter right now.'

'That's the spirit.' Might as well go with the flow. 'Tell him I love him like crazy and that the engagement is very much on. Tell him that I'm putting together an apology surprise for him and that you'll pick him up an hour before sunset for a helicopter joyride with me at the end of it. That's all you need to say. Can you do that?'

'Better coming from you.'

'Apart from that, which I will see to, trust me, I need your helicopter and your services as a pilot for the rest of the day. I'll pay triple the going rate. And sheets. I need every sheet you've got that's not already on a bed.'

'Sheets,' he echoed doubtfully.

'For when I run out of rocks and fallen branches. Oh, and do you have any toilet paper?'

'No way am I giving up my share of the toilet paper. You've gotta be family for that.'

'Bring it anyway,' she urged.

'You're sounding a little bit mad today. Are you aware of this?' He really was a sweet and mostly biddable man.

'I am mad. I'm mad at myself for letting your brother doubt his worth for a second.'

'I'm going to put you on speaker phone now because Judah's just walked in, and you're going to put him out of his misery by telling him that.'

'Wait! Will you help me? It'll be worth it, I promise. I'm aiming to create a truly memorable moment.'

'Speaker phone. Now.'

'Wait!' But she didn't think Reid had been open to influence on this particular issue. 'Judah?'

'Bridie,' he replied evenly.

Right, so…speakerphone. 'I'm, uh, hi!' So not ready to confront him yet.

Silence.

Bridie closed her eyes, took a deep breath and began. 'So, yesterday was tough to navigate. Lots of new and surprising information to think about, you know?' She rushed on without waiting for more astonishingly loud silence. 'But I don't want to call off our engagement. You are without question the finest man I know. I want to marry you, cheer for you, laugh with you and cherish all the little pieces that make you who you are. I still want that for us.'

No one spoke.

Bridie cringed, wishing she could see how her words were being received. 'Do you—is that what you want?'

She heard a heavy sigh, but wasn't sure whose it was. 'Did someone just huff?'

'That was me,' confessed Reid. 'I'm trying to get my white-knuckled, tongue-tied brother to say something at this very special moment in time but he's not responding to my cues.'

And then Judah spoke. 'Bridie, you don't have to do this. You don't owe me a damn thing.'

'Wait!' yelped Reid. 'What?' There was the sound of a scuffle and muffled words she couldn't quite hear and then Reid in her ear again. 'Sorry I interrupted. My brother hasn't quite finished speaking yet.'

She waited. And waited.

And held her breath and *waited*.

'I'm yours.' Rough-cut words that sounded as if Judah had carved them out of his heart just for her. 'Yes, that's what I want. So much.'

'Great. That's perfect. *You're* perfect.' Even if he wasn't one for fancy words. She could be the fancy-word provider. Not a problem. 'Will you join me for an hour before sunset? And probably after the sun sets too? I want to spoil you to make up for my…confusion…yesterday.'

'No need,' Judah rumbled. 'It's forgotten.'

'No, it's not, even though we'll never mention it again. Will you please let Reid bring you to me this afternoon, no questions asked?'

'Yes.'

Yes! She punched the air with her fist. 'See you then. Oh, and, Reid?'

'My rotor blades are at your service, future favourite sister-in-law.'

'I'm really glad I get a little brother out of this deal too.' And not just because she really needed his help if she had any hope of pulling her rapidly forming plans together in a day. 'How soon can you get here? I have so much for you to do.'

Reid found Judah in his office shortly after five that afternoon. Judah studied his brother, looking for clues as to what he'd been up to, but Reid's aviator sunglasses hid his eyes and nothing else about him looked any different than it had this morning. Well-worn jeans, loose T-shirt, work boots, ready grin. Reid had been back twice throughout the afternoon to refuel, so he'd sure as hell been covering some ground in his compact two-seater helicopter.

'Ready to go find your intended?'

Reid had taken to all but bouncing up and down on the balls of his feet. Nervous energy was a new look for Reid and instantly made Judah even more suspicious about what the afternoon held in store. 'Am I going to like this surprise?'

'God, I hope so,' muttered Reid. 'If you don't, I'm thinking of relocating to Canada for a recovery holiday. Got your wallet?'

'What for?' Who needed a wallet around here?

'ID in case we crash. I've been reading up on my aviation rules.'

His brother's words were almost believable. Only not.

'Just bring your wallet.' Reid spread his arms out imploringly. One of his forearms had an ugly red scrape on it that Judah was pretty sure hadn't been there this morning. 'C'mon, I've been humouring Bridie all afternoon and it was a very tough gig. Is it too much to ask that you take your wallet out of your desk drawer and shove it in your back pocket?'

'Testy.' But he did as his brother asked, and Reid's smile re-appeared.

'How about a shirt with a collar?' Reid suggested next and Judah eyed him narrowly.

'Why?'

'Have I mentioned the amount of *effort* I've expended this afternoon on your behalf? Not to mention the effort Bridie's put in. Last I saw her she was absolutely filthy, headed for a shower and obsessing about whether she had anything suitable to wear. Silk was mentioned, along with whether she had time to wash and dry her hair and do anything with it. I have never run away faster, but out of the goodness of my very kind heart I'm sharing this information with you in case you want to go and change your shirt.'

So Judah went to the adjacent walk-in cupboard and changed his shirt. 'Anything else?'

'Decent boots. Not work boots.'

'Is this a formal dinner situation?' Because he'd been expecting something a little more casual. Picnic from the back of her Land Rover somewhere out on the plains while the sun went down.

'I am sworn to secrecy. But if we don't get cracking we're going to be late. Sunset waits for no man.'

It wasn't until they were walking to the helicopter that Judah spoke again. 'Where are we going?'

'Up.'

'Can you be any more specific?'

'Nope.'

Reid flew helicopters with the confidence only youth and long hours in the seat could bring. Mustering would see them flying low and darting about, but this time he took them high and smooth and put them on a north-east course towards river bend. Not so far to go, then, and he wondered why Bridie hadn't simply asked him to drive there. But Reid overshot the mark, so maybe river bend wasn't their destination at all. Reid then confused him twice over by swinging them around to approach the river again, this time with the sun behind them.

And then he saw it: a word spelled out on the ground with a combination of rocks, dead branches and some kind of white material.

The word was STRENGTH.

'I'm working from a script here, so let me get it right,' Reid told him through their headset two-ways. 'This is what Bridie sees in you. A man of strength. I see it too.'

Before Judah could comment, Reid swung the helicopter around in a show-off move and headed west.

Another word waited for them in the channel country, and it was as if a demented fairy had scoured the land for as many moveable rocks as they could find.

COURAGE was the word.

'This too,' said Reid, and circled it twice before taking them north.

'There's more?'

'Better believe it. Which is the point of this whole exercise. That you come to believe what she sees in you. Good thing she ran out of fabric.'

The next word said HONOUR.

'I like that one for you,' said Reid. 'I think it's my favourite.'

The next word was RESILIENCE, and it had been shaped out of some kind of heavy-duty canvas, pinned down by tent pegs and rocks.

'That one nearly did her in,' said tour guide Reid, while Judah sat there awash in words and none of them his. 'I had to help her with it because she was nowhere near done when I came to pick her up. Too many letters, man, way too many letters and not enough rocks in the world. Try PEP, I said. What about GRIT? I didn't do badly in my English exams, I had suggestions, but no. It had to be RESILIENCE. There's not a scrap of tarpaulin left in her shed.' Reid paused. 'Or ours.'

The next word was HOPE.

'She says a man without hope can't begin to imagine the future the way you do. Or work so hard to make it happen the way you do. Can't say I disagree with her. She had more words—it was a very long list, but there's only one more.'

'Good.' Because they were doing him in.

The last word was JOY.

'Joy?' he asked gruffly. 'Me? Now I'm sure she needs glasses.'

'Yeah.' Reid laughed. 'I queried that one too, but she swears there's a lifetime of it in store for you if you'll take her on. I'm to give you this now.' Reid handed him a white envelope. 'To read.'

In the envelope was a sheet of office paperwork, and words printed in a fancy font inviting him to the wedding of Miss Bridie Elizabeth Starr and Lord Judah Leopold Blake.

Date: Today
Time: Sunset
RSVP: Landing means I Do

'I'm your best man if that's what you want,' said Reid. 'And there's a wedding party waiting for you just over those trees. Gert is matron of honour and Tomas is the FOB—that's father of the bride—and he'll be giving Bridie away. I am bang up on wedding abbreviations after today. Old Ernie reckons he can legitimately marry you as long as you have some ID. I think he's dreaming, but what do I know?'

'Take us down.'

But Reid didn't take them down. Instead he flew over the clump of trees to reveal a pathway of rocks that led to a small group of people. Bridie stood out like a beacon in a slim white gown with tiny shoulder straps and the rest of it pretty much fell straight to the ground. Her riot of hair had been pulled away from her face and styled instead to cascade down her back. She held a posy stuffed haphazardly with desert flowers, the kind he'd taken to finding for her after a night beneath the stars.

'Reid. *Take us down.*'

'Those are the words I wanted to hear. Right after *Yes, oh, wise, hardworking and patient brother, I want you to be my best man.*'

'I want you to be my best man.'

'What happened to wise, hardworking and patient? You can't hog *all* the good words.'

'Reid, that woman down there is my North Star, my refuge and my soul. Get me down there before she changes her mind.'

'They're landing,' said Gert, and Bridie's heart soared.

Proving her love for Judah by springing a surprise wedding on him had seemed like a good idea at the time, but as everything came together, with Reid dropping her back at the homestead before flitting off to collect Gert, and then Ernie, and finally Judah, second thoughts had taken hold. What if Judah didn't want to marry her yet? What if he did want to marry her but wanted a different kind of wedding altogether? One that took a year or two to plan and involved many aristocratic guests? Maybe his inherited title meant he had to follow lots of rules before it was official?

Not that he was necessarily one for rules. He had his own unwavering code of honour and she loved him all the more for it.

She took a deep breath. In, out. In, out. While a brilliant afternoon sun gently kissed the horizon.

'It's normal to be a little bit nervous,' said Gert. 'And usually, it's the man standing here waiting for his bride.'

'Yay for equality,' offered Bridie weakly. She hadn't really thought this part of the afternoon through. Standing there scouring the sky and waiting for him to show had been *excruciating.*

She took a deep breath and exhaled noisily. She *had* given him the chance to simply fly away. Give him the invitation when you're on the last word, she'd told Reid. And then take him wherever he wants to go.

She'd had no plan B for if he didn't arrive, other than painfully, publicly falling to pieces. Why was it taking Reid so damn long to land the helicopter?

'Turn around and let me fuss over you,' said Gert, taking charge. The older woman's concerned blue gaze met hers as she tucked a strand of Bridie's hair behind her ear. 'You look so beautiful. So very ready to make that man happy, and there's no one who deserves happiness more than him.'

'I know.' She blew out another breath. Heaven knew what she'd be like in childbirth. Probably hyperventilating all over the place. 'I've got this.' She took Gert's hand and placed it over her racing heart. 'See?'

'Relax, child. He's here.'

She was never not going to associate the sound of the helicopter powering down with this moment. 'Is he heading our way?'

The older woman nodded and squeezed Bridie's hand before letting go. 'Tomas, you stand over here next to Ernie and I'll stand here, and all Judah and Reid have to do when they get here is step into place.'

Which they did.

Judah turned towards her, outback strong in dusty boots, well-worn jeans, collared shirt with the sleeves rolled up and eyes that searched her face. 'Hey.'

'Hey.' Forget butterflies in her stomach. She croaked like a frog.

'Beautiful sunset,' he said next, and Reid elbowed him in the ribs.

'North Star,' Reid muttered around a fit of totally fake coughing.

Judah jostled him back, his gaze not leaving her face. 'And still nowhere near as incredible as you,' he added quietly. 'Are you ready to take on the world with me?'

'I'm ready.' So very ready to love this man for ever.

So Ernie married them.

EPILOGUE

JUDAH WATCHED FROM his vantage point at one end of the ground-floor veranda as his guests spilled out of the crowded ballroom and into the night. Jeddah Creek station glowed with the care that only endless money and strong vision could bring. Planes were parked wing to wing in the outer home paddock and tents had sprung up beside the planes that didn't have sleeping quarters built in. Last year's welcome home ball had only whetted people's appetite for another taste of Judah Blake, philanthropist, and the vast land protection initiatives he spearheaded.

A warm and playful breeze whipped at the wraps and the hair of the ladies present and the stars in the sky that he never took for granted drew gasps from the city folk not used to such a generous display.

This past year had been a rewarding one. Almost as if every mad idea for a better future he'd ever had in the past nine years was being acted out in front of him. Money, so much money available for his projects. Remote area cabins that were architectural marvels. Scientific research projects. Channel country preservation. His brilliant, talented, beautiful wife...

Bridie was inside the ballroom somewhere, but chances were she'd find him soon enough. She still wasn't one for big crowds, and her growing status as an artist made her nervous at times, but she was his fiercest defender and she was in there tonight talking paint colours with his godmother, Eleanor. Bridie wasn't just his North Star. She was all the stars in the sky.

He checked his clothes. White shirt cuffs with a quarter inch showing below the sleeve of his suit. His father's watch, and his grandfather's before that, partly visible when he extended his hand. Such things mattered to some of the people he was courting here tonight.

Bridie wore a pale blue gown tonight, her shoulders bare, a fitted bodice and a sleek fall of silk starting somewhere around her waist and finishing at the floor. A stunning blue opal, outlined in silver filigree, hung from a ribbon around her neck, her father's work. Bridie had already fielded a number of questions about the piece and had gleefully turned them towards her father, especially the single ladies of good nature and mature age. Tomas, who epitomised the rugged, wary outback loner, had suffered the first few ladies with dogged, near-mute politeness, which only seemed to make the ladies try even harder to put him at ease.

Tomas had last been seen fleeing from the ballroom, with Bridie's delighted laughter lingering in his wake.

Bridie laughed a lot these days and Judah never tired of the sound.

And then there was her beauty. Call him biased, but these days her considerable physical beauty seemed somehow lit from within. Contentment, she called it. *Or maybe it's wonder,* she'd once said to him. So many new experiences had come her way this past year and she seemed determined to approach every one of them with wonder and gratitude.

Approaches like that were contagious, no question, given that he'd recently started doing the same.

It was all too easy to be grateful for the life he was living now.

'Your wife has requested your presence at her side,' said Reid, sliding into place beside him. Reid was a hair taller than Judah these days and broader across the shoulders. Responsibility sat more easily on those shoulders, and with it came an easy confidence his brother had more than earned.

If Judah was the visionary and dealmaker of the trio, then Reid was the project manager with the people skills to make it happen. Bridie was their media manager with full control over visual promotional material and how and where it was displayed.

Sometimes, when he was feeling especially smug, Judah thought that together the three of them could change the world.

'She still with Lady Eleanor?'

Reid nodded.

'Have you persuaded your school friend to come and chef for us yet?'

'He says he can give us six months. I'm holding out for twelve so that he's here when the visiting astrophysicists arrive. Have you seen their list of dietary requirements? Talk about special.'

'Double what you're offering him.'

'I love spending your money. Consider it done.' Reid smiled cheerfully. 'Shouldn't you be on your way to rescue your North Star, your refuge and your soul?'

He was never going to live that down.

He was, however, moving towards the ballroom door.

He found her to one side of the dance floor, his godmother nowhere in sight. She watched him walk towards her with a smile she just didn't give anyone else. He tried to figure out what was different about the ones she saved for him but so far he hadn't been able to.

Hooked him every time.

'Dance with me,' he said when he reached her and held out his hand, and she slid hers into it, warm and utterly sure of her welcome.

And why wouldn't she be? She had him wrapped around her little finger.

'I'd like the photographer here tonight to take some photos of us dancing,' she said. 'That okay by you?'

'What for?'

'Private use only. You, me, the family photo album. They'd come after the brilliant ones of our first kiss and the blurry ones Reid took of our wedding.'

She'd kept her promise about always asking before taking pictures of him. He'd never quite got over how exposed he'd felt when looking at a picture of himself, never mind that he carried one small, well-creased picture of them kissing in the rain in his wallet. Every time he looked at it, he was transported back to the purest moment of freedom he'd ever felt.

He also knew how much Bridie regretted not having a single decent photo of their wedding. Didn't matter to him so much.

He'd memorised every moment. 'Okay.'

She nodded and sent a thumbs up to someone off to the side, presumably the photographer, and then he turned her in his arms and put a hand to the back of her waist.

They still hadn't learned how to dance properly. Maybe by their sixtieth wedding anniversary they'd have done this often enough to tear up the dance floor with their prowess.

'Something funny?' she murmured.

'Just thinking of our future.'

'Oh? And how's it looking?'

'Our sixtieth wedding anniversary's going to be a cracker.'

'Slow down. We have so many moments to look forward to before that.' She slid her hand from his shoulder, down his arm to his wrist, and brought his hand around to her front, placing his palm against her belly. 'You know how we started giving birth control a miss?'

His heart stopped. His feet stopped.

Everything stopped.

Her fingers sliding effortlessly into the spaces between his, caressing her belly, and he tried to speak but he didn't have the words and probably never would have words for this.

'Judah?' she asked uncertainly. 'Breathe. Breathing would be good.'

Breathing could wait. He closed his eyes and used the hand not already cradling their baby to tilt her face towards his. His eyes closed as her lips met his and he didn't care that they were in a public place and that every man, woman and dog could see his tumbling, vulnerable steps towards parenthood. Let them see.

He wasn't backing away from this moment of purest love and worship between him and Bridie for any reason. He was hers.

She broke the kiss, which had deepened considerably. 'Judah, we're in public.'

'Don't care.'

'We're being photographed.'

No flying ducks given. The smile wouldn't leave his face. He was going to be a family man. 'I'd like many children.'

'*So* getting ahead of yourself there on the baby front.'

'How about the kissing front?'

She kissed him again and he lifted her off the ground and whirled her around and she laughed and flung her head back, her hair cascading down her back and over his arms. There was nothing he would do differently when it came to all the decisions that had led him to this moment. Not one single thing.

'I'm so happy,' she said when he finally let her feet touch the ground again. 'You're breathing again.'

He was. Go, him.

'There will be no photos of the actual birth,' she warned, but she fair glowed with happiness. 'I'm beginning to comprehend what it means to be utterly exposed.'

'Not even for the family album?'

She was wavering. He could tell. 'I'll let you know.' She tried for ladylike primness, failed miserably, and he loved her all the more for it.

'Your call, North Star,' he rumbled as they started dancing again. 'But I'm thinking there'll be photos in that album.'

* * * * *

Best Friend Bride

Kat Cantrell

USA TODAY bestselling author **Kat Cantrell** read her first Harlequin novel in third grade and has been scribbling in notebooks since she learned to spell. She's a Harlequin So You Think You Can Write winner and a Romance Writers of America Golden Heart® Award finalist. Kat, her husband and their two boys live in north Texas.

Books by Kat Cantrell

Harlequin Desire

Marriage with Benefits
The Things She Says
The Baby Deal
Pregnant by Morning
The Princess and the Player
Triplets Under the Tree
The SEAL's Secret Heirs
An Heir for the Billionaire
The Marriage Contract

Happily Ever After, Inc.

Matched to a Billionaire
Matched to a Prince
Matched to Her Rival

Love and Lipstick

The CEO's Little Surprise
A Pregnancy Scandal
The Pregnancy Project
From Enemies to Expecting

In Name Only

Best Friend Bride

Visit her Author Profile page at
millsandboon.com.au,
or katcantrell.com, for more titles.

Dear Reader,

Interconnected stories are my favorite, especially when they're centered on the heroes. So when I started brainstorming for my next series, I got really excited as three best friends from college popped into my head. I couldn't wait to find out what they had in common, what bonded them together and why they'd be tough nuts to crack in the romance department. Boy, did my guys surprise me! It turns out they share a deep, dark aversion to love due to a tragedy the three endured their senior year. As adults, they continue to avoid relationships, but luckily, three special ladies arrive on the scene to help them understand that love is not so easily dismissed.

Best Friend Bride stars our first hero, Jonas Kim, who needs a temporary wife but not the hassle of a relationship he doesn't intend to prolong. Fortunately, he has a friend who fills the bill. Viviana Dawson is happy to do Jonas this favor for reasons of her own...namely that she has a huge secret crush on him! If he finds out, it's all over. But it's harder than either of them imagined to stay in the friend zone once they get behind closed doors. And how will the tragedy in Jonas's past affect their burgeoning romance? Hint: *a lot*!

I hope you enjoy the In Name Only series! The next two books are coming to you soon. Find me online at katcantrell.com.

Kat Cantrell

Marrying my best friend was the best decision of my life. Love you, Michael.

CHAPTER ONE

JONAS KIM WOULD typically describe himself as humble, but even he was impressed with the plan he'd conceived to outwit the smartest man he knew—his grandfather. Instead of marrying Sun, the nice woman from a prominent Korean family, a bride Grandfather had picked out, Jonas had proposed to Viviana Dawson. She was nice, too, but also his friend and, more importantly, someone he could trust not to contest the annulment when it came time to file it.

Not only was Viv amazing for agreeing to this ridiculous idea, she made excellent cupcakes. It was a win all the way around. Though he could have done without the bachelor party. So not his thing.

At least no strippers had shown up. Yet.

He and his two best buddies had flown to Vegas this morning and though Jonas had never been to the city of sin before, he was pretty sure it wouldn't take much to have naked women draped all over the suite. He could think of little he'd like less. Except for marrying Sun. That he would hate, and not only because she'd been selected on his behalf. Sun was a disaster waiting to happen that would happen to someone else because Jonas was marrying Viv tomorrow in what would go down as the greatest favor one friend had ever done for another.

"Sure you wanna do this?" Warren asked as he popped open the bottle of champagne.

Also a bachelor party staple that Jonas could have done without, but his friends would just laugh and make jokes about how Jonas needed to loosen up, despite being well aware that he had been raised in an ultraconservative family. Grandfather had a lot of traditional ideas about how a CEO should act, and Jonas hadn't landed that job, not yet. Besides, there was nothing wrong with having a sense of propriety.

"Which part?" Jonas shot back. "The bachelor party or inviting you morons along?"

Hendrix, the other moron, grinned and took his glass of champagne from Warren. "You can't get married without a bachelor party. That would be sad."

"It's not a real wedding. Therefore, one would assume that the traditions don't really have to be observed."

Warren shook his head. "It is a real wedding. You're going to marry this woman simply to get out of having a different bride. Hence my question. Are you sure this is the only way? I don't get why you can't just tell your grandfather thanks but no thanks. Don't let him push you around."

They'd literally been having the exact same argument for two weeks. Grandfather still held the reins of the Kim empire closely to his chest. In Korea. If Jonas had any hope of Grandfather passing those reins to him so he could move the entire operation to North Carolina, he had to watch his step. Marrying a Korean woman from a powerful family would only solidify Jonas's ties to a country that he did not consider his home.

"I respect my elders," Jonas reminded Warren mildly. "And I also respect that Sun's grandfather and my grandfather are lifelong friends. I can't expose her or it might disrupt everything."

Sun had been thrilled with the idea of marrying Jonas; she had a secret—and highly unsuitable—lover she didn't want anyone to find out about and she'd pounced on the idea of a husband to mask her affair. Meanwhile, their grandfathers were cackling over their proposed business merger once the two families were united in marriage.

Jonas wanted no part of any of that. Better to solve the problem on his own terms. If he was already married, no one could expect him to honor his grandfather's agreement. And once the merger had gone through, he and Viv could annul their marriage and go on with Jonas's integrity intact.

It was brilliant. Viv was the most awesome person on the planet for saving his butt from being burned in this deal. Tomorrow, they'd say some words, sign a piece of paper and poof. No more problems.

"Can you guys just be happy that you got a trip to Vegas out of this and shut up?" Jonas asked, and clinked glasses with the two men he'd bonded with freshman year at Duke University.

Jonas Kim, Hendrix Harris and Warren Garinger had become instant friends when they'd been assigned to the same project group along with Marcus Powell. The four teenagers had raised a lot of hell together—most of which Jonas had watched from the sidelines—and propped each other up through everything the college experience could throw at them. Until Marcus had fallen head over heels for a cheerleader who didn't return his love. The aftermath of that still affected the surviving three members of their quartet to this day.

"Can't. You said no strippers," Hendrix grumbled, and downed his champagne in one practiced swallow. "Really don't see the point of a bachelor party in Las Vegas if you're not going to take full advantage of what's readily available."

Jonas rolled his eyes. "Like you don't have a wide array of women back in Raleigh who would get naked for you on demand."

"Yeah, but I've already seen them," he argued with a wink. "There are thousands of women whose breasts I've yet to ogle and I've been on my best behavior at home. What happens in Vegas doesn't affect my mom's campaign, right?"

Hendrix's mom was running for governor of North Carolina

and had made him swear on a stack of Bibles that he would not do anything to jeopardize her chances. For Hendrix, that meant a complete overhaul of his social life, and he was feeling the pinch. So far, his uncanny ability to get photographed with scantily clad women hadn't surfaced, but he'd just begun his vow of chastity, so there was plenty of opportunity to cause a scandal if he really put his mind to it.

"Maybe we could focus on the matter at hand?" Warren suggested, and ran his fingers through his wavy brown hair as he plopped down on the love seat near the floor-to-ceiling glass wall of the Sky Suite they'd booked at the Aria. The dizzying lights of Vegas spread out in a panoramic view sixty stories below.

"Which is?"

Warren pointed his glass at Jonas. "You're getting married. Despite the pact."

The pact.

After the cheerleader had thoroughly eviscerated Marcus, he'd faded further and further away until eventually, he'd opted to end his pain permanently. In the aftermath of his death, the three friends had sworn to never let love destroy them as it had Marcus. The reminder sobered them all.

"Hey, man. The pact is sacred," Jonas said with a scowl. "But we never vowed to remain single the rest of our lives. Just that we'd never let a woman take us down like that. Love is the problem, not marriage."

Once a year, the three of them dropped whatever they were doing and spent the evening honoring the memory of their late friend. It was part homage, part reiteration of the pact. The profoundly painful incident had affected them in different ways, but no one would argue that Warren had taken his roommate's suicide harder than anyone save Marcus's mother.

That was the only reason Jonas gave him a pass for the insult. Jonas had followed the pact to the letter, which was easier than he'd ever let on. First of all, a promise meant something to him.

Second, Jonas never got near a woman he could envision falling in love with. That kind of loss of control…the concept made his skin crawl. Jonas had too much to lose to let a woman destroy everything he'd worked for.

Warren didn't look convinced. "Marriage is the gateway, my friend. You can't put a ring on a woman's finger and expect that she won't start dreaming of romantic garbage."

"Ah, but I can," Jonas corrected as he let Hendrix top off his champagne. "That's why this plan is so great. Viv knows the score. We talked about exactly what was going to happen. She's got her cupcake business and has no room for a boyfriend, let alone a permanent husband. I wouldn't have asked her to do this for me if she wasn't a good friend."

A friend who wasn't interested in taking things deeper. That was the key and the only reason Jonas had continued their friendship for so long. If there was even a possibility of getting emotional about her, he'd have axed their association immediately, just like he had with every other woman who posed a threat to the tight rein he held on his heart.

Hendrix drank straight from the champagne bottle to get the last few drops, his nearly colorless hazel eyes narrowed in contemplation as he set the empty bottle on the coffee table. "If she's such a good friend, how come we haven't met her?"

"Really? It's confusing to you why I'd want to keep her away from the man voted most likely to corrupt a nun four years in a row?"

With a grin, Hendrix jerked his head at Warren. "So Straight and Narrow over there should get the thumbs-up. Yet she's not allowed to meet him either?"

Jonas shrugged. "I'll introduce you at the ceremony tomorrow."

When it would be unavoidable. How was he supposed to explain that Viv was special to a couple of knuckleheads like his friends? From the first moment he'd met her, he'd been drawn to her sunny smile and generosity.

The little bakery near the Kim Building called Cupcaked had come highly recommended by Jonas's admin, so he'd stopped in to pick up a thank-you for his staff. As he'd stood in the surprisingly long line to place his order, a pretty brown-haired woman had exited from the back. She'd have captured his interest regardless, but when she'd stepped outside to slip a cupcake to a kid on the street who'd been standing nose pressed to her window for the better part of fifteen minutes, Jonas couldn't resist talking to her.

He'd been dropping in to get her amazing lemon cupcakes for almost a year now. Sometimes Viv let him take her for coffee to someplace where she didn't have to jump behind the counter on the fly, and occasionally she dropped by the Kim Building to take Jonas to lunch.

It was an easy, no-pressure friendship that he valued because there was no danger of him falling in too deep when she so clearly wasn't interested in more. They weren't sleeping together, and that kind of relationship wouldn't compute to his friends.

Didn't matter. He was happy with the status quo. Viv was doing him a favor and in return, he'd make it up to her with free business consulting advice for the rest of her life. After all, Jonas had singlehandedly launched Kim Electronics in the American market and had grown revenue to the tune of $4.7 billion last year. She could do worse than to have his undivided attention on her balance sheet whenever she asked, which he'd gladly make time for.

All he had to do was get her name on a marriage certificate and lie low until his grandfather's merger went through. Then Viv could go back to her single cupcake-baker status and Jonas could celebrate dodging the bullet.

Warren's point about marriage giving a girl ideas about love and romance was pure baloney. Jonas wasn't worried about sticking to the pact. Honor was his moral compass, as it was his grandfather's. Love represented a loss of control that other men might fall prey to, but not Jonas. He would never betray his friends or the memory of the one they'd lost.

All he had to do was marry a woman who had no romantic feelings for him.

Viviana Dawson had dreamed about her wedding day a bunch of times and not once had she imagined the swirl in her gut, which could only be described as a cocktail of nerves and *holy crap*.

Jonas was going to be her husband in a few short minutes and the anticipation of *what if* was killing her.

Jonas Kim had asked her to marry him. *Jonas.* The man who had kept Viv dateless for almost a year because who could measure up to perfection? Nobody.

Oh, sure, he'd framed it all as a favor and she'd accepted under the premise that they'd be filing for annulment ASAP. But still. She'd be Mrs. Kim for as long as it lasted.

Which might be short indeed if he figured out she had a huge crush on him.

He wasn't going to figure it out. Because *oh, my God*. If he did find out...

Well, he couldn't. It would ruin their friendship for one. And also? She had no business getting into a serious relationship, not until she figured out how to do and be whatever the opposite was of what she'd been doing and being with men thus far in her adult dating life.

Her sisters called it clingy. She called it committed. Men called it quits.

Jonas was the antidote to all that.

The cheesy chapel wasn't anything close to the venue of her fantasies, but she'd have married Jonas in a wastewater treatment plant if he'd asked her to. She pushed open the door, alone and not too happy about it. In retrospect, she should have insisted one of her sisters come to Vegas with her. Maybe to act as her maid of honor.

She could really use a hand to hold right about now, but

no. She hadn't told any of her sisters she was getting married, not even Grace, who was closest to her in age and had always been her confidante. Well, until Grace had disappeared into her own family in much the same fashion as their other two sisters had done.

Viv was the cute pony in the Dawson family stable of Thoroughbreds. Which was the whole reason Viv hadn't mentioned her quickie Vegas wedding to a man who'd never so much as kissed her.

She squared her shoulders. A fake marriage was exactly what she wanted. Mostly.

Well, of course she wanted a real marriage eventually. But this one would get her into the secret club that the rest of the married Dawson sisters already belonged to. Plus, Jonas needed her. Total win across the board.

The chapel was hushed and far more sacrosanct than she'd have expected in what was essentially the drive-through lane of weddings. The quiet scuttled across her skin, turning it clammy. She was really doing this. It had all been conceptual before. Now it was real.

Could you have a nervous breakdown and recover in less than two minutes? She didn't want to miss a second of her wedding. But she might need to sit down first.

And then everything fell away as she saw Jonas in a slim-fitting dark suit that showcased his wiry frame. His energy swept out and engulfed her, as it always had from that first time she'd turned to see him standing outside her shop, his attention firmly on her instead of the sweet treats in the window.

Quick with a smile, quicker with a laugh, Jonas Kim's beautiful angular face had laced Viv's dreams many a night. He had a pretty rocking body, too. He kept in great shape playing racquetball with his friends, and she'd spent hours picturing him shirtless, his chest glistening as he swung a racket. In short, he was a truly gorgeous individual who she could never study long enough to sate herself.

Jonas's dark, expressive eyes lit up as he caught sight of her and he crossed the small vestibule to sweep her into a hug. Her arms came up around his waist automatically. How, she had no idea, when this was literally the first time he'd ever touched her.

He even smelled gorgeous.

And now would be a great time to unstick her tongue from the roof of her mouth. "Hey."

Wonderful. They'd had spirited debates on everything from the travesty of pairing red wine with fish to the merits of the beach over the mountains. Shakespeare, *The Simpsons*. But put her in the arms of the man she'd been salivating over for months and the power of speech deserted her.

He stepped back. Didn't help. And now she was cold.

"I'm so glad you're here," he said, his smooth voice ruffling all her nerve endings in the most delicious way. Despite being born in North Carolina, he had almost no accent. Good thing. He was already devastating enough.

"Can't have a wedding with no bride," she informed him. Oh, thank God, she could still talk, Captain Obvious moment aside. "Am I dressed okay for a fake marriage?"

His intense eyes honed in on her. "You look amazing. I love that you bought a new dress for this."

Yeah, that was why she passed up the idiots who hit on her with lame lines like "Give me your number and I'll frost your cupcakes for you." Jonas paid attention to her and actually noticed things like what she wore. She'd picked out this yellow dress because he'd mentioned once that he liked the color.

Which made it all the more strange that he'd never clued in that she had a huge thing for him. She was either better at hiding it than she'd had a right to hope for, or he knew and mercifully hadn't mentioned it.

Her pulse sped out of control. He didn't know, she repeated silently. Maybe a little desperately.

There was no way he could know. He'd never have asked her to do this marriage favor otherwise.

She'd been faking it this long. No reason to panic.

"I wanted to look good," she told him. *For you.* "For the pictures."

He smiled. "Mission accomplished. I want you to meet Warren."

Jonas turned, absently putting his arm around her and oh, that was nice. They were a unit already, and it had seemed to come so naturally. Did he feel it, too?

That's when she realized there was another man in the vestibule. Funny, she hadn't even noticed him, though she supposed women must fawn all over him, with those cheekbones and that expensive haircut. She held out her hand to the friend Jonas had talked endlessly about. "Nice to meet you. Jonas speaks very highly of you."

"Likewise," Warren said with a cryptic glance at Jonas. "And I'm sure whatever he's told you is embellished."

Doubtful when she didn't need Jonas's help to know that the energy drink company his friend ran did very well. You couldn't escape the logo for Flying Squirrel no matter where you looked.

Jonas waved that off with a smirk. "Whatever, man. Where's Hendrix?"

"Not my turn to babysit him." Warren shrugged, pulling out his phone. "I'll text him. He'll be here."

Somehow, Jonas seemed to have forgotten his arm was still around Viv's waist and she wasn't about to remind him. But then he guided her toward the open double doors that led to the interior of the chapel with firm fingers. Well, if this almost-intimacy was part of the wedding package, she'd take it.

"I'm not waiting on his sorry ass," Jonas called over his shoulder. "There are a thousand more couples in line behind us and I'm not losing my spot."

Warren nodded and waved, still buried in his phone.

"Some friends," Jonas murmured to her with a laugh, his head bent close. He was still taller than her even when she wore heels, but it had never been as apparent as it was today, since she was still tucked against his side as if he never meant to let go. "This is an important day in my life and you see how they are."

"I'm here." For as long as he needed her.

Especially if he planned to put his arm around her a whole bunch more. His warm palm on her waist had oddly settled her nerves. And put a whole different kind of butterfly south of her stomach.

Wow, was it hot in here or what? She resisted the urge to fan herself as the spark zipped around in places that *could not* be so affected by this man's touch.

His smile widened. "Yes, you are. Have I mentioned lately how much I appreciate that? The slot for very best friend in the whole world has just become yours, since clearly you're the only one who deserves it."

As reminders went, it was both brutal and necessary. This was a favor. Not an excuse for a man to get handsy with her.

Fine. Good. She and Jonas were friends, which was perfect. She had a habit of pouring entirely too much of herself into a man who didn't return her level of commitment. Mark had stuck it out slightly longer than Zachary, and she didn't like to think about how quickly she'd shed Gary and Judd. A sad commentary on her twenties that she'd had fewer boyfriends than fingers on one hand.

A favor marriage was the best kind because she knew exactly how it would end. It was like reading the last page of the book ahead of time, and for someone who loved surprise flowers but hated surprise discussions that started with "we have to talk," the whole thing sounded really great.

No pressure. No reason to get clingy and drive Jonas away with her neediness. She could be independent and witty and build her confidence with this marriage. It was a practice run with all the best benefits. He'd already asked her to move into his penthouse on Boylan Avenue. As long as she didn't mess up and let on how much she wanted to cling to every last inch of the man, it was all good.

Back on track, she smiled at the friend she was about to marry. They were friends with benefits that had nothing to do with sex. A point she definitely needed to keep in the forefront of her brain.

A lady in a puke-green suit approached them and verified they were the happy couple, then ran down the order of the ceremony. If this had been a real marriage, Viv might be a little disappointed in the lack of fanfare. In less than a minute, traditional organ music piped through the overhead speakers and the lady shoved a drooping bouquet at Viv. She clutched it to her chest, wondering if she'd get to keep it. One flower was enough. She'd press it into a book as a reminder of her wedding to a great man who treated her with nothing but kindness and respect.

Jonas walked her down the aisle, completely unruffled. Of course. Why would he be nervous? This was all his show and he'd always had a supreme amount of confidence no matter the situation.

His friend Warren stood next to an elderly man holding a Bible. Jonas halted where they'd been told to stand and glanced at her with a reassuring smile.

"Dearly beloved," the man began and was immediately interrupted by a commotion at the back. Viv and Jonas both turned to see green-suit lady grappling with the door as someone tried to get into the room.

"Sir, the ceremony has already started," she called out to no avail as the man who must be Hendrix Harris easily shoved his way inside and joined them at the front.

Yep. He looked just like the many, many pictures she'd seen of him strewn across the media, and not just because his mother was running for governor. Usually he had a gorgeous woman glued to his side and they were doing something overly sensual, like kissing as if no one was watching.

"Sorry," he muttered to Jonas. His eyes were bloodshot and

he looked like he'd slept in his expensively tailored shirt and pants.

"Figured you'd find a way to make my wedding memorable," Jonas said without malice, because that's the kind of man he was. She'd have a hard time being so generous with someone who couldn't be bothered to show up on time.

The officiant started over, and in a few minutes, she and Jonas exchanged vows. All fake, she chanted to herself as she promised to love and cherish.

"You may kiss the bride," the officiant said with so little in-flection that it took a minute for it to sink in that he meant *Jonas* could kiss *her*. Her pulse hit the roof.

Somehow, they hadn't established what would happen here. She glanced at Jonas and raised a brow. Jonas hesitated.

"This is the part where you kiss her, idiot," Hendrix mut-tered with a salacious grin.

This was her one chance, the only time she had every right to put her lips on this man, and she wasn't missing the oppor-tunity. The other people in the room vanished as she flattened her palms on Jonas's lapels. He leaned in and put one hand on her jaw, guiding it upward. His warmth bled through her skin, enlivening it, and then her brain ceased to function as his mouth touched hers.

Instantly, that wasn't enough and she pressed forward, seek-ing more of him. The kiss deepened as his lips aligned properly and oh, yes, that was it.

Her crush exploded into a million little pieces as she tasted what it was like to kiss Jonas. That nice, safe attraction she had been so sure she could hide gained teeth, slicing through her midsection with sharp heat. The dimensions of sensation opened around her, giving her a tantalizing glimpse of how truly spec-tacular it would feel if he didn't stop.

But he did stop, stepping back so quickly that she almost toppled over. He caught her forearms and held her steady...

though he looked none too steady himself, his gaze enigmatic and heated in a way she'd never witnessed before.

Clearly that experience had knocked them both for a loop. What did you say to someone you'd just kissed and who you wanted to kiss again, but really, that hadn't been part of the deal?

"That was nice," Jonas murmured. "Thanks."

Nice was not the word on her mind. So they were going to pretend that hadn't just happened, apparently.

Good. That was exactly what they should do. Treat it like a part of the ceremony and move on.

Except her lips still tingled, and how in the world was Jonas just standing there holding her hand like nothing momentous had occurred? She needed to learn the answer to that, stat. Especially if they were going to be under the same roof. Otherwise, their friendship—and this marriage—would be toast the second he clued in to how hot and bothered he got her. He'd specifically told her that he could trust her because they were *friends* and he needed her to be one.

"I now pronounce you husband and wife," the officiant intoned, completely oblivious to how the earth had just swelled beneath Viv's feet.

Jonas turned and led her back up the aisle, where they signed the marriage license. They ended up in the same vestibule they'd been in minutes before, but now they were married.

Her signature underneath Jonas's neat script made it official, but as she'd expected, it was just a piece of paper. The kiss, on the other hand? That had shaken her to the core.

How was she going to stop herself from angling for another one?

"Well," Hendrix said brightly. "I'd say this calls for a drink. I'll buy."

CHAPTER TWO

JONAS HAD NEVER thought of his six-thousand-square-foot penthouse condo as small. Until today. It was full of Viviana Dawson. Er, *Kim*. Viviana Kim. She'd officially changed her name
at the Department of Motor Vehicles, and soon, she'd have a
new driver's license that said she had the legal right to call herself that. By design. His sense of honor wouldn't permit him to
outright lie about his relationship with Viv; therefore, she was
Mrs. Kim in every sense of the word.

Except one.

The concept was surreal. As surreal as the idea that she was
his wife and he could introduce her as such to anyone who
asked.

Except for himself apparently because he was having a hard
time thinking of her that way no matter how many times he repeated the word *wife* when he glimpsed her through the arch-
way leading to the kitchen. Boxes upon boxes covered every
inch of the granite countertops, and though she'd been working on unpacking them for an hour, it looked like she'd barely
made a dent.

He should quit skulking around and get in there to help. But
he hadn't because he couldn't figure out how to manage the
weird vibe that had sprung up between them.

That *kiss*.

It had opened up a Pandora's box that he didn't know how to close. Before, he'd had a sort of objective understanding that Viv was a beautiful woman whose company he enjoyed.

Ever since the ceremony, no more. There was a thin veil of awareness that he couldn't shake. But he needed to. They were living together as *friends* because she'd agreed to a favor that didn't include backing her up against the counter so he could explore her lush mouth.

He liked Viv. Add a previously undiscovered attraction and she was exactly the kind of woman he'd studiously avoided for nearly a decade. The kind he could easily envision taking him deeper and deeper until he was emotionally overwhelmed enough to give up everything.

The problem of course being that he couldn't stop calling her, like he usually did with women who threatened his vow. He'd married this one.

He was being ridiculous. What was he, seventeen? He could handle a little spark between friends, right? Best way to manage that was to ignore it. And definitely not let on that he'd felt something other than friendly ever since kissing her.

All he and Viv had to do was live together until he could convince his grandfather to go through with the merger anyway. Once the two companies signed agreements, neither would back out and Jonas was home free. Since he was covering Viv's rent until then, she could move back into her apartment at that point.

This plan would work, and soon enough, he could look back on it smugly and pinpoint the exact moment when he'd outsmarted his grandfather.

Casually, he leaned on the exposed-brick column between the dining room and the kitchen and crossed his arms like everything was cool between them. It *would* be cool. "What can I do?"

Viv jerked and spun around to face him, eyes wide. "You scared me. Obviously."

Her nervous laugh ruffled his spine. So they were both feeling the weirdness, but it was clearly different weirdness on her side than on his. She was jumpy and nervous, not hot and bothered. He had not seen that coming. That was…not good. "Sorry. I didn't mean to. We've both been living alone for so long that I guess we have to get through an adjustment period."

Which was the opposite of what he'd expected. They'd always been so relaxed with each other. How could they get back to that?

She nodded. "Yes, that's what I've been telling myself."

Was it that bad? Her forlorn voice tripped something inside him and it was not okay that she was uncomfortable around him now. "Best way to adjust is to spend time together. Let me help you put away these…" He grabbed a square glass dish from the counter. "Pans?"

"Pyrex." She smiled and it seemed like it came easier. "I can't imagine you care anything about where I put my bakeware."

He waggled his brows. "That depends on whether that's something you use to make cupcakes or not."

Her cupcakes weren't like the store-bought ones in the hard plastic clamshells. Those tasted like sugared flour with oily frosting. Viv's lemon cupcakes—a flavor he'd never have said he'd like—had a clean, bright taste like she'd captured lemonade in cake form.

"It's not. Casseroles."

"Not a fan of those." He made a face before he thought better of it.

Maybe she loved casseroles and he was insulting her taste. And her cooking skills. But he'd never said one word about her whipping up dinner for him each night, nor did he expect her to. She knew that. Right?

They had so much to learn about each other, especially if they were going to make this marriage seem as real as possible to everyone, except select few people they could trust, like

Warren and Hendrix. If word got back to his grandfather that something wasn't kosher, the charade would be over.

And he'd invested way too much in this marriage to let it fail now.

His phone beeped from his pocket, and since the CEO never slept, he handed over the glass dish to check the message.

Grandfather. At 6:00 a.m. Seoul time. Jonas tapped the message. All the blood drained from his head.

"Jonas, what's wrong?" Viv's palm came to rest on his forearm and he appreciated the small bit of comfort even as it stirred things it shouldn't.

"My grandfather. My dad told him that we got married." Because Jonas had asked him to. The whole point had been to circumvent his grandfather's arranged-marriage plan. But this—

"Oh, no. He's upset, isn't he?" Viv worried her lip with her teeth, distracting him for a moment.

"On the contrary," Jonas spit out hoarsely. "He's thrilled. He's so excited to meet you, he got on a plane last night. He's here. In Raleigh. Best part? He talked my dad into having a house party to welcome you into the family. This weekend."

It was a totally unforeseen move. Wily. He didn't believe for a second that his grandfather was thrilled with Jonas's quick marriage or that the CEO of one of the largest conglomerates in Korea had willingly walked away from his board meetings to fly seven thousand miles to meet his new granddaughter-in-law.

This was something else. A test. An "I'll believe it when I see it." Maybe Grandfather scented a whiff of the truth and all it would take was one slipup before he'd pounce. If pressed, Jonas would feel honor bound to be truthful about Viv's role. The marriage could be history before dark.

A healthy amount of caution leaped into Viv's expression. "This weekend? As in we have two days to figure out how to act like a married couple?"

"Now you're starting to see why my face looks like this." He swirled an index finger near his nose, unbelievably grateful that she had instantly realized the problem. "Viv, I'm sorry. I had no idea he was going to do this."

The logistics alone... How could he tell his mom to give them separate bedrooms when they were essentially still supposed to be in the honeymoon phase? He couldn't. It was ludicrous to even think in that direction when what he should be doing was making a list of all the ways this whole plan was about to fall apart. So he could mitigate each and every one.

"Hey."

Jonas glanced up as Viv laced her fingers with his as if she'd done it many times, when in fact she hadn't. She shouldn't. He liked it too much.

"I'm here," she said, an echo of her sentiment at the wedding ceremony. "I'm not going anywhere. My comment wasn't supposed to be taken as a 'holy cow how are we going to do this.' It was an 'oh, so we've got two days to figure this out.' We will."

There was literally no way to express how crappy that made him feel. Viv was such a trouper, diving into this marriage without any thought to herself and her own sense of comfort and propriety. He already owed her so much. He couldn't ask her to fake intimacy on top of everything else.

Neither did he like the instant heat that crowded into his belly at the thought of potential intimate details. *He* couldn't fake intimacy either. It would feel too much like lying.

The only way he could fathom acting like he and Viv were lovers would be if they were.

"You don't know my grandfather. He's probably already suspicious. This house party is intended to sniff out the truth."

"So?" She shrugged that off far too easily. "Let him sniff. What's he going to find out, that we're really legally married?"

"That the marriage is in name only."

To drive the point home, he reached out to cup Viv's jaw and brought her head up until her gaze clashed with his, her mouth mere centimeters away from his in an almost-kiss that would be a real one with the slightest movement. She nearly jumped out of her skin and stumbled back a good foot until she hit the counter. And then she tried to keep going, eyes wide with… something.

"See?" he said. "I can't even touch you without all sorts of alarms going off. How are we going to survive a whole weekend?"

"Sorry. I wasn't—" She swallowed. "I wasn't expecting you to do that. So clearly the answer is that we need to practice."

"Practice what?" And then her meaning sank in. "Touching?"

"Kissing, too." Her chest rose and fell unevenly as if she couldn't quite catch her breath. "You said we would best get through the adjustment period by spending time together. Maybe we should do that the old-fashioned way. Take me on a date, Jonas."

Speechless, he stared at her, looking for the punch line, but her warm brown eyes held nothing but sincerity. The idea unwound in his gut with a long, liquid pull of anticipation that he didn't need any help interpreting.

A date with his wife. No, with Viv. And the whole goal would be to get her comfortable with his hands on her, to kiss her at random intervals until it was so natural, neither of them thought anything of it.

Crazy. And brilliant. Not to mention impossible.

"Will you wear a new dress?" That should not have been the next thing out of his mouth. *No* would be more advisable when he'd already identified a great big zone of danger surrounding his wife. But *yes* was the only answer if he wanted to pull off this plan.

She nodded, a smile stealing over her face. "The only caveat is no work. For either of us. Which means I get dessert that's not cupcakes."

Oddly, a date with Viv where kissing was expected felt like enough of a reward that he didn't mind that addendum so much, though giving up cupcakes seemed like a pretty big sacrifice. But as her brown eyes seared him thoroughly, the real sacrifice was going to be his sanity. Because he could get her comfortable with his hands on her, but there was no way to get *him* there.

The date would be nothing but torture—and an opportunity to practice making sure no one else realized that, an opportunity he could not pass up. Having an overdeveloped sense of ethics was very inconvenient sometimes.

"It's a deal. Pick you up at eight?"

That made her laugh for some reason. "My bedroom is next door to yours, silly. Are we going to have a secret knock?"

"Maybe." The vibe between them had loosened gradually to where they were almost back to normal, at least as far as she was concerned. Strange that the concept of taking Viv on a date should be the thing to do it. "What should it be?"

Rapping out a short-short-pause-short pattern, she raised her brows. "That means we're leaving in five minutes so get your butt in gear."

"And then that's my cue to hang out in the living room with a sporting event on TV because you're going to take an extra twenty?"

Tossing her head, she grinned. "You catch on fast. Now, I have to go get ready, which means you get to unload the rest of these boxes."

Though he groaned good-naturedly as she scampered out of the kitchen, he didn't mind taking over the chore. Actually, she should be sitting on the couch with a drink and a book while he slaved for hours to get the house exactly the way she liked it. He would have, too, simply because he owed her for this, but she'd insisted that she wanted to do it in order to learn where everything was. Looked like a date was enough to trump that concept.

As the faint sound of running water drifted through the walls, he found spots in his cavernous kitchen for the various pieces Viv had brought with her to this new, temporary life. Unpacking her boxes ended up being a more intimate task than he'd anticipated. She had an odd collection of things. He couldn't fathom the purpose of many of them, but they told him fascinating things about the woman he'd married. She made cupcakes for her business but she didn't have so much as one cupcake pan in her personal stash. Not only that, each item had a well-used sheen, random scrapes, dents, bent handles.

Either she'd spent hours in her kitchen trying to figure out what she liked to bake the most or she'd cleaned out an estate sale in one fell swoop. He couldn't wait to find out, because what better topic to broach on a date with a woman he needed to know inside and out before Friday night?

As he worked, he couldn't help but think of Viv on the other side of the walls, taking a shower. The ensuing images that slammed through his mind were not conducive to the task at hand and it got a little hard to breathe. He should not be picturing her "getting ready" when, in all honesty, he had no idea what that entailed. Odds were good she didn't lather herself up and spend extra time stroking the foam over her body like his brain seemed bent on imagining.

What was his *problem*? He never sat around and fantasized about a woman. He'd never felt strongly enough about one to do so. When was the last time he'd even gone on a date? He might stick Warren with the workaholic label but that could easily be turned back on Jonas. Running the entire American arm of a global company wasn't for wimps, and he had something to prove on top of that. Didn't leave a lot of room for dating, especially when the pact was first and foremost in his mind.

Of course the women he dated always made noises about not looking for anything serious and keeping their options open. And Jonas was always completely honest, but it didn't seem to matter if he flat-out said he wasn't ever going to fall in love. Mostly they took it as a challenge, and things got sticky fast, especially when said woman figured out he wasn't kidding.

Jonas was a champion at untangling himself before things went too far. Before *he* went too far. There were always warning signs that he was starting to like a woman too much. That's when he bailed.

So he had a lot of one-night stands that he'd never intended to be such. It made for stretches of lonely nights, which was perhaps the best side benefit of marriage. He didn't hate the idea of having someone to watch a movie with on a random Tuesday night, or drinking coffee with Viv in the morning before work. He hoped she liked that part of their marriage, too.

Especially since that was all they could ever have between them. It would be devastating to lose her friendship, which would surely happen if they took things to the next level. Once she found out about the pact, either she'd view it as a challenge or she'd immediately shut down. The latter was more likely. He'd hate either one.

At seven forty he stacked the empty boxes near the door so he could take them to the recycling center in the basement of the building later, then went to his room to change clothes for his date.

He rapped on Viv's door with the prescribed knock, grinning as he pictured her on the other side deliberately waiting for as long as she could to answer because they'd made a joke out of this new ritual. But she didn't follow the script and opened the door almost immediately.

Everything fled his mind but her as she filled the doorway, her fresh beauty heightened by the colors of her dress. She'd arranged her hair up on her head, leaving her neck bare. It was such a different look that he couldn't stop drinking her in, frozen by the small smile playing around her mouth.

"I didn't see much point in making you wait when I'm already ready," she commented. "Is it okay to tell you I'm a little nervous?"

He nodded, shocked his muscles still worked. "Yes. It's okay to tell me that. Not okay to be that way."

"I can't help it. I haven't been on a date in…" She bit her lip. "Well, it's been a little while. The shop is my life."

For some reason, that pleased him enormously. Though he

shouldn't be so happy that they were cut from the same workaholic cloth. "For me, too. We'll be nervous together."

But then he already knew she had a lack in her social life since she'd readily agreed to this sham marriage, telling him she was too busy to date. Maybe together, they could find ways to work less. To put finer pleasures first, just for the interim while they were living together. That could definitely be one of the benefits of their friendship.

She rolled her eyes. "You're not nervous. But you're sweet to say so."

Maybe not nervous. But something.

His palms itched and he knew good and well the only way to cure that was to put them on her bare arms so he could test out the feel of her skin. It looked soft.

Wasn't the point of the date to touch her? He had every reason to do exactly that. The urge to reach out grew bigger and rawer with each passing second.

"Maybe we could start the date right now?" she suggested, and all at once, the hallway outside her room got very small as she stepped closer, engulfing him in lavender that could only be her soap.

His body reacted accordingly, treating him to some more made-up images of her in the shower, and now that he had a scent to associate with it, the spike through his gut was that much more powerful. And that much more of a huge warning sign that things were spiraling out of control. He just couldn't see a good way to stop.

"Yeah?" he murmured, his throat raw with unfulfilled need. "Which part?"

There was no mistaking what she had in mind when she reached out to graze her fingertips across his cheek. Nerve endings fired under her touch and he leaned into her palm, craving more of her.

"The only part that matters," she whispered back. "The part where you don't even think twice about getting close to me.

Where it's no big thing if you put your arm around my waist or steal a kiss as I walk by."

If that was the goal, he was failing miserably because it was a big thing. A huge thing. And getting bigger as she leaned in, apparently oblivious to the way her lithe body brushed against his. His control snapped.

Before he came up with reasons why he shouldn't, he pulled her into his arms. Her mouth rose to meet his and, when it did, dropped them both into a long kiss. More than a kiss. An exploration.

With no witnesses this time, he had free rein to delve far deeper into the wonders of his wife than he had at the wedding ceremony.

Her enthusiastic response was killing him. *His* response was even worse. How had they been friends for so long without ever crossing this line? Well, he knew how—because if they had, he would have run in the other direction.

He groaned as her fingers threaded through his hair, sensitizing everything she touched. Then she iced that cake with a tentative push of her tongue that nearly put him on his knees. So unexpected and so very hot. Eagerly, he matched her sweet thrust with his own. Deeper and deeper they spiraled until he couldn't have said which way was up. Who was doing the giving and who was greedily lapping it up.

He wanted more and took it, easing her head back with firm fingers until he found the right angle to get more of her against his tongue. And now he wanted more of her against his body.

He slid a hand down the curve of her spine until he hit a spot that his palm fit into and pressed until her hips nestled against his erection. Amazing. Perfect.

The opposite of friendly.

That was enough to get his brain in gear again. This was not how it should be between them, with all this raw need that he couldn't control.

He ended the kiss through some force of will he'd never understand and pulled back, but she tried to follow, nearly knocking herself off balance. Like she had at the ceremony. And in a similar fashion, he gripped her arms to keep her off the floor. It was dizzying how caught up she seemed to get. A rush he could get used to and shouldn't.

"Sorry," he said gruffly. "I got a little carried away."

"That's what was supposed to happen," she informed him breathlessly, "if we have any hope of your grandfather believing that we're deliriously happy together."

Yeah, that wasn't the problem he was most worried about at this moment. Viv's kiss-swollen lips were the color of raspberries and twice as tempting. All for show. He'd gotten caught up in the playacting far too easily, which wasn't fair to her. Or to his Viv-starved body that had suddenly found something it liked better than her cupcakes.

"I don't think anyone would question whether we spark, Viv," he muttered.

The real issue was that he needed to kill that spark and was pretty certain that would be impossible now.

Especially given the way she was gazing up at him with something a whole lot hotter than warmth in her brown eyes. She'd liked kissing him as much as he'd liked it. She might even be on board with taking things a step further. But they couldn't consummate this marriage or he could forget the annulment. Neither did he want to lead her on, which left him between a rock and an extremely hard place that felt like it would never be anything but hard for the rest of his life.

"In fact," he continued, "we should really keep things platonic behind closed doors. That's better for our friendship, don't you think?"

He'd kissed his wife and put his hands on her body because she'd told him to. And he was very much afraid he'd do it again whether it was for show or not unless he had some boundaries. Walking away from Viv wasn't an option. He had to do something that guaranteed he never got so sucked into a woman that she had power over his emotional center.

Thankfully, she nodded. "Whatever works best for you, Jonas. This is your fake marriage."

And how messed up was it that he was more than a little disappointed she'd agreed so readily?

CHAPTER THREE

VIV HUMMED AS she pulled the twenty-four-count pan from the oven and stuck the next batch of Confetti Surprise in its place. Customers thronged the showroom beyond the swinging door, but she kept an eye on things via the closed-circuit camera she'd had installed when she first started turning a profit.

Couldn't be too careful and besides, it made her happy to watch Camilla and Josie interact with the cupcake buyers while Viv did the dirty work in the back. She'd gotten so lucky to find the two college-aged girls who worked for her part-time. Both of them were eager students, and soon Viv would teach them the back-office stuff like bookkeeping and ordering. For now, it was great to have them running the register so Viv could focus on product.

Not that she was doing much focusing. Her mind wandered constantly to the man who'd kissed her so passionately last night.

Jonas had been so into the moment, so into her, and it had been heady indeed. Score one for Viv to have landed in his arms due to her casual suggestion that they needed to "practice." Hopefully he'd never clue in that she jumped when he touched her because he zapped a shock of heat and awareness straight to her core every dang time, no matter how much she tried to control it.

Of course, he'd shut it all down, rightfully so. They were friends. If he'd been interested in more, he would have made a move long before now.

Didn't stop her from wishing for a repeat.

A stone settled into her stomach as three dressed-to-the-nines women breezed through the door of her shop. On the monitor, she watched her sisters approach the counter and speak to Josie, oblivious to the line of customers they'd just cut in front of. Likely they were cheerfully requesting to speak with Viv despite being told countless times that this wasn't a hobby. She ran a business, which meant she didn't have time to dash off with them for tea, something the three housewives she shared parentage with but little else didn't seem to fully grasp.

Except she couldn't avoid the conversation they were almost certainly here for. She'd finally broken down and called her mother to admit she'd gotten married without inviting anyone to the wedding. Of course that news had taken all of five minutes to blast its way to her sisters' ears.

Dusting off her hands, Viv set a timer on her phone and dropped it into her pocket. Those cupcakes in the oven would provide a handy out if things got a little intense, and knowing Hope, Joy and Grace, that was likely. She pushed open the swinging door and pasted a smile on her face.

"My favorite ladies," she called with a wave and crossed the room to hug first Grace, her next-oldest sister, then Joy and Hope last. More than a few heads turned to check out the additions to the showroom. Individually, they were beautiful women, but as a group, her sisters were impressive indeed, with style and elegance galore.

Viv had been a late-life accident, but her parents tried hard not to make her feel like one. Though it was obvious they'd expected to have three children when they couldn't come up with a fourth virtue to name their youngest daughter. She'd spent her childhood trying to fit in to her own family and nothing had changed.

Until today. Finally, Viviana Kim had a new last name and a husband. Thanks to Jonas and his fake marriage deal, she was part of the club that had excluded her thus far. Just one of many reasons she'd agreed.

"Mom told us," Hope murmured, her social polish in full force. She was nothing if not always mindful of propriety, and Viv appreciated it for once, as the roomful of customers didn't need to hear about Viv's love life. "She's hurt that you ran off to Vegas without telling anyone."

"Are you happy?" Grace butted in. She'd gotten married to the love of her life less than a year ago and saw hearts and flowers everywhere. "That's the important thing."

"Mom said you married Jonas Kim," Joy threw in before Viv could answer, not that she'd intended to interrupt before everyone had their say. That was a rookie mistake she'd learned to avoid years ago. "Surely his family would have been willing to make a discreet contribution to the ceremony. You could have had the wedding of the year."

Which was the real crime in Joy's mind—why spend *less* money when you could spend more, particularly when it belonged to someone else? Joy's own wedding had garnered a photo spread in *Bride* magazine five years ago, a feat no other Raleigh bride had scored since.

It had been a beautiful wedding and Joy had been a gorgeous bride. Of course, because she'd been so happy. All three of her sisters were married to handsome, successful men who treated them like royalty, which was great if you could find that. Viv had made do with what had been offered to her, but they didn't have to know that. In fact, she'd do everything in her power not to tip off her sisters that her marriage was anything but amazing. Was it so wrong to want them to believe she'd ended up exactly where she'd yearned to be for so long?

"Also, he's Korean," Hope added as if this might be news to

Viv. "Mom is very concerned about how you'll handle the cultural differences. Have you discussed this with him?"

That was crossing a line. For several reasons. And Viv had had enough. "Jonas is American. He was born in the same hospital as you, so I'm pretty sure the cultural differences are minimal. Can you just be happy for me and stop with the third degree?"

All three women stared at her agape, even Grace, and Viv was ashamed at how good the speech had made her feel. She rarely stood up to the steamroller of her sisters, mostly because she really did love them. But she was married now, just like they were, and her choices deserved respect.

"Jonas does make me happy," she continued, shooting Grace a smile. "But there's nothing to be concerned about. We've known each other for about a year and our relationship recently grew closer. That's all there is to it."

Despite the fact that it was absolute truth, prickles swept across her cheeks at the memory of how *close* they'd gotten last night.

An unconvinced expression stole over Hope's face. As the oldest, she took her role as the protector seriously. "We still don't understand why the secrecy. None of us even remember you so much as mentioning his name before."

"Of course we know who he *is*," Joy clarified. "Everyone in Raleigh appreciates that he's brought a global company to this area. But we had no idea you'd caught his eye."

Viv could read between those lines easily enough. She didn't wear nine-thousand-dollar Alexander McQueen suits to brunch and attend the opera with a priceless antique diamond necklace decorating her cleavage. "He's been coming in to buy cupcakes for quite some time. We go to lunch. It's not that big of a mystery."

Did it seem like a mystery to others? A lick of panic curled through her stomach. She couldn't ruin this for Jonas. If other people got suspicious because she wasn't the type of woman a billionaire CEO should want to marry, then everything might fall apart.

Breathe. He'd made that decision. Not her. He'd picked Viv and anyone who thought she wasn't good enough for him could jump in a lake.

"But he married you." Grace clapped her hands, eyes twinkling. "Tell us how he proposed, what you wore at the wedding. Ooooh, show us pictures."

Since his proposal had begun with the line "This is going to sound crazy, but hear me out," Viv avoided that subject by holding out her left hand to dazzle her sisters with the huge diamond and then grabbing her phone to thumb up the shots Warren had taken at Jonas's request. The yellow of her dress popped next to Jonas's dark suit and they made an incredibly striking couple if she did say so herself. Mostly because she had the best-looking husband on the planet, so no one even noticed her.

"Is that Hendrix Harris in the shot?" Hope sniffed and the disapproval on her face spoke volumes against the man whose picture graced local gossip rags on a regular basis.

"Jonas and Hendrix are friends," Viv said mildly as she flipped through a few more pictures that mercifully did not include North Carolina's biggest scandalmonger. "They went to Duke together. I'll try not to let him corrupt me if we socialize."

As far as she could tell, Hendrix had scarcely noticed her at the wedding, and he'd seemed preoccupied at the cocktail lounge where they'd gone to have drinks after the ceremony. The man was pretty harmless.

"Just be careful," Hope implored her, smoothing an invisible wrinkle from her skirt. "You married Jonas so quickly and it appears as if he may have some unsavory associations. I say this with love, but you haven't demonstrated a great track record when it comes to the men you fall for."

That shouldn't have cut so deeply. It was true. But still.

"What Hope means is that you tend to leap before you look, Viv," Grace corrected, her eyes rolling in their sister's direction, but only Viv could see the show of support. It soothed the ragged places inside that Hope's comment had made. A little.

"It's not a crime to be passionate about someone." Hands on her hips, Viv surveyed the three women, none of whom seemed to remember what it was like to be single and alone. "But for your information, Jonas and I were friends first. We share common interests. He gives me advice about my business. We have a solid foundation to build on."

"Oh." Hope processed that. "I didn't realize you were being so practical about this. I'm impressed that you managed to marry a man without stars in your eyes. That's a relief."

Great. She'd gotten the seal of approval from Hope solely because she'd skirted the truth with a bland recitation of unromantic facts about her marriage. Her heart clenched. That was the opposite of what she wanted. But this was the marriage she had, the one she could handle. For now. Tomorrow, Jonas would take her to his father's house to meet his grandfather and she hoped to "practice" being married a whole lot more.

Thankfully, she'd kept Jonas in the dark about her feelings. If he could kiss her like he had last night and not figure out that she'd been this close to melting into a little puddle, she could easily snow his family with a few public displays of affection.

It was behind closed doors that she was worried about. That's where she feared she might forget that her marriage was fake. And as she'd just been unceremoniously reminded, she had a tendency to get serious way too fast, which in her experience was a stellar way to get a man to start looking for the exit.

That was the part that hurt the most. She wanted to care about someone, to let him know he was her whole world and have him say that in return. It wasn't neediness. She wasn't being clingy. That's what love looked like to her and she refused to believe otherwise.

But she'd yet to find a man who agreed with her, and Jonas was no exception. They had a deal and she would stick to it.

* * *

The house Jonas had grown up in lay on the outskirts of Raleigh in an upscale neighborhood that was homey and unpretentious. Jonas's father, who had changed his name to Brian when he became a legal US citizen upon marrying his American wife, hadn't gone into the family business, choosing to become a professor at Duke University instead.

That had left a hole in the Kim empire, one Jonas had gladly filled. He and Grandfather got along well, likely because they were so similar. They both had a drive to succeed, a natural professionalism and a sense of honor that harbored trust in others who did business with Kim Electronics.

Though they corresponded nearly every day in some electronic form, the time difference prevented them from speaking often, and an in-person visit was even rarer. The last time Jonas had seen Grandfather had been during a trip to Seoul for a board meeting about eighteen months ago. He'd invited his parents to come with him, as they hadn't visited Korea in several years.

"Are you nervous?" Jonas glanced over at Viv, who had clutched her hands together in her lap the second the car had hit Glenwood Avenue. Her knuckles couldn't get any whiter.

"Oh, God. You can tell," she wailed. "I was trying so hard to be cool."

He bit back a grin and passed a slow-moving minivan. "Viv, they're just people. I promise they will like you."

"I'm not worried about that. Everyone likes me, especially after I give them cupcakes," she informed him loftily.

There was a waxed paper box at her feet on the floorboard that she'd treated as carefully as a newborn baby. When he'd reached for it, she'd nearly taken his hand off at the wrist, telling him in no uncertain terms the cupcakes were for her new family. Jonas was welcome to come by Cupcaked next week and pick out whatever he wanted, but the contents of that box were off-limits.

He kind of liked Bossy Viv. Of course he liked Sweet Viv,

Uncertain Viv, Eager-to-Help Viv. He'd seen plenty of new facets in the last week since they'd moved in together, more than he'd have expected given that they'd known each other so long. It was fascinating.

"What are you worried about then?" he asked.

"You know good and well." Without warning, she slid a hand over his thigh and squeezed. Fire rocketed up his leg and scored his groin, nearly doubling him over with the sudden and unexpected need.

Only his superior reflexes kept the Mercedes on the road. But he couldn't stop the curse that flew from his mouth.

"Sorry," he muttered but she didn't seem bothered by his language.

"See, you're just as bad as me." Her tone was laced with irony. "All that practice and we're even jumpier than we were before."

Because the practice had ended before he started peeling off her clothes. Ironic how his marriage of convenience meant his wife was right there in his house—conveniently located in the bedroom next to his. He could hear her moving around between the walls and sometimes, he lay awake at night listening for the slightest movement to indicate she was likewise awake, aching to try one of those kisses with a lot less fabric in the way.

That kind of need was so foreign to him that he wasn't handling it well.

"I'm not jumpy," he lied. "I'm just…"

Frustrated.

There was no good way to finish that sentence without opening up a conversation about changing their relationship into something that it wasn't supposed to be. An annulment was so much less sticky than a divorce, though he'd finally accepted that he was using that as an excuse.

The last thing he could afford to do was give in to the simmering awareness between them. Jonas had convinced himself it was easy to honor the pact because he really didn't feel much when it came to relationships. Sure, he enjoyed sex, but it had always been easy to walk away when the woman pushed for more.

With Viv, the spiral of heat and need was dizzyingly strong. He felt too much, and Marcus's experience was like a big neon sign, reminding him that it was better never to go down that path. What was he supposed to do, stop being friends with Viv if things went haywire between them? Neither was there a good way to end their relationship before the merger.

So he was stuck. He couldn't act on his sudden and fierce longing to pull this car over into a shadowy bower of oak trees and find out if all of Viv tasted like sugar and spice and everything nice.

"Maybe we shouldn't touch each other," he suggested.

That was a good solution. Except for the part where they were married. Married people touched each other. He bit back the nasty word that had sprung to his lips. Barely.

"Oh." She nodded. "If you think that won't cause problems, sure."

Of course it was going to cause problems. He nearly groaned. But the problems had nothing to do with what she assumed. "Stop being so reasonable. I'm pulling you away from your life with very little compensation in return. You should be demanding and difficult."

Brilliant. He'd managed to make it sound like touching her was one of the compensation methods. He really needed to get out of this car now that he had a hyperawareness of how easily she could—and would—reach out to slide a hand full of questing fingers into his lap.

Viv grinned and crossed her arms, removing that possibility. "In that case, I'm feeling very bereft in the jewelry department, Mr. Kim. As your wife, I should be draped in gems, don't you think?"

"Absolutely." What did it say about how messed up he was that the way *Mr. Kim* rolled off her tongue turned him on? "Total oversight on my part. Which I will rectify immediately."

The fourteen-carat diamond on her finger was on loan from a guy Jonas knew in the business, though the hefty fee he'd paid to procure it could have bought enough bling to blind her. Regardless, if Viv wanted jewelry, that's what she'd get.

They drove into his parents' neighborhood right on time and he parked in the long drive that led to the house. "Ready?"

She nodded. "All that talk about jewelry got me over my nerves. Thanks."

That made one of them.

His mom opened the door before they'd even hit the stone steps at the entryway, likely because she'd been watching for the car. But instead of engulfing Jonas in the first of what would be many hugs, she ignored her only child in favor of her new daughter-in-law.

"You must be Viviana," his mother gushed, and swept Viv up in an embrace that was part friendly and part *Thank you, God, I finally have a daughter.* "I'm so happy to meet you."

Viv took it in stride. "Hi, Mrs. Kim. I'm happy to meet you, too. Please call me Viv."

Of course she wasn't ruffled. There was so little that seemed to trip her up—except when Jonas touched her. All practicing had done was create surprisingly acute sexual tension that even a casual observer would recognize as smoldering awareness.

He was currently pretending it didn't exist. Because that would make it not so, right?

"Hi, Mom," he threw in blithely since she hadn't even glanced in his direction.

"Your grandfather is inside. He'd like to talk to you while I get to know Viviana. Tell me everything," she said to her new daughter-in-law as she accepted the box of cupcakes with a smile. "Have you started thinking about kids yet?"

Jonas barely bit back another curse. "Mom, please. We just got here. Viv doesn't need the third degree about personal stuff."

Right out of the gate with the baby questions? Really? He'd expected a little decorum from his mom. In vain, obviously, and a mistake because he hadn't had a chance to go over that with Viv. Should they say they didn't want children? That she couldn't have any?

He and Viv clearly should have spent less time "practicing" and more in deep conversation about all aspects of potential questions that might come up this weekend. Which they'd have to rectify tonight before going to bed. In the same room.

His mother shot him a glare. "Grandchildren are not personal. The hope of one day getting some is the only reason I keep you around, after all."

That made Viv laugh, which delighted his mother, so really, there was nothing left to do but throw up his hands and go seek out Grandfather for his own version of the third degree.

Grandfather held court in the Kim living room, talking to his son. The older Jonas's dad got, the more he resembled Grandfather, but the similarities ended there. Where Brian Kim had adopted an American name to match his new homeland, Kim Jung-Su wore his Korean heritage like the badge of honor it was.

Kim Electronics had been born after the war, during a boom in Korean capitalism that only a select few had wisely taken advantage of. Jonas loved his dad, but Grandfather had been his mentor, his partner as Jonas had taken what Jung-Su had built and expanded it into the critical US market. They'd created a chaebol, a family-run conglomerate, where none had existed, and they'd done it together.

And he was about to lie to his grandfather's face solely to avoid marrying a disaster of a woman who might cause the Kim family shame.

It was a terrible paradox and not for the first time he heard Warren's voice of reason in his head asking why he couldn't just tell Grandfather the truth. But then he remembered that Sun's grandfather and Jonas's grandfather had fought in the war together and were closer than brothers. Jonas refused to out Sun and her unsuitable lover strictly for his own benefit. No, this way was easier.

And it wasn't a lie. He and Viv were married. That was all anyone needed to know.

Grandfather greeted Jonas in Korean and then switched to English as a courtesy since he was in an English-speaking house. "You are looking well."

"As are you." Jonas bowed to show his respect and then hugged his dad, settling in next to him on the couch. "It's a pleasure to see you."

Grandfather arched a thick brow. "An unexpected pleasure I assume? I wanted to meet your new wife personally. To welcome her into the family."

"She is very honored. Mom waylaid her or she'd be here to meet you, as well."

"I asked your mother to. I wanted to speak with you privately."

As if it had been some prearranged signal, Jonas's dad excused himself and the laser sights of Jung-Su had zero distractions. The temperature of the room shot up about a thousand degrees. One misstep and the whole plan would come crashing down. And Jonas suddenly hated the idea of losing this tenuous link with Viv, no matter how precarious that link was.

"Now, then." Grandfather steepled his hands together and smiled. "I'm very pleased you have decided to marry. It is a big step that will bring you many years of happiness. Belated congratulations."

Jonas swallowed his surprise. What was the wily old man up to? He'd expected a cross-examination designed to uncover the plot that Grandfather surely suspected. "Thank you. Your approval means a lot to me."

"As a wedding gift, I'd like to give you the Kim ancestral home."

"What? I mean, that's a very generous gesture, Grandfather." And crafty, as the property in question lay outside of Seoul, seven thousand miles away from North Carolina. Jonas couldn't refuse or Grandfather would be insulted. But there was an angle here that Jonas couldn't quite work out.

"Of course I'd hoped you'd live in it with Sun Park, but I understand that you cannot curb the impulses of the heart."

Jonas stared at his grandfather as if he'd suddenly started speaking Klingon. The impulses of the heart? That was the exact opposite of the impression he'd wanted to convey. Sure, he'd hoped to convince everyone that they were a couple, but only so that no one's suspicions were aroused. Solid and unbreakable would be more to his liking when describing his marriage, not *impulsive* and certainly not because he'd fallen madly in love.

This was the worst sort of twist. Never would he have thought he'd be expected to sell his marriage as a love match. Was that something that he and Viv were going to have to practice, too? His stomach twisted itself inside out. How the hell was he supposed to know what love looked like?

Regardless of the curveball, it was the confirmation Jonas had been looking for. Grandfather was on board with Viv, and Jonas had cleared the first hurdle after receiving that ominous text message the other day. "I'm glad you understand. I've been seeing Viv for almost a year and I simply couldn't imagine marrying anyone else."

That much at least was true, albeit a careful hedge about the nature of his intentions toward Viv during that year. And thankfully they'd become good enough friends that he felt comfortable asking her to help him avoid exactly what he'd suspected Grandfather had in mind. Apparently throwing Sun in his path *had* been an attempt to get Jonas to Korea more often, if not permanently. It was counter to Jonas's long-term strategy, the one he still hadn't brought to Grandfather because the merger hadn't happened yet. Once Park Industries and Kim Electronics became one, they could leverage the foothold Jonas had already built in America by moving the headquarters to North Carolina, yet keep manufacturing in Korea under the Park branch.

It was also the opportune time to pass the reins, naming Jonas the CEO of the entire operation. The dominoes were in much better position now, thanks to the huge bullet Viv had helped him dodge without upsetting anyone. It was…everything.

Grandfather chatted for a few more minutes about his plans while in the US, including a request for a tour of the Kim Building, and then asked Jonas to introduce him to Viv.

He found her in the kitchen writing down her cupcake recipe for his mother.

"You got her secret recipe already, Mom?" Jonas asked with a laugh. "I guess I don't have to ask whether everyone is getting along."

His mother patted his arm. "You obviously underestimate how much your wife cares for you. I didn't even have to ask twice."

Viv blushed and it was so pretty on her, he couldn't tear his gaze from her face all at once, even though he was speaking to his mom. "On the contrary, I'm quite aware of how incredibly lucky I am that Viv married me."

"You didn't have to ask me *that* twice either," Viv pointed out. "Apparently I lack the ability to say no to anyone with the name Kim."

An excellent point that he really wished she hadn't brought up on the heels of his discovery of how much he enjoyed it when she called him Mr. Kim. All at once, a dozen suggestions designed to get her to say yes over and over sprang to his lips. But with his mom's keen-eyed gaze cutting between the two of them, he needed to get himself under control immediately.

"Come and say hi to my grandfather," he said instead, and she nodded eagerly.

She was far too good to him. For the first time, it bothered him. What was she getting out of this farce? Some advice about how to run her business? That had seemed inadequate before they'd gotten married. Now? It was nearly insulting how little he was doing for her.

She had to have another reason for being here. And all at once, he wanted to know what it was.

CHAPTER FOUR

TEN MINUTES INTO DINNER, Jonas figured out his grandfather's angle. The wily old man was trying to drive him insane with doubt about pulling off this ruse, especially now that he had *impulses of the heart* echoing through his head. Jonas was almost dizzy from trying to track all the verbal land mines that might or might not be strewn through random conversational openers.

Even "pass the butter" had implications. Grandfather hated butter.

And if Grandfather failed at putting Jonas in the loony bin, Viv was doing her part to finish the job, sitting next to him looking fresh and beautiful as she reminded him on a second-by-second basis that she was well within touching distance. Not just easily accessible. But *available* to be touched. It was *expected*. Would a loving husband sling his arm across the back of her chair? Seemed reasonable.

But the moment he did it as he waited for his mom to serve the kimchi stew she'd made in honor of Grandfather's visit, Viv settled into the crook of his elbow, which had not been his intent at all. She fit so well, he couldn't help but let his arm relax so that it fully embraced her and somehow his fingers ended up doing this little dance down her bare arm, testing whether the silkiness felt as good all the way down as it did near her shoulder.

It did.

"...don't you think, Jonas?"

Blinking, Jonas tore his attention away from his wife's skin and focused on his dad. "Sure. I definitely think so."

"That's great," Brian said with a nod and a wink. "It wasn't a stretch to think you'd be on board."

Fantastic. What in the world had he just agreed to that had his father winking, of all things? Jonas pulled his arm from around Viv's shoulders. At this point, it seemed like everyone was convinced they were a couple and all the touching had done nothing but distract him.

Viv leaned in, her hand resting on his thigh. It was dangerously close to being in his lap. One small shift would do it, and his muscles strained to repeat the experience. But before he could sort her intention, she murmured in his ear, "We're playing Uno later. As a team. You'll have to teach me."

Card games with a hard-on. That sounded like the opposite of fun. But at least he knew what he'd absently agreed to, and shot Viv a grateful smile. Her return smile did all sorts of things that it shouldn't have, not the least of which was give him the sense that they were coconspirators. They were in this farce together and he appreciated that more than he could say. At least they could laugh about this later. Or something.

Grandfather was watching him closely as he spooned up a bite of stew, and Jonas braced for the next round of insanity. Sure enough, Grandfather cleared his throat.

"Will you and your bride be starting a family soon?"

Not this again and from his grandfather, too? Obviously Jonas's mother had a vested interest in the answer strictly because she wanted babies to spoil, but Grandfather wasn't asking for anything close to that reason. It was all part of the test.

"Not soon," he hedged because family was important to the Kims. It was a source of frustration for both his parents and his grandparents that they'd only had one child apiece, and Jonas imagined they'd all be thrilled if he said Viv wanted a dozen. "Viv owns a bakery and it's doing very well. She'd like to focus on her career for a while."

Yes. That was the reason they weren't having kids right away. Why had he been racking his brain over that? Except now he was thinking about the conversation where he had to tell everyone that while he cared about Viv, they were better as friends, so the marriage was over. While it soothed his sense of honor that it was the truth, he'd never considered that the annulment would upset his family.

"We're having her cupcakes for dessert," his mother threw in with a beaming smile. "They look scrumptious."

Perfect segue and took some heat off a subject that Jonas suddenly did not want to contemplate. "The lemon are my favorite. One bite and that was when I decided I couldn't let Viv get away."

The adoring glance she shot him thumped him in the gut. The little secret smile playing about her lips worked in tandem, spreading tendrils of heat through him in ways that should be uncomfortable at a table full of Kims who were all watching him closely. But the sensation was too enjoyable to squelch.

"Honestly, that was when I knew he was special," Viv admitted, and Jonas nearly did a double take at the wistful note in her voice. "He appreciates my cupcakes in a way regular customers don't. A lot goes into the recipes and I don't just mean my time. It's a labor of love, born out of a desire to make people happy, and I can see on his face that I've done that. Most customers just devour the thing without stopping to breathe, but Jonas always takes one bite and immediately stops to savor it. Then he tells me how great it is before taking another bite."

Well, yeah, because he could taste the sunshine in it, as if she'd somehow condensed a few rays and woven them through the ingredients. How could he not take his time to fully appreciate the unique experience of a Viviana Dawson cupcake?

Jonas blinked, dragging his lids down over his suddenly dry eyes. He didn't do that *every* time, not the way she was describing it, as if a cupcake held all that meaning.

He glanced at his mom, who looked a little misty.

"That sounds like a magical courtship," she said.

"Oh, it was," Viv agreed enthusiastically. "It was like one of those movies where the hero pretends he only wants the cupcakes when he comes into the shop, but it's really to see the baker. But I always knew from the first that the way to his heart was through my frosting."

His mother laughed and Jonas checked his eye roll because the whole point was to sell this nonsense. Everyone was eating it up, no pun intended, so why mess with the ridiculous story Viv was spinning?

Except the whole thing made him uncomfortable.

Surely his grandfather wouldn't appreciate hearing his successor described with such romanticism. If anything, Viv could help Jonas's case by telling everyone how hard he worked and how difficult it was to pry him away from his cell phone when they went to lunch.

He sighed. She couldn't say that. It would be a big, fat lie. When he did anything with Viv, he always switched his phone to do not disturb. He loved listening to stories about her sisters, or a new recipe she was working through. But it didn't mean he was gaga over her like a besotted fool.

Yet…that's what he needed his grandfather to buy, as difficult as it was to envision. Grandfather hadn't accepted Jonas's marriage to Viv because she'd helped him increase profits or created an advantageous business alliance. Viv was an *impulse of the heart.*

How had he gotten caught in the middle of trying to prove to his grandfather that Jonas was a committed, solid CEO candidate, while also attempting to convince him that he and Viv had fallen in love? And Jonas had no illusions about the necessity of maintaining the current vibe, not after his grandfather

smiled over Viv's enthusiastic retelling of what would probably forever be called the Cupcake Courtship. It was madness.

"Will you bring your wife to Seoul to visit the Kim ancestral
home?" Grandfather asked in the lull. "It's yours now. Perhaps
you'll want to redecorate?"

Jonas nearly groaned. He hadn't had four seconds to mention the gift to Viv. Her eyebrows lifted in silent question and
he blessed her discretion.

"We're actually looking for a house together in Raleigh,"
Jonas improvised much more smoothly than he would have
guessed he could. Viv's eyebrows did another reach-for-the-sky
move as he rushed on. "So probably we won't make it to Korea
anytime soon. But we do both appreciate the gift."

Nothing like a good reminder that Jonas's home was in
America. The future of the company lay here, not in Seoul.
The more he could root himself in North Carolina, the better.
Of course the answer was to buy a property here. With Viv. A
new ancestral home in North Carolina. Then his statement to
his grandfather wouldn't be a lie.

"Yes, thank you so much, Mr. Kim," Viv said sweetly. "We'll
discuss our work schedules and find a mutual time we can
travel. I would be honored to see your ancestral home. Mrs.
Kim, perhaps you'd advise me on whether the decor needs re-
furbishing?"

Jonas's mom smiled so widely that it was a wonder she didn't
crack her face. "That's a lovely idea. I would be thrilled to go
to lunch and discuss the house, as I've always loved the locale."

Speechless, Jonas watched the exchange with a very real
sense of his life sliding out of control and no way to put on the
brakes. In the last two minutes, he'd managed to rope himself
into shopping for a house in Raleigh, then traveling to Korea
so Viv could visit Seoul with the express intent of redecorating
a house neither of them wanted...with his mom. What next?

"While you're in Korea," Grandfather said, and his tone was
so leading that everyone's head turned toward him, "we should

discuss taking next steps toward increasing your responsibilities at Kim Electronics. The board will look very favorably on how you've matured, Jonas. Your accomplishments with the American market are impressive. I would be happy to recommend you as the next CEO when I retire."

The crazy train screeched to a halt in the dead center of Are You Kidding Me Station. *Say something. Tell him you're honored.*

But Jonas's throat froze as his brain tried to sort through his grandfather's loaded statements.

Everything he'd worked for had just been handed to him on a silver platter—that Viv was holding in her delicate fingers. The implications were staggering. Grandfather liked that Jonas was married. It was a huge wrinkle he had never seen coming.

Now he couldn't annul the marriage or he'd risk losing Grandfather's approval with the board. How was he supposed to tell Viv that the favor he'd asked of her had just been extended by about a year?

And what did it mean that his insides were doing a secret dance of happiness at getting to keep Viv longer than planned?

The spare bedroom lay at the end of a quiet hall and had its own en suite bathroom. Nice. Viv wasn't too keen on the idea of wandering around in her bathrobe. At least not outside the bedroom. Inside was another story.

Because Jonas was on this side of the closed door. Time to ramp it up.

If she hoped to build her confidence with a man, there was no better scenario to play that out than this one, especially since she already knew they were attracted to each other And headed for a divorce. None of this was real, so she could practice without fear.

She shivered as her gorgeous husband loosened his tie and threw himself onto the bed with a groan. *Shivered*. What was that but a commentary on this whole situation?

"Bad day, sweetie?" she deadpanned, carefully keeping her voice light. But holy cow, Jonas was so sexy with his shirt-sleeves rolled up and his bare feet crossed at the ankle as he tossed an elbow over his eyes.

"That was one of the most difficult dinners I've ever endured," he confessed, as if there was nothing odd about being in a bedroom together with the door closed, while he lounged on the bed looking like a commercial for something sensual and expensive.

"Your family is great." She eased onto the bed because she wanted to and she could. It wasn't like there were a ton of other seats in the cute little bedroom. Well, except for the matching chairs near the bay window that flanked an inlaid end table. But she didn't want to sit way over there when the centerpiece of the room lay on the bed.

As the mattress shifted under her weight, he peeked out from beneath his elbow, his dark eyes seeking hers. "You're only saying that to be nice. You should stage a fight and go home. It would serve me right to have to stay here and field questions about the stability of our marriage."

As if she'd ever do that when the best part of this fake marriage had just started. She was sharing a bedroom with Jonas Kim and he was her husband and the night was rife with possibilities.

There came the shiver again and it was delicious.

Careful.

This was the part where she always messed up with men by seeming too eager. Messing up with Jonas was not happening. There was no do-over.

Of course, scoring with Jonas had its issues, too. Like the fact that she couldn't keep him. This was just practice, she reminded herself. That was the only way she could get it together.

"I'm not staging a fight." She shook her head and risked reaching out to stroke Jonas's hair in a totally casual gesture meant to soothe him, because after all, he did seem pretty stressed. "What would we fight about? Money?"

"I don't know. No." The elbow came off his face and he let his eyes drift closed as she ran her fingers over his temples. "That feels nice. You don't have to do that."

Oh, yes. She did. This was her chance to touch Jonas in a totally innocuous way and study her husband's body while he wasn't aware.

"It's possible for me to do something because I want to in-stead of out of a sense of obligation, you know."

He chuckled. "Point taken. I'm entirely too sensitive to how big a favor this is and how difficult navigating my family can be."

Stroking his hair might go down as one of the greatest plea-sures of her life. It was soft and silky and thick. The inky strands slid across her fingertips as she buried them deep and rubbed lightly against his scalp, which earned her a groan that was amazingly sexy.

"Relax," she murmured, and was only half talking to herself as her insides contracted. "I don't find your family difficult. Your mom is great and I don't know if you know this or not, but your grandfather does not in fact breathe fire."

"He gave us a house." His eyes popped open and he glanced over at her, shrinking the slight distance between them. "There are all sorts of underlying expectations associated with that, not the least of which is how upset he's going to be when I have to give it back."

She shrugged, pretending like it wasn't difficult to get air into her lungs when he focused on her so intently. "Don't give it back. Keep it and we'll go visit, like we promised."

"Viv." He sat up, taking his beautiful body out of reach, which was a shame. "You're being entirely too accommodat-ing. Were you not listening to the conversation at dinner? This is only going to get more complicated the longer we drag it out. And we *are* going to be dragging it out apparently."

Normally, this would be where she threw herself prostrate at a man's feet and wept with joy over the fact that he wasn't calling things off. But she wasn't clingy anymore. Newly Minted Independent Viv needed to play this a whole different way if she wanted to get to a place where she had a man slavishly devoted to her. And she would not apologize for wishing for a man who loved her so much that he would never dream of calling the duration of their marriage "dragging it out."

"You say that like being married to me is a chore," she scolded lightly. "I was listening at dinner. I heard the words *CEO* and *Jonas* in the same sentence. Did you? Because that sounded good to me."

"It is good. For me. Not you. I'm now essentially in the position of using you to further my career goals for an extended period of time. Not just until the merger happens. But until my grandfather retires and fully transitions the role of CEO to me. That could take months. A year."

Oh, God. A whole year of living with Jonas in his amazing loft and being his wife? That was a lot of practicing for something that would never be real. How could she possibly hide her feelings for Jonas that long? Worse, they'd probably grow stronger the longer she stayed in his orbit. How fair was it to keep torturing herself like this?

On the flip side, she'd promised to do this for Jonas as a favor. As a *friend*. He wasn't interested in more or he'd have told her. Practice was all she could reasonably expect from this experience. It had to be enough.

"That's a significant development, no doubt. But I don't feel used. And I'm not going anywhere."

Jonas scowled instead of overflowing with gratitude. "I can't figure out what you're getting out of this. It was already a huge sacrifice, even when it was only for a few weeks until my grandfather got his deal going with Park. Now this. Are you dying of cancer or something?"

She forced a laugh but there was nothing funny about his

assumptions. Or the fact that she didn't have a good answer for why she didn't hate the idea of sticking around as long as Jonas would have her. Maybe there was something wrong with that, but it was her business, not his. "What, like I'm trying to check off everything on my bucket list before I die and being married to Jonas Kim was in the top three? That's a little arrogant, don't you think?"

When he flinched, she almost took it back, but that's how Newly Minted Viv rolled. The last thing he needed to hear was that being married to him occupied the top spot on all her lists. And on that note, it was definitely time to put a few more logs on the pile before she set it on fire.

"Running a cupcake business is hard," she told him firmly. "You've built Kim Electronics from the ground up. You should know how it is. You work seventy hours a week and barely make a dent. Who has time for a relationship? But I get lonely, same as anyone. This deal is perfect for me because we can hang out with no pressure. I like you. Is that so hard to believe?"

Good. Deflect. Give him just enough truth to make it plausible.

His face relaxed into an easy grin. "Only a little. I owe you so much. Not sure my scintillating personality makes up for being stuck sharing a bedroom with me."

"Yeah, that part sucks, all right," she murmured, and let her gaze trail down his body. What better way to "practice" being less clingy than to get good and needy and then force herself to walk away? "We should use this opportunity to get a little more comfortable with each other."

The atmosphere got intense as his expression darkened, and she could tell the idea intrigued him.

"What? Why? We've already sold the coupledom story to my family. It's a done deal and went way better than I was expecting. We don't have to do the thing where we touch each other anymore."

Well, that stung. She'd had the distinct impression he liked touching her.

"Oh, I wish that was true." She stuck an extra tinge of dismay into her tone, just to be sure it was really clear that she wasn't panting after him. Even though she was lying through her teeth. "But we still have all of tomorrow with your family. And you're planning to meet mine, right? We have to sell that we're hopelessly in love all over again. I'm really concerned about tongues wagging. After all, Joy's husband knows everyone who's anyone. The business world is small."

Jonas's eyes went a little wide. "We just have to sell being married. No one said anything about love."

"But that's why people get married, Jonas." Something flickered through his expression that looked a lot like panic. And it set a bunch of gears in motion in her head. Maybe they should be using this time to get matters straight instead of doing a lot of touching. Because all at once, she was really curious about an important aspect of this deal that she'd thus far failed to question. "Don't you think so?"

"That people should only get married if they're in love? I don't know." But he shifted his gaze away so quickly that it was obvious he had something going on inside. "I've never been married before."

That was a careful way to answer the question. Did that mean he had been in love but not enough to marry the girl? Or he'd never been in love? Maybe he was nursing a serious broken heart and it was too painful to discuss. "Your parents are married. Aren't they in love?"

"Sure. It's just not something I've given a lot of thought to."

"So think about it." She was pushing him, plain and simple, but this was important compatibility stuff that she'd never questioned. Everyone believed in love. Right? "I'm just wondering now why you needed a fake wife. Maybe you should have been looking for someone to fall in love with this whole time instead of taking me to lunch for a year."

He hadn't been dating anyone, this she knew for a fact because she'd asked. Multiple times. Her curiosity on the matter might even be described as morbid.

"Viv." His voice had gone quiet and she liked the way he said her name with so much texture. "If I'd wanted to spend time with someone other than you over the last year, I would have. I like you. Is that so hard to believe?"

Her mouth curved up before she could catch it. But why should she? Jonas made her smile, even when he was deflecting her question. Probably because he didn't think about her "that way" no matter how hot the kiss outside her bedroom had been. One-sided then. They were friends. Period. And she should definitely not be sad about that. He was a wonderful, kind man who made not thinking wicked thoughts impossible the longer they sat on a bed together behind closed doors.

Yeah, she could pretend she was practicing for a relationship with some other man all she wanted. Didn't change the fact that deep in her heart Viv wished she could be the person Jonas would fall madly in love with.

But she knew she couldn't keep Jonas. At least she was in the right place to fix her relationship pitfalls.

Now, how did one go about seducing a man while giving him the distinct impression she could take him or leave him?

CHAPTER FIVE

THE BED IN Jonas's mother's guest room must have razor blades sewn into the comforter. It was the only explanation for why his skin felt like it was on fire as he forced himself to lie there chatting with Viv as if they really were a real married couple having a debrief after his family's third degree.

They *were* a real married couple having a chat.

If only she hadn't brought up the *L* word. The one concept he had zero desire to talk about when it came to marriage. Surely Viv knew real married couples who didn't love each other. It couldn't be that huge of a departure, otherwise the divorce rate would be a lot lower.

But they were a married couple, albeit not a traditional one behind closed doors. If they were a traditional married couple, Jonas would be sliding his fingers across the mattress and taking hold of Viv's thigh so he could brace her for the exploration to come. His lips would fit so well in the hollow near her throat. So far, she hadn't seemed to clue in that every muscle beneath his skin strained toward her, and he had no idea how she wasn't as affected by the sizzling awareness as he was.

They were on a bed. They were married. The door was closed. What did that equal? Easy math—and it was killing him that they were getting it so wrong. Why wasn't he rolling his wife beneath him and getting frisky with breathless anticipation as they shushed each other before someone heard them through the walls?

"Since we like each other so much, maybe we should talk about the actual sleeping arrangements," she suggested. "There's not really a good way to avoid sharing the bed and we're keeping things platonic when no one's around."

Oh, right, because this was an exercise in insanity, just like dinner. He really shouldn't be picturing Viv sliding between cool sheets, naked of course, and peeking up at him from under her lashes as she clutched the pale blue fabric to her breasts.

"I can sleep on the floor," he croaked. She cocked a brow, eyeing him as if she could see right through his zipper to the hard-on he wasn't hiding very well. "I insist. You're doing me a favor. It's the least I can do."

"I wasn't expecting anyone to sleep on the floor. We're friends. We can sleep in the same bed and keep our hands off each other. Right?" Then she blinked and something happened to her eyes. Her gaze deepened, elongating the moment, and heat teased along the edges of his nerve endings. "Unless you think it would be too much of a temptation."

He swallowed. Was she a mind reader now? How had she figured out that he had less than pure thoughts about sharing a bed with his wife? How easy it would be to reach out in the middle of the night, half-asleep, and pull her closer for a midnight kiss that wouldn't have any daylight consequences because nothing counted in the dark.

Except everything with Viv counted. That was the problem. They had a friendship he didn't want to lose and he had taken a vow with Warren and Hendrix that he couldn't violate.

"No, of course not," he blurted out without checking his emphatic delivery. "I mean, definitely it'll be hard—" *Dear God.* "Nothing will be hard! Everything will be..." *Not easy. Don't say easy.* "I have to go check on...something."

Before he could fully internalize how much of an ass he was

making of himself, he bolted from the bed and fled the room, calling over his shoulder, "Feel free to use the bathroom. I'll wait my turn."

Which was a shame because what he really needed was a cold shower. Prowling around the house like a cat burglar because he didn't want to alert anyone he'd just kicked himself out of his own newlywed bedroom, Jonas poked around in his dad's study but felt like he was intruding in the hallowed halls of academia.

He and his dad were night and day. They loved each other, but Brian Kim wasn't a businessman in any way, shape or form. It was like the entrepreneurial gene had skipped a generation. Put Brian in a lecture hall and he was in his element. In truth, the only reason Jonas had gone to Duke was because his father was on faculty and his parents had gotten a discount on tuition. They'd refused to take a dime of Grandfather's money since Brian hadn't filled a position at Kim Electronics.

If his dad had taken a job at any other university, Jonas never would have met Warren, Hendrix and Marcus. His friendship with those guys had shaped his twenties, more so than he'd ever realized, until now.

The funeral had been brutal. So hard to believe his friend was inside that casket. His mom had held his hand the entire time and even as a twenty-one-year-old junior in college who desperately wanted to be hip, he hadn't let go once. Marcus had been down in the dumps for weeks, but they'd all shrugged it off. Typical male pride and bruised feelings. Who hadn't been the victim of a woman's fickle tastes?

But Marcus had been spiraling down and none of them had seen it. That was the problem with love. It made you do crazy, out-of-character things. Like suicide.

Jonas slid into his dad's chair and swiveled it to face the window, letting the memory claw through his gut as he stared blindly at the koi pond outside in the garden. There was no shame in having missed the signs. Everyone had. But that reassurance rang as hollow today as it had ten years ago. What could he have done? Talked sense into the guy? Obviously the pain had been too great, and the lesson for Jonas was clear: don't let a woman get her hooks into you.

That was why he couldn't touch Viv anymore. The temptation wasn't just too much. It was deadly. Besides, she was his friend. He'd already crossed a bunch of lines in the name of ensuring his family bought into the marriage, but it was all just an excuse to have his cake and eat Viv, too.

Bad, bad thing to be thinking about. There was a part of him that couldn't believe Viv would be dangerous to his mental state. But the risks were too great, especially to their friendship. They'd gone a whole year without being tempted. What was different now? Proximity? Awareness? The fact that he'd already kissed her and couldn't undo the effect on his body every time he got within touching distance of her?

That one.

Sleeping with her in the bed was going to be torture. He really didn't know if he had it in him. Probably the best thing to do was sleep on the couch in the living room and set an alarm for something ridiculous like 5:00 a.m. Then he could go for a jog and come back like he'd slept in Viv's bed all night long. Of course he'd never jogged in his life…but he could start. Might burn off some of the awareness he couldn't shake.

That was the best plan. He headed back to the bedroom they shared to tell her.

But when he eased open the door and slipped inside, she was still in the bathroom. He settled onto the bed to wait, next to her open suitcase. There was literally no reason for him to glance inside other than it was right there. Open. With a frothy bunch of racy lingerie laid out across the other clothes.

Holy crap. Jonas's eyes burned the longer he stared at the thin straps and drapes of lace. Was that the *top*? Viv's breasts were supposed to be covered by that? Something that skimpy should be illegal. And red. But the lace was lemon yellow, the color of the frosting Viv slathered all over the cupcakes she always brought him when they had lunch. His mouth watered at the thought of tasting Viv through all that lace. It would be easy. The pattern would show 90 percent of her skin.

The little panties lay innocuously to the side as if an afterthought. Probably because there wasn't enough lace making up the bottom half of the outfit to rightfully call them panties. He could picture them perfectly on his wife's body and he could envision slowly stripping them off even more vividly.

Wait. What was Viv doing with such smoking-hot lingerie?

Was she planning to wear it for *him*? His brain had no ability to make sense of this revelation. She'd brought lingerie. To wear. Of course the only man in the vicinity was Jonas. Who else would she be wearing it for?

That was totally against the rules.

And totally against what he was capable of giving her in this marriage. She might as well drape herself in hearts and flowers. Viv clearly thought love was a recipe for marriage. Stir well and live happily ever after. He wasn't the right ingredient for that mix.

The sound of running water being shut off rattled through the walls. Viv had just emerged from the shower. He should get the hell out of that bedroom right now. But before he could stand, she walked out of the bathroom holding a towel loosely around her body. Her *naked* body. She was still wet. His gaze traced the line of one drop as it slid down her shoulder and disappeared behind the towel.

"Oh. I didn't know you'd come back," she announced unnecessarily as he was reasonably certain she wouldn't have waltzed into the room mostly naked if she'd known he was sitting on the bed.

"Sorry," he muttered, and meant to avert his eyes but the towel had slipped a little, which she'd done nothing to correct.

Maybe she wanted him to catch a glimpse of her perfect breasts. Not that he knew for sure that they were perfect. But the little half-moon slices peeking above the towel flashed at him more brightly than a neon sign, and his whole body went up in flames.

Anything that powerful at only a quarter strength had to be perfect in its entirety.

"Did you want to take a turn in the bathroom?" she asked casually. Still standing there. Wet. In a towel. Naked.

"Uh, sure." He didn't stand. He should cross the room and barricade himself in the bathroom, where it wouldn't matter if she'd used all the hot water because the shower needed to be glacial.

"Okay. Can you give me two minutes? I need to dry my hair." And then she laughed with a little peal that punched him the gut. "Normally I would wrap it up in the towel but there are only two and I didn't want to hog them all."

Then she pulled on the edge of the towel, loosening it from the column it formed around her body and lifted the tail end to the ends of her dripping hair. A long slice of skin peeked through the opening she'd unwittingly created and the answering flash of heat that exploded in his groin would have put him on his knees if he'd been standing. Good thing he hadn't moved.

"You should get dressed," he suggested, but she didn't hear him because his voice wasn't working. Besides, *dressed* could have a lot of different meanings, and the frothy yellow concoction in her suitcase appeared to be the next outfit of choice. If she hadn't been planning to slip it on, it wouldn't be on top, laid out so carefully.

Oh, man. Would she have been wearing it when he got into bed later? No warning, just bam!

He should pretend he hadn't seen the yellow concoction. How else could he find out if that had been her plan? That had to be her plan. Please, God, let it be her plan.

He was so hard, it was a wonder his erection hadn't busted out of his zipper.

Clearing his throat, he tested out speaking again. "I can come back."

That, she heard. "Oh, you don't have to. Really, I've taken way too long already. We're sharing and I'm not used to that. The shower was lovely and I couldn't help standing there under the spray, just letting my mind drift."

Great. Now his mind was drifting—into the shower with her as she stood there. Naked. Letting the water sluice down her body, eyes closed with a small, rapturous smile gracing her face.

He groaned. What was he doing to himself?

"Are you okay?" Her attention honed in on him and she apparently forgot she wasn't wearing anything but a damp towel because she immediately crossed the room to loom over him, her expression laced with concern.

It would take less than a second to reach out and snag her by the waist, pulling her down into his lap. That towel would fall, revealing her perfect breasts, and they'd be right there, ripe and available to taste. No yellow concoction needed. But that would be criminal. She should get to wear her newlywed lingerie if she wanted.

"Oh." Viv blushed all at once, the pink stain spreading across her cheeks, and Jonas could not tear his eyes off her face. But she was staring at the open suitcase. "You didn't see that ridiculous thing Grace gave me, did you?"

She picked up the yellow lacy top and held it up to her body, draping it over the towel one-handed, which had the immediate consequence of smooshing her breasts higher. "Can you imagine me wearing this?"

With absolute, brilliant clarity.

"I don't know what she was thinking," Viv continued as if his entire body wasn't poised to explode. "'Open this with Jonas,' she says with a sly wink. I thought it was going to be a joke, like a gravy boat, and besides, this isn't a real marriage, so I didn't think you'd actually want to help open gifts. Sorry I didn't wait for you."

She rolled her eyes with another laugh that did not help things down below.

"That's okay. Next time." What was he saying? *Sure, I'll help open future gifts full of shockingly transparent clothing that would make a porn star blush?* "Your sister meant well. She doesn't know we're not sleeping together."

Or rather they weren't yet. In a scant few minutes, they'd be in the bed. Together. Maybe some sleeping would occur but it wasn't looking too likely unless he got his body cooled down to something well below its current thermonuclear state.

"Well, true. But obviously she expects us to be hot and heavy, right? I mean, this is the kind of stuff a woman wears for a man who can't keep his hands off her." Suddenly, she swept him with a glance that held a glittery sort of challenge. "We should probably practice that, don't you think?"

"What?" he squawked. "You want me to practice not being able to keep my hands off you?"

Actually, he needed to practice self-control, not the other way around. Restraint was the name of the game. Perfect. He could focus on that instead of the fact that the lingerie had been a gift, not a carefully crafted plan to drive him over the brink.

It was a testament to how messed up he was that he couldn't squelch his disappointment.

She nodded. "My sister just got married not too long ago and she's pretty open with me about how hot the sex is. I think she envisions all newlyweds being like that."

"That doesn't mean she expects us to strip down in your parents' foyer," he countered a little too forcefully. Mostly because he was envisioning how hot *this* newlywed couple could be. They could give Grace and her husband a run for her money, all right.

No. No, they could not.

Viv was not wearing the yellow lacy gateway to heaven for him tonight or any night. She wasn't challenging him to out-sex her sister's marriage. There was no sex at all in their future because Viv had a career she cared about and really didn't have time for a man's inconvenient attraction. Even if the man was her husband. Especially if the man was her husband who had promised to keep things platonic.

Of course he'd done that largely for himself. He'd never experienced such a strong physical pull before and he wasn't giving in to it no matter how badly he wanted to. There was a slippery edge between keeping himself out of trouble so he could honor his promise to his late friend and maintaining his integrity with Viv and his family about the nature of his marriage.

On that note, he needed to change the subject really fast. And get his rampant need under control before he lost everything.

Viv couldn't quite catch her breath. Her lungs ached to expand but the towel was in a precarious spot. If she breathed any deeper, it would slip completely from her nerveless fingers.

Though based on how long it was taking Jonas to clue in that this was a seduction scene, maybe throwing her boobs in his face would get the point across.

God, she sucked at this. Obviously. The girls on TV made it look so simple. She'd bet a million dollars that if this scene had happened on *Scandal*, the seductress would already be in the middle of her third orgasm.

Maybe she *should* have opened the wedding gift with Jonas instead of laying it out so he could find it. For some reason, she'd thought it would give him ideas. That he'd maybe take the lead and they could get something going while they had the perfect setup to indulge in the sparks that only burned hotter the longer they didn't consummate their marriage.

How was she supposed to prove she could be the opposite of clingy with a man she wanted more than oxygen if he wouldn't take her up on the invitation she'd been dangling in his face?

"Instead of practicing anything physical," Jonas said, "we should get our stories straight. We're not going to be hanging out with your family anytime soon but mine is just on the other side of the door. I don't want any missteps like the one at dinner where we didn't plan our responses ahead of time and somehow ended up promising to go to Korea."

"I don't mind going to Korea, Jonas. I would love to see it."

He shook his head with bemusement. "It's a sixteen-hour trip and that's only if there's a not a horribly long line in customs, which even a Kim cannot cut through. Trust me, I'm doing you a favor by not taking you."

How had they shifted from talking about hot sex to visiting his grandfather? That was not how this was supposed to go.

"Well, we have plenty of time to talk about our stories, too," she said brightly. "And the good news is that my hair is almost dry so the bathroom is yours. I like to read before going to sleep so I'll just be here whenever you're ready."

"Oh. Um…" Jonas glanced at the bed and back at her. "Okay. I was thinking about sleeping on the couch and setting an alarm—"

"You can't do that," she cut him off in a rush. That would ruin everything. "What if someone gets up for a midnight snack? Also, the couch would be so uncomfortable. Sleep here. I insist."

She shooed him toward the bathroom and the moment he shut the door, she dragged air into her lungs in deep gulps as she dropped the towel and twisted her hair into a modified updo at her crown, spilling tendrils down her cheeks. Then she slithered into the shameless yellow teddy and panties set that she'd picked out with Grace yesterday. Strictly so she could rub it in that she had a hot husband to wear it for, of course. And then she'd had Grace gift wrap it. The sly wink had been all her sister's idea, so she really hadn't fibbed much when she'd related the story to Jonas.

The lace chafed at her bare nipples, sending ripples of heat through her core. The panties rode high and tight, the strings threading between her cheeks. Not a place she was used to having pressure and friction, but it was oddly exciting.

No wonder women wore this stuff. She felt sexy and more than a little turned on just by virtue of getting dressed. Who knew?

The sound of running water drifted through the walls as Jonas went through his nightly routine. She dove into bed and pulled up the covers until they were tight around her shoulders. Wait. That wasn't going to work. Experimentally, she draped the sheet across her chest like a toga, and threw her shoulders back. Huh. The one breast looked spectacular in the low-cut lace teddy, but the other one was covered up, which didn't seem like the point. Inching the sheet down, she settled into place against the pillow until she was happy with how she looked.

That was a lot of skin on *display*. Much more than she was used to. The lace left little to the imagination.

Surely this would be enough to entice Jonas into making the most of this opportunity to share a bedroom.

Light. She leaped up and slammed down the switch, leaving only the bedside lamp illuminated and leaped back under the covers. The doorknob to the bathroom rattled and she lost her nerve, yanking the sheet back up to cover the yellow lace until X-ray vision would be the only way Jonas could tell what she was wearing. He strode into the room.

Oh, God. Was a more delicious man ever created in the history of time? He'd untucked his button-down and the tail hung casually below his waist. Plenty of access for a woman to slide her hands underneath. There was a gaping hole where his tie had been. A V framed a slice of his chest and he'd rolled his sleeves up to midforearm. It was the most undressed she'd ever seen him and her pulse quickened the closer he came.

This gorgeous creature was about to strip all that off and *get into bed*. With her. This was such a bad idea. Alluring and aloof was not in her wheelhouse and at that moment, she wanted Jonas with a full body ache that felt completely foreign and completely right at the same time.

"I thought you were going to be reading," he said, and stopped in the middle of the room as if he'd hit an invisible wall.

So close. And yet so far.

She shook her head, scrambling for a plausible excuse when she'd just said that was what she planned to do. Couldn't hold an e-reader and pretend you weren't wearing sexy lingerie that screamed *put your hands on me* at the same time.

In retrospect, that might have been a nice scene. She could have been reading with the tablet propped up on her stomach, which would have left her torso completely bare without making it look like she'd set up the scene that way. Dang it. Too late now.

"I couldn't find anything that held my attention."

"Oh. Okay."

And then the entire world fell away along with most of her senses as Jonas started unbuttoning his shirt. It was a slow, torturous event as he slipped the buttons free and each one revealed more of his beautiful body.

Thank God she hadn't stuck a book in front of her face. Otherwise she'd have missed the Jonas Striptease.

She glanced up to see his dark eyes on hers. Their gazes connected and she had the distinct impression he hadn't expected her to be watching him undress. But he didn't seem terribly unhappy about the audience, since he kept going. She didn't look away either.

He let the shirt fall, revealing first one shoulder, then the other. It shouldn't have been such a shock to see the indentations of muscles in his biceps as his arms worked off the shirt. She knew he hit the gym on a regular basis. They'd been friends for a year and talked about all manner of subjects. Sometimes he told her about his workout routine or mentioned that he'd switched it up and his arms were sore. Little had she realized what a visual panorama had been in store for her as a result.

"I feel like I should be wearing something sparkly underneath my pants," Jonas said with wry amusement. "Would it be possible for you to not watch me?"

"Oh. Um…sure." Cheeks on fire, she flipped over and faced the wall, careful to keep the sheet up around her neck. With the motion, it stretched tight. More mummy than Marilyn Monroe, but this was her first seduction. Surely even a woman like Marilyn had a few practice runs before she got it right. This one was Viv's.

And she needed a lot of practice, clearly, since she'd been caught staring and made Jonas uncomfortable at the same time. The whisper of fabric hitting the carpet made her doubly sorry she hadn't been facedown in a book when he came out of the bathroom because she could easily have pretended to be reading while watching the slow reveal out of the corner of her eye.

The bed creaked and the mattress shifted with Jonas's weight. "Still think this is a good idea?"

"I never said it was a good idea," she shot back over her shoulder. "I said our friendship could take it."

Which wasn't a given now that he was so close and so male and so much the subject of her fantasies that started and ended in a bed very much like this one. And she'd been forced to miss half of it due to Jonas's inconvenient sense of propriety. Well, he was done undressing now, right? This was her seduction and she wanted to face him. Except just as she rolled, he snapped off the bedside lamp, plunging the room into darkness.

"Good night," Jonas said, his voice sinfully rich in the dark.

The covers pulled a little as he turned over and settled into position. To go to sleep.

As mood killers went, that was a big one. She'd totally botched this.

Okay. Not totally. This was just a minor setback, most likely because she was trying to play hard to get, which was not as easy as it sounded, and frankly, not her typical method of operation. Plus? This was not a typical relationship. Jonas needed to keep her around, so by default this wasn't going to go like it had with her ex-boyfriends.

She had to approach this like a new recipe that hadn't quite turned out because she'd gone against her instincts and added an ingredient that she didn't like. And if she didn't like it, what was the point?

This was her cupcake to bake. Being the opposite of clingy and needy had only gotten her a disinterested husband—and rightfully so. How was he even supposed to know she wished he'd roll back over and explore the lingerie-clad body she'd hidden under the covers like a blushing virgin bride? Viv wasn't the kind of woman to inspire a man to slavish passion or it would have happened already.

She had to be smart if she couldn't be a femme fatale.

She blinked against the dark and tried not to focus on how the sound of Jonas breathing fluttered against her skin in a very distracting way. Somehow she was going to have to announce her interest in taking things to the next level in big bold letters without also giving him the impression she couldn't live without him. Though perhaps that last part wouldn't be too difficult; after all, she'd already been pretending for a year.

CHAPTER SIX

AFTER THE WEEKEND of torture, Jonas went to work on Monday with renewed determination to get his grandfather moving on the Park Industries merger. The sooner the ink was dry on that deal, the better. Then Jonas could get over his irritation that his marriage to Viv was what had tipped the scales toward his grandfather's decision to retire.

Grandfather recognized Jonas's accomplishments with Kim Electronics. Deep down, he knew that. But it rankled that the conversation about naming Jonas as the next CEO had come about *after* Grandfather had met Viv.

Didn't matter. The subject had come up. That was enough. And Jonas intended to make sure the subject didn't get dropped, because if he was forced to stay married to Viv, he should get something out of it. An Academy Award wouldn't be out of line after the stellar performance he'd turned in at his parents' house. How he'd acted like he'd been sleeping all night while lying next to his wife was still a mystery to him and he was the one who'd pulled it off.

Her scent still haunted him at odd moments. Like now. This conference call he'd supposedly been participating in had gotten maybe a quarter of his attention. Which was not a good way to prove he deserved the position of CEO.

But it was a perfect way to indulge in the memory of the sweet way she'd curled up next to him, her even breathing oddly arousing and lulling at the same time. He'd expected it to be weird the next morning, like maybe they wouldn't look each other in the eye, but Viv had awoken refreshed and beautiful, as if she'd gotten a great night's sleep. He pretended the same and they settled into an easy camaraderie around his parents that hadn't raised a single brow.

At least that part was over. Viv's mom and dad had invited them for dinner on Friday and he was plenty nervous about that experience. It would probably be fine. As long as he didn't have to act like he couldn't keep his hands off Viv. Or act like he didn't want to touch her. Actually, he'd lost track of *what* he was supposed to be doing. Hence the reason he hated lying. The truth was so much easier.

But when he got home that evening after a long day that had included a two-hour debrief with Legal regarding the merger proposal, Viv was sitting on the couch with two glasses of wine. She smiled at him and he felt entirely incapable of faking anything. Especially if it came down to pretending he didn't want to be with her.

His answering smile broadened hers and that set off all sorts of fireworks inside that should have been a big fat warning to back off, but he was tired and there was absolutely nothing wrong with having a glass of wine with his friend Viv after work. That was his story and he was sticking to it.

"Are we celebrating something?" he asked as he hung his work bag on the hook near the refrigerator.

"Yes, that I can in fact open a bottle of wine all by myself." She laughed with that little peal he'd never noticed before he'd married her, but seemed to be a common occurrence lately. Or had she always laughed like that and he'd been too stuck in his own head to notice how warm it was?

"Was that in question?" He took the long-stemmed glass from her outstretched fingers and eased onto the couch next to her.

Instantly, that turned into a big mistake as her scent wrapped around him. It slammed through his gut and his arm jerked, nearly spilling the wine.

For God's sake. This ridiculousness had to stop, especially before Friday or the second family trial by fire would end in a blaze.

"I'm just not talented in the cork-pulling arena," she answered casually as if she hadn't noticed his idiocy. "My skills start and end with baking."

Yes. Baking. They could talk about cupcakes while he got back on track. "Speaking of which, I wasn't expecting you home. Doesn't the shop stay open until seven on Mondays?"

She smiled. "You've been memorizing my work schedule? That's sweet. Josie is closing up for me. I wanted to be here when you got home."

"You did? Why?"

Because I couldn't stay away, Jonas. You're so much more interesting to me than cupcakes, Jonas. I want to strip you naked and have my wicked way with you, Jonas.

There came her gorgeous laugh again. He couldn't hear it enough, especially when he was in the middle of being such a doofus. If she was laughing, that was a good thing. Otherwise, he'd owe her an apology. Not that she could read his thoughts, thank God.

"I wanted to see you. We're still friends, right?"

Oh, yeah. "Right."

"Also, I wasn't kidding when I said my sisters are going to have an eagle eye on our relationship this Friday." Viv sipped her wine, her gaze on his over the rim. "We're still a little jumpy around each other. I'm not sure why, but sharing a bed didn't seem to help."

Huge mystery there. Maybe because his awareness level had shot up into the stratosphere since he'd woken up with a woman whom he hadn't touched one single time. Or it could be because he'd been kicking himself over his regret ever since. He shouldn't regret not touching her. It was the right move.

"No, it didn't help," he muttered. "That wasn't ever going to be the result of sleeping together platonically."

She nodded sagely. "Yes, I realized that sometime between then and now. Don't worry. I have a new plan."

"I wasn't worried. What is it?"

"We're trying too hard. We need to dial it back and spend time as friends. We were comfortable around each other then. It can totally be that way again."

That sounded really great to him. And also like there was a catch he couldn't quite see. Cautiously he eyed her. "What, like I take you to lunch and we just talk about stuff?"

"Sure." She shrugged and reached out to lace her fingers through his free hand. "See, we can hold hands and it doesn't mean anything. I'm just hanging out with my friend Jonas, whom I like. Hey, Jonas, guess what?"

He had to grin. This was not the worst plan he'd ever heard. In fact, it was pretty great. He'd missed their easy camaraderie and the lack of pretension. Never had she made him feel like he should be anything other than himself when they hung out. "Hey, Viv. What?"

"I made reservations at this new restaurant in Cary that sounds fab. It's Thai."

"That's my favorite." Which she well knew. It was hers, too. He took the first deep breath in what seemed like hours. They were friends. He could dang well act like one and stop nosing around Viv like a hormonal teenager.

"Drink your wine and then we'll go. My treat."

"No way. You opened the bottle of wine. The least I can do is spring for dinner."

"Well, it was a major accomplishment," she allowed, and clinked her glass to his as he held out the stemware. "I'm thrilled to have it recognized as such."

And the evening only got better from there. Jonas drove Viv

to the restaurant and they chattered all the way about everything and nothing, which he'd have called a major accomplishment, too, since he managed to concentrate on the conversation
and not on the expanse of Viv's bare leg mere inches from his
hand resting on the gearshift. The food was good and the service exceptional.

As they walked in the door of the condo later, Jonas paused
and helped Viv take off her jacket, then turned to hang it up for
her in the foyer coat closet.

"I have to say," he called over his shoulder as he slid the
hanger into place. "Dinner was a great idea."

He shut the door and Viv was still standing there in the foyer
with a small smile.

"It's the best date I've been on in a long time," she said.
"And seems like the plan worked. Neither of us is acting weird
or jumpy."

"True." He'd relaxed a while back and didn't miss the edgi-
ness that had plagued him since the wedding ceremony. He
and Viv were friends and that was never going to change. That
was the whole reason he'd come up with this idea in the first
place. "We may not set off the fire alarms when we visit with
your family on Friday, but we can certainly pull off the fact
that we like each other, which is not something all married
couples can say."

That was fine with him. Better that way anyway. His reaction to the pull between him and Viv was ridiculous. So unlike
him. He had little experience with something so strong that it
dug under his skin, and he'd handled it badly.

Fortunately, he hadn't done anything irreversible that would
have ruined their friendship. Though there'd been more than a
handful of moments in that bed at his parents' that he'd been
really afraid it was going to go the other way.

But then she stepped a little closer to him in the foyer, waltz-
ing into his space without hesitation. The foyer was just a small
area at the entrance of the condo with a coat closet and nothing

more to recommend it. So there was little else to take his attention off the woman who'd suddenly filled it with her presence.

"We've been friends a long time," she said, and it was such a strange, unnecessary comment, but he nodded anyway because something had shifted in the atmosphere.

He couldn't put his finger on it. The relaxed, easy vibe from the restaurant had morphed into something else—a quickened sense of anticipation that he couldn't explain, but didn't hate. As if this really was a date and they'd moved on to the second part of the evening's activities.

"We've done a lot of firsts in the last little while," she continued, also unnecessarily because he was well aware that he'd shifted the dynamic of their relationship by marrying her.

"Yeah. Tonight went a long way toward getting us back to normal. To being friends without all the weirdness that sprang up when I kissed you."

That was probably the dumbest thing he could have said. He'd thrown that down between them and it was like opening the electrical panel of a television, where all the live components were exposed, and all it would take was one wrong move to fry the delicate circuitry.

Better to keep the thing covered.

But it was too late. Her gaze landed square on his mouth as if she was reliving the kiss, too. Not the nice and unexpectedly sweet kiss at the wedding ceremony. But the hot, tongue-on-tongue kiss outside her bedroom when they'd been practicing being a couple. The necessity of that practice had waned since his family had bought the marriage hook, line and sinker. Sure, they still had to get through her family, but he wasn't worried about it, racy lingerie gifts aside.

Now the only reason to ever kiss Viv again would be because he couldn't stop himself.

Which was the worst reason he could think of. And keep thinking about, over and over again.

"I don't think it was weirdness, Jonas," she murmured.

Instantly, he wished there was still some circumstance that required her to call him Mr. Kim. Why that was such a turn-on remained a mystery to him. But really, everything about Viv was a turn-on. Her laugh. Her cupcakes. The way her hair lay so shiny and soft against her shoulders.

"Trust me, it was weird," he muttered. "I gave myself entirely too many inappropriate thoughts with that kiss."

And that was the danger of being lulled back into a false sense of security with the sociable, uneventful dinner. He'd fallen into friendship mode, where he could say anything on his mind without consequence.

The admission that had just come out of his mouth was going to have consequences.

Her smile went from zero to sixty in less than a second and all at once, he wasn't sure the consequences were going to be anything close to what he'd envisioned. She waltzed even closer and reached up to adjust his tie in a provocative move that shouldn't have been as affecting as it was.

The tie hadn't needed adjusting. The knot was precisely where he'd placed it hours ago when he'd gotten dressed for work. It slid down a few centimeters and then a few more as she loosened it.

Loosened it. As if she intended to take it off.

But she stopped short of committing, which was good. Really...good. He swallowed as she speared him with her contemplative gaze, her hands still at his collar in an intimate touch. She was so close he could pull her into his arms if he wanted to.

He wanted to. Always.

Dinner hadn't changed that.

"The thing is, Jonas," she said. "I've had some thoughts, too. And if yours are the same as mine, I'm trying to figure out why they're inappropriate."

She flattened her hands on his lapels. The pressure sang through him and it would feel even better if he didn't have a whole suit jacket and two shirts between her palms and his skin.

The direction of this conversation floored him. And if she kept it up, the floor was exactly where they were going to end up.

"What are you saying, Viv?" he asked hoarsely, scrambling to understand. "That you lie awake at night and think about that kiss, aching to do it again?"

She nodded and something so powerful swept through his body that he could hardly breathe. This was the opposite of what should be happening. She should be backing off and citing her inability to focus on a man and her career at the same time. She was too busy, too involved in her business to date. This was the absolute he'd banked on for long agonizing hours, the thing that was keeping him from indulging in the forbidden draw between them.

Because if he gave in, he'd have no control over what happened next. That certainty had already been proven with what little they'd experimented so far. More would be catastrophic.

And so, so fantastically amazing.

"After tonight, I'm convinced we're missing an opportunity here," she said, her voice dripping with something sensual that he'd never have expected from his sunny friend Viviana Dawson. *Kim.*

Viv wasn't his friend. She was his wife. He'd been ignoring that fact for an entire day, but it roared back to the forefront with an implication he couldn't ignore. Except he didn't know what it meant to him, not really. Not just a means to an end, though it was an inescapable fact that she'd married him as a favor.

And he wanted to exploit that favor to get her naked and under him? It was improper, ridiculous. So very illicit that his body tightened with thick anticipation.

"What opportunity is that?" he murmured, letting his gaze flick over her face, searching for some sign that the answer about to come out of her mouth *was not* a green light to get naked.

Because he'd have a very difficult time saying no. In fact, he couldn't quite remember why he should say no. He shouldn't say no. If nothing else, taking this next step meant he wasn't lying to anyone about their marriage.

Her limpid brown eyes locked on to his. "We're both too busy to date. And even if we weren't, I have a feeling that 'oh, by the way, I'm married' isn't a great pickup line. You said it yourself. We spark. If our friendship can take a kiss, maybe it can take more. We should find out."

More. He liked the word *more* a lot. Especially if her dictionary defined it as lots and lots of sex while maintaining their friendship. If things got too intense, he could back off with no harm, no foul. It was like the absolute best of all worlds.

Unless that wasn't what she meant.

Clarification would be in order, just to be sure they were speaking the same language. "More?"

"Come on, Jonas." She laughed a little breathlessly and it trilled through him. "Are you going to make me spell it out?"

"Yes, I absolutely am," he growled, because the whole concept of Viv talking dirty to him was doing things to his insides that he was enjoying the hell out of. If he'd known dinner was *this* kind of date, he'd have skipped dessert. "I want to be crystal clear about what's on the table here."

Instead of suggesting things Jonas could do to her—all of which he'd immediately commit to memory so he didn't miss a single one—she watched him as she hooked the neckline of her dress and pulled it to the side. A flash of yellow seared his vision as his entire body tensed in recognition.

"I'm wearing my sister's gift," she murmured, and that admission was as much of a turn-on as any dirty talk. Maybe more so because he'd been fantasizing about that scrap of yellow lace for a million years.

"I bet it looks amazing on you."

"Only one way to find out," she shot back and curled her fingers around his lapels to yank him forward.

He met her mouth in a searing kiss without hesitation. All of his reservations melted in an instant as he sank into her, shaping her lips with his as he consumed her heat, letting it spread deep inside.

Why had he resisted this? Viv didn't want anything from him, didn't expect an emotional outpouring or even anything permanent. This was all going to end at some point and thus didn't count. No chance for romantic nonsense. No declarations of love would ever be forthcoming—on either side. Jonas's sense of honor would be intact, as would his sworn vow to Warren and Hendrix.

Instead of two friends pretending to be a married couple having sex, they were going to be married friends who *were* having sex. Living the truth appealed to him enormously. Desire swept through him as he got great handfuls of Viv's skin under his palms and everything but his wife drained from his mind.

Viv would have sworn on a truckload of Bibles that the kiss outside her bedroom last week had been the hottest one she'd ever participate in.

She'd have been wrong.

That kiss had been startling in its perfection. Unexpected in its heat. It had gotten her motor humming pretty fast. She'd been angling for another one just like that. Thank God she hadn't gotten her wish.

This kiss exploded in her core like a cannon. Desire crackled through the air as Jonas backed her up against the wall, crowding her against it with his hard body, demanding that her every curve conform to him. Her flesh rapidly obeyed. She nearly wept with the glory of Jonas pressed against her exactly as she'd fantasized hundreds of times.

He angled her jaw with his strong fingers until he got her situated the way he apparently wanted and then plunged in with the wickedest of caresses. His tongue slicked across hers so sensuously that she moaned against it, would have sagged if he hadn't had her pinned to the wall.

His hands nipped at her waist, skimmed upward and hooked

both sides of the neckline. The fabric tore at the seams as he separated it from her shoulders, and she gasped.

"I need to see you," he murmured fiercely. "I'll buy you two to make up for this one."

And with that, the dress came apart in his hands. He peeled it from between them, following the line of the reveal with his hot mouth, laving at her exposed flesh until he caught the silk strap of the yellow teddy in his teeth, scraping the sensitive hollow of her shoulder.

The sensation shot through her center with tight, heated pulls. *Oh, my.* His fingers tangled in the strap, binding his palm to her shoulder as he explored the skin beneath the yellow lace with his tongue, dipping and diving into the holes of the pattern. Then his lips closed around her nipple through the fabric and her whole body jerked. Hot, wet heat dampened the scrap between her legs. The awareness that Jonas had drenched her panties so quickly only excited her more.

What had happened to the kind, generous man she'd been so intent on seducing? He'd become a hungry, untamed creature who wanted to devour her. She loved every second. His tongue flicked out to tease her nipple, wetting the lace, and it was wickedly effective. Moans poured from her throat as her head thunked back against the wall.

All at once, he sank to his knees and trailed his lips across the gap between the top and the bottom of her sexy lingerie set, murmuring her full name. *Viviana.* The sound of it rang in her ears as he worshipped her stomach with his mouth, and it was poetry.

Her thighs pressed together, seeking relief from the ache his touch had created, and she arched into his lips, his hands, crying out as his fingers worked under the hem of her soaked panties. The gorgeous man she'd married glanced up at her from his supine position, his gaze so wickedly hot that she experienced a small quake at that alone, but then he slid one finger along her crease, teasing her core until she opened wider, begging him to fill her.

He did. Oh, how he did, one quick motion, then back out again. The exquisite friction burned through her core a second time and she cried out.

"Please, Jonas" dripped from her mouth with little gasping sighs and she whimpered as she pleaded with him for whatever he planned to give her next.

She didn't know she could be this wanton, that the man she'd married could drive her to neediness so easily. It was so hot that she felt the gathering of her release before she was ready for the exquisite torture to end. No way to hold back. She crested the peak and came with hard ripples against Jonas's fingers. The orgasm drained her of everything but him.

Falling apart at his hands was better than what she'd dreamed of, hoped for, imagined—and then some. And it still wasn't over.

He nipped at her lace-covered sex and swept her up in his arms, still quaking, to carry her to his bedroom. Blindly, she tried to clear her senses long enough to gain some semblance of control. Why, she wasn't sure, but being wound up in Jonas's arms wearing nothing but wet lace while he was still fully dressed felt a lot like she'd surrendered more than she'd intended to.

But he wasn't finished with the revelations.

He laid her out on the comforter and watched her as he stripped out of his suit jacket and tie. She shivered long and hard as he began unbuttoning his shirt, but she didn't dare blink for fear of missing the greatest show on earth—the sight of her husband shedding his clothes. For her. Because she'd finally gotten him to see reason.

They were friends. What better foundation was there to get naked with someone than because you liked each other? It was sheer brilliance, if she did say so herself. The fact that she'd been racking her brain over how to best get to this place when the answer had been staring her in the face for a year? She'd rather not dwell on that.

Good thing she had plenty else to occupy her mind. That beautiful torso of his came into sight, still covered by a white undershirt that clung to his biceps and lean waist, and she wanted to touch him so badly her fingers tingled. But then his hands moved to his belt and she didn't move. Couldn't. Her lungs rattled with the need to expand. Slowly, the belt loosened and he pulled it from the loops. After an eternity, it dropped to the floor, followed shortly by the pants, and then came the pièce de résistance. Jonas stripped off his undershirt and worked off his boxers in the most spectacular reveal of all. Better than Christmas, her birthday and flipping the sign in Cupcaked's window to Open for the first time.

Her husband's body was gorgeous, long, lean. Vibrating with need that hungrily sniffed out hers as he crawled onto the bed and onto her, easily knocking her back to the mattress, covering her body with his.

And then she wasn't so coherent after that. His arms encircled her as easily as his dominant presence did. His kiss claimed her lips irrevocably, imprinting them with his particular brand of possession, the likes of which she'd never known. Never understood could exist.

The sensuous haze he dropped her into was delicious and she soaked it in, content to let him take his time as he explored her body with his hands more thoroughly than she'd have imagined possible when she still wore the yellow lace. She was so lost in him that it took her a minute to remember that she could indulge herself, too, if she wished.

Viv flattened her palms to his chest, memorizing the peaks and valleys of his body, reveling in the heat under her fingertips. She slid downward to cup his buttocks, shifting to align their hips because the ache at her core had only been awakened, not sated, and he had precisely what she needed.

He groaned deep in his throat as she circled against his thick, gorgeous erection, grinding her hips for maximum impact. The answering tilt of his hips enflamed her. As did the quickening of his breath.

"I need to be inside you," he murmured. "Before I lose my mind."

Rolling with her in his arms, he reached one hand out to sling open the bedside table and extracted a box of condoms with ruthless precision. In seconds, he'd sheathed himself and rolled back into place against her.

His thumb slid into the indentation in her chin, levering her head up to lock his hot-eyed gaze onto her as he notched himself at her entrance.

The tip of his shaft tormented her, sensitizing everything it touched as he paused in the worst sort of tease.

"Jonas," she gasped.

"Right here, sweetheart. Tell me what you want."

"Everything." And she couldn't take it back, no matter how much of a mistake it was to admit that she wasn't the kind of woman who could be in the midst of such passion and hold back.

Except she wasn't entirely sure he meant for her to as he gripped her hip with his strong fingers, lifted and pushed in with a groan, spreading her wide as he filled her. The luscious solid length of him stretched her tight, and before she could question it, one tear slipped from the corner of her eye. It was a testament to the perfection of how he felt moving inside her, how wholly encompassing the sensations were that washed over her as Jonas made love to her.

And she was ten kinds of a fool if she thought she could keep pretending this was practice for her next relationship.

"Amazing. Beautiful. Mine." Words rained down on her from Jonas's mouth as he increased the tempo. "I can't believe how this feels...you're so wet, so silky. I can't stop. Can't hold back."

For a woman who had never incited much more than mild interest in a man, to be treated to this kind of evidence that she was more than he could take—it was everything. "Give it all to me."

Unbelievably, there *was* more and he gave it to her, driving her to a soaring crescendo that made her feel more alive than anything in her memory. No longer was this bed a proving ground to show she could be with a man and not pour all of herself into him. He demanded her participation, wrung every drop of her essence out of her body.

She gladly surrendered it. Jonas was it for her, the man she'd married, the man she'd wanted for so very long.

As they both roared toward a climax, she had half a second to capture his face in her palms and kiss him with all the passion she could muster before they both shattered. She swallowed his groan and took the shudders of his body, absorbing them into hers even as she rippled through her own release. Everything was so much bigger, stronger, crisper than she'd have ever imagined and his mouth under hers curved into a blissful smile that her soul echoed.

And as he nestled her into his arms for a few badly needed moments of recovery time, she bit her lip against the wash of emotions that threatened to spill out all over their friendship.

She'd told him their relationship could take this. Now she had to stick to her promise. How in the world she was going to keep him from figuring out that she was in love with him?

CHAPTER SEVEN

FOR THE SECOND day in a row, Jonas struggled to maintain his composure at work. It was for an entirely different reason today than it had been yesterday. But still. His wife swirled at the center of it and he wasn't sure what to do with that.

Last night had been legendary. Off the charts. Far more explosive than he would have ever guessed—and he'd spent a lot of time contemplating exactly how hot things with Viv could be.

She'd surpassed everything he'd ever experienced. Even here in his somewhat sterile office that had all the hallmarks of a CEO who ran a billion-dollar global company, his loins tightened the second he let his thoughts stray. She'd made him thoroughly question what he knew about how it could be between a man and a woman. How it could be between Jonas and Viv, more importantly, because he had a feeling they weren't done.

How could they be done? He'd barely peeled back the first layer of possibilities, and he was nothing if not ravenous to get started on the second and third layers. Hot Viv. Sensual Viv. The list could be endless.

Instead of drooling like an idiot over the woman he'd married, Jonas squared his shoulders and pushed the erotic images from his mind. The merger with Park was still just a nebulous concept and no one had signed anything. This was the deal of the century, and Jonas had to get it done before anyone thought twice about marriage alliances. Sun Park's grandfather could still pull the plug if he'd had his heart set on a much more intimate merger. Thus far, Jonas had done little but meet with Legal on it.

Four hours later, he had sketched out a proposed hierarchy for the business entities, worked through the human resources tangle of potential duplicate positions and then run the numbers on whether the Kim Building could support the influx of new people. His grandfather would be coming by soon to take a tour and this was exactly the data Jonas needed at his fingertips. Data that would solidify his place as the rightful CEO of Kim Electronics, with or without an *impulse of the heart* on his résumé.

So that was still a sore spot apparently. Jonas tried to shrug it off and prepare for his grandfather's arrival, but wasn't at all surprised that Jung-Su showed up twenty minutes early. Probably a deliberate move to see if Jonas was prepared.

He was nothing if not ready, willing and able to prove that he was the right choice. He'd been preparing to be his grandfather's successor since college.

He strolled to the reception area, where his admin had made Grandfather comfortable. Technically Jung-Su was the boss of everyone in this building, but he hadn't visited America in several years. Jonas held the helm here and he appreciated that Grandfather didn't throw his weight around. They had professional, mutual respect for each other, which Jonas had to believe would ultimately hold sway.

Jung-Su glanced up as Jonas came forward, his weathered face breaking into a polite smile. Grandfather stood and they shook hands.

"Please follow me," Jonas said, and indicated the direction. "I'd like to show you the executive offices."

Jung-Su nodded and inclined his head, but instead of following Jonas, he drew abreast and walked in lockstep toward the elevator. Over the weekend, they'd done a lot of sitting down and Jonas hadn't noticed how much his grandfather had shrunk. Jonas had always been taller and more slender to his grandfather's stocky build, but more so now, and it was a visual cue that his grandfather had aged. As much as Jonas had focused on getting his grandfather comfortable with passing the mantel, he'd given little thought to the idea that becoming the next CEO of the global company meant his mentorship with Jung-Su would be over.

"Tell me," Grandfather said as they reached the elevator. "How is your lovely wife?"

"She's…" *A vixen in disguise.* Not the kind of information his grandfather was looking for with the innocuous question. "Great. Her shop is constantly busy."

And Viv had ducked out early to take him on the ride of his life last night. For the first time, he wondered if she'd planned the evening to end as it had or if it had been as spontaneous on her part as it had been on his. Maybe she'd been thinking about getting naked since the weekend of torture, too. If so, he liked that she'd been similarly affected.

They rode two floors up to the executive level. As they exited, Jonas and Jung-Su nodded to the various employees going about the business of electronics in a beehive of activity.

"You've mentioned your wife's business frequently," his grandfather commented just outside the boardroom where Jonas conducted the majority of his virtual meetings. "Doesn't she have other interests?"

The disapproval in his grandfather's voice was faint. "You don't understand. Her bakery is much more than just a business. It's an extension of her."

Cupcakes had been a mechanism to fit in among her older, more accomplished sisters, as she'd told him on numerous occasions. But it had morphed from there into a business that she could be proud of. Hell, it was a venture *he* was proud of.

"Anyone can pull a package of cupcake mix off the shelf at

the grocery store," Jonas continued, infusing as much sincerity into his speech as he could. His grandfather had no call to be throwing shade at his wife's profession. "That's easy. Viv spends hours in her kitchen doing something special to hers that customers can't get enough of."

"It seems as if you are smitten by her cupcakes, as well," Grandfather commented with a tinge of amusement.

Jonas forced a return smile that hopefully didn't look as pained as he suspected it did. *Smitten.* He wasn't smitten with Viv and it rankled that he'd managed to convince his grandfather that he was. Cupcakes, on the other hand—no pretending needed there. "Of course I am. That's what first drew me to her."

Like it was yesterday, he recalled how many times he'd found excuses to drop by Cupcaked to get a glimpse of Viv in those first few weeks after meeting her. Often she was in the back but if she saw him, she popped out for a quick hi, ready with a smile no matter what she had going on in the kitchen. That alone had kept him coming back. There was always someone in the office with a birthday or anniversary, and cupcakes always made an occasion more festive.

"Ah, yes, I recall that conversation at dinner where she mentioned you pretended to go there for her cupcakes but were really there to see her."

"It was both," he corrected easily since it was true. He could own that he liked Viv. They were friends.

Who'd seen each other naked.

Before he could stop it, images of Viv spilled through his mind.

The rush of heat to his body smacked him, sizzling across his skin so fast he had little chance of reeling it back. But he had to. This was the most inappropriate time to be thinking about his wife wearing that see-through yellow lacy concoction strictly for his benefit.

"Pardon me for a moment," Jonas croaked, and ducked into the executive washroom to get himself under control. Or as close to it as he could with an enormous erection that showed no signed of abating.

And while he stood in front of the mirror concentrating on his breathing and doing absolutely nothing constructive, he pulled out his phone to set a reminder to drop by the jewelry store on the way home. Viv had expressly asked for jewels as compensation for the favor she was doing him. She needed something pretty and ridiculously expensive.

Thinking of her draped in jewelry he'd bought wasn't helping.

After the longest five minutes of his life, Jonas finally got the tenting mostly under control. No one had noticed. Or at least that's what he tried to tell himself. His staff didn't walk around with their eyes on his crotch.

The biggest hit was to Jonas's psyche. How had he let Viv get under his skin like that? It was unacceptable. If nothing else, he needed to maintain his professionalism during this period when his grandfather's support meant everything. There were other contenders for Jung-Su's job, such as vice presidents who lived in Korea and had worked alongside the CEO for thirty years. Some of Mr. Park's staff could rise to the top as worthy heads of a global company, and those under the Park umbrella arguably had more experience running the factories that would come into play with the merger.

Jonas had to reel it back with Viv. Way back. There was no excuse for falling prey to baser urges and he definitely didn't want to find out what happened next if he kept going down this path. That was one absolute he trusted—the less he let a woman get tangled up in his emotions, the better.

Resolute, Jonas returned to find his grandfather in deep discussion with Jonas's chief financial officer, a man without whom Kim Electronics would suffer in the American market.

Perfect. This was an opportunity to guide the discussion to Jonas's accomplishments as well as those of his staff, who were a reflection of his ability to run the Americas branch. Back on track, Jonas smiled at the two men and jumped into the conversation as if he hadn't just had a minor freak-out over an incontrollable urge to drive straight home and bury himself in his wife.

That wasn't happening. Boundaries needed to happen. Jonas didn't have the luxury of letting his wife dig further under his skin. But when he got home later that night, it was to an empty house, and boundaries didn't seem like such a fun plan.

More disappointed than he had a right to be, Jonas prowled around the enormous condo to be sure Viv hadn't tucked herself away in a corner to read or watch TV. *Nada.* He glanced at his watch. It was well after seven. She must have gotten caught up at the shop. Totally her right to work late. They didn't answer to each other.

For a half second, he contemplated walking the four blocks to Cupcaked. Strictly so he could give Viv her gift, of course. But that smacked of eagerness to see her that he had no intention of admitting to. So instead, he flopped on the couch and scrolled through his never-ending inbox on his phone, desperate for something to take his mind off the resounding silence in the condo. Wow, was it quiet. Why had he never noticed that before? The high ceilings and exposed beams usually created an echo that reminded him of a museum, but he'd have to be making noise for that echo to happen.

Viv had made a lot of noise last night, but he hadn't been paying a whole lot of attention to whether the sounds of her gasps and sighs had filled the cavernous part of the loft. And now he was back to thinking about his wife, her gorgeous body and why she wasn't currently naked in his lap.

He scowled. They'd done zero to establish how their relationship would progress after last night. They should have. *He* should have. Probably the smartest thing would have been to establish that last night was a onetime thing. He couldn't keep having meltdowns at work or moon around over whether Viv planned to hang out with him at night.

He should find something else to do. Like... He glanced

around the condo, suddenly at a loss. Prior to getting married, what had he done on a random Tuesday when he was bored?

Nothing. Because he was rarely bored. Usually he had work and other stuff to occupy him. *Friends.* Of course the answer was to ping his friends. But Warren didn't respond to his text message and Hendrix was in New York on a business trip.

Viv's key rattled in the lock. Finally. He vaulted off the couch to greet her, totally not okay with how his pulse quickened at the prospect of seeing her and completely unsure how to stop it.

As she came through the door, her smile widened as she spied Jonas standing in the hall, arms crossed, hip casually cocked out against the wall.

"Hi," she said, halting just short of invading his space. "Were you waiting for me?"

No sprang to his lips before he thought better of it. Well, he couldn't really deny that, now could he? If he'd stayed sprawled on the couch and given her a casual "what's up?" as she strolled through the door, he might have had a leg to stand on. Too late.

"Yeah," he admitted, and held up the shiny blue foil bag clutched in his fingers. "I have something for you."

Her eyes widened as she held out her hand to accept the bag. The most delicious smell wafted between them, a vanilla and Viv combo that made him think of frosting and sex and about a million other things that shouldn't go together but did—like marriage and friendship.

Why couldn't he greet his wife at the door if he felt like it? It wasn't a crime. It didn't mean anything.

The anticipation that graced her smile shouldn't have pleased him so much. But he couldn't deny that it whacked him inside in a wholly different way than the sultry smile she'd laid on him last night, right before she informed him that she had on yellow lingerie under her clothes.

Which was not up for a repeat tonight. Boundaries should be the first order of business. Viv had sucked him down a rabbit hole that he didn't like. Well, he *liked* it. It just didn't sit well with how unbelievably tempting she was. If she could tempt him into letting go of his professionalism, what other barriers could she knock down? The risk was not worth it.

But then she opened the box, and her startled gasp put heat in places that he should be able to control a hell of lot better.

"Jonas, this is too much," she protested with a laugh and held out the box like she expected him to take it back or something.

"Not hardly. It's exactly right." Before she got ideas in her head about refusing the gift that had taken him thirty minutes to pick out, he plucked the diamond necklace from its velvet housing and undid the clasp so he could draw it around her neck. "Hush, and turn around."

She did and that put him entirely too close to her sweet flesh. That curve where her shoulder flared out called to him. Except it was covered by her dress. That was a shame.

Dragging her hair out of the way, she waited for him to position the chain. He let the catch of the necklace go and the ten-carat diamond dropped to rest against her chest, just above the swell of her breasts. Which were also covered, but he knew precisely where they began.

His lips ached to taste that swell again. Among other things. Palms flat across her back, he smoothed the chain into place, but that was really just an excuse to touch her.

"If you're sure," she murmured, and she relaxed, letting her body sink backward until it met his and heat flared between them.

"Oh, I'm sure." She'd meant about the diamond. Probably. But his mouth had already hit the bare spot she'd revealed when she'd swept her long brown hair aside and the taste of Viv exploded under his tongue.

Groaning, he let his hands skim down her waist until he found purchase and pulled until their bodies nested together tighter than spoons in a drawer. The soft flesh of her rear cradled the iron shaft in his pants, thickening his erection to the point of pain. He needed a repeat of last night. Now.

He licked the hollow of her collarbone, loving the texture under his tongue. More Viv needed. Her answering gasp encouraged him to keep going.

Gathering handfuls of her dress, he yanked it from between them and bunched it at her waist, pressing harder into the heat of her backside the moment he bared it. His clothes and a pair of thin panties lay between him and paradise, and he wanted all that extraneous fabric gone.

She arched against him as his fingers cruised along the hem of her drenched underwear and he took that as agreement, stripping them off in one motion. Then he nudged her legs wider, opening her sex, and indulged them both by running a fingertip down the length of her crease. Her hands flew out and smacked the wall and she used it to brace as she ground her pelvis into his.

Fire tore through his center and he needed to be inside her with an uncontrollable urge, but the condoms were clear across the cavernous living area in his bedside table. He couldn't wait. Viv cried out his name as he plunged one then two fingers into her center, groaning at the slick, damp heat that greeted him. She was so wet, so perfect.

As he fingered her, she shuddered, circling her hips in a frenzied, friction-induced madness that pushed him to the brink. Her hot channel squeezed his fingers and that was nearly all she wrote. Did she have a clue how much he wanted to yank his zipper down, impale her and empty himself? Every muscle in his body fought him and his will crumbled away rapidly. Reaching between them, he eased open his belt.

But then she came apart in his arms, huffing out little noises that drove him insane as she climaxed. His own release roared to the forefront and all it would take was one tiny push to put him over the edge. Hell, he might not even need a push. Shutting his eyes against the strain, he drew out her release with long strokes that made her whimper.

She collapsed in his arms as she finished and he held her upright, murmuring nonsense to her as she caught her breath.

"Let me take you to bed," he said, and she nodded, but it was more of a nuzzle as she turned her cheek into his.

To hell with boundaries.

He hustled her to his room, shed his clothes and hers without ripping anything this time—because he was in control—and finally she was naked. Sultry smile in place, she crawled onto the bed and rolled into a provocative position that begged him to get between her legs immediately and hammer after his own release. But despite being positive the only thing he could possibly do next was get inside her as fast as humanly possible, he paused, struck immobile all at once.

That was *his wife* decked out on the bed.

The sight bled through him, warming up places inside dangerously fast. Places that weren't what he'd call normal erogenous zones. And that's when he realized his gaze was on her smile. Not her body.

What was wrong with him? A naked woman was on display for his viewing pleasure. He forced his gaze to her breasts, gratified when the pert tips pebbled under his watchfulness. That was more like it. This was about sex and how good two people could make each other feel.

With a growl, he knelt on the bed and kissed his way up her thigh. He could absolutely keep his hands off her if he wanted to. He had total control over his desires, his emotions. There was nothing this woman could do to drive him to the point of desperation, not in bed and certainly not out of it. To prove it, he pushed her thighs open and buried his face between them.

She parted for him easily, her throaty cry washing over him as he plunged his tongue into her slickness. That wet heat was *his*. He'd done that to her and he lapped at it, groaning as her musky scent flooded his senses. The ache in his groin intensified into something so strong it was otherworldly. He needed to feel her tight, slick walls close around him, to watch her face as it happened. He needed it, but denied himself because she didn't own his pleasure. He owned hers.

Her hips rolled and bucked. He shoved his mouth deeper into her center as she silently sought more, and he gave it to her. Over and over he worked his lips and tongue against her swollen flesh until she bowed up with a release that tensed her whole body. And then she collapsed against the mattress, spilling breathy, satisfied sighs all over him. Only then did he permit his own needs to surge to the surface.

Fingering on a condom that he'd retrieved from the drawer, he settled over her and indulged his intense desire to kiss her. She eagerly took his tongue, sucking it into her hot mouth, and he groaned as he transferred her own taste back to her. Their hips came together, legs tangling, and before he could fully register her intent, she gathered him up in her tight fist and guided him into the paradise at her core.

A strong urge to fill her swelled. But he held on by the scrabbly edge of his fingertips, refusing to slam into her as he ached to do. Slowly, so slowly that he nearly came apart, he pushed. Her slickness accepted him easily, wringing the most amazing bliss from a place he scarcely recognized. The deeper he sank, the better it felt.

Her gaze captured his and he fell into her depths. She filled him, not the other way around. How was that physically possible? He couldn't fathom it, but neither could he deny it. Or halt the rush of Viviana through his veins as she streamed straight to his heart in a kill shot that flooded all four chambers at once.

And then there was nothing but her and the unbelievable feel of her skin against his, her desire soaking through his pores in an overwhelming deluge. He meant to hold back, determined to prove something that escaped him as she changed the angle. Somehow that allowed him to go deeper, push harder. Her cries spurred him on, and unbelievably, she took it higher, sucking him under into a maelstrom of sensation and heightened pleasure.

When her hips began pistoning in countermeasure to his,

it nearly tore him in two. Delirious with the need to come, he grabbed one of her legs and pushed at the knee, opening her wider so he had plenty of room to finger her at the source of her pleasure. Two circular strokes and she climaxed, squeezing him so tight that it tripped the wire on his own release.

Bright pinpoints of light streamed behind his eyes as he came so hard that he would have easily believed he'd crossed over into an alternate dimension. In this new dimension, he could let all the things crowding through his chest spill out of his mouth. But those things shouldn't exist in any universe.

If he didn't acknowledge them, they didn't exist. Then he wouldn't be breaking his word.

As his vision cleared and his muscles relaxed, rendering him boneless, he collapsed to the mattress, rolling Viv into his arms.

The heavy diamond swung down from the chain he'd latched around her neck, whacking him on the shoulder. He fingered it back into place silently, weighing out whether he could actually speak or if that spectacular orgasm had in fact stolen his voice.

"I get the sense you've been saving up," Viv commented huskily, her lips moving against his chest, where her face had landed after he'd nestled her close. Probably he shouldn't have done that, but he liked coming down from a post-lovemaking high with her in his arms.

"It's been a while," he allowed. "I mean, other than last night, obviously."

Her mouth curved up in a smile. "Both times were amazing. I could get used to this."

He could, too. That was enough to get the panic really rolling. "We should probably talk about that."

To soften the blow, he threaded some of her pretty, silky hair through his fingers. That felt so nice, he kept going, running all the way down her head to her neck and back again.

"Mmm," she purred, pressing into his fingers, which were somehow massaging her with little strokes that she clearly liked. "I'm listening."

"We're still friends, right?" Pathetic. That hadn't been what he'd intended to say at all, but now that it was out there…it was exactly what he wanted to know. He wanted to hear her say that having an amazing encounter that he'd felt to his soul hadn't really affected her all that much. Then he could keep lying to himself about it and have zero qualms.

"Sure."

She kissed his chest right above his nipple and then flicked her tongue across the flat disk. Flames erupted under his skin, fanning outward to engulf his whole body, including his brain, because he suddenly couldn't recall what he'd been so convinced he needed to establish.

Then she slung a leg over his, nestling her thigh against the semi-erection that grew a lot less semi much faster than he would have credited, considering how empty he'd have sworn he was already.

"Geez, Viv." He bit back the curse word that had sprung to his lips. "You're insatiable."

Not that he was complaining. Though he should be saying something that sounded a lot like "Let's dial it back about one hundred and eighty degrees."

"You make me that way," she said throatily. "I've been celibate for like a billion years and that was totally okay, but all of a sudden, you kiss me and I can't think. I just want to be naked with you 24/7."

"Yeah?" he growled. That pretty much mirrored his thoughts perfectly. "That can be arranged."

No. No, it could not.

He had a merger to manage. Reins to pick up from his grandfather. What was he talking about, letting Viv coerce him into a day-and-night screw fest? That sounded like a recipe for disaster, especially given how strong his reactions to her were. They needed to cool it off.

"We can't." She sighed. "I've got a mountain of paperwork and Josie requested the rest of the week off so she can study for final exams. As nice as this is, we should probably back off for a while. Don't you think?"

"Absolutely not." Wrong answer. *Open your mouth and take it back.* "We're doing fine winging it. Aren't we? There's no pressure. If you come home from work hot and needy and want to strip down in the foyer to let me take care of you, I'm perfectly fine with that."

In fact, he'd gladly etch that date on his planner with a diamond drill bit. Mental note: buy Viv more jewelry and more racy lingerie. If he really tried, he could space out the gifts, one a night for oh, at least two weeks.

She arched a brow. "Really? This isn't feeling a little too real?"

His mood deflated. And now he was caught in a trap of his own making. He couldn't lie to Viv, but neither could he admit that it had been feeling too real since the ceremony. The same one he'd tried to sell to Warren and Hendrix as a fake wedding when Warren had clued in immediately that there was nothing fake about any of this.

This was what he got for not nodding his head the second the words *back off* came out of her mouth.

"See, the thing is," he began and would have sworn he'd been about to say that being friends with no benefits worked better for him. But that's not what happened. "I need this to be real. I don't have to pretend that I'm hot for you, because I am. We don't have to sell that we're burning up the sheets when we have dinner with your family on Friday. Why not keep going? The reasons we started this are still true. Unless I've dissatisfied you in some way?"

"Oh, God. No!" Her hand flew to her mouth. "Not in the slightest. You're the hottest lover I've ever had, bar none."

That pleased him enormously. "Then stop talking about easing off. We can be casual about it. Sometimes you sleep in my bed. Sometimes you don't. No rules. We're just friends who're having really great sex."

"That sounds like a plan."

She shrugged like she could take it or leave it, which raked across his spine with a sharpness that he didn't like. She obviously wasn't feeling any of the same things he was. She'd been a half second from calling it quits. Would have if he hadn't stopped her.

"Great." And somehow he'd managed to appease his sense of honor while agreeing to continue sleeping with his wife in what was shaping up to be the hottest affair he'd ever had.

It was madness. And he couldn't wipe the grin off his face.

CHAPTER EIGHT

IF THERE WAS a way to quit Jonas, Viv didn't want to know about it.

She should be looking for the exit, not congratulating herself on the finest plea for remaining in a man's bed that had ever been created in the history of time. She couldn't help it. The scene after the most explosive sexual encounter of her life had been almost as epic. Jonas had no idea how much it had killed her to act so nonchalant about ending things. He'd been shocked she'd suggested backing off. It had been written all over his face.

That kept her feeling smug well into the dawn hours the next morning. She rolled toward the middle of the bed, hoping to get a few minutes of snuggle time before work. Cold sheets met her questing fingers. Blinking an eye open, she sought the man she'd gone to sleep with.

Empty. Jonas had gotten out of bed already. The condo was quiet. Even when she was in her bedroom, she could hear the shower running through the pipes in the ceiling—a treat she normally enjoyed, as she envisioned the man taking a shower in all his naked glory.

Today, she didn't get that luxury, as Jonas was clearly already gone. Profoundly disappointed that he hadn't kissed her goodbye, said goodbye or thought about her at all, she climbed out from under the sheets and gathered up her clothes for the return trek to her bedroom.

It was fine. They'd established last night that there were no rules. No pressure. When he'd gotten on board with convincing her that they could keep sleeping together—which she still couldn't quite believe she'd orchestrated so well—she'd thought that meant they were going to spend a lot of time together. Be goofy and flirty with each other. Grow closer and closer until he looked up one day and realized that friendship plus marriage plus sex equaled something wonderful, lasting and permanent. Obviously she'd thought wrong.

The whole point had been to give him the impression she wasn't clingy. That Independence was her middle name and she breezed through life just fine, thanks, whether she had a man or not. Apparently he'd bought it. *Go me.*

The sour taste wouldn't quite wash from her mouth no matter how much mouthwash she used. After a long shower to care for her well-used muscles, Viv wandered to the kitchen barefoot to fight with Jonas's espresso machine. She had a machine at Cupcaked but Jonas's was a futuristic prototype that he'd brought home from work to test. There were more buttons and gizmos than on a spaceship. Plus, it hated her. He'd used it a couple of times and made it seem so easy, but he had a natural affinity with things that plugged in, and the machine had his name on it, after all. Finally, she got a passably decent latte out of the monstrosity.

She stood at the granite countertop to drink it, staring at the small, discreet Kim Electronics logo in the lower right-hand corner of the espresso machine. Jonas's name had been emblazoned on her, too, and not just via the marriage license and subsequent trip to the DMV to get a new driver's license. He'd etched his name across her soul well before they'd started sleeping together. Maybe about the third or fourth time they'd had lunch.

Strange then that she could be so successful with snowing him about her feelings. It had never worked with any man before. Of course, she'd never tried so hard to be cool about it. Because it had never mattered so much.

But now she wasn't sure what her goal here really was. Or what it should be. Jonas had "talked" her into keeping sex on the menu of their relationship. She'd convinced him their friendship could withstand it. Really, the path was pretty clear. They were married friends with benefits. If she didn't like that, too bad.

She didn't like it.

This wasn't practice for another relationship and neither was it fake, not for her. Which left her without a lot of options, since it was fake to Jonas.

Of course, she always had the choice to end things. But why in the world would she want to do that? Her husband was the most amazing lover on the planet, whose beautiful body she could not get enough of. He bought her diamonds and complimented her cupcakes. To top it all off, Viv was *married*. She'd been after that holy grail for ages and it had felt really nice to flash her ring at her sisters when they'd come to the shop last week. It was the best possible outcome of agreeing to do this favor for Jonas.

Convinced that she should be happy with that, she walked the four blocks to Cupcaked and buried herself in the kitchen, determined to find a new cupcake flavor to commemorate her marriage. That was how she'd always done things. When something eventful occurred, she baked. It was a way of celebrating in cake form, because wasn't that the whole point of cake? And then she had a cupcake flavor that reminded her of a wonderful event.

The watermelon recipe she'd been dying to try didn't turn out. The red food coloring was supposed to be tasteless but she couldn't help thinking that it had added something to the flavor that made the cupcake taste vaguely like oil. But without it, the batter wasn't the color of watermelon.

Frustrated, she trashed the whole batch and went in search of a different food coloring vendor. Fruitless. All her regular suppliers required an industrial sized order and she couldn't commit to a new brand without testing it first.

She ended up walking to the market and buying three different kinds off the shelf. For no reason, apparently, as all three new batches she made didn't turn out either. Maybe watermelon wasn't a good cupcake flavor. More to the point, maybe she shouldn't be commemorating a fake marriage that was real to her but still not going to last. That was the problem. She was trying to capture something fleeting that shouldn't be immortalized.

After the cupcake failure, her mood slid into the dumps. She threw her apron on the counter and stayed out of the kitchen until lunch, when she opened for business to the public. On the plus side, every display case had been cleaned and polished, and the plate-glass window between Cupcaked and the world had not one smudge on it. Camilla wouldn't be in until after school, so Viv was by herself for the lunch rush, which ended up being a blessing in disguise.

Wednesday wasn't normally a busy day, but the line stretched nearly out the door for over an hour. Which was good. Kept her mind off the man she'd married. Josie had the rest of the week off, and Viv had approved it thinking she and Camilla could handle things, but if this kind of crowd was even close to a new normal, she might have to see about adding another part-time employee. That was a huge decision, but a good sign. If she couldn't have Jonas, she could have her cupcakes. Just like she'd always told him.

After locking the bakery's door, tired but happy with the day's profits, she headed home. On the way, she sternly lectured herself about her expectations. Jonas might be waiting in the hall for her to come in the door like he had been last night. Or he might not. Her stomach fluttered the entire four blocks regardless. Her husband had just been so sexy standing there against the wall with a hot expression on his face as if he planned to devour her whole before she completely shut the door.

And then he pretty much had, going down on her in the most erotic of encounters. She shuddered clear to her core as she recalled the feel of that first hot lick of his tongue.

Oh, who was she kidding? She couldn't stop hoping he'd be waiting for her again tonight. Her steps quickened as she let herself anticipate seeing Jonas in a few minutes.

But he wasn't in the hall. Or at home. That sucked.

Instead of moping, she fished out her phone and called Grace. It took ten minutes, but eventually her sister agreed to have dinner with Viv.

They met at an Italian place on Glenwood that had great outdoor seating that allowed for people watching. The maître d' showed them to a table and Grace gave Viv a whole three seconds before she folded her hands and rested her chin on them.

"Okay, spill," she instructed. "I wasn't expecting to see you before Friday. Is Jonas in the doghouse already?"

"What? No." Viv scowled. Why did something have to be wrong for her to ask her sister to dinner? Besides, that was none of Grace's business anyway. Viv pounced on the flash of green fire on her sister's wrist in a desperate subject change. "Ooooh, new bracelet? Let me see."

The distraction worked. Grace extended her arm dutifully, her smile widening as she twisted her wrist to let the emeralds twinkle in the outdoor lighting. "Alan gave it to me. It's an anniversary present."

"You got married in April," Viv said.

"Not a wedding anniversary. It's a...different kind of anniversary."

Judging by the dreamy smile that accompanied that admission, she meant the first time she and Alan had slept together, and clearly the act had been worthy of commemorating.

Viv could hardly hide her glee. It was going to be one of *those* discussions and she *finally* got to participate. "Turns out Jonas is big on memorializing spectacular sex, too."

"Well, don't hold back. Show and tell." Grace waggled her brows.

Because she wanted to and she could, Viv fished the diamond drop necklace from beneath her dress and let it hang from her fingers. Not to put too fine a point on it, but hers was a flawless white diamond in a simple, elegant setting. Extremely appropriate for the wife of a billionaire. And he'd put it around her neck and then given her the orgasm of her life.

The baubles she could do without and had only mentioned jewelry in the car on the way to Jonas's parents' house because he'd pushed her to name something he could do for her. She hadn't really been serious. But all at once, she loved that Jonas had unwittingly allowed her to stand shoulder to shoulder with her sister when it came to talking about whose marriage was hotter.

"Your husband is giving you jewelry already?" Grace asked, and her tone was colored with something that sounded a lot like she was impressed. "Things must be going awfully well."

"Oh, yeah, of course," Viv commented airily and waved her hand like she imagined a true lady of the manor would. "We didn't even make it out of the foyer where he gave it to me before his hands were all over me."

Shameless. This was the raciest conversation she'd ever had with anyone except maybe Jonas, but that didn't count. She should be blushing. Or something. Instead she was downright giddy.

"That's the best." Grace's dreamy smile curved back into place. "When you have a man who loves you so much that he can't wait. I'm thrilled you finally have that."

Yeah, not so much. Her mood crashed and burned as reality surfaced. Viv nodded with a frozen expression that she hoped passed for agreement.

Obviously Grace knew what it felt like to have a man dote on her and give her jewelry because he cared, not because they were faking a relationship. Grace could let all her feelings hang out as much as she wanted and Alan would eat it up. Because they were in love.

Something that felt a lot like jealousy reared its ugly head in the pit of Viv's stomach. Which was unfair and petty, but recognizing it as such didn't make it go away.

"Jonas was worth waiting for," she said truthfully, though it rankled that the statement was the best she could do. While Viv's husband might rival her sister's in the attentive lover department, when it came to matters of the heart, Grace and Alan had Viv and Jonas beat, hands down.

"I'm glad. You had a rough patch for a while. I started to worry that you weren't going to figure out how stop putting a man's emotional needs ahead of yours. It's good to see that you found a relationship that's on equal footing."

Somehow, Viv managed to keep the surprise off her face, but how, she'd never know. "I never did that. What does that even mean?"

"Hon, you're so bad at putting yourself first." Grace waved the waiter over as he breezed by and waited until he refilled both their wineglasses before continuing. "You let everyone else dictate how the relationship is going to go. That last guy you dated? Mark? He wanted to keep things casual, see other people, and even though that's not what you wanted, you agreed. Why did you do that?"

Eyebrows hunched together, Viv gulped from her newly filled wineglass to wet her suddenly parched throat. "Because when I told him that I wanted to be exclusive, he said I was being too possessive. What was I supposed to do, demand that he give me what I want?"

"Uh, *yeah*." Grace clucked. "You should have told him to take a hike instead of waiting around for him to do it for you."

"It really didn't take that long," she muttered, but not very loud, because Grace was still off on her tangent.

Her sister was right. Viv should have broken up with Mark during that exact conversation. But on the heels of being told she was "clingy," "controlling" and "moving too fast" by Zachary, Gary and Judd respectively, she hadn't wanted to rock the boat.

Why was it such a big deal to want to spend time with a man she was dating? It wasn't clingy. Maybe it was the wine talking, but Grace's point wasn't lost on Viv—she shouldn't be practicing her independence but finding a different kind of man. One who couldn't stand being apart from her. One who texted her hearts and smiley faces just to let her know he was thinking of her. One who was in love with her.

In other words—not Jonas.

The thought pushed her mood way out of the realm of fit for company. Dinner with Grace was a mistake. Marrying Jonas had been a mistake. Viv had no idea what she was doing with her life or how she was going to survive a fake marriage she wished was real.

"I just remembered," she mumbled. "I have to…do a thing."

Pushing back from the table, Viv stood so fast that her head spun. She'd planned to walk home but maybe a cab would be a better idea.

"What?" Grace scowled. "You called me. I canceled drinks with the ladies from my auxiliary group. How could you forget that you had something else?"

Because Viv wasn't perfect like Grace with the perfect husband who loved her, and frankly, she was sick of not getting what she wanted. "Jonas has scrambled my wits."

Let her sister make what she would out of that. Viv apologized and exited the restaurant as quickly as she could before she started crying. After not seeing Jonas this morning and the watermelon-slash-red-food-coloring disaster and the incredibly busy day at the store and then realizing that she had not in fact gotten to join the club her sisters were in, crying was definitely imminent.

The icing on the cake happened when she got home and Jonas was sprawled on the couch watching TV, wearing jeans with a faded Duke T-shirt that clung to his torso like a second skin.

His smile as he glanced up at her was instant and brilliant and that was all it took to unleash the waterworks.

With tears streaming down her face, Viv stood in the foyer of the condo she shared with Jonas until whatever point in the future he decided to pull the plug on their marriage and it was all suddenly not okay.

"Hey, now. None of that." Jonas flicked off the TV and vaulted to his feet, crossing the ocean of open space between the living room and the foyer in about four strides.

He didn't hesitate to gather Viv in his strong arms, cradling her against his chest, and dang it, that T-shirt was really soft against her face. It was a testament to how mixed-up she was that she let him guide her to the leather couch and tuck her in against his side as he held her while softly crooning in his baritone that she'd heard in her sleep for aeons.

What was wrong with her that she was exactly where she wanted to be—in his arms? She should be pushing away and disappearing into her bedroom. No pressure, no love, no nothing.

"What's wrong, sweetheart?" he asked softly into her hair. "Bad day at work?"

"I wasn't at work," she shot back inanely, sniffling oh so attractively against his shoulder.

"Oh. Well, I wondered where you were when you weren't here."

"You weren't here either," she reminded him crossly. "So I went to dinner with Grace."

He pulled back, the expression on his face both confused and slightly alarmed. "Did we have plans that I forgot about or something? Because if so, I'm sorry. I didn't have anything on my calendar and my grandfather asked me to take him to the airport. I texted you."

He had? And how desperate would it appear to pull out her phone to check? Which was totally dumb anyway. It was obvious he was telling her the truth, which he didn't even have to do. God, she was such a mess. But after he'd disappeared this morning and then she'd come home to an empty house and…so what? He was here now, wasn't he? She was making a mountain out of a molehill.

"It's okay, we didn't have plans. You called it. Bad day at work," she said a bit more brightly as she latched on to his excuse that wasn't even a lie. Sales had been good, sure, but Cupcaked meant more to her than just profits. "I tried out a new recipe and it was a complete failure."

All smiles again, Jonas stroked her hair and then laid a sweet kiss on her temple. "I hate days like that. What can I do to fix it?"

About a hundred suggestions sprang to her mind all at once, and every last one could easily be considered X-rated. But she couldn't bear to shift the current vibe into something more physical when Jonas was meeting a different kind of need, one she'd only nebulously identified at dinner. This was it in a nutshell—she wanted someone to be there for her, hold her and support her through the trials of life.

Why had she gotten so upset? Because Jonas hadn't fallen prostrate at her feet with declarations of undying love? They were essentially still in the early stages of their relationship, regardless of the label on it. Being married didn't automatically mean they were where Grace and her husband were. Maybe Viv and Jonas were taking a different route to get to the same destination and she was trying too hard.

Also known as the reason her last few relationships hadn't worked out.

"You're already fixing it," she murmured as his fingers drifted to her neck and lightly massaged.

Oh, God, that was a gloriously unfulfilled need, too. After a long day on her feet, just sitting here with Jonas as he worked her tired muscles counted as one of the highest points of pleasure she'd experienced at his hands. Her eyelids drifted closed and she floated.

"Did I wake you up this morning?" he asked after a few minutes of bliss.

"No. I was actually surprised to find that you were gone." Thank God he'd lulled her into a near coma. That admission had actually sounded a lot more casual than she would have expected, given how his absence had been lodged under skin like a saddle burr all day.

"That's good." He seemed a lot more relieved than the question warranted. "I'm not used to sleeping with someone and I was really worried that I'd mess with your schedule."

What schedule? "We slept in the same bed at your parents' house."

"Yeah, but that was over the weekend when no one had to get up and go to work. This is different. It's real life and I'm nothing if not conscious that you're here solely because I asked you to be. You deserve to sleep well."

Warmth gushed through her heart and made her feel entirely too sappy. What a thoroughly unexpected man she had married. "I did sleep well. Thank you for being concerned. But I think I slept so well because of how you treated me before I went to sleep. Not because you tiptoed well while getting dressed."

He did treat her like a queen. That was the thing she'd apparently forgotten. They were friends who cared about each other. Maybe he might eventually fall in love with her, but he certainly wouldn't if she kept being obsessive and reading into his every move.

Jonas chuckled. "Last night was pretty amazing. I wasn't sure you thought so. I have to be honest and tell you that I was concerned I'd done something to make you angry and that's why you weren't here when I got home after taking my grandfather to the airport. I could have called him a car."

"No!" Horrified, she swiveled around to face him, even though it meant his wonderful hands slipped from her shoulders. "We just talked about no pressure and I was—well, I just thought because you weren't here…"

Ugh. How in the world was she supposed to explain that she'd gone out to dinner with Grace because of a hissy fit over something so ridiculous as Jonas not being here because he'd taken his grandfather to the airport? Maybe instead of using the excuse that she'd missed his text messages, she should tell him how she felt. Just flat out say, *Jonas, I'm in love with you.*

"We did talk about no pressure," Jonas threw out in a rush. "And I'm definitely not trying to add any. I like our relationship where it is. I like *you.* It's what makes the extra stuff so much better."

Extra stuff. She absorbed that for a second. Extra stuff like deeper feelings he didn't know he was going to uncover? Extra stuff like being there for each other?

"I value our friendship," she said cautiously, weighing out how honest she could be. How honest she wanted to be given how she managed to screw up even the simplest of relationship interactions.

And just as she was about to open her mouth and confess that she appreciated the extra stuff, too, maybe even tell him that she had a plethora of extra stuff that she could hardly hold inside, he smoothed a hand over her hair and grinned. "I know. I'm being all touchy-feely and that's not what we signed up for. Instead, let's talk about Cupcaked."

"Um...okay?" He'd literally switched gears so fast, she could scarcely keep up.

That was him being touchy-feely? Jonas wasn't one to be gushy about his feelings and usually erred on the side of being reserved; she knew that from the year of lunches and coffee. Clearly, he was uncomfortable with the direction of the discussion. She definitely should not add a level of weirdness, not on top of her storming in here and having a minor meltdown.

This was her relationship to make or break. All at once, it became so obvious what she should be focusing on here.

No, this wasn't practice for the next man she dated. She was practicing for *this* one. If she hoped to get to a point where they were both comfortable with declarations of love, she had to tread carefully. While she didn't think Jonas was going to divorce her if she moved too fast, neither did she have a good handle on how to be less intense.

She needed to back off. Way off. Otherwise, she was going to freak him out. And suddenly she could not fathom giving up this marriage under any circumstances.

"I'd love to talk about Cupcaked," she said with a smile. "Seems like you owe me some advice."

"Yes, exactly." His return smile bordered on relieved. "You've been so patient and I'm a selfish jerk for not focusing on your career when that's the one thing you're getting out of this deal."

"The sex is nice, too," she teased. Look at that. She could be cool.

Jonas shot her a wicked once-over. "That's what makes you so perfect. We can hang out as friends, but if I wanted to, say, slip my hand under your dress, you'd gladly climb in my lap for a little one-on-one time. It's the best."

She shrugged to cover how his compliment had thrilled her to the marrow. "I promised it wouldn't make things weird."

Now she'd stick to that. At the end of the day, Cupcaked *was* important to her. She'd just have to make sure that eventually Jonas realized that he was important to her, as well.

Jonas ducked out of a meeting on Friday with a guilty conscience. While he knew Viv would understand if he put off a thorough analysis of her business plan, he wasn't okay with ignoring his promise. Unfortunately, Park had come through with some amendments to the merger agreement Jonas had drafted, which had taken his time and attention for the whole of the week.

The moment he stepped outside the Kim Building, the sunshine raised his spirits. He was on his way to see his wife at Cupcaked, which oddly would mark the first time he'd graced the store since they'd gotten married. Before the wedding, he found excuses to drop by on a frequent basis. But now he didn't have to. The cupcake baker slept in his bed and if he wanted to see her, all he had to do was turn his head.

It was pretty great. Or at least that's what he'd been telling himself. In reality, the look on Viv's face when she'd told him she valued their friendship had been like a big fat wake-up call. Basically, she was telling him no pressure worked for her regardless of how hot he could get her with nothing more than a well-placed caress.

Well, that *was* great. He didn't have any desire to pressure her into anything. But he couldn't deny that he might like to put more structure around things. Would she think it was weird if he expected her to be his plus-one for events? His admin was planning a big party for the whole company to commemorate the anniversary of opening the Kim Americas branch. He wanted Viv by his side. But it was yet another favor. If they were dating instead of married he wouldn't think twice about asking her.

Everything was backward and weird and had been since that no-pressure discussion, which he'd initiated because he needed the boundaries. For no reason apparently. Viv so clearly wasn't charging over the imaginary lines he'd drawn in the sand. In fact, she'd drawn a few lines of her own. Yet how could he change those lines when Viv had gotten so prickly about the subject? In fact, she'd already tried to call off the intimate aspects of their relationship once. He needed to tread very carefully with her before he got in too deep for them both.

When he got to Cupcaked, the door was locked. Not open yet. He texted Viv that he was outside and within thirty seconds, she'd popped out of the kitchen and hurried to the plate-glass door with a cute smile.

"I didn't know you were coming by," she commented unnecessarily since he was well aware it was a surprise. After she let him in, she locked the door and turned, her brown hair shining in the sunlight that streamed through the glass.

Something was wrong with his lungs. He couldn't breathe.

Or think. All he could do was soak in the most beautiful woman he'd ever seen in his life. And all of his good intentions designed to help her with her business flew out the window in a snap.

Without hesitation, he pulled her into his arms and kissed her. She softened instantly and the scent of vanilla and Viv wound through his senses, robbing him of the ability to reason, because the only thing he could think about was getting more of her against him.

Almost as if she'd read his mind, she opened under his mouth, eagerly deepening the kiss, welcoming the broad stroke of his tongue with her own brand of heat. Slowly she licked into his mouth in kind, teasing him with little flutters of her fingers against his back.

That was not going to work. He wanted to feel her fingers against his flesh, not through the forty-seven layers of clothing between them.

Walking her backward, he half kissed, half maneuvered her until they reached the kitchen, and then he spun her through the swinging door to the more private area, where the entire city of Raleigh couldn't see them.

Her mouth was back on his without missing a beat, and he pushed her up against the metal counter, trapping her body with his. Her sweet little curves nestled into the planes of his body and he wasn't sure if he could stand how long it was taking to get her naked.

The zipper of her dress took three tries to find and then slid down easily, allowing him to actually push the fabric from her shoulders instead of ripping it, a near miracle. There was something about her that drove him to a place he didn't recognize, and it bothered him to be this crazy over her. But then her dress slipped off, puddling to the floor, and he forgot about everything but her as she unhooked her bra, throwing it to the ground on top of her dress.

Groaning, he looked his fill of her gorgeous breasts, scarcely able to believe how hard and pointy they were from nothing other than his gaze. Bending to capture one, he swirled his tongue around the perfection of her nipple and the sound she made shot through his erection like an arrow of heat.

"Hurry," she gasped. "I'm about to come apart."

Oh, well, that was something he'd very much like to witness. In a flash, he pushed her panties to her ankles and boosted her up on the counter. Spreading her legs wide, he brushed a thumb through her crease and, yes, she was so ready for him.

She bucked and rolled against his fingers, her eyes darkening with the pleasure he was giving her, and he wanted her more than anything he could recall. As much as he'd like to do any number of things to bring her to climax, there was one clear winner. Ripping out of his own clothes in record time, he stepped back between her thighs and hissed as she nipped at his shoulder.

"Tell me you have a condom," she commanded, and then smiled as he held it up between his fingers.

He'd stashed a couple in his wallet and he really didn't want to examine that particular foresight right now. Instead, he wanted to examine the wonders of Viv and sheathed himself as fast as humanly possible, notching himself at the slick entrance to her channel. Her wet heat welcomed him, begged him to come inside, but he paused to kiss her because that was one of his favorite parts.

Their tongues tangled and he got a little lost in the kiss. She didn't. She wrapped her legs around him, heels firm against his butt, and pushed him forward, gasping as he slammed into her. So that's how she wanted it. Two could play that game.

He engulfed her in his arms and braced her for a demanding rhythm, then gave it to her. She took each and every thrust eagerly, her mouth working the flesh at his throat, his ear, nipping sensuously. *He* was the one about to come apart.

Viv flew through his soul, winging her essence into every diameter of his body. Wiggling a hand between their slick bodies, he fingered her at the source of her pleasure, gratified when she cried out. Her release crashed against his, shocking him with both the speed and intensity.

She slumped against him, still quaking as she held on. He was busy losing the entire contents of his body as everything inside rushed out in a flash to fill her. Fanciful to be sure since there was a barrier preventing anything of the sort. But she'd wrung him out, taken everything and more, and he couldn't have stopped the train as it barreled down the track, even if he wanted to. Why would he want to?

He turned his head, seeking her lips, and there they were, molding to his instantly. Viv was amazing, a woman he liked, cared for deeply even, and they had the most spectacular chemistry. He could hardly fathom how much he still wanted her four seconds after having her. It was everything he said he wanted.

Except the warmth in his chest that had nothing to do with sex wasn't supposed to be there. He wasn't an idiot. He knew what was happening. He'd let her in, pretending that being friends gave him a measure of protection against falling for her. Instead, he'd managed to do the one thing he'd sworn he'd never do—develop feelings for someone who didn't return them.

This was a huge problem, one he didn't have a good solution for. One he could never let her know he was facing because he'd promised not to pressure her.

Best thing would be to ignore it. It wasn't happening if he didn't acknowledge it. And then he wouldn't be lying to her or dishonoring the pact he'd made with his friends, neither of which could ever happen. If he didn't nurture these fledging tendrils of disaster that wound through his chest, he could kill them before they ruined everything.

Actually, the best thing would be to stop being around Viv so much. *Without* letting on to her that he was deliberately creating distance.

The thought hurt. But it was necessary for his sanity.

CHAPTER NINE

JONAS HELPED VIV off the metal countertop that she'd have to bleach within an inch of its life and pray the fourteen different health-code violations never came to light.

It had been worth it. Whenever Jonas got like that, so into her and excited and feverish as if he'd die if he didn't have her that instant...that was the best part of this fake marriage. Men were never that gaga over her. Except this one. And she secretly loved it. She couldn't tell him. What would she say?

Slow and steady wins the race, she reminded herself. Not-Clingy was her new middle name and she was going to own it. Even if it killed her not to blubber all over him about how it was so beautiful it hurt when he was inside her.

They spent a few minutes setting their clothes back to rights, no small feat without a mirror. She gladly helped Jonas locate his missing tie and then buttoned his suit jacket for him when he forgot.

"Gorgeous," she commented after slipping the last button into its slot and perusing the final product of her husband in his power suit that she immediately wanted to strip him out of again.

He grinned. "Yes, you are."

Great, now she was blushing, judging by the prickles in her

cheeks. Dead giveaway about the things going on inside that she'd rather keep a secret.

"Now, stop distracting me," he continued. "I'm here to get started on my promise to review your books. Lead me to them."

Oh. For some reason, she'd thought he'd come by strictly to have an explosive sexual encounter in her bakery. But in reality, he was here for business reasons. That took a little of the wind from her sails though it shouldn't have. Of course he'd honor his promise to help her, despite absolutely no prompting on her part. "Sure, my office is in the back. We can squeeze in there."

She led him to the tiny hole in the wall where she paid bills and ordered inventory. It wasn't much, not like the Kim Building, where Jonas had an entire office suite expressly designed for the CEO. But she wasn't running a billion-dollar electronics company here, and they both knew that.

He didn't complain about the lack of comfort and space, easily sliding into the folding chair she pulled from behind the door and focusing on her with his dark eyes. "Let me see your balance sheet."

Dutifully, she keyed up her accounting software and ran the report, then pushed the monitor of her ancient computer toward him so he could see it. His gaze slid down the columns and back up again. Within a moment, he'd reviewed the entire thing and then launched into a dizzying speech about how her asset column was blah blah and her inventory was blah blah something else. After five minutes of nodding and understanding almost nothing of what he said, she held up a hand.

"Jonas, while I appreciate your attention on this, you lost me back around 'leveraging your cash.' Can we take a step back and focus on the goal of this?"

She knew what her goal was. Spend time with Jonas. But clearly he'd taken the idea of helping her seriously.

"Sure, sorry." He looked chagrined and adorable as he ran a hand through his hair. "I shouldn't have gone so deep into financial strategy that quickly. Maybe I should ask you what *your* goal is since your career is the most important thing to you. What do you want to see happen with Cupcaked?"

Oh, yeah, right. Her career. The thing she'd sold to him as the reason she didn't date. "I haven't really thought about it."

Should she be thinking about it? She wasn't rich by any stretch, but she made enough and got to bake cupcakes for a living. What else was there?

"Okay." His smile broadened. "I hear you saying that you need help coming up with a five-year plan. Part of that should include a robust marketing strategy and expansion."

Expansion? Her eyebrows lifted almost by themselves. "Are you suggesting I could become a chain?"

The idea seemed so far-fetched. She just made cupcakes and had no ambitions beyond being able to recognize regular customers. But she didn't hate the idea of seeing more Cupcaked signs around Raleigh. Maybe even in Chapel Hill or by the university. The thought of owning a mini-cupcake empire made her smile. Poor substitute for Jonas. But not a terrible one.

"I'm not suggesting it. I'm flat out saying if that's what you want, I will make it happen for you. Sky's the limit, Mrs. Kim." He waggled his brows. "You should take as much advantage of me as you possibly can. Ask for anything."

Mrs. Kim. What if she told him that she'd like to ask him to call her that for the rest of her life? What would he say?

Before she could open her mouth, he launched into another long litany of things to consider for her shop and his gleeful tone told her he was having fun helping her think through the items that might appear on her five-year plan. They talked about any number of ideas from branded cupcake mix to be sold in grocery stores to licensing her flavors to other cupcake bakeries.

Frankly, the discussion was fun for her, too. Partially because she was having it with Jonas and she loved watching his mind churn through the possibilities. But she couldn't deny a certain anticipation regarding the leaps and bounds Cupcaked could take through the doors her husband might open for her.

Camilla popped in to say hi and make sure Viv was okay with her opening the bakery to customers. Viv nodded her assent and dove back into the fascinating concept of franchising, of which Jonas admitted having only a rudimentary knowledge, but he knew way more than she did. She wanted to know more.

His phone rang and he lifted a finger in the universal "one minute" gesture, jabbering away to the caller with a bunch of terms that sounded vaguely legal. Eventually, he ended the call and stood.

"I'm so sorry, but I have to get back to the world of electronics."

She waved off his apology. "You've been here for two hours. I know you're busy. I should give Camilla a hand anyway. If today is anything like the rest of the week, she'll need the help."

Jonas laid a scorching kiss on her and left. Dazed and more than a little hot and bothered, she lost herself in cupcakes until the day got away from her. As planned, she and Jonas went to dinner at her parents' house that night. Given that he shot her smoking-hot glances when he thought no one was watching, and her sisters were nothing if not eagle-eyed when it came to potential gossip, she didn't think they had anything to worry about when it came to revelations about the nature of their marriage.

Or rather, the revelations weren't going to be publicized to the rest of the world. Just to Jonas. As soon as she figured out when she could start clueing him in to the idea that friendship wasn't the only thing happening between them, of course. This was the problem with playing it cool. She wasn't sure when to bring up concepts like *love*, *forever* and *no divorce*.

She bided her time and didn't utter a peep when Jonas carried her to his bed after the successful dinner with her parents. He spent extra time pleasuring her, claiming that tomorrow was Saturday so she had plenty of opportunity to sleep later. Not that she was complaining about his attention. Or anything else, for that matter. Her life was almost perfect.

On Monday, she learned exactly how many people in the

business world jumped when her husband said jump. By nine o'clock, she had appointments lined up every day for the entire week with accounting people, retail space experts and a pastry chef who had ties with the Food Network. A marketing consultant arrived shortly thereafter and introduced herself as Franca, then parked herself in Viv's office, apparently now a permanent part of her staff, as she'd informed Mrs. Kim, courtesy of Mr. Kim.

Franca lived to talk, as best Viv could work out between marathon strategy sessions that filled nearly every waking hour of the day. And some of the hours Viv would have normally said were for sleeping. At midnight, Franca sent a detailed list of the short-term and long-term goals that they'd discussed and asked Viv to vet it thoroughly because once she approved, the list would form the basis of Cupcaked's new five-year plan. Which would apparently be carved in stone.

By Friday, Viv hadn't spent more than five minutes with Jonas. They slept in the same bed, but sometimes he climbed into it well after she had, which was quite a feat since she hadn't hit the sheets until 1:00 a.m. most nights. He'd claimed her busyness came at a great time for him because he was able to focus on the merger with Park Industries without feeling guilty for ignoring her. The hours bled into days and she'd never been so exhausted in her life.

It sucked. Except for the part where sometimes Jonas texted her funny memes about ships passing in the night or had a dozen tulips delivered to the shop to commemorate their one-month anniversary. Once he popped up with Chinese takeout for dinner as a "forced" break for them both. He gave her his fortune cookie and told her a story about how one of the ladies in his procurement department had gone into labor during a meeting. Those stolen moments meant the world to her because she could almost believe that he missed her as much as she missed him.

The pièce de résistance came when the pastry chef she'd met with a couple of weeks ago contacted her via Franca to let her know that he'd loved her cupcakes and gotten her a spot on one of the cupcake shows on the Food Network. Agape, Viv stared at Franca as the tireless woman reeled off the travel plans she'd made for Viv to fly to Los Angeles.

"I can't go to Los Angeles," Viv insisted with a head shake. "I have a business to run."

Franca tapped her phone on Viv's new desk. "Which will become nationally known once you appear on the show."

She'd had Viv's office completely redone and expanded at Jonas's expense and the top-of-the-line computer that had replaced the old one now recessed underneath the surface of the desk with the click of a button. It was very slick and gave them a lot more working space, which Franca used frequently, as she spread brochures and promo items galore across the top of it at least twice a week.

"How long would I be gone?" Viv asked. Josie and Camilla had never run the bakery by themselves for a whole day, let alone several. They needed her. Or did they? She was often in the back strategizing with Franca anyway. They had four or five irons in the fire at any given time and the woman was indefatigable when it came to details. There was literally nothing she couldn't organize or plan and often took on more of a personal assistant role for Viv.

"Depends on whether you make the first cut." Franca shrugged and flipped her ponytail behind her back, a move she made when she was about to get serious. "It's a competition. You lose the first round, you come home. You win, you stay. I would advise you to win."

Viv made a face. "You're talking days."

"Sure. I hope so anyway. We're going to launch the new website with online ordering at the same time. It'll be an amazing kick start to the virtual storefront."

Sagging a little, Viv gave herself about four seconds to pretend she was going to refuse when in reality, she couldn't pass up the opportunity. It really didn't matter if she won or not because it was free advertising and all it would cost her was some time away from Jonas. Whom she rarely saw awake anyway.

"When do I leave?"

Franca grinned like she'd known the direction Viv would end up going the whole time. "I'll get the rest of the arrangements settled and let you know."

With a nod, Viv texted the news to Jonas, who instantly responded with at least four exclamation marks and a *congrats* in all caps. Funny, they were basically back to being friends with no benefits, thanks to her stupid career. She had all the success she'd lied to Jonas about wanting and none of the happiness that she'd pretended would come along with it.

Worse, if she hadn't been so busy, she'd be sitting around the condo by herself as Jonas worked his own fingers to the bone. This was really, really not the marriage she'd signed up for.

Or rather it was absolutely the one she'd agreed to but not the one she wanted.

The day before she was supposed to fly to Los Angeles for the taping, Viv came home early to pack. Shockingly, Jonas was sitting on the couch still decked out in his gorgeous suit but on the phone, as he nearly always was anytime she'd been in the same room with him lately.

For half a second, she watched him, soaking in his pretty mouth as it formed words. Shuddered as she recalled what that mouth could do to her when he put his mind to it. God, she missed him. In the short amount of time they'd been married, they'd gone from zero to sixty to zero again. She'd prefer a hundred and twenty.

She waved, loath to interrupt him, but before she could skirt past him to her bedroom, where her clothes still were since she'd never really "moved in" to Jonas's room, he snagged her by the hips and settled her on the couch near him as he wrapped up his phone call.

Tossing his phone on the glass-and-steel conglomeration that he called a coffee table, he contemplated her with the sort of attention she hadn't experienced in a long while. It was delicious.

"You're going to LA in the morning?" he said by way of greeting, and picked up her hand to hold it in his, brushing his thumb across her knuckles.

"Yeah. I don't know for how long. Franca left the plane ticket open-ended." The little strokes of his thumb stirred something inside that had been dormant for a million years. He'd been so distant lately. Dare she hope that they might be coming back together?

No reason she had to let him be the instigator. She lifted his hand to her mouth and kissed it, but he pulled away and sat back on the couch. "That sounds like fun. I hope you have a good time."

Cautiously, she eyed him. Why had he caught her before she left the room if he hadn't been after spending time with her? "Is everything okay? I wasn't expecting you to be here."

"I…came home on purpose. To see you," he admitted. "Before you left."

Her heart did a funny a little dance. But then why all the weird hot and cold? He obviously cared about her—but how much? Enough? She had no idea because they never talked about what was really going on here.

It was high time they had it out. She was leaving for LA in the morning and they rarely saw each other. She had to make this small opportunity work.

"I'm glad. I missed you." There. It was out in the open.

But he just smiled without a hint of anything. "I miss hanging out with you, too. We haven't had coffee in ages."

Or sex. The distinction between the two was legion and she didn't think for a minute that he'd misspoken or forgotten that they'd been intimate. It was a deliberate choice of words. "We haven't had a coffee relationship in ages."

His expression didn't change. "I know. It's been crazy. We're both so busy."

"By design, feels like."

That got a reaction, but why, she couldn't fathom. She watched as unease filtered through his gaze and he shifted positions on the couch, casually folding one leg over the other but also moving away from her. "We're both workaholics, that's for sure."

"I'm not," she corrected. "Not normally. But I've been dropped into an alternate reality where Franca drives me fourteen hours a day to reach these lofty goals that don't represent what I really want out of life."

Jonas frowned, his gaze sweeping over her in assessment. "You're finally getting your career off the ground. She's been keeping me apprised and I've been pleased with the direction she's taking you. But if you're not, we should discuss it. I can hire a different marketing expert, one that's more in line—"

"It's not the direction of the marketing," she broke in before he called in yet another career savant who would be brilliant at taking her away from her husband. "It's that I was happier when Cupcaked was a little bakery on Jones Street and we had sex in the foyer."

Something flitted through his gaze that she wished felt more like an invitation. Because she would have stripped down right here, right now if that had gotten the reaction she'd hoped for. Instead, his expression had a huge heaping dose of caution. "We agreed that we'd take that part as it came. No pressure. You're focusing on your career, just like I am. If Franca's not guiding you toward the right next level, then what do you want her to do?"

"I want her to go away!" Viv burst out. "She's exhausting and so chipper and can do more from 10:00 p.m. to midnight than a general, two single moms and the president combined. I want to have dinner with you, and lie in bed on a Saturday morning and watch cartoons with my head on your shoulder. I want you to rip my dress at the seams because you're so eager to get me naked. Most of all, I don't want to think about cupcakes."

But he was shaking his head. "That's not me. I'm not the kind of guy who rips a woman's dress off."

"But you are. You did," she argued inanely because what a stupid thing to say. He was totally that man and she loved it when he was like that. "I don't understand why we were so hot and heavy and then you backed off."

There came another shadow through his gaze that darkened his whole demeanor. "Because we're friends and I'm nothing if not interested in preserving that relationship."

"I am, too," she shot back a little desperately. This conversation was sliding away from her at an alarming pace, turning into something it shouldn't be, and she wasn't sure how that had happened. Or how to fix it. "But I'm also not happy just being friends. I love the text messages and I'm thrilled with what you've done for my business. But it's not enough."

"What are you saying?" he asked cautiously, his expression blank.

"That I want a real marriage. A family. I want more than just cupcakes."

Jonas let the phrase soak through him. Everything inside shifted, rolling over. In six words, Viv had reshaped the entire dynamic between them, and the effects might be more destructive than a nuclear bomb.

His chest certainly felt like one had gone off inside. While he'd been fighting to keep from treating Viv to a repeat of the dress-ripping incident, she'd been quietly planning to cut him off at the knees. Apparently he'd been creating distance for no reason.

Viv's gorgeous face froze when he didn't immediately respond. But what was he supposed to say?

Oh, that's right. *What the hell?*

"Viv, I've known you for over a year. We've been married for almost five weeks. For pretty much the entire length of our acquaintance, you've told me how important your career is to you. I have never once heard you mention that you wanted a family. Can you possibly expand on that statement?"

The weird vibe went even more haywire and he had the impression she regretted what she'd said. Then, she dropped her head into her hands, covering her eyes for a long beat. The longer she hid from him, the more alarmed he got. What was she afraid he'd see?

"Not much to expand on," she mumbled to her palms. "I like cupcakes, but I want a husband and a family, too."

Which was pretty much what she'd just said, only rephrased in such a way as to still not make any sense. "Let me ask this a different way. Why have you never told me this? I thought we were friends."

Yeah, that was a little bitterness fighting to get free.

How well did he really know the woman he'd married if this was just now coming out after all this time? After all the intimacies that they'd shared?

The lick of temper uncurling inside was completely foreign. He'd asked her to marry him strictly because he'd been sure— *positive* even—that she wasn't the slightest bit interested in having a long-term relationship.

Otherwise, he never would have asked her to do this favor. Never would have let himself start to care more than he should have.

His anger fizzled. He could have been more forthcoming with his own truths but hadn't for reasons that he didn't feel that self-righteous about all at once.

"I never told you because it…never came up." Guilt flickered in her tone and when she lifted her face from her hands, it was there in her expression, too. "I'm only telling you now because you asked."

Actually, he hadn't. He'd been sorting through her comments about the marketing consultant he'd hired, desperately trying to figure out if Viv and Franca just didn't get along or if the references he'd received regarding the consultant's brilliance had been embellished. Instead, she'd dropped a whole different issue in his lap. One that was knifing through his chest like a dull machete.

Viv wanted a real husband. A family. This fake marriage was in her way. *Jonas* was in her way. It was shattering. Far more than he would have said.

He didn't want to lose her. But neither could he keep her, not at the expense of giving her what she really wanted. Obviously he should have given more weight to the conversation they'd had at his parents' house about love being a good basis for marriage. Clearly that was what she wanted from a husband.

And he couldn't give her that, nor was she asking him to. He'd made a promise that he'd never let a woman have enough sway to affect his emotions. Judging by the swirl of confusion beneath his breastbone, it was already too late for that.

If she just hadn't said anything. He could have kept pretending that the solution to all his problems was to keep her busy until he figured out how to make all his inappropriate feelings go away.

But this…he couldn't ignore what he knew was the right thing to do.

"Viv." Vising his forehead between his fingers, he tried like hell to figure out how they'd gotten so off track. "You've been telling me for over a year that your career sucked up all your time and that's why you didn't date. How were you planning to meet said husband?"

"I don't know," she shot back defensively. "And cupcakes are important to me. It's just not the only thing, and this marathon of business-plan goals kind of solidified that fact for me. I love the idea of sharing my recipes with a bigger block of customers. But not at the expense of the kind of marriage I think would make me happy. I want—need—to back off."

Back off. From him, she meant. Jonas blinked as something wrenched loose in his chest, and it felt an awful lot like she'd gripped his heart in her fingers, then twisted until it fell out.

"I understand. You deserve to have the kind of marriage you want and I can't give that to you."

Her face froze, going so glacial all at once he scarcely recognized her.

"You've never thought about having a real marriage?" she asked in a whisper.

Not once. Until now. And now it was all he could think about. What was a real marriage to her? Love, honor and cherish for the rest of her days? He could do two out of three. Would she accept that? Then he could keep her friendship, keep this marriage and…how crappy was that, to even contemplate how far he could take this without breaking his word to anyone? It was ridiculous. They should have hashed out this stuff long ago. Like before they got married. And he would have if she'd told him that she harbored secret dreams of hearts and googly eyes. Too bad that kind of stuff led to emotional evisceration when everything went south.

Like now.

"Viv." She shifted to look at him, apparently clueing in that he had something serious to say. "I married you specifically because I have no intention of having a real marriage. It was deliberate."

Something that looked a lot like pain flashed through her gaze. "Because I'm not real marriage material?"

A sound gurgled in his throat as he got caught between a vehement denial and an explanation that hopefully didn't make him sound like an ass.

"Not because you're unlovable or something." God, what was wrong with him? He was hurting her with his thoughtlessness. She'd spilled her guts to him, obviously because she trusted him with the truth, and the best he could do was smash her dreams? "I care about you. That's why we're having this conversation, which we should have had a long time ago. I never told you about Marcus."

Eyes wide, she shook her head but stayed silent as he spit

out the tale of his friend who had loved and lost and then never recovered. When he wound it up with the tragedy and subsequent pact, she blinked away a sheen of tears that he had no idea what to do with.

"So you, Warren and Hendrix are all part of this...club?" she asked. "The Never Going to Fall in Love club?"

It sounded silly when she said it like that. "It's not a club. We swore solemn vows and I take that seriously."

She nodded once, but confusion completely screwed up her beautiful face. "I see. Instead of having something wonderful with a life partner, you intend to stick to a promise you made under duress a decade ago."

"No," he countered quietly. "I intend to stand by a promise I made, period. Because that's who I am. It's a measure of my ethical standards. A testament to the kind of man I want to be."

"Alone? That's the kind of man you want to be?"

"That's not fair." Why was she so concerned about his emotional state all at once? "I don't want to be alone. That's why I like being married to you so much. We have fun together. Eat dinner. Watch TV."

"Not lately," she said pointedly, and it was an arrow through his heart. If he was going to throw around his ethics like a blunt instrument, then he couldn't very well pretend he didn't know what she meant.

"Not lately," he agreed. "I'd like to say it's because we've both been busy. But that's not the whole truth. I...started to get a little too attached to you. Distance was necessary."

The sheen was back over her eyes. "Because of the pact. You've been pulling back on purpose."

He nodded. The look on her face was killing him, and he'd like nothing more than to yank her into his arms and tell her to forget that nonsense. Because he wanted his friend back. His lover. His everything.

But he couldn't. In the most unfair turnabout, he'd told her about the pact and instead of her running in the other direction like a lot of women, *he* was the one shutting down. "It was the only way I could keep you as my wife and honor the promises I made to myself and to my friends. And to you. I said no pressure. I meant to keep it that way. Which still stands, by the way."

She laughed, but he didn't think it was because she found any of this funny. "I think this is about the lowest-pressure marriage on the planet."

"You misunderstand. I'm saying no pressure to stay married."

Her gaze cut to him and he took the quick, hard punch to the gut in stride without letting on to her how difficult it had been to utter those words.

Take them back. Right now.

But he couldn't.

"Jonas, we can't get divorced. You'd lose your grandfather's support to take over his role."

The fact that she'd even consider that put the whole conversation in perspective. They were friends who cared about each other. Which meant he had to let her go, no matter how hard it was. "I know. But it's not fair to you to stay in this marriage given that you want something different."

"I do want something different," she agreed quietly. "I have to go to LA. I can't think about any of this right now."

He let her fingers slip from his, and when she shut herself in her bedroom, the quiet click of the door burst through his chest like a gunshot to the heart. He wished he felt like congratulating himself on his fine upstanding character, but all he felt like doing was crawling into bed and throwing a blanket over his head. The absence of Viv left a cold, dark place inside that even a million blankets couldn't warm.

CHAPTER TEN

THE TRIP TO LA was a disaster. Oh, the cooking show was fine. She won the first round. But Viv hated having to fake smile, hated pretending her marriage wasn't fake, hated the fakeness of baking on camera with a script full of fake dialogue.

There was nothing real about her, apparently. And it had been slowly sapping her happiness away until she couldn't stand it if one more person called her Mrs. Kim. Why had she changed her name? Even that was temporary until some ambiguous point in the future.

Well, there was one thing that was real. The way she felt about Jonas, as evidenced by the numbness inside that she carried 24/7. Finally, she had someone to care about and *he* cared about *her*. Yay. He cared so much that he was willing to let her out of the favor of being married to him so she could *find someone else*.

How ironic that she'd ended up exactly where she'd intended to be. All practiced up for her next relationship, except she didn't want to move on. She wanted Jonas, just like she had for over a year, and she wanted him to feel the same about her.

The cooking show, or rather the more correctly labeled entertainment venue disguised as a cupcake battle, wrapped up the next day. Viv won the final round and Franca cheered from the sidelines, pointing to her phone, where she was presumably checking out the stats on Cupcaked's new digital storefront. Every time the show's camera zoomed in on Viv's face, they put a graphic overlay on the screen with her name and the name of her cupcake bakery. Whatever results that had produced made Franca giddy, apparently.

It was all too overwhelming. None of this was what she wanted. Instead of cooking shows, Viv should have been spending fourteen hours a day working on her marriage. The what-ifs were all she could think about.

On the plane ride home, Franca jabbered about things like click-through rates, branding and production schedules. They'd already decided to outsource the baking for the digital storefront because Viv's current setup couldn't handle the anticipated volume. Judging by the numbers Franca was throwing out, it had been a good decision.

Except for the part where none of this was what Viv wanted. And it was high time she fixed that.

When she got home, she drafted a letter to Franca thanking her for all of her hard work on Viv's behalf but explaining that her career was not in fact the most important thing in her life, so Franca's services were no longer needed. The improvements to Cupcaked were great and Viv intended to use the strategies that they'd both developed. But she couldn't continue to invest so much energy into her business, not if she hoped to fix whatever was broken in Jonas's head that made him think that saying a few words a decade ago could ever compare with the joy of having the kind of marriage she'd watched her sisters experience. Viv had been shuffled to the side once again and she wasn't okay with that.

Jonas came home late. No surprise there. That seemed to be the norm. But she was not prepared to see the lines of fatigue around his eyes. Or the slight shock flickering through his expression when he caught sight of her sitting on the couch.

"Hey," he called. "Didn't know you were back."

"Surprise." Served him right. "Sit down so we can talk."

Caution drenched his demeanor and he took his time slinging his leather bag over the back of a chair. "Can it wait? I have a presentation to the board tomorrow and I'd like to go over—"

"You're prepared," she told him and patted the cushion next to her. "I've known you for a long time and I would bet every last cupcake pan I own that you've been working on that PowerPoint every spare second for days. You're going to kill it. Sit."

It was a huge kick that he obeyed, and she nearly swooned when the masculine scent of her husband washed over her. He was too far away to touch, but she could rectify that easily. When it was time. She was flying a little blind here, but she did know one thing—she was starting over from scratch. No familiar ingredients. No beloved pan. The oven wasn't even heated up yet. But she had her apron on and the battle lines drawn. Somehow, she needed to bake a marriage until it came out the way she liked.

"What's up? How was the show?" he asked conversationally, but strictly to change the subject, she was pretty sure.

"Fine. I won. It was fabulous. I fired Franca."

That got his attention. "What? Why would you do that?"

"Because she's too good for me. She needs to go help someone run an empire." She smiled as she gave Jonas a once-over. "You should hire her, in fact."

"Maybe I will." His dark eyes had a flat, guarded quality that she didn't like. While she knew academically that she had to take a whole different track with him, it was another thing entirely to be this close but yet so far.

"Jonas, we have to finish our conversation. The one from the other day."

"I wasn't confused about which one you meant." A brief lift of his lips encouraged her to continue, but then the shield between them snapped back into place. "You've decided to go."

"No. I'm not going anywhere." Crossing her arms so she couldn't reach out to him ranked as one of the hardest things she'd done. But it was necessary to be clear about this without adding a bunch of other stuff into the mix. "I said I was going to do you this favor and as strongly as you believe in keeping your word, it inspires me to do the same. I'm here for the duration."

Confusion replaced the guardedness and she wasn't sure which one she liked less. "You're staying? As my wife?"

"And your friend." She shrugged. "Nothing you said changed anything for me. I still want the marriage I envision and I definitely won't get that if I divorce you."

Jonas flinched and a million different things sprang into the atmosphere between them. "You're not thinking clearly. You'll never meet someone who can give you what you want if you stay married to me."

"For a smart man, you're being slow to catch on." The little noise of disgust sounded in her chest before she could check it. But *men*. So dense. "I want a real marriage with *you*, not some random guy off the street. What do you think we've been doing here but building this into something amazing? I know you want to honor your word to your friends—"

"Viv." The quiet reverberation of her name stopped her cold and she glanced at him. He'd gone so still that her pulse tumbled. "It's not just a promise I made to my friends. I have no room in my life for a real marriage. The pact was easy for me to make. It's not that I swore to never fall in love. It's that I refuse to. It's a destructive emotion that leads to more destruction. That's not something I'm willing to chance."

Her mouth unhinged and she literally couldn't make a sound to save her life. Something cold swept along her skin as she absorbed his sincerity.

"Am I making sense?" he asked after a long pause.

That she could answer easily. "None. Absolutely no sense."

His mouth firmed into a long line and he nodded. "It's a hard concept for someone like you who wants to put your faith and trust in someone else. I don't. I can't. I've built something from nothing, expanded Kim Electronics into a billion-dollar enterprise in the American market, and I'm poised to take that to the next level. I cannot let a woman nor the emotions one might introduce ruin everything."

She'd only thought nothing could make her colder than his opening statement. But the ice forming from this last round of crazy made her shiver. "You're lumping *me* in that category? *I'm* this nebulous entity known as 'woman' who might go Helen of Troy on your business? I don't even know what to say to that."

Grimly, he shook his head. "There's nothing to say. Consider this from my perspective. I didn't even know you wanted anything beyond your career until a couple of days ago. What else don't I know? I can't take that risk. Not with you."

"What?" Her voice cracked. "You're saying you don't trust me because I didn't blather on about hearts and flowers from the first moment I met you?"

Pathetic. Not-clingy hadn't worked. In fact, it might have backfired. If she'd just told him how she felt from the beginning, she could have used the last five weeks to combat his stupid pact.

Something white-hot and angry rose up in her throat. Seriously, this was so unfair. She couldn't be herself with *anyone*. Instead there were all these rules and games and potholes and loopholes, none of which she understood or cared about.

"Viv." He reached out and then jerked his hand back before touching her, as if he'd only just realized that they weren't in a place where that was okay. "It's not a matter of trust. It's…me. I can't manage how insane you make me."

She eyed him, sniffling back a tsunami of tears. "So now I make you crazy? Listen, buster, I'm not the one talking crazy here—"

A strangled sound stopped her rant. Jonas shook his head, clearly bemused. "Not crazy. Give me a break. I was expecting you to walk out the door, not grill me on things I don't know how to explain. Just stop for a second."

His head dropped into his hands and he massaged his temples.

"Insane and crazy are the same thing."

"I mean how much I want you!" he burst out. "All the time. You make me insane with wanting to touch you, and roll into you in the middle of the night to hold you. Kiss you until you can't breathe. So, yeah, I'll give you that. It makes me crazy. In this case, it does mean the same thing."

Reeling, she stared at him, dumbstruck, numb, so off balance she couldn't figure out how to make her brain work. What in the world was wrong with *any* of that?

"I don't understand what you're telling me, Jonas."

"It's already way too much." He threw up his hands. "How much worse will it get? I refuse to let my emotions control me like that."

This was awful. He was consciously rejecting the concept of allowing anything deeper to grow between them. Period. No questions asked. She let that reality seep into her soul as her nails dug into her palms with little pinpricks of pain that somehow centered her. If this was his decision, she had to find a way to live with it.

"So, what happens next?" she whispered. "I don't want a divorce. Do you?"

At that, he visibly crumpled, folding in on himself as if everything hurt. She knew the feeling.

"I can't even answer that." His voice dipped so low that she could scarcely make it out. "My grandfather asked me to come to Korea as soon as possible. He got some bad news from his doctor and he's retiring earlier than expected."

"Oh, no." Viv's hand flew to her mouth as she took in the devastation flitting through Jonas's expression. "Is he going to be okay?"

"I don't know. He wants you to come. How can I ask that of you?" His gaze held a world of pain and indecision and a million other things that her own expression probably mirrored. "It's not fair to you."

This was where the rubber met the road. He wasn't asking

her to go, nor would he. He was simply stating facts and giving the choice to her. If she wanted to claim a real marriage for herself, she had to stand by her husband through thick and thin, sickness and health, vows of honor and family emergencies.

This was the ultimate test. Did she love Jonas enough to ignore her own needs in order to fulfill his? If nothing else, it was her sole opportunity to do and be whatever she wanted in a relationship. Her marriage, her rules. If she had a mind to cling like Saran Wrap to Jonas, it was her right.

In what was probably the easiest move of the entire conversation, she reached out to lace her fingers with his and held on tight. "If you strip everything else away, I'm still your wife. Your grandfather could still pass his support to someone else if he suspects something isn't right between us. If you want me to go, I'll go."

Clearly equal parts shocked and grateful, he stared at her. "Why would you do that for me?"

She squared her shoulders. "Because I said I would."

No matter how hard it would be.

Jonas kept sneaking glances at Viv as she slept in the reclined leather seat opposite his. She'd smiled for nearly ten minutes after claiming a spot aboard the Kim private jet that Grandfather had sent to Raleigh to fetch them. It was fun to watch her navigate the spacious fuselage and interact with the attentive staff, who treated her like royalty. Obviously his grandfather had prepped them in advance.

But after the initial round of post-takeoff champagne, Viv had slipped back into the morose silence that cloaked them both since their conversation. He'd done everything in his power to drive her away so he didn't hurt her and what had she done? Repacked the suitcase that she'd just pulled off a conveyor belt at the airport hours before and announced she was coming with him to Korea. No hesitation.

What was he going to do with her?

Not much, apparently. The distance between them was nearly palpable. Viv normally had this vibe of openness about her as if she'd never met a stranger and he could talk to her about anything. Which he had, many times. Since he'd laid down the law about what kind of marriage they could have in that desperate bid to stop the inevitable, there might as well have been an impenetrable steel wall between them.

Good. That was perfect. Exactly what he'd hoped for.

He hated it.

This purgatory was exactly what he deserved, though. If Viv wasn't being her beautiful, kind, amazing self, there was no chance of his emotions engaging. Or rather, engaging further. He was pretty sure there was a little something already stirring around inside. Okay a lot of something, but if he could hold on to that last 50 percent, he could still look Warren and Hendrix in the eye next time they were in the same room.

If he could just cast aside his honor, all of this would be so much easier.

Seoul's Incheon Airport spread out beneath them in all its dazzling silvery glory, welcoming him back to Korea. He appreciated the birthplace of his father and the homeland of his grandfather. Seoul was a vibrant city rich in history with friendly people who chattered in the streets as they passed. It was cosmopolitan in a way that Raleigh could never be, but Jonas preferred the more laid-back feel of his own homeland.

"It's beautiful," Viv commented quietly as the limo Grandfather had sent wound through the streets thronged with people and vehicles.

"I'll take you a few places while we're here," he offered. "You shouldn't miss Gyeongbokgung Palace."

They could walk through Insa-dong, the historic neighborhood that sold art and food, then maybe breeze by the Seoul Tower. He could perfectly envision the delighted smile on her face as she discovered the treasures of the Eastern world that comprised a portion of his lineage. Maybe he'd even find an opportunity to take her hand as they strolled, and he could pretend everything was fine between them.

But Viv was already shaking her head. "You don't have to do that. I don't need souvenirs. You're here for your grandfather and I'm here for you."

That made him feel like crap. But it was an inescapable fact that she'd come because he needed her. Warmth crowded into his chest as he gazed at her, the beauty of Seoul rushing past the limousine window beyond the glass.

"Why?" he asked simply, too overcome to be more articulate.

Her gaze sought his, and for a brief moment, her normal expressiveness spilled onto her face. Just as quickly, she whisked it away. "No matter what, you're still my friend."

The sentiment caught in his throat. Her sacrifice and the unbelievable willingness to be there for him would have put him on his knees if he wasn't already sitting down. Still might. It didn't make any sense for her to be so unselfish with her time, her body, her cupcakes even without some gain other than the righteous promise of *friendship*. "I don't believe that's the whole reason."

A tiny frown marred her gorgeous mouth and he wished he could kiss it away. But he didn't move. This was something he should have questioned before they got on the plane.

"Is this another conversation about how you don't trust me?" she asked in a small voice.

Deserved that. He shook his head. "This is not a trust issue. It's that I don't understand what you're getting out of all of this. I've always wondered. I promised you that I would help you with your business since you claimed that as your passion. Then you politely declined all the success my efforts have produced. I give you the option to leave and you don't take it. Friendship doesn't seem like enough of a motivator."

Guilt crowded through her gaze. What was that all about? But she looked away before he got confirmation that it was indeed guilt, and he had a burning need to understand all at once.

The vows he'd taken with Warren and Hendrix after Marcus's death seemed like a pinky swear on the playground in comparison to Viv's friendship standards, yet he'd based his adult life on that vow. If there was something to learn from her about the bonds of friendship, he'd be an instant student.

Hooking her chin with his finger, he guided her face back toward his, feathering a thumb across her cheek before he'd barely gotten purchase. God, she felt so good. It was all he could do to keep from spreading his entire palm across her cheek, lifting her lips into a kiss that would resolve nothing other than the constant ache under his skin.

He'd enjoy every minute of the forbidden, though.

Since she still hadn't answered, he prompted her. "What's your real reason, Viv? Tell me why you'd do this for me after all I've said and done."

She blinked. "I agreed to this deal. You of all people should know that keeping your word is a choice. Anyone can break a promise but mine to you means something."

That wasn't it, or rather it wasn't the full extent. He could tell. While he appreciated her conviction, she was hedging. He hadn't expanded Kim Electronics into the American market and grown profits into the ten-figure range by missing signs that the person on the other side of the table wasn't being entirely forthcoming. But she wasn't a factory owner looking to make an extra million or two or a parts distributor with shady sources.

She was his wife. Why couldn't he take what she said at face value and leave it at that?

Because she hadn't told him about wanting a real marriage, that was why. It stuck under his rib cage, begging him to do something with that knowledge, and the answer wasn't pulling her into his arms like he wanted to. He should be cutting her free by his choice, not hers.

Yet Viv was quietly showing him how to be a real friend regardless of the cost. It was humbling, and as the limo snaked through the crowded streets of Seoul toward his grandfather's house, his chest got so tight and full of that constant ache he got whenever he looked at Viv that he could hardly breathe.

Caught in the trap of his own making, he let his hand drop away from her face. He had a wife he couldn't let himself love and two friends he couldn't let himself disappoint. At what point did Jonas get what he wanted? And when had his desire for something more shifted so far away from what he had?

There was no good answer to that. The limo paused by his grandfather's gates as they opened and then the driver pulled onto the hushed property draped with trees and beautiful gardens. The ancestral home that Grandfather had given Jonas and Viv lay a kilometer down the road up on a hill. Both properties were palatial, befitting a businessman who entertained people from all over the world, as Jung-Su did. As Jonas would be expected to do when he stepped into Grandfather's shoes. He'd need a wife to help navigate the social aspects of being the CEO of a global company.

But the painful truth was that he couldn't imagine anyone other than Viv by his side. He needed *her*, not a wife, and for far more reasons than because it might or might not secure the promotion he'd been working toward. At the same time, as much as he'd denied that his questions were about trust, he was caught in a horrible catch-22. Trust *was* at the root of it.

Also a trap of his own making. He was predisposed to believe that a woman would string him along until she got tired of him and then she'd break his heart. So he looked for signs of that and pounced the moment he found evidence, when in reality, he'd have to actually give his heart to a woman before it could be broken. And that was what he was struggling to avoid.

Grandfather's *jibsa* ushered them into the house and showed them to their rooms. A different member of the staff discreetly saw to their needs and eventually guided Jonas and Viv to where his grandfather sat in the garden outside, enjoying the sunshine. The garden had been started by Jonas's grandmother, lovingly overseen until her death several years ago. Her essence still flitted among the mugunghwa blooms and bellflowers, and he liked remembering her out here.

His grandfather looked well, considering he'd recently been diagnosed with some precursors to heart disease and had begun rounds of medication to reverse the potential for a heart attack.

"Jonas. Miss Viviana." Grandfather smiled at them each in turn and Viv bent to kiss his cheek, which made the old man positively beam. "I'm pleased to see you looking well after your flight. It is not an easy one."

Viv waved that off and took a seat next to Jung-Su on the long stone bench. His grandfather sat on a cushion that was easier on his bones but Viv didn't seem to notice that she was seated directly on the cold rock ledge. Discreetly, Jonas flicked his fingers at one of the many uniformed servants in his grandfather's employ, and true to form, the man returned quickly with another cushion for her.

She took it with a smile and resituated herself, still chatting with Grandfather about the flight and her impressions of Korea thus far. Grandfather's gaze never left her face and Jonas didn't blame him. She was mesmerizing. Surrounded by the lush tropical beauty of the garden and animated by a subject that clearly intrigued her, she was downright breathtaking. Of course, Jonas was biased. Especially since he hadn't been able to take a deep breath pretty much since the moment he'd said *I do* to this woman.

"Jonas. Don't hover." Grandfather's brows came together as he shot a scowl over the head of his new granddaughter-in-law. "Sit with us. Your lovely wife was just telling me about baking cupcakes on the American television show."

"Yes, she was brilliant," Jonas acknowledged. But he didn't sit on the bench. The only open spot was next to Viv and it was entirely too much temptation for his starving body to be that near her.

"Jonas is too kind." Viv's nose wrinkled as she shook her head. "The show hasn't even aired yet."

"So? I don't have to see it to know that you killed it." Plus, she'd told him she'd won, like it was no big deal, when in fact, it was. Though the result was hardly shocking. "*Brilliant* is an understatement."

Viv ducked her head but not before he caught the pleased gleam in her eye. He should have told her that already and more than once. Instead, he'd been caught up in his own misery. She deserved to hear how wonderful she was on a continual basis.

"It's true," he continued. "She does something special with her recipes. No one else can touch her talent when it comes to baking."

Grandfather watched them both, his gaze traveling back and forth between them as if taking in a fascinating tennis match. "It's very telling that you are your wife's biggest fan."

Well, maybe so. But what it told, Jonas had no idea. He shrugged. "That's not a secret."

"It's a sign of maturity that I appreciate," his grandfather said. "For years I have watched you do nothing but work and I worried that you would never have a personal life. Now I see you are truly committed to your wife and I like seeing you happy. It only solidifies my decision to retire early."

Yeah. *Committed* described Jonas to a T. Committed to honor. Committed to making himself insane. Committed to the asylum might well be next, especially since his grandfather was so off the mark with his observation. But what was he supposed to do, correct him?

"It's only fair," Viv murmured before Jonas could formulate a response. "I'm his biggest fan, as well."

"Yes, I can see that, too," Jung-Su said with a laugh.

He could? Jonas glanced at Viv out of the corner of his eye in case there was some kind of sign emanating from her that he'd managed to miss. Except she had her sights firmly fixed on him and caught him eyeing her. Their gazes locked and he couldn't look away.

"You're a fan of workaholic, absentee husbands?" he asked

with a wry smile of his own. Might as well own his faults in front of God and everyone.

"I'm a fan of your commitment, just like your grandfather said. You do everything with your heart. It's what I first noticed about you. You came into the shop to get cupcakes for your staff, and every time, I'd ask you 'What's the occasion today?' and you always knew the smallest details. 'It's Mrs. Nguyen's fiftieth birthday' or 'Today marks my admin's fourth anniversary working for me.' None of my other customers pay attention to stuff like that."

He shifted uncomfortably. Of course he knew those things. They'd been carefully researched excuses to buy cupcakes so he could see Viv without admitting he was there to see her. Granted, she'd already figured that out and blathered on about it to his parents during their first official married-couple dinner. Why bring that up again now?

"That's why he'll make the best CEO of Kim Global," she said to his grandfather as an aside. "Because he cares about people and cares about doing the right thing. He always keeps his word. His character is above reproach and honestly, that's why I fell for him."

That was laying it on a bit thick, but his grandfather just nodded. "Jonas is an honorable man. I'm pleased he's found a woman who loves him for the right reasons."

Except it was all fake. Jonas did a double take as Viv nodded, her eyes bright with something that looked a lot like unshed tears. "He's an easy man to love. My feelings for him have only grown now that we're married."

Jonas started to interrupt because…come on. There was play-acting and there was outright lying to his grandfather for the sake of supporting Jonas's bid to become the next CEO. But as one tear slipped from her left eye, she glanced at him and whatever he'd been about to say vanished from his vocabulary. She wasn't lying.

He swallowed. Viv was in love with him? A band tightened

around his lungs as he stared at her, soaking in the admission. It shouldn't be such a shock. She looked at him like that all the time. But not seconds after saying something so shocking, so provocative *out loud*. She couldn't take it back. It was out there, pinging around inside him like an arrow looking for a target.

A servant interrupted them, capturing Grandfather's attention, and everything fell apart as it became apparent that they were being called for dinner. Jonas took Viv's hand to help her to her feet as he'd done a hundred times before but her hand in his felt different, heavier somehow as if weighted with implications. She squeezed his hand as if she knew he needed her calming touch.

It was anything but calming. She was in love with him. The revelation bled through him. It was yet another thing that she'd held back from him that changed everything. He worked it over in his mind during dinner, longing to grab her and carry her out of this public room so he could ask her a few pointed questions. But Grandfather talked and talked and talked, and he'd invited a few business associates over as well, men Jonas couldn't ignore, given that the whole reason he was in Korea was to work through the transition as his grandfather stepped down.

Finally all the obstacles were out of the way and he cornered his wife in their room. She glanced up as he shut the door, leaning against it as he zeroed in on the woman sitting on the bed.

"That went well," she commented, her gaze cutting away from his. "Your grandfather seems like he's in good spirits after his diagnosis."

"I don't want to talk about that." He loved his grandfather, but they'd talked about his illness at length before Jonas had left the States, and he was satisfied he knew everything necessary about Jung-Su's health. Jonas's wife, on the other hand, needed to do a whole lot more talking and he needed a whole lot more understanding. "Why did you tell my grandfather that you're in love with me?"

"It just kind of…came out," she said. "But don't worry, I'm pretty sure he bought it."

"*I bought it,*" he bit out. "It wasn't just something you said. You meant it. How long have you been in love with me?"

She shrugged. "It's not a big deal."

"It is a big deal!" Frustrated with the lack of headway, he crossed the room and stopped short of lifting her face so he could read for himself what she was feeling. But he didn't touch her, because he wanted her to own up to what was really going on inside. For once. "That's why you married me. Why you came to Korea. Why you're still here even though I told you about the pact."

That's when she met his gaze, steady and true. "Yes."

Something wonderful and beautiful and strong burst through his heart. It all made a lot more sense now. What he'd been calling friendship was something else entirely.

Now would be a *really* good time to sit down. So he did. "Why didn't you tell me? That's information that I should have had a long time ago."

"No, Jonas, it's not." She jammed her hands on her hips. "What does it change? Nothing. You're determined to keep your vow to your friends and I can't stop being in love with you. So we're both stuck."

Yes. *Stuck.* He'd been between a rock and a hard place for an eternity because he couldn't stop being in love with her either.

He'd tried. He'd pretended that he wasn't, called it friendship, pushed her away, stayed away himself, thrown his honor down between them. But none of it had worked because he'd been falling for her since the first cupcake.

Maybe it was time to try something else.

"Viv." He stood and waited until he had her full attention. But then when she locked gazes with him, her expressive eyes held a world of possibilities. Not pain. Not destruction. None of the things that he'd tried to guard against.

That was the reason she should leave. Instead of feeling

stuck, she should divorce him simply because he was a moron. The character she'd spoken of to his grandfather didn't include being courageous. He was a coward, refusing to acknowledge that avoiding love hadn't saved him any heartache. In fact, it had caused him a lot more than he'd credited. Had caused Viv a lot, too.

Worse, he'd avoided the wonderful parts, and ensured that he'd be lonely to boot. And what had he robbed himself of thus far? Lots of sex with his wife, a chance to have a real marriage and many, many moments where she looked at him like she was looking at him right now. As if he really was worthy of her devotion, despite his stupidity.

He'd had plenty of pain already. Avoiding the truth hadn't stopped that. The lesson here? No more pretending.

"Tell me," he commanded. "No more hiding how you really feel. I want to hear it from you, no holds barred."

"Why are you doing this?" Another tear slipped down her face and she brushed it away before he could, which seemed to be a common theme. She had things inside that she didn't trust him with and he didn't blame her.

"Because we haven't been honest with each other. In fact, I'd say my behavior thus far in our marriage hasn't been anything close to honorable, and it's time to end that. You know what? I should go first then." He captured her hand and held it between his. "Viv. You're my friend, my lover, my wife, my everything. When I made a vow to never fall in love, it was from a place of ignorance. Because I thought love was a bad thing. Something to be avoided. You taught me differently. And I ignored the fact that I took vows with you. Vows that totally overshadow the promise I made to Warren and Hendrix before I fully understood what I was agreeing to give up. I'm not okay with that anymore. Not okay with pretending. What I'm trying to say, and not doing a very good job at, is that I love you, too."

Like magic, all of his fear vanished simply by virtue of saying it out loud. At last, he could breathe. The clearest sense of happiness radiated from somewhere deep inside and he truly couldn't fathom why it had taken him so long to get to this place.

Viv eyed him suspiciously instead of falling into his waiting arms. "What?"

He laughed but it didn't change her expression. "I love you. I wouldn't blame you if you needed to hear it a hundred more times to believe me."

Her lips quirked. "I was actually questioning the part where you said you weren't doing a good job explaining. Because it seemed pretty adequate to me."

That seemed like as good an invitation as any to sweep her into his arms. In a tangle, they fell back against the mattress, and before he could blink, she was kissing him, her mouth shaping his with demanding little pulls, as if she wanted everything inside him. He didn't mind. It all belonged to her anyway.

Just as he finally got his hands under her dress, nearly groaning at the hot expanse of skin that he couldn't wait to taste, she broke the kiss and rolled him under her.

That totally worked for him. But she didn't dive back in like his body screamed for her to. Instead, she let him drown in her warm brown eyes as she smiled. "What's going to happen when we get home and you have to explain to Warren and Hendrix that you broke your word to them?"

"Nothing. Because that's not what I'm going to say." He smoothed back a lock of her hair that had fallen into her face, and shifted until her body fell into the grooves of his perfectly. This position was his new favorite. "We made that pact because we didn't want to lose each other. Our friendship isn't threatened because I finally figured out that I'm in love with you. I'll help them realize that."

"Good. I don't want to be the woman who came between you and your friends."

"You couldn't possibly. Because you're the woman who *is* my friend. I never want that to change."

And then there was no more talking as Viv made short work

of getting them both undressed, which was only fair since she was on top. He liked Take Charge Viv almost as much as he liked In Love with Him Viv.

She was everything he never expected when he fell in love with his best friend.

EPILOGUE

JONAS WALKED INTO the bar where he'd asked Warren and Hendrix to meet him. He'd tried to get Viv to come with him, but she'd declined with a laugh, arguing that the last person who should be present at the discussion of how Jonas had broken the pact was the woman he'd fallen in love with.

While he agreed, he still wasn't looking forward to it. Despite what he'd told Viv, he didn't think Warren and Hendrix were going to take his admission lightly.

His friends were already seated in a high-backed booth, which Jonas appreciated given the private nature of what he intended to discuss. They'd already taken the liberty of ordering, and three beers sat on the table. But when he slid into the booth across from Warren, Hendrix cleared his throat.

"I'm glad you called," Hendrix threw out before Jonas could open his mouth. "I have something really important to ask you both."

Thrilled to have an out, Jonas folded his hands and toyed with his wedding band, which he did anytime he thought about Viv. He did it so often, the metal had worn a raw place on his finger. "I'm all ears, man."

Warren set his phone down, but no less than five notifications blinked from the screen. "Talk fast. I have a crisis at work."

Hendrix rolled his eyes. "You always have a crisis. It's usually that you're not there. Whatever it is can wait five minutes." He let out a breath with a very un-Hendrix-like moan. "I need you guys to do me a favor and I need you to promise not to give me any grief over it."

"That's pretty much a guarantee that we will," Warren advised him with cocked eyebrow. "So spill before I drag it out of you."

"I'm getting married."

Jonas nearly spit out the beer he'd just sipped. "To one woman?"

"Yes, to one woman." Hendrix shot him a withering glare. "It's not that shocking."

"The hell you say." Warren hit the side of his head with the flat of his palm. Twice. "I think my brain is scrambled. Because I'd swear you just said you were getting married."

"I did, jerkoff." Hendrix shifted his scowl to Warren. "It's going to be very good for me."

"Did you steal that speech from your mom?" Warren jeered, his phone completely forgotten in favor of the real-life drama happening in their booth. "Because it sounds like you're talking about eating your veggies, not holy matrimony."

"You didn't give Jonas this much crap when he got married," Hendrix reminded him as Warren grinned.

"Um, whatever." Jonas held up a finger as he zeroed in on the small downturn of Hendrix's mouth. "That is completely false, first of all. You have a short memory. And second, if this is like my marriage, you're doing it for a reason, one you're not entirely happy about. What's this really about?"

Hendrix shrugged, wiping his expression clear. "I'm marrying Rosalind Carpenter. That should pretty much answer all of your questions."

It *so* did not. Warren and Jonas stared at him, but Warren beat him to the punch. "Whoa, dude. That's epic. Is she as much a knockout in person as she is in all those men's magazines?"

He got an elbow in his ribs for his trouble, but it wasn't Warren's fault that there were so many sexy pictures of Rosalind Carpenter to consider.

"Shut up. That's my fiancée you're talking about."

Jonas pounded on the table to get their attention. "On that note…if the question is will we be in the wedding party, of course we will." They had plenty of time to get the full story. After Jonas steered them back to the reason why he'd called them with an invitation for drinks. "Get back to us when you've made plans. Now chill out while we talk about my thing."

"Which is?" Warren gave him the side-eye while checking his messages.

"I broke the pact."

The phone slipped out of Warren's hand and thunked against the leather seat. "You did what? With Viv?"

Jonas nodded and kept his mouth shut as his friends lambasted him with their best shots at his character, the depths of his betrayal and the shallowness of his definition of the word *vow*. He took it all with grace because he didn't blame them for their anger. They just needed to experience the wonders of the right woman for themselves and then they'd get it.

When they were mostly done maligning him, Jonas put his palms flat on the table and leaned forward. "No one is more surprised by this than me. But it's the truth. I love her and I broke the pact. But it's not like it was with Marcus. She loves me back and we're happy. I hope you can be happy for us, too. Because we're going to be married and in love for a long time."

At least that was his plan. And by some miracle, it was Viv's, too.

"I can't believe you're doing this to us," Warren shot back as if he hadn't heard a word Jonas said. "Does keeping your word mean nothing to you?"

"Integrity is important to me," he told them without blinking. "That's why I'm telling you the truth. Lying about it would dishonor my relationship with Viv. And I can't stop loving her just to stick to a pact we made. I tried and it made us both miserable."

"Seems appropriate for a guy who turns on his buddies," Hendrix grumbled.

"Yeah, we'll see how you feel after you get married," Jonas told him mildly. Hendrix would come around. They both would eventually. They'd been friends for too long to let something like a lifetime of happiness come between them, strictly over principle.

Warren griped about the pact for another solid five minutes and then blew out a breath. "I've said my piece and now I have to go deal with a distribution nightmare. This is not over."

With that ominous threat, Warren shoved out of the booth and stormed from the restaurant.

Hendrix, on the other hand, just grinned. "I know you didn't mean to break the pact. It's cool. Things happen. Thank God that'll never be me, but I'm happy that you're happy."

"Thanks, man." They shook on it and drank to a decade of friendship.

When Jonas got home, Viv was waiting in the foyer. His favorite. He flashed her the thumbs-up so she would know everything was okay between him and his friends—which it would be once Warren calmed down—then wrapped Viv in his arms and let her warmth infuse him. "I have another favor to ask."

"Anything."

No hesitation. That might be his favorite quality of hers. She was all in no matter what he asked of her—because she loved him. How had he gotten so lucky? "You're not even going to ask what it is?"

She shrugged. "If it's anything like the last favor, which landed me the hottest husband on the planet, by the way, why would I say no? Your favors are really a huge win for me so…"

Laughing, he kissed her and that made her giggle, too. His heart was so full, he worried for a moment that it might burst.

"Well, I'm not sure this qualifies as a win. I was just going to ask you to never stop loving me."

"Oh, you're right. I get nothing out of that," she teased. "It's torture. You make me happier than I would have ever dreamed. Guess I can find a way to put up with that for the rest of my life."

"Good answer," he murmured, and kissed his wife, his lover, his friend. His everything.

* * * * *

From Best Friend
To Daddy

Jules Bennett

National bestselling author **Jules Bennett** has penned over forty contemporary romance novels. She lives in the Midwest with her high-school-sweetheart husband and their two kids. Jules can often be found on Twitter chatting with readers, and you can also connect with her via her website, julesbennett.com.

Books by Jules Bennett

Harlequin Special Edition

Return to Stonerock

The Cowboy's Second-Chance Family

The St. Johns of Stonerock

Dr. Daddy's Perfect Christmas
The Fireman's Ready-Made Family
From Best Friend to Bride

Harlequin Desire

What the Prince Wants
A Royal Amnesia Scandal
Maid for a Magnate
His Secret Baby Bombshell
Best Man Under the Mistletoe

Mafia Moguls

Trapped with the Tycoon
From Friend to Fake Fiancé
Holiday Baby Scandal
The Heir's Unexpected Baby

The Rancher's Heirs

Twin Secrets
Claimed by the Rancher
Taming the Texan

Visit her Author Profile page at millsandboon.com.au, or julesbennett.com, for more titles.

Dear Reader,

Who doesn't love a good friends-to-lovers story? I knew from the moment I met Gray in *The Cowboy's Second-Chance Family* that he would need a special woman. He's infatuated with Kate but has never acted on his feelings. He's remained a faithful friend and a self-appointed protector.

Kate has had her share of heartache, and who better to lean on than Gray? She has her girlfriends, but Gray is different. She values their friendship and the special bond they've had since childhood.

But one night after their friends' wedding rehearsal changes everything. Suddenly they're more than friends...they're about to become parents.

I hope you enjoy Kate and Gray because I truly loved writing their story. Considering I married my best friend, I have a special place in my heart for this couple.

Happy reading!

Jules

Marrying my best friend was the best decision
of my life. Love you, Michael.

CHAPTER ONE

"IT'S JUST ONE GLASS."

Kate McCoy stared at the champagne flute the best man held. He'd flirted with her all night during the wedding rehearsal dinner—and by her estimate in smelling his overwhelming breath, he'd had more than enough for both of them. Thankfully he was just Noah's cousin and visiting from out of town. As in, he'd be leaving after the nuptials tomorrow afternoon.

One of Kate's three best friends, Lucy, was marrying her very own cowboy, and Kate couldn't be happier. She could, however, do without Noah's cousin all up in her face.

"She doesn't drink."

That low, growly tone belonged to Gray Gallagher, her only male best friend and the man who always came to her rescue whether she needed him to or not. She could've handled herself, but she wasn't about to turn away backup since Bryan with a Y wasn't taking her subtle hints.

Kate glanced over her shoulder and smiled, but Gray's eyes weren't on her. That dark, narrowed gaze was focused downward at the best man. Which wasn't difficult. Gray easily had five inches and an exorbitant amount of muscle tone on Best Man Bryan.

"Oh, well." Bryan awkwardly held two flutes in his hand,

tossing one back with a shrug. "Perhaps I could get you a soda or some water."

"We were just leaving," Gray growled.

He slid his arm around her waist and escorted her from the dining area of the country club. Apparently they were indeed leaving because he kept heading toward the exit.

"I need to at least get my purse before you manhandle me out the door," she said, swiping her clutch off the table closest to the door, where she'd been chatting with some guests. "And for your information, I was going to have a glass."

Gray stopped short in the hallway and turned to her. "You wanted to have a drink with that lame guy? You've never drank in your life."

Kate shrugged. "It's my thirtieth birthday."

"I'm aware of that." Eyes as dark as midnight narrowed. "You're not drinking with him."

Should she clue Gray in on her reasoning for wanting to have her first drink on her birthday and at her friend's wedding?

True, Kate hadn't so much as tried a drop of alcohol since her parents had been tragically killed in an accident. Her father had been thirty-five, her mother only thirty-two.

Now that Kate had hit the big 3-0, she'd started reevaluating everything about her carefully detailed life.

"C'mon." Gray slid his hand around her arm and escorted her out the door into the humid Tennessee heat. "If you're going to have a drink, it's not going to be with someone who can't handle champagne at a damn formal dinner."

Kate couldn't help but laugh. "That wasn't nice."

"Wasn't meant to be. I don't like how he looked at you."

What was up with this grouchy attitude tonight? Well, not just tonight. Gray seemed to be out of sorts for months now and with each passing day, he seemed to be getting worse and worse.

Gray headed toward his truck. He'd picked her up earlier and presented her with a box of chocolate-covered strawberries for her birthday. He knew those were her weakness and it was a tradition he'd started years ago when he'd first come back from the army only days before her birthday. Gray had told her he'd actually ordered her something this year, but it hadn't arrived yet.

"I'm picking you up for the wedding tomorrow, too."

Kate McCoy calculated everything, from matching her underwear to her outfit to the precise inches of curling ribbon she needed when wrapping packages. She had every detail in her life down to perfection and even owned a company that specialized in organizing the lives of others—everything from closets to finances. The Savvy Scheduler was still fairly new, but it was growing thanks to her social media accounts that drove interested viewers to her blog and ultimately resulted in many new clients.

Kate had anal-retentive down to a science. So she didn't like when her plans got changed.

"I'm driving myself in the morning."

Gray knew she calculated everything in her life well in advance. Hell, her planner had a planner. Everything in her personal life and business was not only on paper but also in e-format.

He was perfectly aware of how meticulous she was with every detail. They'd met in grade school on the playground when she made fun of his new haircut. Considering he'd hated it as well, they had a good laugh and bonded when other children would've fought over the mocking. They knew each other better than most married couples, which was why she couldn't pinpoint why he'd been surlier than usual tonight.

From scowling when he'd picked her up and muttered something about her dress, to the rude way he'd just escorted her out without saying goodbye to their friends, Gray's manners were seriously lacking.

"Plans change," he said with a shrug as he released his hold and walked ahead. "Relax."

Relax? The man had been uptight all night, glaring at any

male guest who talked to her, but she was supposed to relax? What was up with him?

The wind picked up, threatening to blow her short skirt higher than was within her comfort zone and expose said matching panties. Kate fisted the bottom of her flare dress in one hand as she marched across the parking lot after Gray—which wasn't easy, considering she'd gone with three-inch stilettos for the special occasion.

Stubborn man. He always wanted to bicker, and tonight was apparently no exception. But his unexplained behavior was starting to wear on her nerves.

Honestly, though, she didn't have time to analyze Gray's snarly attitude. It was late and she was tired and sweaty from this damn heat. Coupled with the unforgiving humidity wave hitting Stonerock, she was becoming rather grouchy herself. What happened to spring?

"I *planned* on getting to the church early to make sure everything was ready for when Lucy got there in the morning." Why was she yelling at his retreating back? "Would you stop and listen to me?"

Gray didn't stop until he got to the passenger door of his black truck. When he turned to face her, he released an exasperated sigh. He hadn't shaved for a few days, had that whole messy head of dark hair going on, and his tattoos peeked from beneath each sleeve that he'd cuffed up over his forearms. If she went for the dark, mysterious type, Gray would fit the bill perfectly. Well, also if he weren't her best friend.

Kate could easily see why women flocked to Gallagher's to flirt and throw themselves at the third-generation bar owner. He was a sexy man, had the whole "I don't give a damn" attitude, but she knew something those women didn't. Gray was loyal to a fault and didn't do flings. He may have looked like the quintessential bad boy, but he was all heart and a true Southern gentleman.

"Noah asked if I would bring you," he told her. "He said Lucy was worried about parking for the guests and he was trying to make things as simple as possible by having the wedding party carpool. I'll pick you up whatever time you want. Is this seriously something we have to argue about?"

One dark brow quirked and she thought for a scant second that maybe this was something they didn't have to argue about. Not that she was ready to concede the upper hand. First the angry attitude, now a lame argument?

"I'll pick you up," she stated, swiping away a hair that had landed right on her lip gloss. "I want my own vehicle there."

"Fine. Hop in." He motioned toward the truck. "I have to swing by the bar and get champagne out of the back stock since more was consumed tonight than originally planned. I'll give you a drink of whatever you want. But your first one will be with me."

"It's late, Gray. You don't have to do that. My list isn't going anywhere."

"List?" He shook his head, muttering something under his breath she couldn't quite make out. "Get in the truck. I should've known you'd have a damn list about taking a sip of alcohol."

Kate blew out a sigh. "I'm not sure, though. Maybe I should just mark it off and move on to the next item."

Gray reached out and tucked a strand behind her ear. "First of all, one drink of champagne or wine is a far cry from the ten empty vodka bottles found in the car of the person who hit your parents. Second, I'd never let you get in over your head. Third, what the hell is this list you keep referring to?"

The breeze kicked up, thankfully sending some relief over her bare shoulders, but making it impossible to let go of her dress. She'd left her hair down, which was a huge mistake. With that thick mass sticking to her neck and back, she'd give anything for a rubber band about now.

"It's silly."

"I live for silly."

Even without the dry humor, she knew Gray was as far re-moved from silly as any human being.

"Since I was turning thirty, I decided to make a list of things I want to do. Kind of a way to give myself a life makeover." She shrugged, because saying this out loud sounded even more ridiculous. "Trying a drink is on there."

"What else made the list?"

His eyes raked over her. Sometimes he did that. Like she was fragile. Just because life had knocked her down at times didn't mean she couldn't handle herself.

"Nothing for you to worry about."

She started to edge around him and reach for her handle when he stepped in her path. "Tell me."

Her eyes met his and she could tell by the hard stare that he wasn't backing down.

"I don't know what's up with you lately. You've been a bit of a Neanderthal." Might as well point out the proverbial ele-phant in the room. "You're pushy and hovering and…well, de-manding. Just because some guy flirts with me doesn't mean I'm going to repeat old mistakes. And if I want a drink, I can do that for myself, too. I know you want to protect me, but you can't always do that, Gray. I'm a big girl and—"

In a quick move he spun her around and had her caged be-tween the truck door and his hard chest. Mercy, he was ripped… and strong.

"Wh-what are you—"

"Putting that mouth to better use."

The words had barely processed before he covered her lips with his. There was nothing gentle, nothing sweet or calm about Gray. He was a storm, sweeping her up before she even knew what hit her.

Wait. She shouldn't be kissing her best friend. Should she?

He touched her nowhere else and she still clutched her dress in one hand. On a low growl, he shifted and changed the angle of the kiss before diving back in for more. The way he towered over her, covering her body from lips to hips, made her feel protected and ravaged all at the same time.

Heat flooded through her in a way that had nothing to do with the weather.

Just as fiercely as he started, Gray pulled back. Cursing under his breath, he raked a hand through his already messy hair. Clearly he was waging some war with himself. Well, he could just get in line, because she had no idea what to do about what had just happened.

"Gray—"

"Get in the truck, Kate."

His raspy voice slid over her, making her shiver despite the heat.

What the hell did that mean? What did any of the past few minutes mean? Kate couldn't wrap her mind around his actions, his words. One minute she was trying to get to the bottom of his behavior and the next...well, she was being kissed by her best friend, and not just any kiss. No, he'd all but devoured her, almost as if he were trying to ruin her for another man.

Gray reached around her for the door handle, giving her no choice but to move. She settled inside and stared ahead, completely dazed. With his taste still on her lips and countless questions swirling through her mind, Kate didn't dare say another word out loud as she buckled her seat belt.

What on earth had triggered such an intense response? And then to just leave like that? She'd already told him that they couldn't be more than friends, but damn it, that kiss sparked something inside her she'd never experienced before.

Why did he have to go and do that to her? Why did he have to make her question her stance on their relationship and leave her aching for more?

More wasn't an option.

CHAPTER TWO

THE RIDE FROM the country club to Gallagher's had been too damn quiet. Tension had settled between them like an unwanted third party. Never before had things been this tense between them. They bantered, they bickered...that's just who they were.

But now, thanks to his inability to control himself, the dynamics had shifted completely.

Gray wasn't even going to question what had gotten into him. He knew full well that years of pent-up frustration from being relegated to the friend category, seeing her flirt and dance with other men at his bar and then being engaged and heartbroken, and finally that damn dress and heels tonight had all caused him to snap. There was only so much a man could take...especially from a woman like Kate.

And then the list. He wanted to know what the hell was on it and why she thought she needed to revamp herself. Not a thing was wrong with her. Who was she proving herself to?

Losing his cool and kissing her may not have been his finest moment, but every man had a breaking point and Kate McCoy had been his for far too long.

Damn, she'd tasted good and she'd felt even better all pressed against him. He wasn't sorry he'd kissed her, wasn't regretting in the slightest that he'd finally taken what he'd wanted. She'd leaned into him and obviously had wanted it just as much.

No, what angered him was the shocked look on her face and the fact he'd just pulled them both across a line they could never come back from. He was her friend, her self-appointed protector. She didn't have many constants in her life and she counted on him, damn it. She *trusted* him.

Now Kate stood at the bar, her eyes never meeting his. No doubt she was replaying that kiss just as he'd been over the past ten minutes.

Gray didn't say anything as he went to the back and pulled out a bottle of champagne that none of his customers would ever be interested in, but it was perfect for Kate. Once he got her home and came back, though, he was going to need something much stronger. Thankfully he could just crawl upstairs to his apartment after throwing one back.

Gray returned to the bar to find Kate exactly how he'd left her. He reached for a glass and carried that and the bottle around to the front side of the bar.

"I assume you still want that drink."

Finally, her blue eyes darted to his. "If anything in my life warranted a drink, this night would be it."

He poured her a small amount and slid the glass over to her. Kate stared at the peach-toned liquid for only a moment before picking it up and smelling the contents.

All of that long, dark hair curtained her face as she leaned down. With those creamy shoulders exposed, he was having a difficult time not reaching out to touch her.

Had he severed that right? Had he ruined everything innocent about their friendship when he'd put his lips on hers?

Damn it. He didn't like the idea of another man coming into her life. It had damn near killed him when she'd gotten engaged while he'd been in the army. Then, when the jerk had broken her heart, it had taken all of Gray's willpower not to pummel the guy.

Tonight he'd nearly lost it when Noah's best man had gotten flirty. Gray saw how Bryan looked at her, like she was going to be easy to take home. That wasn't his Kate. She didn't go home with random strangers.

Kate slammed her empty glass on the bar. "More."

He added a bit more to her glass and was a little surprised when she tipped it back and swallowed it in one drink. Then belched like a champ.

"Wow. That's bubbly."

Gray couldn't help but smile. "It is. Had enough?"

"I can still taste your lips, so probably not."

His gut tightened as arousal spiraled through him. "Don't say things like that."

She lifted a slender shoulder. "Why not? It's the truth."

Gray took her glass away and set it aside with the bottle. The last thing she needed was to start buzzing, get all talkative and then regret spilling her secrets come morning. Though part of him—the part that had kissed her—would love to keep pouring and get her true feelings to come out into the open.

The low lighting behind the bottles lining the mirror along the bar wall sent a warm glow throughout the space. The main dining section and dance floor were still dark and Gray had never been more aware of a woman or his desire.

Over the years he'd purposely never allowed himself to be in a compromising situation with Kate, yet here he was only moments after plastering her against the side of his truck and claiming her lips.

"You can't be attracted to me," she murmured. "You *can't*, Gray."

If her words had any heat to them, if he thought for a second she didn't feel anything toward him, he'd ignore his need. But the only emotion he heard in her tone was fear and she'd kissed him right back earlier, so...

"You know I'm attracted to you." He closed the space between them. "I've never made it a secret."

"I'm the only woman who comes in your bar and hasn't thrown herself at you. I'm a conquest."

Anger settled heavily inside him. "Never call yourself that."

"Then what's the reasoning?" she tossed back. "Why me? After all these years, you're telling me…what? I need you to talk to me instead of being so damn irritated. Why now?"

"Maybe I'm tired of seeing other guys flirt with you. Maybe I'm sick of you dating losers since your breakup because you know your heart won't get involved."

She'd been burned and her defense mechanism to set her standards low was slowly driving him out of his ever-loving mind. Couldn't she see that she deserved more? She should actually be expecting more.

"Why did you kiss me back?" he asked, shifting the direction back to her.

Gray adjusted his body to cage her in against the bar with one hand on either side of her hips. He didn't want her to dodge him or look away or find an excuse not to hash this out right here, right now.

Maybe it was the late hour, maybe it was the near-darkness surrounding them. Or perhaps it was just time that his war with himself came to an end one way or another.

Kate's eyes widened, then darted to his mouth. That innocent act had arousal pumping through him. His frustrating friend could stir up quite the gamut of emotions. One of the reasons he had always been so fascinated by her. Nobody could get to him the way she could. And nobody could match him in conversation the way Kate could.

She flattened her palms on his chest. "Gray, I can't lose you as a friend."

"I never said I was going anywhere." He leaned in just a bit closer, close enough to see those navy flecks in her bright blue eyes. Close enough for her to realize he wasn't messing around anymore. "Tell me you don't want me kissing you again."

Because as much as he worried he was pushing her, he kept returning to the fact that she'd kissed him back.

Kate's mouth opened, then closed. That was all the green light he needed.

Gray didn't waste time gripping her hips and capturing her mouth. Those fingertips against his chest curled in, biting into his skin through the fabric. She let out a soft moan as her body melted against his. He wanted to hoist her up onto this bar and see exactly what she wore beneath this damn dress that had driven him crazy all night. He wanted those legs wrapped around him, her body arched against his.

Kate tore her mouth away. "We can't... Why does this feel so good? It can't go anywhere."

Like hell it couldn't. She was just as turned on as he was if the way she'd rubbed herself against him proved anything.

Gray slid his hands over the curve of her hips, to the dip in her waist, and back down. "Tell me to stop and I will."

He leaned in, trailing his lips over her collarbone, breathing in that jasmine scent that belonged only on her.

"Tell me, Kate," he whispered, smiling when she trembled beneath his touch. "I have to hear the words."

He was torturing himself. If she told him to stop right now he would. But damn it, being pulled away after having a sample would be hell.

Slowly her hands slid up around his neck, and her fingers threaded through his hair. "Gray," she murmured.

Music to his ears. He'd always wondered how his name would sound sliding through her lips on a whispered sigh. Now he knew...and he wanted more.

Gray hovered with his mouth right over hers, his hands circling her waist. "You want me."

She nodded.

"Say it."

"I want you," she murmured. "But I need you as a friend. Please. Tell me we won't lose that."

He didn't want to lose anything. He wanted to build on what they had. They couldn't ignore this pull between them, so taking this risk to see where things went was the only option.

When he said nothing, she eased back as much as she could with the bar at her back. "Gray, this night is all we can have. We'll still be friends come morning."

One night? Did she think she'd be done with him that soon?

"And nobody can know," she added. "I don't want Lucy or Tara to know."

Her girl posse. He understood the need for privacy, but at the same time, he didn't want to be her dirty little secret and he sure as hell wanted more than one night.

He was a guy. Wasn't he supposed to be thrilled at the idea of a one-night stand with no strings? He should've had her dress off by now.

But this was Kate and she was special. Always had been.

"I wondered."

Her words stopped every single thought. "What?"

Bright blue eyes came up to his. "About this. I wondered before."

"Kate," he growled.

"I mean it, Gray. Just this night and it stays here, between us."

There was so much he wanted to say, so much he wanted to fight for because Kate was worth fighting for. He'd worry about the semantics tomorrow. He'd come too far and had a willing woman in his arms right now. There was only one thing to do.

Gray lifted her up onto the bar and kissed her.

CHAPTER THREE

KATE DIDN'T WANT to think about why this could potentially be a disastrous idea. How could she form a coherent thought when her best friend had his mouth and hands all over her? She'd never felt this good in her life and her clothes were still on.

Was it the champagne? Surely not. She'd only had two small glasses.

No, it couldn't be the alcohol. Gray was more potent than any drink he could give her. Why was she just discovering this fact?

Kate's head spun as she continued to clutch his shirt. She didn't want to analyze this moment or her emotions. She only wanted to feel.

Part of her wanted to rip off his clothes, but she'd never been that brazen a woman. The few lovers she'd had were all calm, tame…and she'd never tingled like this for any of them.

She'd never ached with desire for her best friend, either, but here they were. A new wave of emotions swept her up, giving her no choice but to go along for the ride and enjoy every glorious moment.

Gray's firm hands rested on her knees as he spread them wide and stepped into the open space. He continued kissing her as his fingertips slid beneath her short skirt. Every single nerve ending inside her sizzled. When was the last time she'd sizzled?

Oh, right. Never. How did he know exactly what to do and how was she just realizing that her bestie had skills?

Kate tipped her head back as Gray's lips traveled over her chin and down the column of her throat. She circled his waist with her legs, toeing off her heels. The double thumps of her shoes hitting the hardwood floor sliced through the moment. Gray eased back and pinned her with his dark gaze. She'd never seen that look on his face before—pure hunger, passion, desire. All directed toward her.

Kate looked in his eyes and the need that stared back had her figuring maybe this wasn't a bad idea at all. No one had ever looked at her with such a need before. Something churned within her, not just arousal, but some emotion she wasn't ready to identify that coupled right along beside it, making her feel more alive and needed than ever.

Keeping his eyes locked on hers, Gray flipped her skirt up and jerked her by the waist toward the edge of the bar. Kate was completely captivated by the man before her. This passionate, sexual side of Gray had her reaching for the buckle on his belt, more than ready to hurry this process along. He quickly shoved her hands aside and reached for his wallet.

The second he procured a foil packet everything clicked in her mind. This was real. All of this was actually happening. She was about to have sex with her best friend…and she'd never been more thrilled, more excited in her life.

Shouldn't she be freaking out? Where had all of this come from? Clearly the desire had built up over time.

But she didn't. Kate waited, anticipation coiling through her. She'd address those questions later. Right now, she had a need, an ache, and judging by Gray's urgency, he did, too.

He tossed the packet next to her hip on the bar and unfastened his pants. Then, in a move that both shocked and aroused her, he reached beneath her dress, gripped the strip of satin that lay against her hip, and gave a jerk until the rip resounded through the quiet bar. So much for that pair of panties. They were a worthy sacrifice to the cause.

Kate didn't even get to enjoy the view before Gray sheathed himself and stepped toward her. With his hands firmly circling her waist, he nudged her forward once again, until he slowly joined their bodies.

Oh...my...

On a groan, Kate took a moment to allow her body time to adjust, but Gray clearly was in a hurry. He framed her face with his strong hands, tipped her head and covered her mouth as his hips jerked forward once again.

There was not much she could do but lock her ankles behind his back and match the perfect rhythm he set with their bodies.

"Kate," he muttered against her mouth.

She didn't want words. She had no clue what he was about to say, but she didn't want anything breaking into this moment. Words couldn't even begin to cover the tumultuous emotions flowing between them and she just wanted to feel. For right now, she wanted this man and nothing else.

Fisting his hair in her hands, Kate slammed his mouth back down onto hers. His hips pumped harder and in the next second, Kate's entire body trembled. She arched against Gray, pulling from the kiss. Her head dropped back, eyes shut as the euphoria spiraled through her.

She felt him lifting her before he settled her onto the bar. He whispered something just as his fingertips dug into her waist and he rose to tower above her. For a moment she marveled at his strength, but he started shifting again, moving faster and giving her no choice but to clutch his muscular arms.

Gray's body stilled as he rested his forearms on either side of her head, aligning their torsos. His mouth came down onto her shoulder. The sudden nip of his teeth against her flesh stunned her, arousing her even as she came down from her high. He kissed her there and trailed his lips across her heated skin.

Kate held onto Gray's shoulders even when their bodies completely stopped trembling. She had no idea what to say at this point. They lay on top of his bar half-dressed and had never so much as kissed more than in a friendly manner before, yet they'd just had explosive sex.

That was one hell of a birthday present.

Okay, maybe those shouldn't be the first words out of her mouth. But really, what was the protocol for a situation like this? She prided herself on always being prepared, but nothing could prepare her for what just took place. On a bar top, no less.

Gray came up onto his hands and looked down at her. Fear curled low in her belly. Was he waiting on her to say something and cut through the tension? Did they joke about this or did they fix their clothes like nothing happened?

Considering she analyzed everything from every angle, they would have to talk about this at some point. Maybe not right now when her emotions were too raw and she was still reeling from the fact that Gray had pursued her and torn off her underwear. Just the memory had chills popping up over her skin.

Exactly how long had he wanted her like this? There had been quite a bit of pent-up sexual need inside her bestie. Not that she was complaining. Definitely not complaining. Just... confused, and there were so many questions whirling inside her head, she had no clue where to start.

The muscle in Gray's jaw clenched and the way he continued to study her had Kate fidgeting. The top of her dress had slid down, so she adjusted to cover herself. She lifted onto her elbows and glanced around, anything but having to look right into those dark eyes to see...

She didn't know what she'd see, but she knew awkward tension had already started settling in.

Gray eased down off the bar and took a step back. Kate started to climb down, but he reached up, lifted her carefully into his arms, and placed her on the floor. The cool wood beneath her feet had her shivering, as did the sweet gesture of how he'd just handled her.

Of course, she could be shivering because her underwear was in shreds on the floor and her best friend was walking away. So much for him being sweet.

Apparently he wasn't one for chatter after sex, either. The silence only left her alone with thoughts she wasn't quite ready to tackle.

Kate's pale pink heels lay on their sides and she padded over to retrieve them. She clutched them against her chest like they could ward off the unknown, because she truly had no clue what was going to happen next.

Hell, it wasn't only the next few minutes she was concerned with. What about long-term? Did this change everything between them? She hadn't been lying when she said she couldn't lose him. Gray was her everything. Absolutely everything.

The only constant in her life other than Tara and Lucy, but Gray was different. He was…well, he was special.

Right now, though, Kate could use some space to think and here on his turf, where her tattered panties lay mocking her, was not the place to clear her head and regroup.

Of all the times not to have her car. Damn it. This was why she always planned things, always had a plan B. But neither plan A nor B had been to leave the rehearsal dinner and have a quickie on the bar top at Gallagher's.

She was at the mercy of Gray whenever he came back and chose to take her home. Maybe then they'd talk and she'd get a feel for what was going on in that head of his.

Kate was stunned at the way her body still tingled. Gray had awakened something inside her, something she hadn't even known existed. But she'd made him promise just one night and that's exactly what she was going to hold on to.

She couldn't afford to lose him as a friend simply because she'd just experienced the best sex of her life. Gray was the one constant male in her life. He had been in that role since they were in junior high, and he'd come to rescue her from some bullying jerk who was new at the school. Not that she'd needed rescuing, but she'd appreciated it at the time, and he'd been her self-appointed white knight since.

So who was going to save her from him? Because now that she'd had him, Kate knew he'd ruined her for other men.

Gray Gallagher had infiltrated her, body and soul, and she'd better just live with the tantalizing memories, because they were definitely one and done.

She couldn't emotionally afford to have it any other way.

Gray took a minute longer than necessary in his private bathroom attached to the back office. The second he'd come back to reality and looked down into Kate's eyes, he'd seen her withdrawing. He'd instantly wanted her to reconsider that one-night rule. But he hadn't even gotten her completely undressed. He'd ripped her panties off, and they'd had a quickie on his bar.

Yeah, real smooth. Perfect way to show her she was special and he wanted to do it all over again. He'd be lucky if she didn't haul off and smack him when he walked back in there. Hadn't he always told her she deserved better? That she deserved to be treated like she was the most valuable woman in a man's life?

Gray slammed his hand against the wall and cursed himself for being such a jerk to the one woman he cared most about. Now he was going to have to go out and face her, make some excuse as to his behavior, and then drive her home in what he was sure would be uncomfortable silence.

What a fantastic way to end an already crappy day. He'd already been in a bitch of a mood when he'd seen that best man flirting with her. He shouldn't be jealous, but damn it, he couldn't help how he felt.

He'd faced death when he'd lost his mother at the tender age of five. He'd faced the enemy when he'd been overseas in the army. He faced his father, who was disappointed because Gray hadn't settled down and started a family. But Gray was not looking forward to facing his best friend, because if he saw even the slightest hint of regret or disappointment in her eyes, he would absolutely be destroyed.

Knowing he couldn't stay hidden forever, he made sure his clothes were adjusted before he headed out. The second he rounded the corner from the back hallway, he stilled.

Kate stood frozen just where he'd left her. She clutched her shoes, worried her bottom lip with her teeth, and stared at the spot where he'd taken her like some horny teen with no experience.

But it was the pale pink bite mark on her shoulder that had him cringing and cursing himself all over again.

Damn it. What the hell was wrong with him? His Kate was a lady. She was classy. She was so far above him and he'd treated her like a one-night stand.

Oh, wait. That's exactly what this was, per her last-minute request. It wasn't like he gave her ample time to get used to the idea of the two of them together.

Still, Kate deserved better and he damn well was going to show her. Screw the one-night rule. If anyone should be proving to her exactly how she should be treated, it was him.

"I'll take you home."

Kate jumped and turned to face him, her eyes wide. His voice came out gruffer than he'd intended.

With a simple nod, she headed toward the back door. Gray didn't move from his position and ultimately blocked the opening to the hallway. He waited until she stopped right before him. He shouldn't touch her, shouldn't push this topic, but damn if he couldn't help himself. There had to be something he could do to redeem his actions.

Reaching out, he traced one fingertip over the faint mark on her shoulder.

"We good?"

Wow. He'd had several minutes to think of something tender, kind, and apologetic to say, and that's the best he could come up with?

Yes, he saw confusion looking back at him, but there was more. Kate wasn't upset, not at all. She had questions, of that he was sure, but she wasn't angry. Thankfully he hadn't botched this night up too much.

Kate attempted a smile. "We're good," she murmured as her eyes darted away.

She may not be angry, but she was no doubt wondering what they should do next. Kate planned everything and this whole experience had definitely not been planned.

Enter the awkward tension he swore wouldn't be there. He promised her they wouldn't change. He promised they'd be friends just like before.

Yet she couldn't even look him in the eyes.

"Kate."

Her focus darted back to him, but he didn't see regret. Kate's pretty blue eyes were full of desire... Damn if that didn't just confuse the hell out of him. She might be wanting to ask him about what just happened, but she also wasn't sorry.

Gray didn't know what else to say at this moment. The dynamics had changed, the intimacy too fresh. Maybe once they had some time apart and saw each other at the wedding tomorrow they'd laugh and joke and go back to the Gray and Kate they'd been hours ago.

Or maybe they'd find the nearest closet and rip each other's clothes off. Things could go either way at this point.

Gray moved out of her way so she could pass. Her hair hung down her back in dark waves, her dress was slightly askew, and she still clutched her shoes. He'd turned a moment of intimacy with his best friend into forcing her to do a walk of shame from his bar.

He was no better than the prick who'd cheated on her and broke her heart. But Gray would make this up to her. He had to.

Kate adjusted her one-shoulder bridesmaid's dress for the fifth time in as many minutes. Thankfully Lucy hadn't chosen strapless dresses. Kate needed this chiffon strap to cover Gray's mark. She didn't know what she would've done had he chosen the other shoulder.

Part of her loved the mark. She'd be lying if she said otherwise. She'd never had a man lose such control, and the fact he hadn't even been able to get them out of their clothes was thrilling. Sex should be thrilling, or so she'd heard before, and she'd always wondered if that was a myth. Now she knew.

Analyzing this over and over wasn't going to change the future. Gray wasn't going to happen again. On that they'd agreed, so now she had to figure out how to not compare any other man to her best friend. But at least the standards were set and she wasn't going to settle for someone who didn't at least give her a little spark.

Kate had definitely had a happy birthday. At least she had until he'd come from the bathroom and couldn't get her out of the bar fast enough. Did he regret what they'd done? Or worse. Was she a disappointment?

"Hey, you okay?" Tara whispered.

"Fine."

Kate smiled for the camera and hoped they were nearly done with all the photos. What did it matter if Gray found her lacking in the skill department? They weren't doing anything again anyway.

He'd barely said a word when she'd picked him up this morning and she hadn't seen him at the wedding. But the church had been packed, so that wasn't a surprise. She'd see him at the reception for sure. He was in charge of all the drinks and had brought a few of his employees to serve as waiters.

She felt a bit odd not sharing her epic, mind-blowing, toe-curling experience with Lucy and Tara. If this had been any other man she'd had wild sex with late at night in a closed bar, she would've texted them immediately after, but this was Gray. He was different and what they shared was…well, it was something she still couldn't describe.

"I think we got them," the photographer announced. "We'll do more at the reception."

Kate resisted the urge to groan. This was Lucy and Noah's day. She shouldn't be so grouchy, but smiling and posing and pretending to be in a good mood was not working for her. All she could think of was Gray: what they'd done, what she had missed from him that led up to that moment, how he'd react seeing her again.

Kate lifted the long skirt of her dress and stepped off the stage. A hand slid over her elbow.

"Wait a second," Tara said.

Turning her attention to her friend, Kate dropped her dress and clutched the bouquet. "What's up?"

"That's what I want to know."

Tara's questioning gaze held Kate in place. "I'm just going to hop on the shuttle to take me to the reception so I can get some food. I'm starving."

Rolling her eyes, Tara stepped closer. "You've been acting weird all day. What happened from last night to this morning?"

What happened? Oh, just a quickie on the bar top at Gallagher's, third stool from the left. Well, Gray had shoved the stool out of the way when he'd climbed up to her, but still. She'd never be able to look at that space again without bursting into internal flames. Her panties would probably melt right off.

"I just had a late night." Kate opted to go with some form of the truth. "Gray and I left the rehearsal and headed back to the bar so he could pull more champagne and wine from the back stock. I just didn't get much sleep before we had to be up and ready."

Tara's bright blue eyes studied Kate a moment longer than she was comfortable with. Gathering her skirt in her hand once again, Kate forced a smile.

"C'mon," she said, nodding toward the front of the church. "Let's go get on the shuttle so they can take us over to the food and dancing. I'm ready to get rid of these heels."

Tara nodded. "Will you get some pictures of me dancing with Marley?"

Marley, Tara's five-year-old daughter. She shared custody with her ex, Sam Bailey. Sam had brought Marley to the wedding since this was his weekend to have her. Tara had been surprised that Sam had taken Marley to get her hair done and her nails painted.

Kate knew Sam had some issues several months ago, but she saw the man was trying. Okay, using the word "issues" was really sugarcoating things. But addiction was such a delicate topic and Kate still wasn't sure how to approach it with Tara.

But Kate saw Sam fighting to get his family back. The man had gone to rehab, he'd gotten a new job, he'd gone to counseling. There was a determination in him now that Kate hadn't seen before. Tara wasn't ready to see it and Kate worried irreparable damage had been done and their marriage was over for good.

None of that was Kate's business and she had her own issues to worry about right now. Like seeing Gray at the reception. She didn't like the silence that had settled between them this morning. That wasn't like them. They were always bantering or arguing or joking about something. It was their thing. They lived to annoy the hell out of each other and for some strange reason, it worked for them.

Damn it. She knew sleeping with him would change things, but she'd been unable to prevent herself from giving in. One second they were friends, and the next he'd kissed her against his truck and made her want things she never realized she was missing.

Well, she had to just suck it up and get over this awkward hurdle. She wanted her friend back and she wasn't going to let great sex stand in their way.

CHAPTER FOUR

GRAY CHECKED ON the status of the bottles, confident they'd be just fine with the extras he'd brought. He asked around with his staff to see if they were doing okay or if anyone needed a break. None of them took him up on his offer.

He had such amazing, loyal employees at his bar who would work any venue when he asked. Honestly, they could run the whole place themselves and probably didn't even need him around.

Damn it. He was out of things to do other than watch Bryan try to hit on Kate again. Didn't the guy take the not-so-subtle hint from the rehearsal dinner?

Gray had been jealous last night, but seeing him make a play again tonight had him feeling all sorts of rage. Which was absurd. Kate was a grown woman and they were just friends. They'd slept together and now he was letting that incident cloud his judgment.

Actually, he didn't care. Kate was better than Bryan and Gray didn't like the way the guy kept looking at her.

Gray walked around the perimeter of the country club dining area and glared at Bryan as he stepped in behind Kate on the dance floor. What the hell was wrong with that guy?

Kate turned and glanced at Bryan, then shook her head and

held up her hands as if to ward him off. Bryan smiled and reached out to touch her bare shoulder. Seeing that man's hand against Kate's creamy skin had Gray making his way across the floor.

The jerk stepped into her when a slow song started and the tension on Kate's face made Gray's anger skyrocket. He was sure his face showed his every emotion but right now he didn't give a damn who saw him or what others thought. He was putting a stop to this now.

"Go have another drink, Bryan. This dance is mine."

Gray instantly wrapped an arm around Kate's waist and took her hand in his. From the corner of his eye, Gray saw Bryan still standing there. Spinning Kate in a circle, Gray stepped on Bryan's foot and was rewarded with a grunt.

"Still there?" Gray asked over his shoulder.

The guy finally disappeared through the crowd of dancers.

Kate's eyes were wide, but Gray would rather she be uncomfortable with him than with some idiot who didn't know what a treasure Kate was.

"He's harmless."

Gray narrowed his gaze. "And I'm not?"

She merely tipped her chin in defiance. "I could've handled it myself."

Gray offered her a smile. "You always say that."

"Because I can."

"I'm aware." He spun her around again, keeping his firm hold on her. His Kate was extra prickly today. "But we haven't danced yet and I had a few minutes to spare."

Her eyes continued to hold his. "And what were you doing those few minutes you were glaring this way?"

Damn if she wasn't adorable when she was fired up. "Some people take a smoke break. I don't smoke, so I take a glare break."

Kate stared for another moment before she finally shook her

head and let out a soft laugh. "You're incorrigible. You know that, right?"

A bit of tension eased from his chest at her sweet laugh. "It's only because I care and Bryan is not the guy for you. Not even as a dance partner. Hell, he's not even your drink provider."

Kate arched a brow. "So now you're screening my guys?"

Screening them? Hell, if that was a possibility he damn well would be first in line to sign up for that job. If he hadn't been overseas during her ill-fated engagement, perhaps he could've prevented her heartache. But Gray hadn't even met the ex because he'd come and gone while Gray had been serving. So, yeah, perhaps he was looking out for her. Isn't that what friends did?

"Maybe dancing with a guy like Bryan made my list."

Here she went with that damn list again. He'd like to see exactly what was on that thing.

"Tell me more about this infamous list."

He spun her around again, slowly leading the way toward the edge of the dance floor, where there weren't as many people. He found he didn't want to share Kate right now. He wanted to keep her talking, keep her dancing. Though dancing wasn't his thing, it was an excuse to get her in his arms.

He glanced around as he led her. He recognized many people from town. The St. John brothers and their wives were all dancing. Several other couples who frequented his bar were also dancing and having a good time.

Gray actually hadn't seen the bride and groom for a while, though. Perhaps they'd already slipped out once the bouquet and the garter had been tossed. Most likely they'd been in a hurry to get to their honeymoon.

"I'm keeping my list to myself for now," she replied.

Gray stared down into her blue eyes. She hadn't brought up last night and he wasn't about to, either. They hadn't wanted things to change between them, but the tension had become palpable and he wasn't sure how to erase it.

Eventually they would have to discuss what happened. Might as well be now, while he had her undivided attention. Maybe having everyone around would help ease the tension. If they were alone again and trying to talk, Gray wasn't so sure he could prevent himself from touching her again. Touching her now was safe, smart.

"About last night—"

Kate's eyes widened a fraction. "I need to find Tara," she said, breaking from his hold. "We'll talk later."

And then she was gone, leaving him all alone with a slew of couples dancing around him. Gray fisted his hands at his sides. He hadn't expected Kate to run. He hadn't expected their night to scare her away. She'd always been comfortable with him.

But then he'd turned into the guy who had sex with his best friend on top of a bar.

Raking a hand through his hair, Gray left the dance floor and went back to what he could control. The alcohol and the servers. Right now, Kate was utterly out of his control. Perhaps they needed space. Maybe she needed a breather after what had happened.

One thing was certain, though. He'd had her only one time and he knew without a doubt he wanted more.

Kate sank onto the chaise in the seating area of the women's restroom. She slid out of her heels and resisted the urge to moan. Between all the food she ate and dancing and the lack of sleep, she was ready for bed.

It was that whole lack of sleep—or the reason behind it—that had her escaping to the restroom to hide for a bit. She'd known Gray would bring up their situation, but their friend's wedding was sure as hell not the place she wanted to hash things out.

She couldn't think when he was holding her, because now that they'd been intimate, any type of touch triggered her memories…not that the images of last night had ever faded to the background. Would they ever?

Besides, Kate had no clue what she wanted to say anyway. Did she say thank you? Did she compliment him? Or did she broach the fact that she'd had her first taste of alcohol and it wasn't that bad? What exactly did she lead in with after such an epic, mind-boggling night?

The bathroom door opened, but Kate kept her eyes in her lap, not wanting to face any guests.

"Who are we hiding from?"

So much for not facing anyone.

Kate glanced up to see Tara and Lucy holding the skirts of their gowns and coming in from the madness and noise outside. Once the door shut, her friends waited for her answer in silence.

"Tara—"

"Is it Bryan?" Lucy asked, rolling her eyes. "I swear, he and Noah are close, but I had no idea how annoying that man could be when presented with a single woman. Guess he thinks he has a chance with you."

Kate blew out a sigh. If her only problem involved a man who was a complete goober and found her attractive, she'd be golden and certainly wouldn't be hiding in the bathroom.

No, her issues came in the form of a six-foot-four-inch bar owner who could make her tingle just from the slightest brush of his fingertips.

"This isn't about Bryan. I'm just taking a breather," she told them, which was the absolute truth.

Lucy gathered the full skirt of her wedding dress and flopped next to Kate on the chaise. Tara crossed and sat in the floral armchair.

"I told you something was up," Tara stated, looking at Lucy.

"This is her wedding day." Kate glared at her friend. "You told her you thought something was up with me when she should be focusing on how quickly she and Noah can get out of here and head to their honeymoon?"

Tara's eyes widened as she shrugged. "We're friends. She

can go have sex with Noah whenever. I need to know what's going on with you and Gray."

"Are you two arguing again?" Lucy asked. "I swear, you're like an old married couple, just without the sex."

Kate nearly choked on the gasp that lodged in her throat. Fortunately, she recovered before giving herself away. She was nowhere near ready to spill her secret. Her friends would be completely shocked if they learned she'd had sex with Gray. Kate was still reeling from the fact herself.

"What? No, we're not arguing." They couldn't argue when she was running away and dodging the issue. "Why would you think that?"

"Because you two were dancing, then you rushed out in the middle of the song."

Kate stared at Tara. "I didn't see you on the dance floor."

"I wasn't there. I was getting Marley another plate of fruit and dip when you scurried by," Tara explained. She pinned her with those bright eyes. "I'd assumed you were running from Bryan, but I saw Gray's face as he watched you."

Oh, no. *Damn it.* Kate didn't want to ask what emotions Tara had seen on his face, what feelings he'd been unable to mask. She honestly had no clue what he was feeling because he'd been so good at keeping that to himself since last night.

Of course, if she'd waited to hear what he had to say, maybe she'd be better in tune with what was happening in his mind.

"He stepped in and saved me from Bryan. You know how Gray is," Kate explained, smoothing down her chiffon-overlay skirt. She had to convince them there was nothing more than what was on the surface. "We just danced a few minutes until Bryan was gone. That's all."

Silence filled the room, which was good because the door opened again and an elderly lady came in. Kate didn't know her, but she'd seen her on the groom's side during the ceremony. Considering Noah wasn't from here, it would make sense that there were guests Kate didn't know.

"Would you go back out to your husband?" Kate hissed. "I'm just taking a break from those killer heels. Nothing is wrong."

Lucy took Kate's hand and squeezed. "Promise?"

"Of course." Kate nodded. "Go on."

Lucy finally got up and left. Once the other guest left as well, Kate was alone with Tara and her questioning gaze.

"What?" Kate demanded. "Can't a girl just take a break?"

"Lucy can and I can, but not you." Tara crossed her legs and leaned back in the seat. "You are always on the go, always planning the next thing, and I've never seen you relax. So what's really going on? And don't lie. I'm done with lies."

Kate swallowed a lump of guilt. Tara had been dealt too much lately, but there were just some things Kate wasn't about to share. That was not a reflection of their friendship. She'd tell her and Lucy…someday.

"Not now, okay?"

Tara's curiosity quickly turned to concern. "Promise me you'll come to us if you need anything. I know what it's like to be lost in your own thoughts and worry what to do next."

True story. Tara and Sam were going through hell all while trying to keep their daughter out of the fires.

"Same goes." Kate reached over and took her friend's hand. "Sam looked like he was doing really well."

Tara nodded. "He is. He left me a note on my windshield this morning."

How could anyone not find Sam and his handwritten notes simply heart-melting? He'd done that when they'd been married and since their split, he continued to leave her notes. Tara always mentioned them and Kate wondered what it would be like to have a man who cared that much.

The man was a hopeless romantic who'd just made some bad choices. Kate didn't blame Tara for being cautious, though. Some obstacles were just too great to overcome.

"We should get back out there." Kate came to her feet and

stared down at her heels. "If I ever get married, we're all going barefoot."

Tara laughed as she stood up. "Deal."

Kate had pushed marriage thoughts out of her head long ago when her engagement ended. The whole ordeal had left her a bit jaded, but seeing Noah and Lucy come together after they'd both experienced such devastation in their lives gave Kate hope. She wanted to marry one day, to have a husband who loved her, start a family and live in the picturesque mountains of Tennessee.

One day, she vowed. But first she was going to have to figure out how to get back on that friendship ground with Gray. Every time she thought of him now, she only remembered him tearing off her underwear and climbing up on that bar to get to her.

And her body heated all over again. She had a feeling the line they'd crossed had been erased. There was nowhere for them to go that was familiar and comfortable because they were both in unknown territory.

CHAPTER FIVE

GRAY SLID ANOTHER tray of glasses beneath the bar. For the past five days he'd gone about his business and mundane, day-to-day activities. This wasn't the first time, and wouldn't be the last, that he couldn't shake the void inside him. Something was missing, had been for quite some time, but he'd never been able to quite place it.

His father always said it was a wife and children, but Gray didn't believe that. He wasn't looking to settle down and worry about feeding a relationship. His parents had been completely in love up until his mother's death when Gray had been five. He'd seen how the loss had affected his father, seen how the man had mourned for decades. Gray didn't want to subject himself to that type of pain.

Besides, he'd never found anyone who would make him even think about marriage.

He'd been hand-delivered this bar when he'd come home from the army, just like his father before him. Gray's grandfather, Ewan Gallagher, had opened the doors when he'd retired from the army after World War II. Right after that, he'd married the love of his life and started a family. Same with Gray's father, Reece.

They'd both had a plan and been the happiest men Gray had

ever known. Not that Gray wasn't happy. He knew how fortunate he was to have served his country and come home to a business with deep familial roots and heritage. Some men never came home, and some guys who did weren't even close to the men they'd been before they were deployed.

But beyond all of that, something inside him felt empty. The void that accompanied him every single day had settled in deep and he had no clue how to rid himself of it.

Gray pushed those thoughts aside and headed to the back office. He needed to get his payroll done before they opened this afternoon.

He sank into his worn leather office chair and blew out a sigh. He couldn't even lie to himself. It wasn't just the monotonous life he led that had him in a pissy mood. He hadn't seen Kate once since she'd deserted him on the dance floor.

They'd texted a few times, but only about safe topics.

Safe. That word summed up Kate. She did things by the book. Hell, the book she carried with her was like her lifeline to the world. She always had a plan, excelled at making her life organized and perfect.

Gray was anything but organized and perfect. He ran a bar. Things got messy and out of control at times. He'd obliterated her perfect little world when he'd taken their relationship to an entirely unsafe level.

Still, he was going to let her hide for only so long.

"Hello?"

Gray stilled at the unfamiliar voice coming from the front of the bar. He came to his feet and rounded his desk. He always left the doors unlocked while he was here working. Stonerock was a small town where everybody knew everybody. Crime was low and people usually respected his bar's hours.

Sometimes his buddy Sam would stop in during the day to talk or just to unwind. After all that man had been through, Gray wasn't about to lock him out. Sam needed support now more than ever and if he was here, at least Gray could keep an eye on him and be part of that support team.

"Anyone here?"

Definitely not Sam. Gray had no idea who'd decided to waltz right into his bar in the middle of the morning.

He stepped from the back hall and came to stand behind the bar. The man who stood in the middle of Gray's restaurant clearly had the wrong address. Nobody came in here wearing a three-piece suit and carrying a briefcase. Who the hell even owned a suit like that? Nobody in Stonerock, that was for damn sure.

Gray flattened his palms on the bar top. "Can I help you?"

The stranger offered a toothy smile and crossed the space to the bar...third stool from the left. Now his favorite place in the entire building.

"You the owner?"

Gray nodded. People came in looking for donations for schools, ball teams, charity events...but Gray couldn't pinpoint exactly what this guy was nosing around about.

"My name is Preston Anderson. I'm from Knoxville."

Preston Anderson sounded exactly like the type of man who'd own a suit as confining and stiff as this one. Gray eyed the man's extended hand and ultimately gave it a quick shake.

"I have enough staff," Gray replied. "But the bank might be hiring."

The guy laughed and propped his briefcase on a bar stool. "I'm here to see you. I assume you're Gray Gallagher."

"You would assume correctly."

He pulled a business card from his pocket and placed it on the bar. Gray didn't even give it a glance, let alone touch it.

"My partner and I are looking to buy a number of properties here in Stonerock and doing some minor revamping of the town."

Gray crossed his arms over his chest. "Is that so?"

"We'd like to make it a mini-Nashville, if you will. The area is perfect for day tourists to pop over to get away from the city, but still have a city feel."

Pulling in a breath, Gray eyed the business card, then glanced back to Preston. "And you want to buy my bar."

Preston nodded. "We'll make it more than worth your while."

He took a pen from inside his jacket pocket, flipped the card over, and wrote a number. Using his fingertip, he slid the card across the bar. Again, Gray didn't pick it up, but he did eye the number and it took every ounce of his resolve to not react. There was a hell of a lot of numbers after that dollar sign.

"You really want this bar," Gray replied.

Preston nodded. "We're eager to dive into this venture. We'd like to have firm answers within a month and finalize the sales within thirty days after that. All cash. Our goal is to have all of our properties up and running before fall for when the tourists come to the mountains for getaways."

Gray had never thought of selling this place before, and now he had a month to make a decision. His initial reaction was hell no. This was his family's legacy, what his grandfather had dreamed of.

But reality kicked in, too. That void he'd been feeling? He still didn't know what was causing it, but all of those zeroes would go a long way in helping him find what was missing... or at least pass the time until he could figure out what the hell he wanted to be when he grew up.

Gray never had a set goal in mind. He'd done what was expected and never questioned it. But more and more lately he wondered if this was really where he was supposed to be. And if it was, then why did he still feel like something was lacking?

Preston went on to explain they'd still keep the establishment a bar, but it would be modernized for the crowds they were hoping to bring in. Gray had no idea what to say, so he merely nodded and listened.

The figure on the untouched card between them spoke more than anything Preston could've said.

"So, think about it," Preston stated, picking up his briefcase. "My number is on the card if you have any questions. This isn't an opportunity that will present itself again, Mr. Gallagher."

"I imagine not," Gray muttered.

Preston let himself out the front door, leaving Gray to process everything that had happened over the past ten minutes. He reached for the card, turning it from front to back.

What the hell did he do with this proposal? True, he'd never actually wanted the bar, but it was his. And while he may have wanted to pursue other things in his life, there were some loyalties that came with keeping up tradition. Gray would never purposely go against his family.

Family was absolutely everything to him. His father never remarried, so Gray and his dad had been a team. Then Gray's grandfather had passed only a few years ago, leaving Gray and his father once again reeling from loss.

Now that they were all each other had, this business deal wasn't going to be something easy to say yes or no to. This was definitely a decision he needed to discuss with his father. But Gray wanted to weigh his options and have some idea of what he wanted before that discussion took place.

Gray already knew where his father would stand on this from a sentimental standpoint, but his father also didn't know that Gray hadn't been happy for a while now.

Ultimately, the final decision would belong to Gray.

There was one other person he wanted to talk to. One other person who'd been his voice of reason since junior high, when she talked him out of beating the hell out of some new jock who had mouthed off one too many times.

Sliding Preston's card into the pocket of his jeans, Gray went back to working on the payroll. Kate had one more day to come to him…and then he was going to her.

Kate's color-coded binder lay open to the red section. The red section was reserved for her most important clients. Not that all of them weren't important, but some needed more attention than others.

Mrs. Clements was by far her best client. That woman wanted help with everything from organizing her daughter's bridal shower to setting up her new home office. Kate also had a standing seasonal job with the middle-aged lady when it was time to change out her closets for the weather.

Kate stared at the time on her phone. It was nearly two in the morning, but she wasn't the slightest bit tired. This plan for Mrs. Clements wasn't due for nineteen days, but Kate wanted it to be perfect before she presented it to her.

Pulling her green fine-tip marker from the matching green pouch, Kate started jotting down possible strategies. The definite plans were always in blue and those were already completed and in the folder.

Kate tapped on her phone to fire up her music playlist before she started compiling a list of possible caterers.

The knock on her door had Kate jumping in her seat. She jerked around and waited. Who would be knocking on her door in the middle of the night? Probably some crazy teenagers out pulling pranks. But the knock sounded again, more determined than just a random tap.

She contemplated ignoring the unwanted guest, but figured murderers didn't go around knocking on doors. Plus, this was Stonerock. She knew the entire police force. She could have anyone over here in a flash if something was wrong.

Kate paused her music and carried her phone to the door in case she needed to call upon one of those said officers. Of course Noah was still on his honeymoon with Lucy, so he wasn't an option.

As she padded through the hall, Kate tipped her head slightly to glance out the sidelight. Her heart kicked up. Gray. She knew it was only a matter of time, but she certainly didn't expect him in the middle of the night.

This man…always keeping her guessing and on her toes.

Blowing out a breath, Kate set her phone on the accent table by the door. She flicked the dead bolt and turned the knob.

Without waiting for her to invite him in, Gray pulled open the screen door and stepped inside.

"Won't you come in," she muttered.

"Considering I rarely knock anyway, I figured you wouldn't mind."

She closed the door, locking it before she turned to face him. "And what on earth do you possibly need at this time of the night?"

"You weren't asleep. I saw your lights on."

No, she wasn't asleep, and he'd just come from the bar. His black T-shirt with the bar logo on his left pec stretched tightly across his broad shoulders. She could never look at those shoulders the same way again, not after clutching them the other night as he'd given her the most intensely satisfying experience of her life.

Suddenly the foyer in her townhome seemed too small. She couldn't be this close to Gray, not with those memories replaying through her head. The memories that made her question everything and want more than she should.

Clearing her throat, Kate turned and headed to the back of the house, where she'd turned a spare bedroom into her home office.

Gray fell in step behind her. She went back to her cushy chair at her corner desk and spun around to see Gray fold his frame onto the delicate yellow sofa she'd found at a yard sale a couple of years ago.

"Why am I not surprised you're working?" he asked, nodding toward the organized piles on her desk.

"I couldn't sleep."

"There's a surefire remedy for that."

Kate stared at him for a moment before she rolled her eyes. "Did you seriously come here thinking we'd have sex again?"

Gray quirked one dark brow. He stretched his long, denim-clad legs out in front of him and crossed his ankles. He placed one tattooed arm on the armrest. Gray was clearly comfortable with this topic based on the way he looked at her, taking in her thin tank and ratty old shorts.

His gaze was anything but friendly. Well, it was friendly in the sense that he looked like he wanted to strip her out of her clothes again.

Wait. He'd never gotten her out of her clothes the first time. Perhaps that's why he was staring so intently. But he'd seen her in a bathing suit and he'd most definitely seen her lower half.

Boobs. Men always wanted boobs. It was a ridiculous thing she would never understand. Still, he continued to stare across the office as if he knew exactly what she looked like in her birthday suit.

Had he always been this intense? This potent?

Kate shivered and tucked one leg beneath her. "Why did you really stop by?"

"I missed you."

The way those words settled between them had Kate's breath catching in her throat. He said them so simply, as if the question were silly and it should be obvious why he was here.

They hadn't gone this long without seeing each other since he'd served in the army. She appreciated how he put himself out there and used complete and utter honesty.

Another reason why he was her everything. Gray never sugarcoated anything and had always been up front with her. Considering her ex had been so deceitful, having Gray in her life was refreshing and made her realize there were good men out there. This good man, however, just couldn't be for her.

"I missed you, too," she replied, because she wanted to be just as honest right back. "I've been busy with the Savvy Scheduler, the blogs and the scheduling for upcoming giveaways, and then getting ready for the next Helping Hands meeting. With Lucy gone—"

"You're hiding from me."

She really was getting ready for the next meeting. Kate, Tara and Lucy all led a weekly support group that helped to uplift those hurting from loss. They'd all experienced it themselves on some level, so it was a labor of love.

But perhaps she was using her work and the group to hide from Gray. Still, she'd always made time for him before and he'd never pushed her away. Not once.

Fine. So maybe she wasn't being totally honest with him, but how could she be when she was trying to fumble around with her own emotions and figure it all out herself?

Kate glanced down to her lap and stared at her pale pink polish. "I don't know what to do now."

Silence settled in the room. She had no clue what he was thinking, no clue how to get them back on the comfortable ground they'd been walking on for years. How could one moment undo years of friendship? How did sex muddle so much?

When the awkward tension became unbearable, Kate turned slightly and started straightening her desk. There had never been awkwardness between them and she desperately needed to rid this moment of it. She needed her Gray back—her best friend back.

She glanced at the outline for her next week and mentally tried to prepare herself and focus. At least this was something she could control, because she sure as hell couldn't control her feelings—not now that he was in her house and staring at her as if he wanted an encore bar performance.

No. No more sex—at least not with him. She shouldn't pay attention to her body when it started getting all revved up again at just the sight of Gray. She shouldn't keep remembering how he'd felt as he'd joined their bodies. And she sure as hell shouldn't keep wondering if there was any man who could measure up to him.

"We do what we've always done, Kate."

She shivered as his soft words pierced the silence and washed over her. Leave it to him to find a simple resolution to their tension. Maybe he didn't have the juxtaposition of feelings running through him like she did. Maybe he slept just fine at night and hadn't given her or their encounter another thought.

Kate slid the green marker back into the pouch, set Mrs. Clements's folder in her desk organizer labeled Things to Do, and worked the corners of the rest of the folders until they were perfectly lined up. Now what? There was nothing else to straighten or fiddle with.

"Look at me."

Oh, that low, sultry tone. Now that they'd been intimate, she could appreciate it so much more.

Kate gritted her teeth and spun around in her chair. That piercing stare had her gripping the edge of her chair. Anticipation curled low in her belly at what he would say or do next. She'd never been on the edge of her seat with him before.

Honestly, sex changed everything. Hadn't she warned herself about that in the few moments between the kiss and the torn underwear? But her hormones had taken over and Gray had been all too convincing...and she was human.

"We're still Gray and Kate," he reminded her, pinning her with that dark gaze. "We annoy each other for fun. We watch old movies and argue over the classics. I still worry you're going to choose another loser, so I'm extra cautious and overprotective. Yes, we had sex, but we're still us."

He made things sound so simple and easy, as if sex hadn't changed a thing. But it had changed everything. She found herself looking at him differently, seeing him in a completely different light. Because for a short time he'd been not only her best friend, but also her lover.

"That's why you came?" she asked.

"You didn't think I'd let you hide forever, did you?"

Kate smiled. "I would've been at Ladies' Night this week."

That side grin flashed over his face. "You missed last week, so I wasn't sure."

Kate picked at one of the threads on the edge of her shorts. "I just needed some space."

"Had enough?"

She chewed the inside of her cheek. "Maybe."

Gray came to his feet and crossed to her. He took her hands and pulled her up against him. Kate tipped her head back to look him directly in the eyes. A punch of lust hit her faster than she'd expected. She'd hoped that need, that ache, had vanished or had been all in her mind. But no. Gray had crossed the line and had settled deep into a place inside her. And she had no clue how to categorize him.

"You're done hiding or running, or whatever the hell else you were doing." He flashed her that devilish grin. "I need you, Kate. We've been together too long to let anything come between our friendship. Can we just get back there again?"

Something akin to relief slid through her at how easily he was putting them both back on stable ground. At the same time, though, she hated that they were going back to being just friends.

How could she just ignore how she felt now that he was this close? How could she forget how he'd kissed her? How he'd looked at her, touched her?

She couldn't forget. Gray had imbedded himself so far into her soul, she truly wasn't sure she could go back. She wasn't even entirely sure she wanted to.

"We are friends," she agreed. "You have to admit this is a bit awkward."

Gray laughed. "So stop making it awkward."

He pulled her into a hug just like he'd done for years. Only this time she couldn't prevent herself from pulling in a deep breath of that masculine scent, remembering how she'd been completely enveloped by that familiar aroma and the man. His potency had been all-consuming when he'd ripped off her panties and taken her on that bar top. Would she ever get that image, that *feeling* from her mind?

"You in a hurry to get home?" she asked into his chest.

"Not really."

Kate tipped her head back and smiled. "How about a movie?"

Gray kissed her forehead. "Perfect."

CHAPTER SIX

"TELL ME ABOUT this list."

Kate stopped tapping her toes on the side of his thigh. He sat on one end of the sofa and she had relaxed on the other, stretching those legs out, propping her dainty feet against his denim-clad thigh, and driving him out of his ever-loving mind.

Gray had known facing her would be difficult. Of course they'd seen each other at the wedding, but this was the first time they'd been alone and forced to really discuss what had happened at the bar. The tension still hovered between them, but he was going to push through because as much as he wanted her physically, he refused to lose her altogether.

Other than the obvious fact she'd been dodging him, he knew she was panicking about where they were now. He knew she'd be trying to analyze things from every which angle and she wouldn't be able to. He'd wanted her for a while, longer than he probably wanted to admit even to himself, so there was no way she could decipher what the hell truly happened when he couldn't explain it himself.

For years, he'd been able to control himself out of respect for her and their friendship. Then, over the past several months, little by little, seeing her at the bar dancing with other guys, then at the rehearsal with Bryan, it had all just become too much and he'd snapped. Every man had a breaking point and she'd definitely hit his.

"It's nothing," she finally replied.

He curled his hand around her bare toes. "Tell me about the infamous list or I'll crack your toes."

Kate's legs jerked from his lap as she laughed. "Watch the movie and leave me alone."

"We've seen this at least a hundred times," he told her as he shifted on the couch to face her. He grabbed the remote from the back of the couch and muted the TV before tossing the device between them on the cushion. "Talk to me, Kate. You can't hide it forever. I'm going to get the truth out of you, you know."

She let out a sigh and shook her head. "Fine."

When she started to get up, Gray reached out and gripped her arm. "You don't have to go get some color-coded spreadsheet that no doubt you've laminated. Just tell me. I want to hear your words, not read some damn paper."

Kate smiled as she settled onto the couch. She swung her legs back up and he instantly started rubbing her feet. Maybe if she was relaxed she'd talk, and if she was talking about this mystery list, then perhaps he would focus on that and not the fact that he wanted his best friend now more than ever.

There was still the matter of discussing the business proposition with her, but right now there were much more important things to work out. It was just another area of his life he was confused as hell about. Once he talked to Kate and his father, he'd have a clearer picture of the future...he hoped.

"Tell me why you made a list," he started, needing to reel himself in from his wayward thoughts.

Kate adjusted the throw pillow between her head and the arm of the couch. Tipping her head sideways, she stared down at him. "My thirtieth birthday just passed."

"Yes, I'm aware of that." His thumb slid up over the arch of her foot. "So, what? You think you're old now that you're thirty? I'm thirty-one. We're barely getting started."

She smiled, which is exactly the response he wanted. He loved seeing that smile, loved knowing he could get such a quick, heartfelt reaction from her.

Lacing her hands over her abdomen, Kate blew out a deep sigh. "I don't think we're old. My mom was only thirty-two when she died, which was way too young. I just… I don't know. I guess I've been thinking too much over the past year. My mom probably thought she had her whole life ahead of her with raising me. Maybe she even wanted more kids. I have no clue. All I know is I don't want to lose out on anything because I was too busy working or assumed I had more time."

Gray's hands stilled. Her words hit hard. She was absolutely right. What if he kept up his day-to-day life, wondering what else was out there, what he was missing out on? Life was fleeting and nothing was guaranteed.

Should he take that business deal? Should he accept the money and sell Gallagher's, finally moving on to fill that void? The possibilities for him would be endless and the money would allow him to fully explore his options.

But at what cost? Disappointment from his father and the unknown of what he'd do next or if he would even stay in Stonerock. The risk from either decision weighed heavily on him.

"You okay?" Kate asked, pulling him away from his thoughts.

"Fine." He switched to her other foot and circled back to her needs. He wasn't quite ready to express his own just yet. "Tell me what you've put on the list."

"You'll think I'm silly."

"We've already established I live for silly."

Kate rolled her eyes and laughed—music to his ears. "Well, I'd like to go camping."

Gray couldn't help but laugh. "Camping? What in the world brought that up?"

"I don't know. It's just something I haven't done." She stretched her legs and rotated her ankles before dropping them back to his lap. "I live in the mountains, for crying out loud, and I've never been camping."

"So you made a bucket list?"

She nodded. "I titled it My Life List."

"Of course you gave it a title. What else is on there?" he asked, resting his hands on her legs.

"I'd like to get a dog and name her Sprout. A kennel dog or a stray. I can't handle the thought of all those abandoned animals while people are paying for novelty pets. It's heartbreaking. So I'll start with one dog. Who knows how many I'll end up with."

Someone as passionate and caring as Kate would want to help the less fortunate. Just another aspect he'd always admired about her. She was always looking at how to spread her light, even when she didn't always shine it on herself.

Kate kept her eyes on his as she discussed the items from her list. "I want to go to the beach since I've never seen the ocean. I'd love to throw a *Great Gatsby*–themed party and dress up and have fun all night. I think I'd like to go on a road trip. Of course I'd have to have it mapped out, but I want to just take off in the car and visit some national landmarks. Once I get closer to checking that one off the list, I'll make a spreadsheet."

As he listened to her, Gray realized her goals were all so obtainable and there was no reason she couldn't do those things.

"I wanted to try alcohol, so that box is already ticked off," she added.

"In bright blue marker, I'm sure."

She reached up to swat his shoulder. "No, smarty-pants. Yellow is clearly the only choice."

Gray couldn't help but laugh. Kate took her feet from his lap and crisscrossed them in front of her on the cushion.

"So what else do you have?" he asked.

"I want to do something utterly spontaneous."

Gray stared at her, waiting for her to smile or give some hint that she was kidding. But she merely stared at him, completely serious.

"Darlin', you do realize you're missing the whole point of being spontaneous if you put it on a list and schedule it."

She toyed with the frayed ends of her shorts. Gray couldn't help but watch her movements, tormenting himself further as he stared at the white threads lying against her tanned skin. He wanted to run his hands up those shapely legs. He wanted to strip her and have her right here on this couch.

Being together in the middle of the night with nothing around to interrupt them was probably not the smartest idea, but he couldn't bring himself to leave. He was dead-tired now, but she was talking. They were getting back to a place of comfort and familiarity. And she wasn't trying to make excuses for the mistake they'd made.

Only having sex hadn't been a mistake. It had been perfect and he was hell-bent on making sure it happened again. But above all, he didn't want her to worry about the future of their relationship. He'd never let anything—including his all-consuming desire for her—jeopardize that, because he needed her just as much.

While he respected her stipulation that their one night of passion stay just that, he wasn't going to let her ignore the attraction. If the opportunity arose again, if she gave the slightest hint she wanted more, he'd be all over it…and her.

"Well, I don't know what the spontaneous moment will be," she explained. "So it's not completely ridiculous that I listed it. I just want to try to be more… I don't know. Like you. You're so laid-back and carefree. I don't even know what that would feel like. But it's a short-term goal."

He wasn't going to state the obvious of the spontaneity on the bar. She'd probably already labeled that under something else.

"If you say so," he chuckled. "Anything else on the list?"

"Well…"

She was driving him crazy. "What? You want to jump out of a plane? See the Mayan ruins? Take an Alaskan cruise? Just spit it out."

"Jump out of a plane?" She jerked back. "First of all, I wouldn't pick something so predictable, and second of all, hell no."

Gray laughed and curled his hands over her toes. "Tell me or I start cracking."

"I want to trace my heritage."

Intrigued at her statement, he relaxed his hands and stared over at her. "Seriously?"

Kate nodded and tipped her head to the side, resting on the back of the couch. "With my parents gone, I just want to know where I came from, you know? I don't have any other family and I was just a teen when they passed. It's not something I ever thought of asking them about."

Gray had never thought of that before. His grandfather had died only two years ago, but his father was alive and well and more than willing to pass down the family stories that could trace all the way back to their roots in Ireland. Kate didn't have anything like that.

While Gray had lost his mother at a young age and always had that hole in his heart, he couldn't imagine how Kate felt, essentially alone other than having friends. But that wasn't the same as family. Nothing could ever replace parents.

She'd lived with her grandmother for a while, but ultimately she passed, too. Thankfully Kate was older when that happened.

"I want to know where I got the combination of black hair and blue eyes," she went on with a slight smile. "It's a little silly, I know, but I guess I just feel like I need those answers. Maybe I have family out there and a long-distance relative I can connect with."

Gray hated that lost tone. She'd never mentioned feeling alone before. She'd never talked like she was hurting. At least, she hadn't said as much to him. Of course, she suffered from her parents' absence. That was something she'd never get over. But he really had no idea she'd been longing to find out where she came from. Kate should have every opportunity to trace her family roots. He'd make damn sure of it.

As she went through her list, he realized that he wanted to be the one to experience those things with her. They were best friends. Yes, she had Tara and Lucy, but Lucy was newly married and Tara was still struggling with Sam and their own sordid mess.

Gray wasn't going to let Kate feel alone any longer. Hell, he'd already helped her knock trying alcohol off her list. The rest would be a joy to share with her.

"We'll do this together," he told her.

Bright blue eyes snapped up, focusing on him. "Don't be ridiculous. I wasn't hinting that I needed a partner. I wasn't going to tell anyone about this list. It's just something I'm doing for me."

"I don't plan on telling anyone," he replied. "Keep all the secrets about it you want, but I'm not going to let you do this alone."

Kate stared at him another minute before swinging her feet to the floor. She grabbed the remote and turned the television off, then put it back on the table.

"I really should get to bed." She stretched her arms above her head, giving him a glimpse of pale skin between her tank and her shorts. "I think I'm finally tired."

Yeah, well, he wasn't. Well, he was tired in the sense that he needed sleep, but he didn't want to leave. He could sit here all night and talk with her like they had when they were younger, with fewer responsibilities. Besides, she couldn't brush him off that easily. She was running scared again. He'd offered to help and she flipped out, jumping off the couch to get away from his touch. How could she choose this over intimacy?

If they just went with the sexual pull, the undeniable attraction, it would have to be less stressful than what was brewing between them now. How could she not see that? Was she simply too afraid to face the truth?

An idea formed in his head, but he kept the piece of brilliance locked away as he came to his feet. He knew she was tired, so he'd go. But he was done letting her hide behind her fear of the unknown and what was happening here.

"You look like you're ready to drop."

Gray took in her sleepy eyes, her relaxed clothing, and there was nothing more he wanted to do than to pick her up and carry her to bed...and stay the rest of the night. Maybe he would one day. Maybe she'd realize that the one time wasn't enough and she wanted more.

He had every intention of respecting her wishes to stay in the friend zone—but that didn't mean he wouldn't keep showing her how perfect they were together. There was nothing wrong with exploring what they'd started. Besides, he knew Kate better than she knew herself at times. She had analyzed that night from every different angle and their intimacy was never far from the front of her mind. He'd bet his bar on it.

Said bar might not be his for much longer, though. But she wasn't in the right mind-set to discuss the potential sale now, and honestly, neither was he. Tomorrow, he vowed. There was too much at stake no matter which way he decided to go. Both choices were life-altering and would change not only his entire world, but that of his father and the town.

Gallagher's had been the pride of three generations now. His grandfather had wanted to set down roots, to have something that brought people together, because he'd seen so much ugliness tearing them apart. Ewan Gallagher had started a tradition, one that the people in this tiny town had come to appreciate and rely upon.

Gray didn't want that niggle of doubt and guilt to sway his decision. He wanted to look at this from a business and personal standpoint, but it was so difficult when the two were so inherently connected.

He dropped an innocent kiss on Kate's forehead and let himself out the front door. Gray waited until he heard her click the lock back into place before he headed to his car.

He knew he needed to grab sleep, but as soon as he got up, he was putting a few plans into motion. Kate was about to check off more items on her bucket list and he was personally going to see that she accomplished exactly what she set out to do.

Morning runs sucked. They sucked even more when little sleep was a factor and really all she'd wanted was to run to the bakery and buy a donut the size of her face. And by run, she meant drive.

Kate took a hearty chug from her water bottle as she pulled her key from the tiny pouch on her running shorts. She'd ended up falling asleep on the couch after Gray left, then stumbled to her room at about six and climbed into bed. When she'd woken up for good at nine, Kate realized she'd slept later than usual, so she'd hopped out of bed and quickly headed out the door to get in her miles.

She hated running. But that was the only way she could enjoy her donuts and still fit in her clothes. Besides, the exercise was a great stress reliever...so were pastries, but whatever.

As Kate opened her front door, she heard a vehicle pulling into her drive. Kate glanced over her shoulder, her heart skipping a beat at the sight of Gray's large black truck. The thing was as menacing as the man himself. He might look like the quintessential bad boy, but he'd listened to her drone on and on about her bucket list all while rubbing her feet.

Damn it. Why did he have to be her best friend? He was the perfect catch for any woman...just not her. She couldn't—no, she *wouldn't*—risk losing him as a friend. If she'd jumped at her initial reaction after the great sex and ignored common sense altogether, she might have made a play for him. But he was the only stable man in her life. He'd filled that role for far too long for her to just throw it aside and take the risk for something more.

Even if she went for more, what would it be? Gray wasn't the type to settle down. In fact, she knew his father mentioned Gray's bachelor status quite often and Gray brushed the notion aside. He seemed just fine keeping busy with his bar. The man rarely dated and even when he did, he kept it all so private. He was definitely not someone looking for happily-ever-after.

Kate took another drink as she waited on the porch for Gray to come up her flower-lined walk.

"Didn't you just leave here?" she joked.

He glanced up, flashing that megawatt smile he didn't always hand out freely. Mercy, the man was too sexy for his own good, and now that she'd had a sample of that sexiness, she was positive no other man would ever measure up.

How did one encounter have such an epic impact? Kate had to push aside what happened. It couldn't have been that great… could it? Surely she was just conjuring up more vivid details than actually happened.

Or maybe not. Gray did in fact tear her panties off and climb up the bar to get to her.

"I feel like I did," he replied as he mounted the steps. "You're sweating."

Kate rolled her eyes. "That happens when I go for a run."

"Well, you have ten minutes to get a bag together." He hooked his thumbs through his belt loops. "And if you want to shower, you better squeeze it in that time frame."

Kate jerked back. "Excuse me? Pack a bag?"

A mischievous smile spread across his face. "We're going camping."

"What?" Shocked, she turned and let herself in her house, trying to wrap her mind around his announcement. "I can't just go camping right now. I have things to do."

Her planner lay on the table just inside the door. She fingered through the colored tabs until she landed on the red. Flipping it over, she quickly glanced at her mounting list—color-coded with her favorite fine-point markers, of course.

"You can see there's no time," she stated as Gray followed her in. She used the tip of her finger to tap on the upcoming days. "I have to finish outlining a bridal shower and start on a new client's vacation schedule. Then I have to try to come up with some way to fit in my neighbor, who swears her closets are full but won't get rid of anything. Same story with her kitchen, so at this point I'm afraid her entire house needs an overhaul. I also have eight online clients I'm working with who found me just last week through my social media sites and referrals."

"And do you plan on doing all of that today?" he asked, crossing his arms and leaning against the wall beside her.

"Well, no, but—"

"You're down to eight minutes, Kate. If you hurry, I can even swing by and get a box of donuts on our way out of town so we can have breakfast in the morning."

"That's a low blow," she stated, narrowing her eyes.

"You need a break."

She slapped her planner shut and faced him. "I can't go camping last minute. I'd need sufficient time to strategize and make a detailed list of all the things I need to take. Hell, I need to research *what* to take. I've never been, so I have no clue."

That smile assaulted her once again. Damn cocky man.

"You're in luck," he replied. "I have been multiple times so I have everything you need, minus your clothes and the donuts I'll stop and get on the road. Look at it this way—you can check off two things on your list. Camping and spontaneity."

Kate shook her head and sighed. "I can't mark off being spontaneous when it was your idea."

And she still hadn't marked it in regards to the bar sex. That needed a whole other label of its own. How could something so life-altering be checked off so simply? No, that encounter deserved more respect than just a quick X by the words spontaneous quickie.

Gray pushed off the wall and started for the steps. "You'll want a pair of jeans for when we go hiking, plus shorts, maybe a swimsuit, comfortable shoes that can get wet. It gets cooler at night so grab a sweatshirt or something with sleeves."

Kate watched as he just headed up to her bedroom like she

hadn't just laid out several reasons she couldn't go. Did the man ever take no for an answer?

Her mind flashed back to the bar as her body trembled with the onslaught of memories.

So no. No, he didn't.

And here she was, contemplating going camping? Being alone with him all night and not invoking how she felt when he'd touched her, kissed her. This was not smart. Not smart at all.

Kate headed for the steps, rushing up to her bedroom.

"You're not getting out of this," he told her before she could open her mouth.

He opened her closet and jerked a sweatshirt off the top shelf. Two more shirts fell to the floor as a result and Kate cringed.

"You're messing up my system here, Gallagher." She crossed over and instantly started sorting the mess back into neat piles. "You cannot just start packing my bag."

He shot her a wink. "Does that mean you're cuddling up to me for warmth and skinny dipping? Hey, I'm game, but you might be more comfortable with clothes."

Kate blew out a breath and leaned back against her open closet door. "You're not going to let this go, are you?"

"Nope." He took a step closer to her, his eyes all serious now. Gone was the playful smile. "Listen, if I didn't push you into this, I'm not sure you'd actually do it. Making a list is one thing, but following through is another."

"I would do it," She felt the need to defend herself because, damn it, she would do it...at some point. "I don't know when, but I would."

He tossed the sweatshirt behind him onto her four-poster bed, then took her by her shoulders. "My truck is packed. I literally have everything we need: a large tent, food, supplies, blankets. I got Jacob to cover at the bar for me tonight. We'll be back late tomorrow evening."

Kate stared into those dark eyes and knew if anyone could help her check items off her list, it was this man. He'd clearly gone to great lengths to set this up for her and she'd be a terrible friend, not to mention flat-out rude, to turn him down.

He'd literally thought of everything and he stood before her, having rearranged his entire life for two days just to make her happy.

Kate's heart flipped in her chest. Gray always did amazing things for her, but since the sex, his actions had taken on a deeper, more intimate meaning.

"Fine," she conceded. "But step away from my neatly organized closet and let me pack. I don't trust you over there and I promise I won't be long. You swear we're stopping for donuts?"

"I promise." Gray leaned forward and wrinkled his nose. "I'll give you an extra five minutes to shower. You smell."

Laughing, Kate smacked his arm. "Get out of my room. I'll be down in twenty minutes."

Once he was gone, Kate closed her bedroom door and started stripping on her way to the shower. She dropped her clothes into the color-coded piles in her laundry sorter just inside her bathroom.

Gray Gallagher was slowly making her reconsider that whole one-night rule. For a half second she thought about packing some pretty underwear, but then snorted.

Seriously? Even if she was after an encore performance, they were camping. She'd never been, but she had a feeling lace and satin didn't pair well with bug spray and campfire smoke.

Kate stepped under the hot shower and mentally started packing. No matter how this trip went down, she had a feeling lasting memories would be made.

CHAPTER SEVEN

"I DID IT," Kate exclaimed, jumping up and down.

Gray glanced over to the tent she'd put together. He'd set everything out and given her instructions, and damn if she hadn't erected their tent like a pro. He knew she wouldn't give up, but she'd definitely gotten it done much quicker than he thought she would. He was proud of her.

This was by far his favorite campground, but the spot he usually chose had already been taken and he'd had to choose another. He found one closest to a hiking trail near his favorite areas in the forest. He couldn't wait to share all of these experiences with Kate.

"Looks good." Gray came to his feet and wiped his hands on his pants. "The fire is ready if you want to roast some hot dogs for lunch."

"I don't recall the last time I had a roasted hot dog."

Gray rolled over another large log and stood it up on its end as a makeshift stool. He'd found several near the designated fire area, but set up only the two.

"We had one at the bonfire last fall," he said. "Remember the fundraiser for Drake?"

Drake St. John had been a firefighter who had encountered several issues with the then mayor. Drake had decided to run for office himself and ultimately won. Drake and his brothers were pillars in the community and Gray had happily voted for him.

"Oh, yeah." Kate picked up one of the roasting sticks and held it out for him to put the hot dog on. "So I guess that was the last time I had one."

"Then you're long overdue," he replied, getting his own roasting stick ready.

The crackling fire kept his focus on cooking his lunch.... and away from the swell of her breasts peeking from the top of her fitted tank. He had no business going there. This was about Kate. He wanted this to be an easy trip, something where she could relax and just be herself, take a break from work and all those damn schedules. He was here to make sure she was taken care of, first and foremost.

Silence settled easily between them, but so much swirled through Gray's mind. Kate, their turning point, the bar, the possibilities...the unknowns came at him from every single angle.

He still hadn't spoken to his father about the proposal. There were pros and cons that Gray could easily see now, but there was no clear answer.

"I jotted down some things for us to do," Kate said after a minute. "I looked on my phone for area suggestions while you were driving and made a list—"

"I saw you. You just had to bring your planner, didn't you?"

Kate gasped and stared at him as if he'd just asked if the sky was purple. "Of course I had to bring it. How else would I know what to do? I can't keep all these places and a timeline of when to visit them straight without writing them down."

Shaking his head, Gray rotated the stick. "You can relax for a day, damn it. I've got the trip planned and details covered. We'll be fine. Chill."

"I'm relaxed," she argued. "Look at me. Cooking a hot dog over a fire, sitting on a tree stump, completely relaxed."

"Where's the planner?"

She pursed her lips and shrugged.

"It's beside you, isn't it?"

Kate blinked. "I don't know what you're talking about."

Gray pulled his charred hot dog from the fire and tested it with his fingers. Black and crispy on the outside, just the way he liked it.

"What would you do if you didn't have that colorful binder?"

"I'd be lost. This is my personal one. But I need both personal and business or I'd never be able to function."

He threw her a sideways glance. "You've got to be kidding."

Kate came to her feet and pulled her hot dog from the fire. "Why is that so strange? I have too much to remember so I just keep it all nice and neat in my planner."

"But that's just your personal one," he stated. "You still have one for work."

Gray pulled the pack of buns out and set them on the old picnic table before grabbing bottles of water from the cooler.

"This is supposed to be a nice, calm overnight trip," he reminded her. "We don't need an itinerary."

She took a seat on one of the benches and grabbed a bun. "I need a plan or I'm going to miss out on things. So, like I was saying—"

"You've got me." Gray threw a leg over the bench and took a seat. "I have plans for us so put your planner in my truck and forget about it until we start to head home."

Kate's eyes widened. "You're joking."

He stared across the table. "Do I look like I'm joking?"

"I don't like camping already," she muttered around a bite.

Gray couldn't help but smile. He was going to get her to relax if it was the last thing he did.

"After we eat there's a little place I want to show you."

"What do I need to wear?"

"You're fine the way you are."

She'd come down the stairs at her house freshly showered. Her hair had been pulled up on top of her head in some wet bun thing she sometimes wore. She'd thrown on a tank that fit her curvy body perfectly, and her shorts showed off those legs she kept toned and shapely by her constant running. Though she'd looked perfectly fine before she'd taken up that hobby. She'd started running after her jerk fiancé left. Gray never did figure out if she was using the exercise as a natural form of therapy or if she thought something was wrong with her body.

Kate was pretty damn perfect no matter her look or her shape…at least in his eyes.

They finished their lunch and cleaned up, making sure to burn what they could before putting the food back in a sealed cooler to keep the hungry animals away.

"We've got things to do that do not involve spreadsheets or strict schedules," he informed her. "I'll wait while you put your planner and cell in my truck."

Kate hesitated, but he quirked his brow and crossed his arms. Groaning, she picked up her things and put them in the cab of his truck before coming back beside him.

"Happy now?"

Gray nodded and turned to head toward the marked trail. He wasn't sure if this camping idea was the greatest or dumbest move he'd ever made. On one hand, at least he was getting her out of her scheduled shell and she was checking things off her list.

On the other, though, they would be sharing a tent. Which wouldn't be a big deal if they hadn't already slept together. He'd warned her not to make things awkward between them, so he needed to take his own advice.

Still, anticipation had settled in deep because he had no idea how the night would play out once they were alone lying mere inches from each other.

"How far are we going?" she asked from behind him.

"About a mile."

She came up beside him. "I could've skipped my run this morning."

"You could skip it every morning and be just fine," he growled.

He hadn't meant to sound grouchy, but she worried about her body when her body was perfect. Why did women obsess about such things? Confidence was more of a turn-on to him than anything. Kate had to know how amazing she looked. Damn that ex of hers for ever making her doubt it.

They walked on a bit more in silence before they came to the top of a hill. He reached for her arm to stop her. With careful movements, he shifted her to stand and turn exactly to the spot he'd been dying for her to see.

"Oh my word," she gasped. "That's gorgeous."

Gray looked down into the valley at the natural waterfall spilling over the rocks. "This is one of my favorite places."

She glanced over her shoulder. "How often do you come here?"

"Not enough. Maybe once a year."

"And you've never brought me?"

Gray shrugged. "I tend to come alone to recharge, plus I never knew you had an interest in camping."

Kate turned her attention back to the breathtaking view. "I didn't know I had an interest, either, but I'm starting to love it. There's not a worry in the world up here. How could anyone even think of their day-to-day lives when this is so...magical?"

Something turned deep inside him. He couldn't put his finger on it, but as he stood behind her, seeing her take in this sight for the first time, Gray knew he'd be bringing her back.

This one night out here with her wouldn't be enough. Just like the one night of sex wouldn't be enough. Kate was a huge part of his life. He couldn't just ignore this continual pull between them.

Gray had always loved being outside, there was a sense of freedom he didn't have when he was behind the bar or doing office work. Knowing that Kate might share this...well, he was starting to wonder just how right they were together in areas he'd never fathomed.

"Can we climb down there and get a closer look?" she asked.

"We can, but you'll want to change."

She turned back to face him. "Why?"

"There's a natural spring you can swim in."

Her face lit up and she smacked his chest. "Then what are we waiting for? Let's get to it."

She circled around him and started heading back down the narrow, wooded trail. Gray watched her go and raked a hand down his face. First camping alone and now getting her in a bathing suit. Yeah, this whole adventurous weekend was a brilliant idea...for a masochist.

Kate smoothed her wet hair back from her face as she climbed back up the shoreline toward the grassy area with a large fallen tree serving as a makeshift bench. She grabbed her towel from the tree and patted her face.

Pulling in a deep breath and starting to dry her legs, she threw a smile at Gray, who had yet to put his shirt back on.

How long was he going to stand there? They'd splashed in the water, floated on their backs, then chatted a bit while just wading. Thankfully the conversation had stayed light, mostly about the beauty of the area and its peacefulness. There was something so calming and perfect about it. Kate was convinced no problems existed here.

Gray had gotten out of the water several minutes ago but still wasn't making any moves to get dressed. And that was pretty much the only reason she'd gotten out. They needed to get back to camp so he could put some damn clothes on and stop driving her out of her mind. Those water droplets glistening all over his well-defined shoulders, pecs and abs. The dark ink curving over his shoulder. There wasn't a thing about her best friend that she didn't find attractive.

Yes. He was definitely driving her out of her mind.

Unfortunately, Kate had a feeling he wasn't even trying.

She pushed aside her lustful thoughts. Okay, she didn't push them aside so much as kept them to herself as she turned her attention toward the brooding man. Something was up with him, but it could just be the sexual tension that continued to thicken between them with each passing day.

"That was amazing," she stated, blowing out a breath and glancing toward the crisp blue sky before looking back at Gray. He said nothing, didn't even so much as crack a smile. "But I guess we can't stay here forever."

Kate tightened the knot on her towel and when she lifted her eyes back up, those dark, mesmerizing eyes were directed right at her. She couldn't quite decipher the look, but whatever it was had her clutching the knot she'd just tied.

"What's wrong?" she asked.

Gray wrapped his towel around his neck, gripping the ends in one hand. "I've had something on my mind I want to discuss with you."

Instantly, Kate stilled. The only major thing between them was the new state of their relationship that they hadn't fully fleshed out. They'd brushed it aside in an attempt to get back on safer ground.

Was he about to open the memory bank and dig deeper? Fine. She needed to just remain calm and do this. They had to hash it out at some point, and better before they fell into bed together than later, so to speak.

Gray sank down onto the large old tree stretched across the ground. Without waiting to see what he was about to say or do, she took a seat beside him.

"What's up?"

Gray rested his forearms on his knees and leaned forward, staring out at the waterfall. The way stress settled over his face, Kate worried something else was wrong. If he wanted to discuss the other night, he'd be more confident. Right now, Gray appeared to be...torn.

Kate honestly had no idea what he was going to say, but the silence certainly wasn't helping her nerves. *Was* there something else wrong? Had he actually brought her out here to tell her he was sick or dying?

"Gray, come on," she said, smacking his leg. "You know my anxiety and overactive imagination can't handle this."

"I had a visitor at the bar yesterday morning."

Okay, so he wasn't dying. That was good. So what had him so upset and speechless?

Kate shifted to block the sun from her eyes. She waited for him to go on, but at this rate it would be nightfall before he finished the story. Whoever this visitor was had Gray struggling for words. Either that or he was battling something major and trying to figure out how to tell her.

"He offered me an insane amount of money to buy the bar."

His words settled heavily between them, rendering her speechless as well. Sell the bar? Is that something he actually wanted to do? She'd never heard him mention wanting away from something that she'd always thought held so much meaning. What would his dad say? Had he even talked to his dad?

There were so many questions crammed into one space and she wanted all of the answers now.

"Are you selling?" she finally asked when it was clear he wasn't going to add more to his verbal bomb.

Gray lifted one bare shoulder and glanced over. "I have no idea. I never wanted the bar, it was just assumed I'd take it over. When I came home from the army, it was there, so I stepped into role of owner."

"What would you do without it?"

He raked a hand over his wet hair and blew out a sigh. "I have no idea, but I've always wondered. I mean, with the amount I was offered, I could do anything."

"You haven't talked to your dad."

Gray shook his head, though she hadn't actually been asking.

"Is that why you brought me camping?" she asked. "So you could get my opinion?"

Gray reached for her hand. "No. I mean, I knew I wanted to talk to you, but the second you mentioned that list and started naming things off, I knew I was going to bring you here as soon as I could get everything lined up. It just happened to be rather quickly."

Kate couldn't help but smile as she glanced down to their joined hands. "Have you made a list of reasons to stay and reasons to go?"

His lips twitched into a grin of their own as he shook his head. "No, ma'am. I leave the list-making to you."

Her mind started rolling on all the good things about owning a family business. There was just so much, but only Gray knew what he loved most about the place.

On the downside, once you owned a business, you were married to it. Randomly he would take a day, like this, but the man was loyal and that bar was his wife, baby. Plus, he carried on the small-town tradition his grandfather had started.

Family heritage meant everything to someone like Gray. Money could only go so far. She was surprised he even considered selling the bar, which meant he must really be looking for something else in his life.

Kate's heart ached for him, for this decision. If she were in his place she wouldn't even have to think about it. She had no family and would kill to carry on this kind of legacy.

"Your silence is making me nervous."

Kate smiled and patted his leg. "You should be nervous. The pros and cons are already lining up inside my head."

Gray led her back to camp and she was somewhat grateful for the distraction. Though she didn't think anything could fully take her mind off the ripped torso covered with tats that he still hadn't covered. She'd be lying if she didn't admit her nerves had settled in at the thought of spending the night in that tent with him.

But first, she'd help him figure out what to do about this business proposition. Surely that would crush any desires... wouldn't it?

Yes, if they just continued to focus on the bar and his proposal, then any desires they shared would be pushed aside and they could reconfigure their friendship.

Kate would keep telling herself that until it became the truth.

CHAPTER EIGHT

THE FIRE CRACKLED, the stars were vibrant in the sky, and beside him, Kate continued to jot down notes. She'd mutter something, then mark out what she'd just written. Every now and then she'd ask him a question and scribble something else down.

Her system was driving him insane. She fidgeted, pulling her hair up into a knot, then taking it down and raking her fingers through it. Then she'd start the process all over again. Watching her was killing him, mostly because her mind was working overtime, but just seeing her in her element was too damn sexy.

Kate let out a groan. "I need my colored markers so I can see the overall picture clearer."

Gray had had enough. He reached over, jerked the planner from her lap and tossed it into the fire.

"Gray!" Kate leaped to her feet and stared down as the pages curled, turned black, and drifted up in ashes. "That was my personal planner. You can't just—"

"Too late. I just did."

Okay, maybe he should feel bad, but she needed to relax because until she did, he couldn't. She'd brought the damn thing camping when this whole night should be about taking a break from reality.

Now she sat here working on his life like he was one of her damn clients. No more.

"Not only does that have my whole life in it, I had the lists for you about the bar."

Kate spun around and propped her hands on her hips as she stared down at him. He picked up the long stick he'd had beside him and poked around at the fire, shoving the last bit of the planner further into the flames for good measure. It was better than seeing that snug little tank pulling across her chest or the creamy patch of skin between the hem of her shirt and the top of her pants.

"You're a jerk."

She stomped off into the darkness, heading toward his truck. Gray bit the inside of his cheek to keep from laughing. She most likely had a backup planner at home and he knew she kept duplicate electronic files. He felt only a little guilty. She'd be fine. Knowing Kate, she had everything logged into her memory bank anyway. Someone who was so focused on details and schedules and color coding the hell out of every minute of life would definitely know her schedule by heart.

The slam of his truck door had Gray glancing in that direction. Seconds later, Kate came stomping back with her cell in hand. She flopped back onto the fat stump she'd been using as her seat. The glow of her phone added a bit more light to their campfire area.

"You can't be serious," he grumbled.

Without looking up, she started typing like a mad woman. "Oh, when it comes to schedules, I'm dead serious. And even though you just ruined my life by burning my planner, I'm still going to help you work this out."

Gray tossed the stick back to the ground. "I'm not making a decision tonight, so relax."

"You keep telling me to relax, but if I don't worry about it and try to come to a conclusion, who will?"

Gray stood and took a step toward her. She jerked her phone behind her back and tipped her chin up in defiance.

"You're not throwing this in the fire," she said, and he thought he saw a ghost of a smile on her lips.

"No," he laughed. "But I'm not worrying and neither are you. I'm tired and it's late so I thought we could get our sleeping bags rolled out and get some rest. I want to get up early and hike to the top of the peak so you can see the sunrise."

"Sounds beautiful."

"Words can't describe it." Gray held out his hand to help her up. "So you may want to get some sleep or you'll be grouchy when I wake you."

"I'm grouchy now," she muttered, placing her hand in his. "You owe me a new planner, but I get to pick it out. I don't trust you anymore."

He helped her up, but didn't let go of her hand. "Now, where's the fun in that? You may love the one I choose."

"Please," she said, and snorted. "You have terrible taste. I've seen that painting over your sofa."

"Hey, *Dogs Playing Poker* is a classic. I paid good money for that."

"From a flea market, maybe," she muttered. Kate shook her head and blew out a sigh. "We better just go to bed and stop arguing."

Gray wasn't sure why he hadn't let her go, or why he continued to watch as the orange glow from the flames tinted her cheeks. Now her hair was down from the knot she'd been wearing. It had air-dried from the swim earlier...a swim that he took way too long to recover from. She'd only worn a simple black one-piece, but he knew exactly what she had hidden beneath that suit. She may as well have been naked. The V in the front and the low scoop in the back had been so damn arousing, he'd had to recite all fifty states in alphabetical order to get himself under control.

Gray kept hold of her hand, pulling it up to his chest. Her

eyes remained locked on his. Sounds from crickets filled the night, the crackling of the fire randomly broke into the moment.

"Gray," she whispered.

"Kate."

Her eyes closed as she pulled in a deep breath. "You're making this difficult."

"None of this has to be difficult," he countered. No reason to pretend he didn't know what she spoke of. They both had the same exact thing on their minds.

"No, it shouldn't be," she agreed, lifting her lids to look at him again. "But when I'm around you, I just remember the bar and how that felt. And then I wonder if my memory is just making the whole scenario better than it actually was."

Good. He'd been banking on her replaying that night, but he hadn't expected such an honest compliment. He sure as hell remembered, too, and not just when he was with her.

Even when he was alone or working, especially working, he recalled how stunning she'd been all spread out across the gleaming mahogany bar top. She was like a fantasy come to life.

There wasn't a doubt in his mind that she wanted him, too. He could see the way her gaze kept dropping to his mouth, the fact she hadn't let go of his hand, the way she'd avoided him for days after their intimacy. She was afraid of her feelings, of taking what she wanted.

"I don't expect anything once we go in that tent," he explained. The last thing he wanted was for her to think that was why he actually brought her here.

"I didn't think that." She licked her lips and curled her fingers more tightly around his hand. "You understand why I made the one-night rule. Right?"

She might need him to know, but that didn't mean he wanted to. All Gray cared about was how they felt, and ignoring such intense emotions was only going to complicate things further down the line. The resulting tension would eat away at their friendship and drive a wedge between them much more than taking a risk would.

"I can't lose you, Gray," she went on, staring up at him like he was everything in her life. "It would destroy me."

Kate had looked at him that way before, when her parents died and when he'd come home from the army. He didn't want to be some type of hero to anybody.

No, that wasn't right. He did want to be her hero, but not someone she thought needed to be on a pedestal. He wanted to be her equal, to prove to her that they were good together.

Fortunately, he didn't need to prove such things. She already knew just how good they were...and that's what scared the hell out of her.

"You're the only constant man in my life." She squeezed his hand. "Do you even know how important that is to me? Tara and Lucy are great, but they're not you."

Gray swallowed the lump in his throat. He didn't get emotional. Ever. But something about her raw honesty, her vulnerability got to him.

"You really think I'd let something happen to our friendship?" he asked, staring into her expressive eyes.

"Neither of us would mean for anything to happen to it," she countered. "But are you willing to take that chance?"

"I'd never risk hurting you," he stated. Gray palmed one side of her face, stroking his thumb beneath her eye. "You think I don't understand where you're coming from? You have to notice you're the only constant woman in my life basically since we met."

A smile played over her mouth. "You date."

"I do, but serious relationships aren't my thing. I'm too busy with work to feed a relationship or worry about a woman." He took a half-step closer until they were toe to toe. "I need this friendship just as much as you do, but I'm not going to ignore these feelings forever, Kate."

Her eyes widened. "You promised—"

"—that I wouldn't let you lose this friendship and that I wasn't pressuring you for anything tonight. But you can't run from your feelings forever. I won't let you deny your own feelings, either."

Unable to resist, Gray dropped a quick kiss on her lips, not lingering nearly as long as he would've liked. After releasing her and taking a step back, he finally turned and headed to the tent.

This was going to be one long, uncomfortable night.

Kate rolled over in her sleeping bag for what seemed like the eighteenth time in as many minutes. Facing Gray now, she narrowed her gaze to adjust to the darkness and make out his silhouette.

How dare he throw down that gauntlet and then lie there and get a good night's sleep? How did the man turn his emotions off and on so easily?

She wanted to know the secret because this jumbled up mess inside her head, inside her heart, was causing some serious anxiety issues. As if she didn't have enough to handle where this man was concerned.

Kate couldn't make out his face in the dark. But she knew it by heart just as well as she knew her own. The faint lines around his eyes and between his brows gave him that distinguished look she found sexier than she should. His dark lashes always made the perfect frame for those dark as night eyes. She'd bet they were fanned out over his cheeks right now as he slept peacefully.

When he'd come home from the army, he'd been harder than when he'd left. Whatever he'd seen overseas had done something to him, something she never could put her finger on. But then he'd jumped right in and taken over the family business.

Some men came home a shell of who they'd once been. While Gray might be harder and more closed off to some, he was alive and thriving in their little town. He might not like the word *hero*, but he was hers. Honestly, he always had been.

Just another reason she couldn't keep exploring these new sexual feelings. The friendship was so, so much more important.

When Gray had implemented Ladies' Night at Gallagher's, the women around town had flocked there, all trying to catch the attention of the town's most eligible bachelor. Ladies from surrounding towns also came in to see the sexy new vet turned bartender.

Kate had always been aware of Gray's ridiculously good looks. She wasn't blind or stupid. She'd just never thought about acting on her attraction. She could be attracted to someone and still be friends…right?

Well, she'd been doing just fine at managing both until he propositioned her on the bar top. The sex couldn't have been as good as she remembered. It simply couldn't. And yet it was all of those overexaggerated flashes in her mind that had her all jumbled and aching now when she had no right to be.

"Are you going to stare at me all night?"

Kate jerked at Gray's mumbled words. He hadn't even cracked an eyelid open, so how did he know she was staring? Her heart beat faster at the abrupt break in the peaceful silence.

"I can't sleep," she answered honestly. No need to tell him her insomnia was due to him. Gray wasn't stupid.

"I can tell from all the flopping around you've been doing."

Now he did open his eyes. Even though she couldn't make out the color in the dark tent, she knew they were fixed on her.

"Sorry I kept you awake," she whispered, though why she was whispering was lost on her. Maybe because everything was so peaceful around them and she needed to hold on to that just a bit longer. Lately, so much in her life didn't seem calm. Well, maybe not so much. Mostly just Gray and their friendship, which trickled down to everything else because she couldn't stop thinking of him, of what had happened, and how to move on.

Gray shifted in his sleeping bag. When his knee bumped hers, a jolt shot through her. Being hyperaware of him in the middle of the night with these sexual urges spiraling through her was not good. Not good at all.

But there wasn't one thing she could do to stop how she felt. Why did these feelings have to be awakened inside her? How long had she had them and not even realized it?

Yes, she'd wondered if they could ever be more than friends. She'd thought of sex with him. He was hot. She was a woman. It was the natural order of things. But she'd always pushed those thoughts aside and focused on their friendship.

That wasn't the case right now.

"Your movement didn't keep me awake," he countered.

Kate curled her fingers around the top of her sleeping bag and tried to resist the urge to reach out. So close. He was so close she would only have to lift her hand slightly to brush the side of his face. She knew from firsthand experience exactly how that bristle would feel against her skin.

Kate swallowed. She shouldn't be fantasizing about that stubbled jaw beneath her palm. She shouldn't wonder if they both could fit into one sleeping bag. And she sure as hell shouldn't be thinking how quickly they could get their clothes off.

"What's keeping you awake?" he asked.

Kate snorted. "You're joking, right?"

"Do I sound like I'm joking?"

No. He sounded sexy with that low, growly voice she'd never fully appreciated until now.

"You've got me so confused and worked up," she confessed. "Why couldn't we just keep things the way they were?"

"Because attraction doesn't follow your rules."

Kate closed her eyes and chewed on her lip. What could she say to that? He was right, but that didn't mean she wouldn't keep trying to compartmentalize her emotions. They had to stay in the friend box. They had to. Everyone in her life had a special area inside her heart, but Gray kept stepping out of his designated spot and causing all sorts of confusion.

"You're not the only one losing sleep over this, Kate."

Oh, mercy. Those were words she wished he hadn't thrown out there to settle between them. Not now, when they were being held hostage by the circumstances surrounding them. The dark night, the enclosed tent, the sexually charged energy that seemed to be pulling them closer together.

Her heart beating a fast, steady rhythm, she reached out. When her fingers found his jawline, she slid her hand up the side of his face. That prickle of his coarse hair beneath her palm had her entire body heating up.

"What if…"

She couldn't finish. This was insane. This entire idea was absolutely insane and not smart. But she ached…for this man.

His warm, strong hand covered hers as he whispered, "What if what?"

"One more time," she murmured. "We do this just once more."

"Are you going to regret it this time?"

Kate eased her body closer. "I didn't regret it last time."

He released her hand and jerked on the zipper of his bag before sliding hers down as well. In another swift move, he was on her, taking her hands and holding them on either side of her head.

"Tell me now if you want me to stop."

Kate arched against him, pulling against his hold. "Now, Gray."

CHAPTER NINE

THE GREEN LIGHT couldn't be brighter. And one time? Sure, he'd heard that before. Whatever. He'd take this time and show her again exactly how perfect their special bond was.

Gray eased up just enough to slide his hands beneath the long-sleeved T-shirt she had on. He hadn't been able to appreciate her before at the bar, and it was so damn dark he could barely see, but he was going to get her naked and not fumble around ripping underwear like some inexperienced, out-of-control teen.

With some careful maneuvering and assistance from Kate, Gray had her clothes off in record time. His hands settled on her bare hips as she reached up to frame his face.

"You're still wearing clothes."

Gray gripped her wrist, kissed her palm and put her hand on his shirt. "Then take them off."

Her hands trembled as she brought them to the hem of his tee. She jerked the material up and over his head. When she grabbed the waistband of his shorts, he sucked in a breath. Those delicate fingers on his body might be more than he could handle. To say he was hanging on by a thread would be a vast understatement.

Since she'd paraded around in that swimsuit, he'd been fighting the ache to take her hard and fast. Gray covered her hands with his and took over. Within seconds, he was just as bare as her.

Kate eased her knees apart, making room for him. Her fingertips grazed up his arms and over his shoulders. "I wish I could see you better."

Gray reached over, taking the lantern-style light he'd brought. He flicked the switch on and left it against the edge of the tent. When he turned his attention back to Kate, his breath got caught in his throat. A vise-like grip formed around his chest.

She lay beneath him, all of that dark hair spread around her, her eyes bright and beautiful and solely focused on him.

"You're stunning."

He hadn't meant to say the words out loud. He'd wanted to keep this simple—or as simple as they could be, considering their circumstances. But now that they were out, he wasn't sorry. Maybe Kate needed to hear this more often. Maybe she needed to realize just how special and amazing she was.

A smile spread across her face. "I'm already naked," she joked. "You don't need to flatter me."

If she wanted to keep things light, that was fine. Having Kate here with him, like this, was more than he thought would happen.

But he didn't want more words coming between them. All he wanted was to feel this woman, to take his time with her, and show her how much she was treasured. Above all else, he never wanted her to feel like she was just a one-night stand. Even if they agreed to stay friends, he needed her to know she was worth more than quick actions and meaningless words.

Gray covered her body. Then he covered her mouth. Her delicate arms and legs wrapped all around him.

"I need to get protection," he muttered against her lips.

Her hold tightened. "I'm on birth control and I trust you."

The whispered declaration had him battling over what he should do. There was nothing more he wanted than to have no barrier between them and he trusted her, too. He'd never gone without because there wasn't a woman he trusted that much.

But he knew his Kate and he wasn't about to move from this spot, not when she was holding on so tight and looking at him like she couldn't take another second without his touch.

Gray settled himself between her thighs, bracing his forearms on either side of her face. He smoothed her hair back, wanting to see every emotion that flashed across her face when he joined their bodies.

And he wasn't disappointed.

The second they became one, her lids fluttered down, her breath came out on a soft sigh, and she arched against him.

Kate's fingertips threaded through his hair as she urged him down, opening for another kiss. How could he ever agree to just one time with her? Hell, he already knew that twice wouldn't be enough.

She muttered something against his lips, but he couldn't make out what. Her hands traveled down to his shoulders, then his back as she tossed her head to the side. Raven hair covered a portion of her face as she cried out, her legs tightening around him.

Gray shoved her hair out of the way, basking in the play of emotions. He'd never seen a more beautiful, expressive woman than Kate. His Kate. No matter what happened, friends or more, she'd always be his.

In no time he was pumping his hips, capturing her mouth beneath his. Kate's nails bit into his back and that was all he needed to send him over the edge. Nothing had ever felt like this…well, nothing except their encounter at his bar.

Gray held on to her, nipping at her lips as he trembled. After several moments, and once his body stilled, he gathered her close and pulled the open sleeping bag over them. He didn't care about their clothes, didn't care that there was a little chill in the mountain air. He leaned over with his free hand and clicked the light off.

"That was the last time," she muttered against his chest. "I mean it."

Gray smiled into the dark. He'd never agreed to that bargain to begin with.

"These new pamphlets turned out so nice."

Kate glanced to Tara, who was waving around the stack of brand-new promotional material for their grief center. Judging by the look on her face, she'd been talking for a while, but Kate had zoned out.

"What? Oh, yes. They're pretty. Lucy did a great job with the design and the colors."

They'd just had new pamphlets done a few months ago, but with the popularity of their weekly meetings, Lucy had taken it upon herself to design the new ones, adding some testimonials from the regulars and having nicer pages printed online.

"You're distracted," Tara stated, dropping the stack to the table at the entryway of the community center. "Does this have anything to do with the camping trip?"

Kate shook her head. "No. Gray and I just went away for a day. It was pretty cool. I can't believe I live in this gorgeous state and have never taken advantage of the mountains. I'm definitely going camping again."

The waterfall had been amazing, but the sunrise only hours after making love had been something special. She wasn't sure where Gray's thoughts were, but for her, something had changed. She needed a breather and she needed to do some serious reevaluating of where she stood on her feelings for her best friend.

What had she been thinking, telling him not to use protection? Not that she didn't believe him that he was safe, but that bold move was, well…bold. They'd taken their intimacy to another level when she knew full well they couldn't do that ever, ever again.

But when she'd been lying beneath him, cradled by his

strength and seeing how he looked at her, she simply hadn't wanted him to move away for anything. She'd wanted him and only him.

Besides, they were fine. She was on the pill and neither of them had ever gone without protection before.

"What's up with the two of you lately?" Tara asked.

Before Kate could answer, she was saved by the adorable five-year-old running around the tables and singing something Kate didn't recognize.

"Marley Jo Bailey," Tara scolded. "You cannot run in here. I brought your bag in and put it back in the kitchen. You have crayons, a coloring book and your new baby doll to play with."

Marley stopped at her mother's abrupt tone, or maybe it was the use of her full name. Either way, the little cutie started skipping toward the back of the building, where the kitchen was located.

"Sorry about that," Tara said, turning her focus back to Kate.

She wasn't sorry one bit. Marley's running got Kate out of answering the question that had been weighing on her, because honestly, Kate had no idea what was going on with Gray.

"Is Sam working?"

Tara nodded. "He's always good to keep her on meeting nights, but he got a new job and he's worried about asking off."

Kate smiled. "Sounds like he's getting things back in order."

"He left me another note."

"He wants forgiveness," Kate stated. "It's obvious he loves you."

Her friend nodded and glanced back toward the kitchen area. "I know he does. That's never been the issue."

Kate couldn't imagine what her friend struggled with. Between losing her husband to addiction only to have him fight and claw his way back, and having a sweet, innocent child in the mix...there was so much to take in and Tara was handling things like a champ.

"So, back to Gray."

Kate resisted moaning. There was no way she was going to offer up everything that had happened between them. She and Gray were still friends and that's what they'd stay, because the other night was it. No more taking her clothes off for her best friend.

"He's just going through some personal things right now and needed to escape and get some advice."

There. That wasn't a total lie. She'd offered him advice, hadn't she? She'd told him to take his clothes off.

"And you gave him advice?" Tara asked, her raised brows almost mocking.

"Well, I was trying to until he tossed my planner into the fire."

Something she was still pissed about, but seemed to have forgotten about the second he'd touched her and made her toes curl all over again. Damn that man for making her want things she couldn't have—and for destroying her beloved planner.

And in answer to her question from days ago, yes. Yes, the sex was just as fabulous as she'd remembered. Maybe more so since they'd both gotten out of their clothes this time. Gray had been rather thorough and her body continued to tingle at just the mere thought of how gloriously his hands had roamed over her as if memorizing every aspect.

"The fire?" Tara gasped, throwing a hand to her chest. "Tell me he didn't burn the cherished planner."

"Very funny." Kate playfully smacked Tara's shoulder. "He said I needed to relax."

Tara laughed. No, she doubled over laughing, which had Marley running from the kitchen with some blond baby doll tucked beneath her arm.

"What's so funny?" Marley asked, her wide eyes bouncing between her mother and Kate.

"Oh, just something Kate said, honey." Tara swiped beneath her eyes and attempted to control her laughter. "So he told you to relax, which I'm sure you immediately did. And then he watched your planner turn to ash?"

Kate crossed her arms. "Pretty much."

"And he's still breathing?"

"Barely," Kate replied. "He owes me a new planner and don't think I'm not going to pick out the most expensive, thickest one I can find. It will have quotes on every page and a gold-embossed font, and I may just have him spring for the twenty-four-month one instead of the twelve."

Uninterested in the grown-ups' conversation, Marley started skipping around the room with her baby in the air.

"Oh, hitting him in his wallet." Tara feigned a shudder. "That will teach him never to mess with your schedules."

Kate dropped her arms to her sides and rolled her shoulders. "I don't know why the closest people in my life mock my work," she joked. "I mean, I make a killer living off organizing lives. I could help with yours if you'd let me."

Tara held up her hands. "I already let you into my closet. I'm still afraid to mess up those white shirts hanging next to the gray for fear you've set some alarm in there and you'll know if I get them out of order."

Kate laughed as she went to the food table on the back wall. "I'm not that bad," she called over her shoulder. "Besides, your closet was a disaster."

After Sam had left, Tara had needed something to occupy her time, and she'd had Kate and Lucy come over for a girls' night. One thing turned into another and the next thing Kate knew, she was knee-deep in a three-day project to revamp her friend's closet.

"I'm still upset you tossed my favorite sweatshirt," Tara griped, coming to lean against the wall by the table.

Kate rolled her eyes as she straightened up the plastic cups next to the lemonade and sweet tea. "That sweatshirt needed a proper burial and I just helped things along."

"It was a classic."

"No, it was from the junior high volleyball camp we went to and it was hideous."

"Still fit," Tara muttered.

Kate patted her friend's arm. "And that's why I threw it away and secretly hate you. You have never gained an ounce of fat other than when you were pregnant."

Tara quirked a brow. "High metabolism and good gene pool?"

"Still, I can hate you." Kate stepped back and glanced around. "I think we're good to go."

The meeting was due to start in fifteen minutes, which meant people should be rolling in anytime. They always had their regulars, accounting for about eight people. Randomly others would filter in. Some stayed only a few sessions. Some they never saw again.

Ironically, this uplifting support group was how Lucy and Noah met. They would've eventually met at work since he was an officer and Lucy had been a dispatcher. But, as fate would have it, Noah had slipped into the back of the meeting one day and Lucy had made a beeline for him when he tried to sneak out. Noah had lost his wife before coming to Stonerock and Lucy had lost her husband in the war a few years ago. If nothing else came from Helping Hands, at least Lucy and Noah had found true love and a second chance at happiness.

Kate wished that Tara and Sam could do the same, but things weren't looking good. Marley skipped back into the room and ran up to her mom. Tara picked her daughter up and squeezed her tight.

Something flipped in Kate's chest. She wanted a family, a husband to share her life with. But she'd been too busy with her career, a failed engagement and the launch of Helping Hands to make it happen.

An image of Gray flashed through her mind.

No. That was not the direction she needed to take her thoughts. Gray wasn't the marrying type. His father had pressured him over the past few years to settle down, but obviously that wasn't something Gray wanted.

And she needed to remember that he was her everything. She couldn't allow herself to hope for more with him. No, when she married and settled down it wouldn't be with a hunky bar owner with a naughty side and a sleeve of tattoos.

CHAPTER TEN

GRAY FINISHED PULLING the wood chairs off the tabletops. He
still needed to complete the invoice for next week's beer order
and return a call to a new vendor before they opened in two
hours.

Owning a bar wasn't just mixing drinks and writing pay-
checks. There was so much more that went into it, but he'd done
it so long—hell, he'd grown up here—he pretty much did everything on autopilot.

Is that how he wanted to spend the rest of his life? Doing the
same thing day in and day out? How could a thirty-one-year-
old man not have a clue what he wanted to do with his life?

The tempting business proposal from the random stranger
still weighed heavily on him and kept him awake at night.

Granted, the looming deadline wasn't the only thing keeping him awake. A raven-haired vixen posing as his best friend
had him questioning everything he'd ever thought to be a truth.

Gray set the last chair on the floor and turned to head toward
his office. The old black-and-white picture hanging behind the
bar stopped him. He'd seen that picture countless times, passed
it constantly, but the image of his grandfather standing in his
army uniform outside the bar on the day he bought it seemed
to hit home this time.

The back door opened and slammed shut. Only a handful of people used the back door. A sliver of hope hit him as he stared at the doorway to the hall, thinking he'd see Kate step through.

But when his father rounded the corner, Gray smiled, hating how disappointment over not seeing Kate had been his first reaction.

She'd retreated again after their trip. Her pattern shouldn't surprise him, but it did. Whatever she was afraid of, he could battle it. Seriously. Did she not think all of this was freaking him out a little, as well? But there was no way in hell he was just going to ignore this pull toward her. He knew without a doubt that she was being pulled just as fiercely.

"Want a beer?" Gray asked as he circled the bar.

Reece Gallagher went to the opposite side of the bar and took a seat on one of the stools. "You know what I like."

Gray smiled as he reached for a frosted mug and flipped the tap of his father's favorite brew. He tipped the mug enough to keep the head of the beer just right. Another thing he simply did without thinking.

He'd been meaning to call his dad, but now that he was here, there was no better time to discuss the future of Gallagher's.

Gray set the beer in front of his dad, the frothy top spilling over. He pulled a rag from below the counter and swiped up the moisture.

"Had a visitor the other day," he told his dad.

"Oh, yeah?" Reece took a hearty drink of his beer before setting the mug back on the bar. "Something tells me there's more to the story."

"He offered me more money than I'd know what to do with if I sell him this bar."

His father's dark eyes instantly met his. "Sell Gallagher's? I hope you told him where he could stick his money. Who the hell was this guy?"

Gray swallowed, resting his palms on the smooth bar top.

"Businessman from Knoxville. He left me his card and told me I had a month to think about it."

His dad's silver brows drew in as he shifted on his stool and seemed as if he was about ready to come over the bar. "What's there to think about, son?"

Gray figured his father would have this reaction. The bar had been in their family for years and selling had never been an option. Hell, Gray had never thought about selling the place until he'd been presented with the option.

He had to be honest with his dad. There was no reason to gloss this over and pretend everything was fine and he wasn't contemplating the change.

"Maybe I'm not meant to run this bar."

Silence settled between them as the words hung in the air. Gray didn't back down. If his father and the military taught him one thing, it was to never back down from what you believed in.

"You're actually considering this."

Gray nodded even though his father hadn't actually asked. "Something is missing in my life," he said.

His father's response was another pull of his beer. Gray figured he should just lay it all out there. His dad might not like the direction of Gray's thoughts, but he did appreciate and expect honesty.

"I'm thankful for this, all of it. I know you and Grandpa worked hard." He pulled in a deep breath. "I'm just not sure this is what I was meant to do in life."

Reece Gallagher tapped the side of his mug. Whatever was rolling around in his mind, Gray knew his father was formulating a plan to convince him to stay.

"How much were you offered?" his dad finally asked.

Gray threw out the number which resulted in a long, slow whistle from his father.

"That's a hell of a number," he agreed. "And you think this money will ultimately buy you what you want in life? Which is what, exactly?"

Gray shrugged. "I have no clue. There's a void, though. I haven't been able to put my finger on it."

"A wife? Kids?" his dad suggested. "Settling down is a logical step."

Gray pushed off the bar. He was going to need a beer of his own if this was the path the conversation was going to head down.

"I'm not looking for a wife, let alone children."

He pulled a bottle from the cooler behind the bar. Quickly he popped the top and tossed it into the trash.

"I know that's what worked for you and Grandpa," he went on, resting his bottle on the bar. "But I'm not you or him. I'm my own person, and is it so bad that I'm not sure what I want?"

"No," his father agreed. "But I also don't want you making decisions based on money alone, and I certainly don't want you letting all of this go only to find that what you were looking for was here all along."

What the hell did that mean? Stonerock was a great town, but it wasn't necessarily where he wanted to spend his future.

"The decision is ultimately up to you," he dad went on. "You have to understand that I'm not giving you my blessing if you choose to sell. What does he want to do with the bar, anyway?"

Gray took a drink of his beer, then leaned onto his elbows. "He and his business partner want to make Stonerock like a mini-Nashville. I guess they're looking to buy more businesses in the area and revamp them to draw more tourists."

Reece wrinkled his nose. "That's absurd. Stonerock is just fine the way it is."

Gray finished his beer and tossed his bottle. Then he grabbed his dad's empty mug and set it in the sink below the bar.

"I won't contact him without talking to you first," Gray assured his dad. "I don't want you to think that your opinion doesn't matter or that I'm only looking at dollar signs."

His dad came to his feet and tapped his fingertips on the bar. "I know money can sound good, especially that much, but family is everything, Gray. At the end of the day you only have a few friends and your family that you can count on. Money is just paper."

Why did his dad have to make him feel guilty? Why did he have to add more doubts in his head when he was so close to making a decision?

Reece headed for the back hallway.

"Wait a second," Gray called out. "What did you stop by for to begin with?"

Tossing a glance over his shoulder, his father shook his head. "It's not important."

His footsteps echoed down the hall until they disappeared behind the closing door. Gray stared out at the empty bar, knowing that in just over an hour it would be bustling. That was definitely the main perk to this place. He'd never had to worry about patrons or making money. Gallagher's was the only bar in town and it was a nice place to hang. He was proud of that accomplishment, of the tradition he carried on here.

Emotions filled his throat and squeezed his chest. No matter the decision he made, he'd always wonder if he'd made the right one. If he left, he'd look back and wonder if his father thought him a disappointment. If he stayed, he'd always be looking for something to fill the void. Could he achieve what his heart desired?

Gray wasn't going to be making any decisions tonight. Between the bar and Kate, he wasn't sure how the hell he was supposed to maintain his sanity.

"I have to go," Kate said around a yawn. "I have to meet a client early in the morning to discuss reorganizing her basement for a play-work area."

Lucy put a hand on Kate's arm. "Don't go. I haven't even gotten to the part about the hammock."

Tara busted out laughing and Kate groaned. "Seriously, Lucy.

Keep the honeymoon stories to yourself. You came back just as pale as when you left so I know what you were doing."

Lucy shrugged. "But the hammock story is hilarious. Can you even imagine how difficult—"

Kate held up her hands. "I'm getting the visual."

Lucy had been back from her honeymoon only a day, but they'd been in need of some long overdue girl time. The wedding planning and showers and anticipation had filled their schedules over the past several months.

Tara had invited them over to her house and opened a bottle of wine, and they'd proceeded to just decompress and gossip. Sweet Marley had gone to bed an hour ago, leaving the women to some much-needed adult conversation that wasn't centered around dresses, registries and invitations.

Kate didn't partake in the wine, though. The last time she drank, the *only* time she'd drunk, had changed her entire life, and she was still reeling from the results. Maybe this would just her new normal and she'd have to get used to these unfamiliar emotions that seemed to have taken up residence in her heart.

"Will you hang a bit longer if I promise to hold off on describing the hammock incident?" Lucy asked as she refilled her own wineglass.

Kate shook her head. "I've seriously got so much to do."

"Did you tell Lucy about the planner and the campfire?"

Kate shot a glare at Tara, who sat across on the opposite sofa. The smirk on her friend's face was not funny. Not funny at all.

"A fire and your planner?" Lucy gasped. "I have to hear this. I swear, tell me this and I won't bring up the hammock again."

Kate realized she wasn't going anywhere anytime soon. She sank back into her corner of the couch and replayed her camping story—minus the sex and lustful glances—to her best friends.

"Wait." Lucy held up her hands. "You went camping? That's almost as shocking as the fact Gray burned your planner."

"He forced my hand on the camping thing," she stated. "Well, he didn't force me. Camping was on my life list and he just showed up unannounced—"

"Hold up," Lucy said, incredulous. "What's this life list? Good grief. A girl gets married, has awkward sex in a hammock and misses so much that has happened. Start at the beginning."

"No hammock talk," Kate reminded her.

Lucy shrugged. "Minor slip."

Tara refilled her glass, then propped her bare feet on the couch. "Yes. The beginning of this camping adventure, please."

Kate rolled her eyes. "You already know everything."

"Still makes for a good bedtime story." Tara shrugged. "Besides, I think something is brewing between you and Gray."

"Nothing is brewing. You know we drive each other insane on a good day."

Kate was quick to Δdefend herself, but she and Gray were friends. No, really. No more sex. Just the one time…times two.

"I made a list," Kate started. "I guess you could call it a bucket list. With turning thirty, I started getting a little anxiety about inching closer to the age my mom was when she died. I figured I better start doing some of the things I really want to try. You just never know how much time you have left."

"Camping made your list?" Lucy asked. "I'm intrigued by what else you've put on there."

Kate slipped off her sandals and pulled her feet back under her. She didn't want to get into the full details of her wishes because…well, she felt that was something she and Gray shared. As strange as that sounded, she'd originally wanted to keep it all to herself, but since he knew, Kate wanted to keep things just between them.

The secrets between her and Gray were mounting up.

"I tried to think of things I'd never done, so, yeah. Camping ranked high," Kate explained. "Once we got settled in and took a hike, I could tell something was bothering Gray. He finally opened up and dropped a bomb on me that someone wants to buy his bar."

"What?" Lucy and Tara both asked.

Kate met her friends' wide eyes and dropped jaws with a nod. "He said some guy came in and offered him an insane amount of money to purchase Gallagher's. Said something about buying properties around the town to update them and make them more city-like."

"Our town doesn't need updating," Lucy stated. "The reason people live here is because they like the small-town atmosphere. If they wanted a city feel, they'd move there. I wonder if Drake is aware of this. Surely these guys had the decency to talk to our mayor."

Kate shrugged. "Just telling you what I know."

Tara set her wineglass on the coffee table and shifted to face Kate. "Is Gray seriously considering giving up the bar?"

"He hasn't turned the offer down."

Which honestly surprised her. He'd explained the whole thing about feeling something missing in his life, but at the same time, this was his family's legacy. A piece of history that had just been handed to him. Did he even realize how lucky he was? She'd give anything to have a piece of her parents handed down to her, some way to still hold on to them.

Which was why tracing her family genealogy had made her list.

"Wow." Lucy took another sip of her wine. "When will he decide what he's doing?"

"The guy gave him a deadline. Next week sometime." Kate stretched her legs out and felt around for her shoes. She really did need to get going. Not just because of the work thing. She didn't want to get back into the camping conversation and Tara's speculation that something was up. "He's going to talk to his dad and feel him out, though I imagine that won't go very well."

No doubt he'd let her know exactly how that talk went. Then he'd probably call her out on dodging him since they'd returned from their trip. She hadn't been dodging him, exactly. She'd been working and she assumed he had, as well.

Besides, she just needed a break after those two days together. The man consumed her every thought lately and when they were together he was…well, even more irresistible and in her face.

What did all of this mean? How could she let her Gray go from being her best friend to lover, then try to put him back in the best friend zone? It shouldn't be that difficult to keep him locked away in that particular section of her heart. Isn't that what she did for a living? Put everything in a neat and tidy order?

So why the hell couldn't she do that with her personal life?

Kate finally said her goodbyes to her best girlfriends and agreed to meet them at Ladies' Night on Wednesday. She hadn't been for a while and was overdue—something Gray had noticed and called her out on. And, well, she could use a night of dancing and just having a good time.

That would prove to Gray that she wasn't dodging him… right?

Kate headed home, her mind working through all she needed to get done over the next couple of days. She was still in need of a good personal planner. She had looked at a few, but hadn't made a commitment yet. Whatever she chose, Gray would feel it in his wallet. That would teach him not to mess with her things anymore.

As she pulled into her drive, she noticed a sporty black car parked on the street directly in front of her house. Her eyes darted to the porch, where a man in a suit sat on one of her white rockers.

Kate barely took her eyes off him as she put the car in Park and killed the engine. Of all people to make an unexpected visit, her cheating, lying ex was the last man she ever expected to see again.

CHAPTER ELEVEN

GRIPPING HER PURSE, Kate headed up her stone walkway. "What are you doing here, Chris?"

Always clean-cut and polished, Chris Percell came to his feet and shoved his hands in his pockets.

Who wore a suit at this time of night? And in this humidity? Not that his wardrobe was a concern of hers. No, the main issues here were that he stood on her porch without an invitation and she hadn't heard a word from him in years. Granted, once he'd left, she hadn't wanted to hear a word from the cheating bastard.

Kate didn't mount the steps. He had about three seconds to state his business and then she was going in her house and locking the door. She hadn't been lying when she told her friends she was tired and still had some work to do, so this unexpected visitor was not putting her in the best of moods.

"You look good, Kate."

Chris started down the steps toward her. Now she did dodge him and go on up to her porch. When she turned, he stood on the bottom step, smiling up at her.

"It's been a long time," he stated.

"Not long enough. What do you want?"

With a shrug, he crossed his arms and shifted his stance. "I was hoping we could talk."

"Most people just text." She'd deleted him from her phone long ago, but still. Showing up unannounced was flat-out rude. Not that he had many morals or even common decency.

"I wasn't sure if you'd respond."

"I wouldn't," she told him.

He propped one foot on the next step and smoothed a hand over his perfectly parted hair. "After all these years, you're still angry?"

She didn't know whether to laugh at his stupidity or throw her purse at him and pray she hit him in the head hard enough to knock some damn sense into him.

No purse should be treated that way, so she adjusted the strap on her shoulder and held it tight.

"Angry?" she asked with a slight laugh. "I'd have to feel something to actually be angry with you."

"Kate." Chris lowered his tone as if to appeal to her good side. She no longer had one where he was concerned. "Could I come in for a bit just to talk?"

"No. And actually, it's a bit creepy that you're on my porch waiting on me to get home."

"I haven't been here long," he assured her. "Maybe I should come back tomorrow. Can I take you for coffee?"

Kate stared down at the clean-cut man who probably still got bimonthly manicures. She couldn't help but wonder what in the hell she'd ever seen in him to begin with. Coffee with a man wearing a suit? She'd prefer champagne served up by a sexy tattooed-up bar owner.

Oh, no.

No, no, no.

Now was not the time to discover that her feelings were sliding into more than just friendship with Gray. Chris continued to stare at her, waiting for her answer, but she was having a minor mental breakdown.

"I'm busy tomorrow," she finally replied. "Good night, Chris."

Without waiting for him to respond, Kate pulled her key from her purse and quickly let herself into the house. She flicked the dead bolt back into place and smacked the porch lights off.

What on earth had flashed through her mind when Chris mentioned taking her for coffee? She loved coffee and Stonerock had the best little coffee house on the edge of town. Not that she would even entertain the thought of having coffee with that slime bag.

But Gray?

Everything in her thought process lately circled back to that man. Her planner, her bucket list, her drinks, her most satisfying sexual experiences.

Kate groaned as she made her way toward her bedroom. What she needed to do was spend more time with Tara and Lucy. So much one-on-one with Gray had obviously clouded her judgment and left her confused and mixing amazing sex with feelings that shouldn't be developing.

But Tara was busy with her own life and Lucy was still in that newlywed bliss phase. Ladies' Night would definitely be her best bet to get back to where she needed to be mentally. Letting lose, being carefree, and not worrying about anything would surely cleanse her mind of all lustful thoughts of her best friend.

Sex really did cloud the mind. And great sex…well, maybe she just needed sleep. If she weren't so exhausted, perhaps Gray wouldn't have filled her mind the second Chris started talking about taking her out.

Gray hadn't even taken her out. They weren't in any way dating. They were going on about their way like always—just adding in a few toe-curling orgasms along the way.

Kate pushed aside all thoughts of Chris showing up, Gray and his ability to make her want more than she should and the fact he may be selling his bar and leaving. She couldn't get wrapped up in lives and circumstances she had no control over. As much as she thrived on micromanaging, realistically, she had to let go.

After pulling on her favorite sleep shirt, Kate slid beneath her sheets and adjusted her pillows against the upholstered headboard. She unplugged her iPad from the nightstand and pulled up her schedule for the following day. Yes, her schedule was in both paper and e-format.

After glancing over her schedule, she went to her personal blog. So many blogs failed, but Kate prided herself on being a marketing genius. She honed in on her niche market, taking full advantage of social media platforms that drove her clients to her site, thus turning them into paying customers.

Not many people could do their dream job and work from home. Kate knew how blessed and lucky she was to have such a fabulous life.

Though seeing Lucy so happy with love and Tara with sweet Marley made Kate wonder if she was missing out.

Tara clicked on the tab to bring up her bucket list. At the bottom she added the word "family" in bold font. Ultimately that would be her main goal once she'd achieved the others. She wasn't going to rush it, she wanted to wait on the right man to come along. She was definitely ready to take that step toward a broader future.

Stifling a yawn, Kate placed her device back on her nightstand and clicked the light off. As she fluffed her pillows and rolled over, she hoped she would fall asleep right away and not dream of the sexy bar owner who had occupied her thoughts every night.

But she found herself smiling. She couldn't help herself. There was no greater man in her life, and even though things were a little unbalanced right now, she fully intended on keeping him at an arm's length. For real this time.

"Thanks, darlin', but I'm busy tonight."

Ladies' Night always brought in the flirtatious women with short skirts and plunging necklines. Being single didn't hurt business, either, but he'd never picked up a woman in his bar. That wasn't good business and certainly not a reputation he wanted hovering over his establishment.

Gray extracted himself from the clutches of the blonde at the table in the corner. That's what he got for coming out from behind his post. His staff had been busy so he'd taken the table their drinks.

Back behind the safety of the bar, Gray tapped on the computer and started filling more drink orders. Jacob ran the finger foods from the kitchen. The menu remained small and simple but enough to keep people thirsty, because the drinks were by far the moneymaker.

The DJ switched the song to one that seriously made Gray's teeth itch. "It's Raining Men" blared through the hidden surround sound speakers. Considering the crowd and the cheers and squeals, Gray was definitely in the minority here.

One night. He could live through terrible music for one night a week. Wednesday nights brought in the most revenue. Women from all walks of life came out in droves. Some were celebrating bachelorette parties. Some were stay-at-home moms who needed a break. Sometimes a group of employees got together to decompress after work. Whatever their situation was, Gray—and his bottom line—was thrilled he'd decided to add this night when he'd taken over.

As he placed three margaritas on the bar for one of his staff to take to table eleven, he glanced at the front door when it opened.

Finally.

Gray didn't even care that his heart skipped a little at the sight of Kate. He was done ignoring the way he felt when she was near. He just...damn it, he wanted her to stop avoiding him. He needed her stability, the security she brought to their friendship.

He hadn't spoken with her since he'd talked to his dad. Just the thought of that conversation had him questioning what to do. Clearly his father would be heartbroken over losing Gallagher's, but Gray just kept thinking back to how free he would be if he was able to explore his own interests.

His eyes drifted back to Kate. She'd settled in a booth with

Tara and Lucy. When her gaze landed on him, she might as well have touched him with her bare hands. Immediate heat spread through him, and the second she flashed that radiant smile, Gray nearly toppled the glass he'd been holding.

After returning her smile, he returned his focus to the orders. No woman had ever made him falter on the job before. Then again, no woman was Kate McCoy.

As he worked on filling orders, he randomly glanced her way. He knew exactly which drinks were going to that table. Those three were so predictable. Tara always wanted a cosmo, Lucy stuck with a light beer and Kate went with soda.

It wasn't long before another song blared through the speakers that had Gray cringing, but the dance floor instantly filled with women. Kate and her friends were right in the midst of the action.

That little dress she wore had his gut tightening. The loose hem slid all over her thighs as she wiggled that sweet body on the dance floor. She'd piled her hair up on top of her head, but the longer she danced, the more stray strands fell around her face, her neck.

Get a grip.

"Hey, baby. You ever take time for a dance?"

Gray flashed a smile to the redhead leaning over the bar at just the right angle to give him a complete visual of her cleavage and bra of choice.

"Who would make all these drinks if I went dancing?" he yelled over the music.

She reached across the bar and ran her fingertip down his chest. "I think if you got on that dance floor, we'd all forget about our drinks. At least for a little while."

Someone slammed a glass next to him, jerking Gray's attention from the flirtatious patron.

He turned just in time to see Kate walking away, her empty glass on the bar.

"Looks like you made someone's drink wrong," the red-head stated, lowering her lids. "You can make me anything you want."

Gray stepped back, causing her hand to fall from his chest. "Where are you and your friends sitting?" he asked. "I'll send over a pitcher of margaritas."

Her smile widened as she gestured to their table. Apparently the idea of free booze was more appealing than him...which was perfectly fine. Right now, he was more intrigued with the way Kate had acted. She'd slammed that glass pretty close to his arm on purpose and then walked away without a word.

Jealous?

Gray couldn't help but smile as he got the pitcher ready. If Kate was jealous, then maybe she was ready to see where this new level of friendship would take them. Perhaps she'd missed him in the days they'd been apart and she'd thought more about their time in the mountains.

Maybe she'd finally realized how good they were together and that it was silly to put restrictions on their intimacy. He spotted her back out on the dance floor talking to Lucy. Lucy nodded in response to whatever she said and Kate walked away.

Gray picked up empty glasses and wiped off the bar where a few ladies had just sat, all the while keeping his gaze on Kate. She went back to the booth and grabbed her purse.

Well, hell. She was pissed and leaving? All because some woman flirted with him?

If she was that upset, then she was definitely jealous. Gray had every intention of playing right into that little nugget of information.

Gray lost track of Kate, but he never saw the front door open, which meant she had to be inside somewhere. He glanced at his watch and realized they still had another two business hours to go. He couldn't get to Kate for a while, but she better be ready for him, because he wasn't backing down from this fight. He was damn well going to call her out on her jealousy and forbid her to make any excuses for why they shouldn't be together.

Gray couldn't wait to get her alone again.

CHAPTER TWELVE

THIS WAS THE most ridiculous thing she'd ever done in her entire life. But hey, at least she could mark spontaneity off her life list.

Kate stared at the clock on Gray's nightstand. The bar had closed thirty minutes ago. She knew he had cleanup down to a science and he should be wrapping things up any minute.

She thought coming up here to cool off would help. Seeing that trampy redhead raking her false nail down Gray's chest had set something off inside Kate she didn't want to label...because it smacked her right in the face with jealousy.

Why was she jealous? Kate knew full well that women found Gray sexy and did nearly anything to get his attention. But things were different now. Yes, they were just friends, but everything had changed.

What would he say when he came up here and found her in his bed? Would he tell her they'd agreed to call it quits after the camping? Would he climb in bed and give her another night to remember?

Kate came to her feet and grabbed the dress she'd flung at the bottom of the bed. This was a mistake. She looked like an utter fool. No, a desperate fool, and she needed to get the hell out of here before Gray came in.

The front door to his apartment clicked shut, followed by the dead bolt. Too late to run.

She clutched the dress to her chest, feeling even more ridiculous now. Why had she put that damn "be more spontaneous" idea on her list? And why had she let that busty tramp bring out the green-eyed monster?

Heavy footsteps sounded down the hall seconds before Gray filled the doorway. His dark eyes widened as they raked over her. There was no way she could move. Just that simple, visual lick he gave her had her rooted in place.

His eyes snapped back up to hers. "Put the dress down."

Kate dropped it at her feet before thinking twice. That low command gave her little choice but to obey. Warmth spread through her. There was no denying exactly why she'd come up here, just as there was no denying that heated look in his eyes.

"You came up here a while ago." He leaned one broad shoulder against the door frame and continued to rake his eyes across her body. "What have you been doing?"

"Second-guessing myself," she murmured.

Gray's lips twitched. "Is that so? I don't recall sneaking into a man's bedroom on your life list."

"I was trying to check off spontaneity."

"Is that so?"

Kate crossed her arms over her chest. "I'm feeling a little silly standing here like this. Are you just going to stay over there and stare at me?"

"Maybe I'm looking at you because you deserve to be valued."

Oh, no. He couldn't say things like that to her. Statements so bold only pushed them deeper into this ...whatever the technical term was. *Friends* seemed too tame of a label considering she stood in his bedroom wearing only her underwear.

"Chris showed up at my house."

Why did she blurt that out? She prided herself on planning everything, even her words. But somehow hearing him mention her being valued made her think of the jerk who thought the opposite.

Gray stood straight up and took a step toward her. "What the hell did he want?"

Kate laughed. "To talk. He invited me to coffee."

The muscle in his jaw clenched. "Did you go?" he all but growled.

"No. I demanded he leave and I haven't heard from him since."

Gray's eyes narrowed. "He's trying to get you back."

"After all this time and after what he did? He's a fool."

"Tell me if he comes back."

Kate stared up into those dark eyes. "You're jealous."

Gray slid his palms up her bare arms, over her shoulders, and hooked his thumbs in her bra straps. "Like you were jealous downstairs?"

Tipping her chin up, she met his mocking stare. "I was not jealous."

Gray's fingertips left the straps and slid over the swell of her breasts. Tingles raced through her body.

"You cracked the glass you slammed down." One finger slid between her breasts and back up. "Seemed like you were upset about something."

"Consider the glass payment for the panties you ripped off me."

If possible, his eyes darkened at the mention of her underwear. In one swift move, he flicked the front closure of her bra and had it off. When he gripped the edge of her panties and met her eyes, she smiled.

"You going for two?" she asked, quirking a brow.

He gave a yank, and the sound of ripping material answered her question. Suddenly she stood before him completely naked and in the bright light of his bedroom while he was completely clothed.

"This is hardly fair," she informed him.

"You snuck up to my apartment and came to my bed," he reminded her. "You're playing by my rules now, Kate."

How did the man continually get sexier? Seriously. Looks were one thing, but the way he treated her, spoke to her…how would she feel when this came to an end?

"I wasn't going to do this again," she muttered, mostly to herself.

"And I wasn't going to let you run, either." He banded an arm around her waist and jerked her body against his. "Why is there a time limit on what we're doing? We both like it. Neither one of us is dating anyone. It makes sense."

Kate closed her eyes. "Because we could lose ourselves and forget who we really are."

He leaned down and nipped her lips. "Maybe we're only just discovering who we really are."

Those words barely registered before he lifted her off her feet and carried her to his bed. He eased her down onto the plain gray sheets that were still rumpled from when he'd gotten out of them. She'd never been in his bedroom. They'd been friends forever, but crossing this threshold was taking things to a whole new territory.

Gray eased back, leaving her lying spread out. She watched as he reached behind his neck and jerked the black tee up and over his head. After he tossed it into the corner, he started unfastening his jeans, all while keeping those heavy-lidded eyes on her.

"You look good here, Kate."

She closed her eyes. Maybe if she didn't look at him when he said such meaningful words, they wouldn't penetrate her soul. But he kept saying little things. No, not little, not in the terms of the impact they had.

Instead of responding, because she truly had no words, she lifted her knees to make room for him. Once he'd gotten protection from his nightstand, she reached out, taking him in her arms. His weight pressed her further into the bed. She wasn't sure how she looked here, but she knew she liked it. Being wrapped up in Gray and knowing they shared something no one else knew about…there was a thrill to what they were doing.

A thrill she wasn't sure she ever wanted to see end.

But was he on the same page? If she threw out that she was having stronger feelings, what would he say? Would he tell her they were done with sex? Would he tell her they could be friends and have sex only as long as they were both single? Because suddenly, she wondered if there could be more.

"Hey."

Kate focused on the man who flanked her head with his forearms and smoothed her hair away from her face.

"Stay with me," he murmured.

Curling her fingers around his bare shoulders, Kate smiled. "I wouldn't be anywhere else."

Gray joined their bodies and Kate locked her ankles behind his back. She wanted to stay just like this, to forget the outside world, to ignore any warning that went off in her head about what could go wrong. Because right now, everything in her world was absolutely perfect.

Gray's lips slid over her skin, along her jawline, down her neck, along her chest. Kate arched into him, needing more and silently begging him to give it to her. Gray murmured something into her ear and she couldn't make it out. He'd done that before and she wondered what he was saying, but that was something she'd ask later. She'd rather enjoy the euphoria and sweet bliss of being in his arms…in his bed.

In a move that shocked her, Gray held on to her and flipped them until he was on his back and she straddled him. The way he looked up at her…

A girl could get used to a man looking at her like she was the only good thing in his world.

Gray gripped her hips and Kate's body instantly responded to his strength. His fingers bit into her as she flattened her palms on his chest and let the moment completely consume her.

Before Kate's body ceased trembling, Gray's stilled beneath her. His lips thinned. His head tipped back. His eyes shut. But his grip on her never lightened. She remained where she was, watching the play of emotions across his face.

Slowly he relaxed beneath her. As he slid his hands up over the dip in her waist and urged her down, Kate smiled. She fell against his chest and closed her eyes.

"What now?" she asked, unable to stop herself.

His chest vibrated with the soft rumble of laughter. "We don't need to plan the next move. Relax."

When she started to set up, he flattened his hand on her back. "You can stay just like this a few more minutes."

She could, but she had questions. So many questions and only he could answer them. Well, they could figure them out together, but what was going to happen when she told him she might want more? He'd never even acted like he wanted a relationship. They had sex. They had never even been on a real date.

Kate couldn't take it anymore. She sat up and shifted off him. With her back to Gray, she sat on the edge of the bed and leaned down to pick up her discarded dress.

"We really need to talk."

Silence filled the air, as she'd expected it would once she uttered those five words that would put any man's hackles up.

Kate threw a glance over her shoulder. Gray lay there naked as you please, with his arms folded behind his head. His eyes held hers, but he still said nothing even when she raised a brow, silently begging him to speak.

"Why are you making this difficult?" she asked.

She came to her feet and threw her dress on, sans all undergarments. When she spun around toward the bed and crossed her arms over her chest, Gray merely smiled. Still naked, still fully in charge of this situation, because he just watched her. The man could be utterly infuriating.

"What are we doing?" she muttered, shaking her head. "Seriously? Are we going to keep doing this? Is there more?"

Her heart beat so fast, she wondered if he could see the pulse in her neck. Again without a word, Gray came to his feet and strutted from the room.

She threw her arms out. "Well, that went well," she whispered to the empty room.

Moments later, he came back in, still not the least bit concerned with his state of undress. He carried two wine stems between his fingers and in the other hand he had a champagne bottle.

"This is another bottle of what you had the other night." He set everything on the nightstand and poured her a glass. "You need another drink if we're going to get into this discussion."

"Drinking isn't the answer," she retorted.

He picked up the glass and handed it to her. "I never said it was. But I brought this bottle up earlier and got sidetracked when I found you naked in my room."

She took the glass but didn't take a sip yet. "Why did you bring it to begin with? I didn't take you for a champagne drinker."

"I'm not, but I knew you were up here so I brought it for you."

Kate jerked. "How did you know I came up here? I was discreet."

Gray laughed as he filled his own glass and then downed it in one gulp. He set the glass back on the nightstand and turned toward her.

"I'm a pretty smart guy, Kate." He pointed toward her glass. "You're going to want to start on that."

She took a small drink, relishing the bubbles that burst in her mouth. Champagne really wasn't bad at all.

"You were jealous," he started, holding up his hand when she opened her mouth to argue. "You were, so be quiet for a minute."

Kate took another drink and sank onto the edge of the bed. "Could you at least put something on? It's hard to concentrate with all that hanging out."

Gray laughed and turned toward his dresser, where a stack

of clean laundry lay neatly folded. He grabbed a pair of black boxer briefs and tugged them on.

"Better?"

Actually, no. The briefs hugged his narrow hips, drawing her attention to that perfect V of muscles leading south. Mercy, how had she missed all of his flawless features in the past?

She took another drink.

"So you were jealous," he went on.

"Move to something else," she growled.

Gray laughed, propping his hands on those hips she tried so hard to stop staring at. "Fine. Then I saw you grab your purse and disappear, only the front door didn't open and I couldn't get a clear view of the back hall. Nobody goes that way, but I had a feeling my Kate had done just that."

She narrowed her eyes. "Jacob told you."

"He didn't have to say anything."

Kate polished off her champagne and set her empty glass next to his. When she glanced back up at him, she shivered at the look in his eyes.

"You didn't like that woman flirting with me. That was a good piece of information to have."

Kate hated that she'd let her emotions get the better of her. "Fine. I was jealous."

Gray knelt down in front of her and clasped her hands in his. "I didn't think you'd admit it."

"Why hide it? We may just be having sex, but that doesn't mean I want to see some woman pawing you."

Kate stared down at their joined hands and willed herself to be strong and just say what she wanted to say. But before she could tell him her thoughts, he placed one hand beneath her chin and tipped her face to meet his.

Gray leaned forward and nipped at her lips before murmuring, "Marry me."

CHAPTER THIRTEEN

WHY WASN'T SHE saying anything?

Gray waited.

"Kate?"

She blinked. "Marry you? But we've never discussed anything like that."

When she came to her feet, her abrupt movement had him standing as well. Then she began to pace his room. She couldn't go far in the small space, but since he had only a bed and dresser, she didn't have much to maneuver around.

"Marry you," she repeated beneath her breath as she turned on her heel to walk in the other direction.

"Why not?" he asked. "We get along, we're good together in bed, and we just understand each other. That's more than most married couples have."

She stopped and stared at him as if he had grown another nose on the side of his head. "Why on earth do you want to marry me?"

"I talked to Dad about selling the bar." Now it was his turn to pace because the thought of everything closing in on him made him twitchy. "He's most definitely not on board and he seems to think I just need to settle down. Perhaps this way, I could sell it and you and I could use that money to start over somewhere. Or hell, build a house here. Whatever. We'd have freedom and that's all that matters."

He'd come to stand directly in front of her, but she continued to stare. No, glare would best describe what she was doing now. There was something he couldn't quite pinpoint in her eyes. Gone was the desire he'd seen moments ago.

"So, what, I'm just a means to pacify your dad so you can collect a check?" she asked. With a shake of her head, she let out a humorless laugh. "I was already going to marry one jerk who obviously didn't get me. It's quite clear you never understood me either if you think I'll marry you."

Anger simmered within him, but he didn't want to lash out.

"What the hell is wrong with marrying me?" he asked.

"I want to know your first thought when I asked why you wanted to marry me. Don't think about what I want to hear. Just tell me the first thing that comes into your head."

This was a trap. Somewhere in that statement she'd set a trap for him and he was about to fall headfirst into it.

"I think it makes sense," he answered honestly. "What's there to think about?"

She stared at him a bit longer and that's when he saw it. Hurt. That emotion he couldn't pin down before had been pain and it stared back at him plain as day. He'd seen that look before from patrons who wanted to drink their worries away. He'd seen it too often. But he was completely baffled by why the hell she stared at him with such anguish.

"What did I say?"

She chewed on her bottom lip for a moment before skirting around him and picking up her underwear and bra. He watched as she dressed fully and then sat on the edge of his bed to pull her sandals on.

"Where are you going?"

Without looking up, she adjusted her shoe and came to her feet. "Home. I've had enough of...whatever this is. We never should've slept together."

He crossed the room and took her shoulders, forcing her to face him. "What the hell are you talking about? Is this because I asked you to marry me?"

Her eyes swam with unshed tears and he wished like hell he knew why she was this upset.

"Do you love me, Gray?"

"What?" Her question stunned him. "Of course I love you. I've loved you since the seventh grade. What kind of a question is that?"

She blinked, causing a tear to spill down her cheek. He swiped the pad of his thumb over her creamy skin. His heart ached at seeing her hurt, but hell if he knew how to fix this.

"It's a legitimate question, considering you proposed," she said, her voice soft, sad. "This isn't working for me anymore."

Kate shrugged from his arms and stepped back. She tilted her chin and squared her shoulders as if going into warrior mode before his eyes.

"You want freedom?" she asked. "Then go. Take that fat check, sell the bar and just go."

"What the hell are you so angry about?" he asked...well, more like yelled, because damn it, he could not figure her out.

"I never thought you'd use me or consider me plan B for your life." She swatted at another tear that streaked down her cheek. "You're only asking me to marry you to pacify your father. That man would do anything for you and he's all you have left. Do you know how lucky you are? Do you understand that if I had a parent in my life, I'd do anything to make them proud of me?"

Now he was pissed. Gray fisted his hands at his sides and towered over her as he took a step forward. "You think my father isn't proud of me? Of what I've done here? You know I'm sorry about your parents, but damn it, Kate, you can't always throw that in my face."

She recoiled as if he'd hit her. Gray muttered a string of curses beneath his breath as he raked a hand through his hair.

"That's not what I meant," he said.

She held up her hands. "You said exactly what you meant. We don't see eye to eye on things anymore. Just another reason why I need to go and this...all of it has to stop."

His heart clenched. "What do you mean, 'all of it'?"

"I knew we couldn't keep our friendship and sex separate," she cried. Tears streamed down her cheeks and she didn't even bother swiping them away. "Then you throw out an engagement like it's a simple fix to your problems. Did you ever think that maybe I'd want to marry someone who actually loves me? That I don't just want to settle?"

"I said I loved you," he practically shouted. "What more do you want?"

The brief smile that flashed amid the tears nearly gutted him. Pain radiated from her and if he knew what he'd done to crush her, he'd fix it.

"You don't mean it," she whispered. "Not in the way I need you to."

A rumble of thunder and a quick flash of lightning interrupted the tense moment. Within seconds, rain pelted the windows. Kate stared at him another second before she turned away and headed toward the door. Gray had a sinking feeling that if she walked out that door, she might never come back... not even as his friend.

"Don't go, Kate. Not like this."

She stilled, but didn't face him.

"We can work this out."

"I think we've said enough," she replied.

He took a step toward her, but didn't reach for her like he desperately wanted to. "At least let me drive you home. You're upset and it's starting to storm."

Those bright blue eyes shining with tears peered over her shoulder. "I'd rather take my chances with the storm outside than the one surrounding us."

And then she was gone.

Gray stared at the spot where she'd just stood, then he glanced to the empty glasses, the rumpled sheets.

What the hell had just happened here?

Well, there was the proposal that had taken them both by surprise. But in his defense, the moment the words were out of his mouth, he hadn't regretted them.

He did love her. They'd been friends forever, so what kind of question was that? And what did she mean by saying he didn't love her the way she needed him to? He'd always been there for her, hadn't he?

Gray turned from the bedroom. He couldn't stay in there, not when the sheets smelled like her, not when just the sight of that bed had him recalling how perfect she'd looked lying there.

He stalked down the hall and into the living room. The storm grew closer as the thunder and lightning hit simultaneously. The electricity flickered once, twice, then went out.

Perfect. Pitch black to match his mood.

Gray went to the window and looked down into the parking lot beside the bar. Kate's car still sat there.

Without thinking, he fumbled his way through the dark to throw on a pair of jeans, not bothering with shoes. He raced down the back steps and out the rear entrance.

Instantly he was soaked, but he didn't care. If Kate was still here, she was sitting in her car, upset. He knew that as well as he knew his name.

He tapped on the driver's window. Kate started the car and slid the window down a sliver.

"Get out of the storm," she yelled.

"I will when I know you're all right."

The damn street lights were out so he couldn't see her face, but he saw enough shimmer in her eyes to know she wasn't fine, not at all.

"You're soaked. Go inside, Gray. We're done."

He jerked open her door, propping one arm up on the car,

and leaned down to get right in her face. "We're not done, Kate. You can't brush me aside."

The lights from her dash lit up her face. She stared at him for a moment before shaking her head.

"I'm going home. I need some space."

He knew what that was code for. She wanted to push him away and try to figure everything out herself. Hell no. Yes, he'd upset her, but he wasn't backing down. This was bigger than selling the bar, pleasing his father or some lame marriage proposal.

Kate had legitimately been hurt by their conversation. She'd opened herself and came to his room. He could only imagine the courage that had taken.

"You can have your space," he told her, swiping the rain from his eyes. "But know that you can't keep me away. I'm not going anywhere, Kate."

He didn't give her a chance to reply. Gray gripped the back of her head and covered her mouth with his. Quick, fierce, impossible to forget, that's the kiss he delivered before he stepped back and closed her car door.

The window slid up as she put the car in Drive and pulled out of the lot. He stood in the midst of the storm, watching her taillights disappear into the dark night.

The thunder continued to rumble and a bolt of lightning streaked across the sky. Gray rubbed his chest as he headed back inside. He'd always ached for her when she'd gotten upset. But this was different.

Somehow with that surprise proposal, he'd severed something they shared. He'd tainted their friendship and put a dark cloud over their lives. All he'd wanted to do was make his father happy and somehow that had blown up in his face.

Gray knew sleep wasn't coming anytime soon, so he started plotting. If the damn electricity would come back on, he could put his plan into motion and maybe salvage some semblance of this friendship.

CHAPTER FOURTEEN

KATE CLICKED SEND on her blog and sat back to admire the new layout she'd implemented on her site. Thanks to sleepless nights, she'd had plenty of time to work on cleaning up her pages a bit. She now had everything organized and easier to maneuver.

But she was in no mood to celebrate. For the past two mornings she'd been sick as a dog. She'd also missed her period and there was a home pregnancy test in her bathroom that mocked her every time she went in. There was no need to take it. She knew.

The birth control she'd switched from pill to patch had come during their camping trip, there was no questioning how this happened.

She hadn't heard from Gray in two weeks. The deadline had passed for him to make a decision on the bar, but he hadn't told her anything. He hadn't texted, hadn't called. He'd warned her he'd give her space and he'd kept his word.

Damn it, why did she have to miss him so much? What was he going to say when she told him about the baby? Most likely he'd take that Neanderthal attitude and try to convince her to marry him.

Kate glanced at the clock. She really needed to get some

lunch. The crackers and ginger ale this morning had worn off. Well, they hadn't stayed down, so they'd worn off immediately.

She scrolled through her newly uploaded blog discussing why organization made for a better attitude. People in general were calmer if the world around them was in order so they didn't feel as if they were living in chaos. She'd even added a new buy button to the site, along with a note stating that all first-time clients would receive a 10 percent discount.

Her newsletter was set to go out this evening, so the timing of this post was perfect. Of course, she'd planned it that way.

Kate pushed her chair back and came to her feet. A slight wave of dizziness overcame her. Gripping the edge of her desk, she closed her eyes and waited for it to pass.

What would Lucy and Tara say? They didn't even know she and Gray had been intimate. They would be hurt that she hadn't confided in them, but she just hadn't been ready and then she thought things were going to go back to normal and now...well, this was her new normal.

Kate's cell buzzed and vibrated on her desk top. She sank back into her chair and stared at the screen, not recognizing the number. New clients contacted her all the time, so ignoring the call wasn't an option.

"Hello?"

"Ms. McCoy?"

She didn't recognize the male voice on the other end. "Yes."

"My name is Steven Sanders. I'm with a group out of Nashville called Lost and Found Family."

Intrigued, Kate eased back in her seat and kept her eyes shut. The room had stopped spinning, but she wasn't taking any chances right now.

"What can I do for you, Mr. Sanders?"

"Actually, it's what I can do for you," he countered. "I was given your contact information by Gray Gallagher. He wanted me to talk with you about tracing your family and finding your heritage. Is this a good time to talk?"

So many things swirled around in her mind. Gray had called someone to help her find her family? But he hadn't talked to her or even texted. Why hadn't he told her about this? Why was he being so nice when she'd turned him down and left in the midst of a storm?

"Sure," she replied. "Um…sorry. This is all just a bit of a surprise."

The man chuckled on the other end of the line. "Gray was adamant I call you as soon as I could, but I was trying to get another case wrapped up before contacting you. He made me vow to give your case special attention."

Something warmed inside her, something that brought tears to her eyes. She leaned forward, resting her elbows on her desk.

"Well, I appreciate that," she replied. "But I understand I'm probably not your only client. What information do you need from me?"

Steven went on to explain the information Gray had already delivered to him. He asked her about her mother's maiden name, her skin color, eye color, hair color. He went through her father's description. Then he asked for birthdays, where they were born and any grandparents' names she might know.

"This gives me a bit to go on to get started," Steven said after about a half hour of gathering information. "Should I call or email you when I have more questions?"

"I'm fine with either," she replied. "I can't thank you enough. I never knew really who to call to get started on this. You can bill me through email and I'll—"

"Oh, no, ma'am. Mr. Gallagher already took care of the bill, and any further charges will be sent to him."

Kate wasn't going to get into an argument with this guy. He had no clue about the whirlwind of emotions that continued to swirl around her and Gray. The poor guy was just doing his job.

"Thanks so much for taking on this case," she replied. "I look forward to hearing from you."

"I'll be in touch."

She disconnected the call and stood back up, thankfully no longer dizzy. As she made her way toward the kitchen, she went over in her mind what she wanted to say to Gray. He'd already helped her by tracking down someone who could research her ancestry. He didn't need to pay for it, too. And he'd done all of this after they'd stopped speaking.

The idea that he'd started working on a portion of her life list had tears burning her eyes. No matter what had transpired between them, he was still determined to be there for her.

Kate made a quick peanut butter sandwich and grabbed a bottle of water and a banana before heading back to her office. There was no dodging Gray anymore. She needed to thank him for hiring the genealogy investigator, plus tell him about the baby.

If she thought their dynamics had been changed before with just sex, this would certainly alter everything they'd ever known. She had to be positive before going to him and she had to know exactly what to say.

Kate would definitely take the test to be sure, but he deserved to know. This was definitely something they needed to work on together.

Looked like she wasn't going to be putting him in that friend category anymore. She wasn't ready to put him in the husband category, either. He'd honestly hurt her when he'd said why he wanted to marry her.

How could he be so blind? How could he not see that she wanted someone who genuinely loved her? Like *in love* with her?

She'd been on the verge of telling him she was falling for him when he blurted out the proposal, destroying any hope she might have had that their bond could go deeper than friendship. And now she was carrying his child. If this wasn't the most warped situation ever, she didn't know what was.

Ladies' Night was tonight and in their group texts, Lucy and Tara had already been vocal about wanting to go. Kate figured now would be as good a time as any to go out, try to have fun and not freak out about her entire life getting turned upside down.

Because as scared, nervous and anxious as she was about this child—along with a gamut of other emotions—the truth of the matter was…she was happy. She had no family, but she was creating her very own. No, this was definitely not planned and, surprisingly, she was okay.

This wasn't a schedule or a job. This was a child. Her child.

Would Gray still want to take the money from the sale of the bar? She couldn't stand the thought of him leaving, but he needed to be aware of just how much their lives were about to change.

Tonight. She'd go tonight and thank him for the genealogy specialist. Then, once the bar closed, she'd take him upstairs and tell him about the baby.

First, though, she had a test to take.

As Wednesday nights went, the bar was crazier than usual. He'd begged one of his waitresses to come in on her night off. He never begged. He'd even offered her an extra paid day off if she just came in for a few hours to help bartend. Jacob was in the kitchen filling in for the cook, who'd come down with some cold or whatever.

It was just a crazy, messed up day.

And Kate had strolled in with her friends and hadn't come up to the bar once to speak to him. In the two weeks he'd given her space, he'd damn near lost his mind.

More orders flooded the system and Gray didn't slow down or stop. If Kate was here, then she was here to talk. She'd missed Ladies' Night last week and, like a fool, he'd watched the door. But he'd been so busy over the past fourteen days trying to get this place ready to sell that he'd let himself get wrapped up in the business.

He still hadn't made up his mind, but he had texted the guy

and bought more time. Gray was inching closer to realizing he might never get a chance like this again. If he ever wanted to get out and see what he'd been missing in his life, now was the time.

What seemed like an eternity later, the crowd started winding down. Gray had caught glimpses of Kate, Lucy and Tara dancing, but now he only saw Kate in the corner booth alone and looking at something on her phone.

He left the bar to his employee and promised to be away only two minutes. Now that things weren't so insane, he wanted to talk to Kate.

As he crossed the bar, weaving through the tables and the stragglers who were still hanging out, Kate looked up and caught his gaze. Her eyes widened and with her tense shoulders and tight smile, Gray knew something was up.

Without asking, he slid into the booth across from her. "Didn't expect you to show up tonight."

She laid her phone in front of her and shrugged. "I needed to get out of the house. Plus, I needed to thank you for having Steven Sanders call me."

Gray eased back in the seat. "So he's on it. Good. I was giving him two more days to contact you before I called him again."

"He has other clients, you know."

Gray didn't care. What he cared about was helping Kate with her list and finding some sort of family for her to call her own.

"I hope he can find what you need," Gray replied.

Silence settled between them as she glanced down at her hands. She'd laced her fingers together and the way her knuckles were turning white made him wonder what was really on her mind.

"You're upset that I contacted him?" he guessed.

"No, no. I'm surprised and thankful," she corrected him.

"What's wrong?" he asked, leaning forward. "Lucy and Tara took off a while ago but you're still here."

Her eyes darted to the dancing women on the dance floor.

"Kate."

She turned her focus to him, but that didn't last long. Her gaze dropped once again to her clasped hands. "We need to talk. Can I wait until you're closed?"

Gray glanced to his watch. "We've got another hour. Do you want to go upstairs? You look like you could fall over."

And she did. She'd gone sans makeup, which wasn't unusual, but he could see the dark circles under her eyes, and she was a bit paler than normal.

"You feeling all right?" he asked.

She attempted a smile, but it was lame and forced. "Fine. I think I will go upstairs if you don't care. I can't leave without talking to you alone."

When she slid out of the booth, Gray came to his feet as well. She reached for the table with one hand and her head with the other as she teetered.

"Kate." He grasped her arms, holding tight. "I didn't make a drink for you. What have you had?"

She waved a hand away as she straightened. "I'm just tired and stood up too fast. I've only had water."

"Do you need something to eat?"

Shaking her head, she tried for a smile once again. "Really, I'm okay. I'll meet you upstairs when you're done."

He watched her head behind the bar and into the back hallway. Never in all his years as owner had he wanted to close up early and tell everyone to get the hell out.

Something was wrong with Kate. After all the running she'd done, something had pulled her back to him and he knew it wasn't the fact he'd called a genealogy specialist.

The next hour seemed to drag as he busted his butt to get the place ready to shut down for the night. He could sweep the floors and do a thorough wipe down in the morning. Once all the alcohol was taken care of, the kitchen was shut down properly and the employees were gone, Gray locked up and headed upstairs.

When he opened the door and stepped into the living room,

he froze. There on his sofa was Kate all curled up in one corner. She'd removed her shoes and her little bare feet were tucked at her side.

She didn't look too comfortable at the angle her head had fallen against the back of the couch. Had she not been sleeping at home? Had she thought about his proposal and was here to…what? Take him up on it?

Gray turned the knob and slowly shut the door, careful not to click it into place. He crossed the room and took a seat directly in front of her on the old metal trunk he used as a coffee table. He watched her for a minute, torn between waking her and letting her get the sleep she seemed to desperately need.

After several minutes of feeling like a creeper, Gray reached out and tapped her leg. She didn't move. He flattened his hand around her thigh and gave a gentle squeeze.

"Kate," he said in a soft tone.

She started to stir. Her lids fluttered, then lifted. She blinked a few times as if focusing. Then she shot up on the sofa.

"Oh my gosh." Her hands immediately went to her hair, pushing wayward strands back from her face. "I didn't mean to fall asleep."

He held out his hands. "Relax. It's no big deal."

She swung her legs around and placed them on the area rug. The side of her knee brushed his as she propped her elbows on her thighs and rubbed her face.

"What's wrong, Kate?" He couldn't stand it any longer. "I gave you the space you asked for, but you show up here looking like a small gust of wind could blow you over. Are you sick? Don't lie to me."

Damn it, fear gripped him and he didn't like this feeling. Not one bit.

"I'm not sick." She dropped her hands in her lap and met his gaze dead-on. "I'm pregnant."

CHAPTER FIFTEEN

KATE STARED AT HIM, worried when the silence stretched longer than was comfortable.

She hadn't meant to just blurt that out, but honestly, was there a lead-in to such a bomb? Gray sat so close, their knees bumped. And for the second time in their years of friendship, she couldn't make out the expression on his face.

His eyes never wavered from her, but he reached out and gripped her hands in his. "Pregnant? Are you sure?"

Before she could answer, he shook his head. "That was stupid. You wouldn't tell me unless you were sure."

"I've suspected for a few days, but just took the test today."

Now his eyes did drop to her stomach. "I don't even know what to say. Are you... I mean, you feel okay?"

"I'm nauseous, tired, look like hell. Other than that, I'm fine."

Gray shifted his focus from her flat abdomen to her eyes. "You've never looked like hell in your life."

"You didn't see me hugging the commode this morning," she muttered.

His thumb raked over the back of her hand. "Did you come here to tell me you'd marry me?"

She'd been so afraid he'd say that. That he would just assume a baby would be a reason to marry. If the marriage wasn't going to be forever, how was joining lives the right thing to do?

"I'm not marrying you, Gray."

His dark brows drew in as he continued to stare at her. "Why not? This is all the more reason to get married. We're going to be parents. I can sell the bar, get the money, and we can go wherever you want. Hell, we'll travel and then decide where to settle down. Name it."

Kate shook her head and removed her hands from his. She leaned back on the couch and curled her feet back up beside her where they'd been.

"That's not the answer," she countered. "I don't want to keep doing this with you. We have time to figure out what the best plan will be for our baby."

"So if I sell the bar and leave, you'll what? Stay here? I want to be part of our child's life."

She knew he would. She expected him to be. Gray would be a wonderful father. He'd be a fabulous husband, just not in the way he was proposing. Literally.

"I'd never keep you away from the baby," she told him. "I'm hurt you would even suggest such a thing. If you leave, that's on you. I'll be right here in Stonerock."

He stared at her another minute and then finally pushed to his feet. "Stay here tonight," he said, looking down at her. "Just stay here so we can figure this out."

Kate smiled, but shook her head. "Sex isn't going to solve anything."

"Maybe I just want you here," he retorted. "Maybe I've missed you and now, knowing that you're carrying my child, I want to take care of you."

The tenderness in his voice warmed her. She knew he'd want to take over and make sure everything was perfect for her. He'd want to make her as comfortable as possible.

Unfortunately, through all of that, he just couldn't love her the way she wanted to be loved. The way she loved him.

Tears pricked her eyes. She dropped her head and brought her hands up to shield her face. Damn hormones.

"Kate." The cushion on the sofa sank next to her. One strong arm wrapped around her and she felt herself being pulled against his side. "Don't cry. Please. I'll figure something out."

Couldn't he see? This had nothing to do with the bar and if he kept it or sold it. If he loved her, truly loved her like a man loved a woman, she'd go anywhere with him. But she couldn't just uproot her life for a man who was settling and only trying to do the right thing.

"Stay," he whispered into her ear as he stroked her hair. "Sleeping. Nothing more."

She tipped her head back to peer up at him.

"Please."

She knew he only wanted to keep an eye on her, plus it was late and she was exhausted. Kate nodded. "I'll stay."

Gray left Kate sleeping and eased out of the bed. He glanced back down to where she lay wearing one of his shirts, her raven hair in a tangled mess around her, dark circles beneath her eyes. She'd been so exhausted when she'd come to the bar last night.

And she'd dropped the biggest bomb of his life.

A baby. He was having a baby with his best friend and she refused to marry him.

Gray had to convince her to. Before she'd changed his entire life with one sentence, he'd nearly talked himself into selling Gallagher's. Now that he knew he was going to be a father, well, he was sure he wanted to sell. He could use that money and make a nice life for his family...just as soon as he convinced Kate to marry him. Didn't she see that this was the most logical step?

He hadn't planned on getting married, but with his dad always hinting that he should, with the new chapter of selling the bar, and with Kate pregnant...hell, he had to move forward with his plan and make her see this was the best option for their future.

Quietly he eased the door shut and went to the kitchen to make breakfast. He had no clue what was on her agenda today, but hopefully after a good night's sleep, they could talk and try to work things out. Well, he'd try to get her to see reason.

Gray checked his fridge and realized he hadn't been to the store in... Honestly, he couldn't remember the last time he went to the store.

He headed down to the bar and raided that kitchen, then ran back upstairs. Now he could actually start cooking something. Kate still slept, so he tried to be quiet. His apartment wasn't that big, but it worked for him.

That is, this space had always worked until now. He couldn't exactly expect Kate to raise a baby here. She valued family and the importance of home. Kate and the baby deserved a house with a yard, somewhere they could put a swing set. Something the total opposite of a bachelor pad above a bar.

Gray fried some potatoes he'd snagged from downstairs and pulled out the ham steaks from his freezer. Kate was more of a pancake girl, but she'd have to adapt today. He would see to it that she was cared for, whether she liked it or not.

He'd just dished up the plates when he heard running down the hall and then the bathroom door slamming shut.

Muttering a curse, he left the breakfast and went to the closed door. Yeah, she was definitely sick. He rubbed his hands down his face and stared up at the ceiling. How the hell could he make her feel better? He couldn't exactly fix this or take it from her.

He stood on the other side of the door and waited until the toilet flushed. He heard water running and, moments later, she opened the door. Gray hated how pale she was, how her hand shook as she shoved her hair away from her face.

"Sorry about that," she murmured, leaning against the door frame. "It hits quick."

He reached out and framed her face in his hands. "Never apologize to me. I made breakfast, but I'm thinking maybe you're not in the mood."

Her eyes shut as she wrinkled her nose. "Do you just have some juice?"

"Downstairs I do. I'll be right back."

In record time he had the juice and was racing back upstairs. As soon as he stepped into the apartment, he heard Kate talking.

"No, Chris. This isn't a good time."

Gray set the bottle on the small dining table and headed down the hall toward her voice. Chris, the bastard ex.

"I never agreed to meet up with you, so if you thought I did, then you're mistaken."

When Gray hit the doorway of his bedroom, he saw Kate sitting on the edge of his bed, her back to him. She had her head down and was rubbing it.

Anger bubbled within him. Who the hell was this guy who suddenly came back into her life? Why did he think she would want anything at all to do with him after the way he'd treated her?

"I don't care how long you're in town," she replied. "I'm busy."

She tapped the screen and tossed her cell on the bed.

"Has he been bothering you?" Gray asked, stepping into the room.

Kate turned to glance over her shoulder. "Just a few calls and texts. He only showed up at my house the one time."

If this jerk planned on staying in town, Gray intended to track him down. It was time for Chris to find out for good that he'd lost his chance at anything with Kate.

"I have your juice in the kitchen," he told her. "How are you feeling?"

She let out a slight laugh. "Confused. Scared. Powerless."

It probably wasn't the best time to tell her he felt the same way. Kate needed him to be strong, needed him to be there like he always had been. Even more so now.

Gray crossed the room and came to stand in front of her. "Don't answer me now, but think about marriage, Kate. There are so many reasons this is a good idea."

She stood, easing around him. "Not now, Gray. Just…not now."

"I'm just asking you to think about it."

He followed her down the hall to the kitchen. Grabbing a glass from the cabinet, he set it on the counter and poured her juice.

"I'm not asking for an answer today," he told her as she drank. "But you can't dismiss the idea completely."

She licked her lips and leveled her gaze. "Are you selling the bar?"

Gray swallowed, knowing he was going to have to say it out loud at some point. "Yes."

Kate pulled in a slow breath and nodded. Then she finished the last of the juice and handed him back the glass.

"Then go do what you need to do," she told him. "You wanted to figure out what your life was missing, and I sure as hell don't want to be the reason you stay. I won't be someone's burden and I won't let this baby feel that way, either."

Gray slammed the glass on the counter and took her by her shoulders. "You're not listening to me, damn it. You're not a burden, Kate. This baby isn't a burden. But selling the bar makes more sense now than ever. What? You want to live up here and raise a child?"

"We're not getting married or living together, so it's a moot point," she threw back at him. "I don't like this, Gray. We're always arguing and I just want my friend back."

Her voice cracked on that last word and he hauled her against his chest. He wanted his friend back, too, but they'd obliterated the friendship line and now they were adding a baby to the mix.

"We can't go back," he told her. "But I won't let you go through this alone. I'm here."

She eased back, piercing him with those blue eyes full of questions, but she asked only one.

"For how long?"

CHAPTER SIXTEEN

WELL, THERE WAS no more dodging the inevitable.

Kate had asked the girls over since she knew Sam had Marley. This was definitely not a conversation for little ears.

She'd ordered pizza, made cookies, had wine and water on hand—everything was all set for the big reveal. Just then, her front door opened and Tara and Lucy came in, chattering.

Kate heard Lucy saying something about her stepdaughter, but couldn't make out exactly what it was. When she'd married Noah, she'd gotten an instant family and was filling the role of mom beautifully. Tara excelled at motherhood, despite the roller coaster she'd had to endure these past several months with Sam and his addiction.

Looked like Kate couldn't have asked for two better women to call on for support. She only hoped they weren't too angry with her for keeping the situation with Gray a secret.

Kate stepped from the kitchen into the living room. "Hey, guys."

"I smell pizza," Tara stated. "Please, tell me you got extra bacon on at least part of it."

Kate rolled her eyes. "Have I ever let you down? I even bought your favorite wine, though wine and pizza always sounded like a bad combo to me."

Lucy set her purse on the accent chair and dropped her keys inside. "Wine goes with everything and so does pizza, so it only makes sense to pair them together."

Kate attempted a smile, but her nerves were spiraling out of control. She could do this. There was nothing to be afraid of and her friends would be there for her. Isn't that what they did? They banded together during the best and worst of times.

"Oh, no." Tara took a slow step forward. "I thought we were just having a random girls' night. What's wrong, Kate?"

"You guys might want to sit down with a glass of wine first."

Lucy crossed her arms over her chest and shook her head. "Not until you tell us what's wrong."

"Nothing is wrong, exactly," she replied. "Gray and I—"

"Finally." Tara threw her hands in the air. "I knew something was going on with the two of you. What is it, though? You seem, I don't know...nervous."

"Are you and Gray together?" Lucy whispered as if this was some sacred secret.

"You could say that."

Kate looked from one friend to the other. They'd barely made it inside the front door, and from the determined look on their faces, they weren't moving any further until she confessed.

"I'm pregnant."

Tara's eyes widened. Lucy's mouth dropped. Neither said a word, but their shock spoke volumes.

"We were just fooling around," Kate went on. "I mean, there was the night of the rehearsal dinner, then camping—"

"I called this," Tara repeated. "Well, not the baby. Damn, Kate. You're having a baby?"

Kate couldn't help the smile and shrug. "Of all people, the CEO of Savvy Scheduler did not plan this."

Lucy stepped forward and extended her arms. Kate shook her head and held her hands out, silently telling her friend no.

"I can't do comfort right now," she explained. "I'm barely hanging on here and I just need to come to grips with this—"

Lucy wrapped her arms around Kate and that was all it took for Kate to finally crumble. Tears fell, fear took hold, and soon Tara's arms were banding around them as well.

"It's going to be okay," Tara stated. "A baby is a wonderful blessing."

"What did Gray say?" Lucy asked, easing back slightly.

Kate sniffed and attempted to gather herself together. "He proposed," she whispered.

"That's great," Tara exclaimed. "I always thought you two would end up together."

Swiping her face with the back of her hand, Kate pulled in a shaky breath. "I turned him down."

Tara gripped her shoulder. "What?"

"I'm not settling," Kate explained. "I want to marry someone who loves me, who isn't marrying me because of some family pressure or a pregnancy."

Kate stepped back to get some space. She didn't want to cry about this, didn't want pity. She wanted to figure out what her next step should be and she needed to be logical about it.

Maneuvering around her friends, who continued to stare at her as if she'd break again, Kate went to the sofa and sank into the corner.

"He proposed before I told him about the baby," she explained. "He's got that offer to sell the bar and his father has been on him for years to settle down. Gray wants to move ahead with the deal and figured if we got married, maybe his dad wouldn't be so upset about losing Gallagher's. Then when I told him about the baby, well, he thinks it's only logical."

Tara sat on the edge of the accent chair across from the sofa. "What's logical is that you should tell him how you really feel so the two of you can move on."

"You do love him, right?" Lucy asked as she sat in the chair right next to Tara's hip. "I don't mean like you love us as your friends. I mean, you love Gray. I know you do or you never would've slept with him."

Kate couldn't deny it—she didn't want to. She was tired of the sneaking, the secrets, the emotions.

"I do," she whispered. "But it's irrelevant because he doesn't see me like that."

"Men are blind." Lucy reached over to pat Kate's knee. "Sometimes you have to bang them over the head in order for them to see the truth. You need to be honest with Gray. He should know how you feel."

Kate had put her love out there before. She'd had a ring on her finger and a dress in her closet, but that love—or what she'd thought was love—had been thrown back in her face.

She loved Gray more than she ever did Chris. Gray was… well, he was everything. How would she handle it if he rejected her? At least if she kept her feelings locked inside her heart, they could remain friends, raise the baby and not muddle up their relationship with one-sided love.

"How are you feeling, other than Gray?" Tara asked. "Physically, I mean. Have you been sick?"

"Gray made me potatoes and ham for breakfast and the smell woke me when my stomach started rolling. Sick doesn't begin to describe my mornings."

Lucy's eyes widened. "He made you breakfast? That's so sweet."

Kate laughed. "He's always taken care of me. That's not the problem."

"The key to any good relationship is communication," Tara stated, and the wistfulness in her tone had Kate turning her focus on her. "Trust me. You need to tell him how you feel."

Kate tucked her hair behind her ears and wondered what would be best. Baring her heart to Gray as to her true feelings or just waiting to see what happened? For all she knew, he would sell the bar, go on some grand adventure to find himself and then discover that he never wanted to return. Then what?

"I honestly don't know what to do," she muttered. "I don't want him to feel sorry for me or think I fell in love with him because of the pregnancy. I've loved him... I don't even know how long. Maybe forever, but I didn't realize it until recently."

Lucy grabbed Kate's hand. "Well, right now let's focus on you and this baby. I'm confident Gray will come around."

Kate wished she had Lucy's confidence and Tara's courage. But this was her life and this pregnancy was the biggest thing that had ever happened to her. And she didn't want to put her heart on the line again because she'd been right from the very beginning. She could lose Gray's friendship if all of this went wrong. Losing the one constant man in her life wasn't an option. Especially now that the same man would be needed as a constant for their baby.

Gray set the glass of sweet tea on the counter in front of Sam. The bar didn't open for another hour and Sam had stopped by after a long week at his new job. Gray admired the man for putting his family first, for selling his own company and humbling himself to get counseling before going to work for another construction company.

He'd helped himself but may never get his wife back. The harsh reality was a bitch to bear, Gray was sure. Sam was a great guy who'd made poor decisions.

"Are you really selling the bar?" Sam asked, gripping the frosted glass.

Gray flattened his palms on the rolled edge of the bar. "I am. I haven't contacted the guy from Knoxville yet, but I plan on calling Monday morning."

"What does your dad say about it?"

Gray didn't like to think of the disappointment he'd seen in his father's eyes. He knew his dad wanted to keep the bar in the family, but would ultimately support Gray no matter what.

The problem was, Gray wasn't a hundred percent sure what he wanted. He did know that the money from the sale would put him in a perfect spot to provide for Kate and the baby.

He hadn't mentioned the baby to his dad because that

would've brought up a whole other set of issues…like the fact that she wouldn't marry him.

But he knew where her doubts were coming from. Kate had been left so shaken when her parents had passed. Then her fiancé had revealed his true colors and broken her heart. Gray never wanted her to question where her foundation was again. He knew she was scared with this pregnancy—hell, he was, too. But there was nothing he wouldn't do for her even if she refused to marry him.

"Dad isn't happy," Gray finally replied. "But he respects my decision. He'd like to see me settled down with a wife and a bunch of little Gallaghers running around and gearing up to pass this place to them."

Sam took a hearty drink of his tea and set the glass back down. "That's not what you want, I take it."

Gray gave a slight shrug, feeling something tug on his heart. "I don't know what I want, but has been on my mind."

Especially now.

"It's not for everyone, that's for sure." Sam slid his thumb over the condensation of his mug. "Tara is everything and when you find a love like that, it's worth fighting for. I really messed up, Gray. Don't learn from my mistakes."

Gray gritted his teeth and tried to sort through the thoughts scrolling through his head.

The most dominant thought was love. Love worth fighting for. He loved Kate. Hadn't he told her as much? They'd loved each other for years, so why was she so adamant about not marrying him? Wasn't any level of love a good basis for a marriage?

But she'd told him she wouldn't settle, that she wanted to be with a man who loved her the way a husband should love his wife.

He didn't even know what that meant. He thought she'd be happy with him, that they could be happy together. Obviously she had other expectations about her future.

"How are things with Tara?" Gray asked.

Sam shrugged. "Still the same. We get along for Marley and we're always civil, but it seems so shallow, you know? We just go through the days, same cycle, same fake smiles, like we're both not hurting."

Gray hated seeing his friends so torn. Yes, Sam had made mistakes, but he was human and he'd fought like hell to get clean and make up for the pain he'd caused.

Is this how Gray and Kate would be? Would they be moving through the days just living civilly and trying not to break? Would they bounce their child back and forth and pretend everything was okay?

And what would happen if Kate wanted to go on a date or brought a man home?

Jealousy spiraled through him at the mere thought of another man in Kate's life. Another man in their child's life.

Gray went about getting the bar ready to open. He chatted with his employees when they came in the back door and he welcomed the first customers who started to filter in. Sam remained on his stool, sipping his tea, then finally beer. Gray made sure to always keep an eye on his friend when he came in, and Sam usually limited his drinking to one or two beers. He seemed to be on the road to getting his life back under control.

Too bad Gray couldn't say the same.

CHAPTER SEVENTEEN

"THIS WAS A MISTAKE," Kate growled as Lucy practically dragged her inside the front door of Gallagher's. "A pregnant woman shouldn't be hanging out at the bar."

Lucy held onto her arm. "This is exactly where that pregnant lady should be when the man she loves is the owner. Besides, Tara is home with Marley tonight and Noah took Piper on a father-daughter date to the movies. I wanted to get out, so you're stuck with me."

Kate shouldn't be here. Then again, she shouldn't have put on her favorite dress and curled her hair, either. She didn't do those things for Gray. Absolutely not. She did them for herself because...

Fine. She did them for Gray because no matter how much she wished it, she couldn't just move on and forget her feelings for him. Pregnancy aside, Kate wanted Gray just as much as ever. Even if she hadn't been carrying his child, she would be completely in love with him.

For years she'd wanted a family of her own. She'd dreamed of it, in fact. Then she'd started her little business and focused on that after her world was rocked when Chris left. Now she was being given a second chance at a family, but Gray wasn't on board...not in the way she needed him to be.

Inside Gallagher's, an upbeat country song was blasting as several couples danced. The tables were full, except for one table right smack-dab in the middle of the floor. Fabulous. Why couldn't their usual corner booth be open? That real estate should always be on reserve for her.

Kate dropped to the hard wooden seat and hung her purse on the back. This was not ideal, not at all. Here she was, front and center of the bar, almost as if fate was mocking her.

A slow, twangy song filled the space and even more couples flooded to the dance floor.

"Fancy seeing you here."

Kate turned around, barely registering the cheesy line and her ex before he whisked her out of her seat and spun her toward the dance floor.

In a blur, she saw Lucy's shocked face.

"Chris, what in the world," she said, trying to wriggle free of his grip on her hand. "I don't want to dance."

Banding an arm around her waist, he took her free hand in his and maneuvered them right into the midst of the dancers.

"Just one dance," he said, smiling down at her as if he had every right to hold her. "Surely you can give me three minutes to talk and then I'll leave you alone."

Kate didn't want to give him three seconds, let alone three minutes. She didn't get a chance to say anything because Chris was jerked from her and then Gray stood towering over him.

"You're Chris?" Gray asked, his body taut with tension.

Kate stepped forward and put her hand on his back. "Don't, Gray."

Ignoring her, he took a half step forward, causing Chris to shove at Gray. "I'm talking to Kate, if you don't mind."

"I actually do mind," Gray growled over the music. A crowd had formed around them.

"It's fine," Kate insisted. She didn't want an altercation.

"You heard the lady," Chris said with a smirk. "It's fine. Now go back to making drinks."

Kate didn't have time to react as Gray's fist drew back and landed right in the middle of Chris's face. Her ex stumbled back, landing on a table and upending another one.

Gray shook his hand out and Kate stepped around to stand in front of him, worried he'd go at Chris again. The last thing Gray needed was to get in a fight in his own bar. That wouldn't be good for business.

"Stop it," she demanded.

The look on his face was pure fury. Finally, he took his gaze from Chris and landed it on her. "Keep your boyfriend out of my bar."

Kate drew her brows in and dropped her hand. "What is wrong with you?"

"What the hell?"

Kate turned around to see some guy helping Chris up. The stranger turned his attention to Gray. "This is how you run a business?"

Gray moved around Kate and walked past Chris, the stranger and the crowd. Kate stared at his retreating back and was startled when a hand fell on her shoulder. She spun around to find Lucy.

"That was...territorial."

Kate shook her head. "What just happened?"

"I'd say your guy got jealous, but who was the other man who stepped in?"

Gray stalked back over to Chris and the other man. Kate watched, waiting and hoping there wasn't going to be another altercation.

"The bar isn't for sale." Gray stood directly in front of the two guys. Chris held his jaw, working it back and forth. "You two can get the hell out of here and don't come back."

Gray and Chris sparring wasn't something she thought she'd ever see. But no doubt about it, Chris wasn't going to win this fight no matter what he threatened.

"I'll sue you," Chris spouted. "My partner and I were going to give you a lot of money for this place."

"Sue me," Gray said, crossing his arms over his massive chest as if he didn't have a care in the world. "But leave."

He turned back around and went back to the bar. Kate watched as he started making drinks like his whole life hadn't just changed. Chris was a bastard, no doubt about it.

He'd wanted to sell the bar. He'd been pretty set on doing just that. What had changed his mind? He hadn't said a word to her. Between Gray's silence and Chris's betrayal, Kate wasn't sure how to feel, but pissed was a great starting point.

Then dread filled her. Had he done this because of the baby? Was he giving up what he truly wanted to make her happy? Because he'd done that with his father, when he'd taken over the bar after his tour of duty just to appease him. And here he was putting his own needs aside again. Kate intended to find out why.

Chris and his business partner turned and left, leaving many talking about what had just happened. Obviously the other guy was the one who'd made Gray the exorbitant offer.

"I can't believe he just hit him," Kate muttered.

Lucy laughed. "I recall him hitting another guy who got in your face several months ago."

Kate ran a hand through her hair as she met Gray's dark eyes across the bar. "At least he's consistent."

"Heard you made a little scene at the bar last night."

Gray rubbed his eyes and attempted to form a coherent sentence. His father had called way too early, knowing full well that Gray would still be asleep. The man had run the same bar for thirty years. He knew the routine.

"Nothing I couldn't handle."

Gray eased up in bed and leaned against the headboard because he knew his father didn't randomly call just to chat.

"Also heard you turned down the offer to sell."

Gray blew out a breath. Yeah. He had. That hadn't been an

easy decision, but definitely the right one. The second he'd seen Kate in another man's arms, Gray had lost it. Then, on his way over, he'd heard Kate call the guy Chris and Gray nearly exploded. Okay, he did explode, but that guy deserved the punch—and more—for what he'd done years ago.

Kate was his family. Kate and their child was his family. The future had seemed so clear in that moment. All the times he'd waited for a sign, waited for some divine intervention to tell him what to do. But Kate and their family was everything. And he'd found that he wanted to continue that tradition with his child, boy or girl.

"I'm keeping the bar," Gray confirmed.

"Who changed your mind?" his dad asked.

Gray instantly pictured Kate. He couldn't help but smile though he was dead tired. He'd screwed up things with her. He'd legit botched up their relationship from the friendship to the intimacy. But he had a plan.

"I just realized nothing is missing from my life," Gray replied. "I'm staying here and Gallagher's will remain in the family."

"That was a lot of money to turn down, son."

Funny, but that didn't bother him anymore. "It was," he agreed. "Family means more."

Family meant *everything*.

He needed to tell his dad about the pregnancy, but he wanted to talk to Kate first. He had quite a bit to talk to her about, actually.

"I'm proud of you," his dad finally said. "Your grandfather would be, too, knowing you decided to stay in Stonerock, keep the tradition alive."

A lump formed in Gray's throat. "I wouldn't be anywhere else."

"Well, I guess I'll let you get back to sleep," his dad chuckled. "But Gray. Let's lay off the hitting. I know you have a thing for Kate, but control yourself."

His dad hung up before Gray could say anything about Kate or his self-control. He tossed his phone onto the rumpled sheet next to his hip. Raking his hands over his face, Gray attempted to sort his thoughts, his plans. Today he was taking back his life. Taking what he'd always wanted, but never knew he was missing.

And Kate wasn't going to get away again.

CHAPTER EIGHTEEN

SHE HADN'T SEEN Gray since the night before last. He'd punched Chris, turned down an enormous business deal and gone back to brooding.

Out of the blue, he'd texted this morning to tell her she'd left something at his apartment. There was no way she'd left anything there because she was meticulous about her stuff and knew where everything was.

Clearly he wanted her there for another reason. Kate found herself sipping her ginger ale and clutching a cracker as she mounted the outside back steps to the bar apartment.

Shoving the rest of the cracker in her mouth, she gripped the knob and eased the door open.

"Gray?" she called out as she stepped inside.

She'd never knocked before, so she didn't now, plus he knew she was coming.

Kate stepped into the living area and stopped short. The picture over the sofa was no longer the tacky *Dogs Playing Poker*. Tears pricked her eyes as she stepped closer to the image, one she'd seen so many times, but never like this.

A young Kate stared back at her. On either side of her in the portrait were her parents. All three smiling, not knowing what the future held. Kate had this exact picture in her bedroom.

"You like it?"

Kate was startled as Gray's easy question pulled her from the moment. Without turning, she nodded. Emotions formed heavy in her throat as her eyes burned with unshed tears.

"I remember that day so vividly," she told him, taking in every feature of her parents' faces. "We'd just gone for a picnic at one of the state parks. Then Dad took us on a small hike. My mom tripped on a rock and tore a hole in her tennis shoe. We laughed because she was always so clumsy."

She could still hear her mother's laugh—so sweet, almost wistful. "Not a day goes by that I don't miss them."

"They'd be proud of you."

Kate smiled as she turned to face Gray. "I hope so. I wonder what they'd think of me becoming a mother. Not having mine right now is…"

She blew out a breath and tried to gather her thoughts.

"I'm sure it's difficult," he told her as he remained in the doorway to the bedroom. "My mother passed when I was little, so I don't remember her. You're going to be a great mother and you've got those fond memories that will help."

She met his gaze, biting her bottom lip to cease the quivering.

"And you've got me," he added.

Kate blinked away the moisture and turned back to look at the picture. "Why is this hanging here?" she asked.

"This is your birthday present. It didn't come in on time, but I want you to have it."

This is what he'd done for her. For years he'd given her chocolate-covered strawberries, and this year had been no different. But he'd gone a step further and done something so thoughtful, so unique. Damn it, why did love have to be a one-way street with him?

"How did you get a copy?" she asked.

"Social media. I pulled it from one of your accounts and had it blown up on the canvas."

Crossing her arms, Kate turned her attention back to Gray. "If it's my birthday present, why is it hanging here?"

"Because you didn't like the other painting."

Confused, Kate shook her head. "I don't understand."

Gray pushed off the doorway and closed the distance between them. He stood directly in front of her, within touching distance, but didn't reach for her. As she studied the fine lines around his eyes, she realized he was tired. Had he not slept lately? Was he regretting his decision not to sell the bar?

"You and this baby are my priority now," he stated simply. "Not the bar, not moving and taking that money. Nothing else matters but my family."

What? Did he mean...

"I don't care where we take the picture I got you," he went on. "If you want to live here, we leave it here. You want to stay in your house, we hang it there. Our child will know your parents and I want to create a family with you."

"Gray," she whispered.

She dropped her face to her hands as another wave of emotions overcame her. He was only saying this to appease his dad, to make his father see that Gray was ready to settle down.

Kate swiped her face and met Gray's eyes. "We've been over this."

Now he did reach for her. Those large, strong hands framed her face. "No, we haven't, because we're about to have a whole new conversation. I need your undivided attention when I tell you I'm in love with you."

Kate's heart clenched. She stared up at him, gripped his wrists, and murmured, "You—you're in love with me? As in..."

"As in I want to make you my wife, not because of the baby and not because I'm staying here and keeping the bar." A ghost of a smile formed on his lips. "All these years I thought there was a void, but there wasn't. You were here all along and the only thing missing was having you even deeper in my life. That was the void. I need you, Kate. I know you'd be fine without me and we could share joint custody of our baby, but I want this life with you. I want this child and more with you."

Tears spilled and there was no way she could even think of holding them back. "You're serious?"

Gray laughed, then nipped at her lips. "You think I'd get rid of my dog picture for just anybody? I love you, Kate. I love this baby."

"But you were so angry the other night and I thought…"

"I wasn't angry with you," he assured her. "I was angry with that jerk who held you in his arms. I was angry with myself for being a dick to you, for not realizing sooner exactly how much you mean to me."

Gripping his wrists tighter, she so hoped he meant that. Every part of her wanted him to love her, to love this baby and to want to be a united family.

"Are you sure this isn't because of the baby?" she repeated.

"It's because of us," he stated, swiping the moisture from her cheeks. "If you weren't pregnant, I'd still be in love with you. I'd still want to spend my life with you."

"Spend your life with me?"

Gray let out a soft chuckle as he stepped back and dropped his hands. "You keep answering me with questions."

Kate watched as he went to the bedroom and came out a moment later holding something behind his back.

"I got something else for you."

Honestly, she wasn't sure how much more she could take. Between the photo and the declaration of love, she had more than she'd ever wanted.

Gray pulled out a thick book from behind his back. No. It wasn't a book at all.

Kate busted out laughing. "A planner?"

Gray got down on one knee and her breath caught in her throat. "Not just any planner, babe. Our life starts now. Marry me."

The front of the planner had a big gold heart on a white background. Gray opened the cover to reveal an attached satin ribbon to use for marking pages.

"Gray," she gasped.

Tied to the satin ribbon was a ring.

"I was just going to propose with the planner because I realize that's more important than jewelry to you," he joked. "But I hope you'll take this ring. It was my mother's. My dad saved it for me to give to the woman I love. There's nobody else I would ever give this ring to."

Kate's nausea chose that moment to make an appearance. She swayed on her feet, and Gray instantly came to his and wrapped an arm around her waist.

"I hope that's the baby and not my proposal," he said, guiding her to the couch.

"Definitely the baby," she told him.

He set the planner down on the old, antique trunk. "What can I get you?"

Kate closed her eyes, willing the dizziness to pass. "The ring on my finger, for starters."

She risked looking over at him and found him smiling, his eyes misting. "Are you going to cry?" she asked.

"Me? No. I don't cry." He sniffed as he untied the ring and held it up to her. "My dad said my mom loved pearls, but if you want a diamond or, hell… I don't know. I'll get anything, Kate. I just want you."

She held out her left hand. "And I want you and this ring that means so much to you."

Gray slid the ring onto her finger and let out a breath. "I so hoped this would fit."

Kate extended her arm and admired the ring. "It's perfect."

He pulled her into his arms. "We're perfect. I'm sorry I didn't see this before. When you said you needed me to love you like you deserve, I didn't get it."

Kate slid her arm around his abdomen and toed off her sandals. She propped her feet on the trunk and nestled deeper into his side.

"I've always loved you," he went on. "I even loved you like a husband should love a wife, but it took a reality check for me to fully realize it."

"Was it Chris coming back to town?"

"Part of it," he replied, trailing his fingertips up and down her arm. "When you weren't here, I felt empty. Once we slept together that first time, everything changed. I wanted you more and more, not just for the sex, but because I felt alone without you."

Kate smiled and eased up. "Then you took me camping to seduce me."

A naughty grin spread across his face. "I took you camping to mark an item off your bucket list. The seducing was just a handy by-product."

His face sobered as he studied her. "I meant what I said before about helping you fulfill your list. Have you heard any more from the genealogy expert?"

"Not yet, but he's starting his research and that's a step in the right direction."

Gray kissed the tip of her nose. "What do you say we go pick out that dog you wanted? Sprout, right?"

Her eyes widened. "Right now?"

With a shrug, Gray sat up. "Why not? The local shelter is open."

Of course he'd want a shelter dog. As if the man couldn't be more perfect. She reached out and fisted his unruly hair in her hands, pulling his mouth down to hers.

"You're so perfect," she muttered against his lips. "Let's go get our Sprout."

"Want to get married, too?"

Kate stilled. "Today?"

"You still looking for something spontaneous for your list?"

The planner inside her started to have anxiety, but the woman who stared at this man wanted him to be hers in every single way.

"Don't worry about the perfect venue or the gown or flowers," he told her. "Marry me, Kate. Now. Today."

She let out a laugh, completely shocked at her response. "Let's do it."

Gray lifted her up into his arms and held her tight. There was no one else on earth who could make her want to ignore her plans and throw caution to the wind. But Gray made her want to live in the moment.

"Maybe I should write this in my planner," she told him.

He set her down on her feet and smiled as he reached down to flip the pages of the planner. "I already did. I had a feeling you'd say yes."

Kate glanced at the open pages. Her heart leaped in her chest at Gray's writing on today's date: Making Kate My Wife.

She smacked a kiss on his cheek. "I'm going to turn you into a personal planner after all."

"As long as you're mine, I'll make a thousand lists with you."

EPILOGUE

SAM STOOD OUTSIDE his front door. Well, not *his* front door, since he and Tara had separated. Everyone thought their divorce was final and he'd never said otherwise. Tara had wanted the divorce, and he deserved all of her anger, but he'd never signed the papers. Sam Bailey never gave up and he sure as hell didn't intend to now—even when his entire world was slipping from his grasp.

He tapped his knuckles on the door—a door he'd installed when they'd bought the house only three years ago, a door he'd walked through thousands of times without thinking twice. Those days were gone. He'd severed his right to just walk in. At this point, he just hoped Tara talked to him.

The dead bolt flicked and Tara eased the door open, pulling her robe tighter around her chest.

"Sam, what are you doing here?"

She always looked gorgeous. Whether she wore her ratty old bathrobe or she had on a formfitting dress. His Tara was a complete knockout. Only she wasn't his anymore.

"Marley called me."

"What?"

"She said you'd been crying." He studied her face but didn't notice any traces of tears. "Everything okay?"

"I wasn't crying," she stated, but her swollen, red eyes gave her away. "Nothing for you to worry about. What else did she tell you?"

Sam swallowed. This wasn't the first time Marley had called him, trying to find a reason to get him to come over. He knew his little girl wanted her parents to live together again, but it just wasn't possible right now.

Even so, he and Tara had made it clear they would put Marley first at all times. They didn't want her to suffer any more than necessary. Keeping her happy, feeling secure, was top of their priority list.

"I'm fine." Tara licked her lips and raked a hand through her hair, then opened the door wider. "Do you want to come in and see her? She's getting ready for bed. Or I thought she was. I'm sorry. I had no idea she called you."

Again.

The word hovered between them because this wasn't the first time, and likely not the last. But Sam would come every single time if there was the slightest chance something was wrong with Tara.

"I shouldn't come in." Though he desperately wanted to. He wanted to walk in that door and tuck his daughter into bed and then go to his own room with his wife. "I don't want her to think she can keep doing this when there's nothing wrong."

But there was so much that was wrong. So much pain, so much heartache. All of it caused by his selfish desires, his addiction. An addiction he'd put ahead of his own family.

Tara glanced over her shoulder, then eased out the front door and closed it at her back. Sam adjusted his stance to make room for her. The glow of the porch lights illuminated her green eyes. It was those wide, expressive eyes that had initially drawn him to her.

"I know you're trying to move forward, to seek forgiveness or even more from me." She looked down to her clasped hands and shook her head. "But you can't keep leaving notes, Sam."

That's how he'd originally started to get her attention when he was serious about dating her. Stonerock was a small town, so they'd known each other for years, but something had shifted. He'd leave random notes asking her out and then, once they were together all the time, he'd leave little love notes. He'd done that for years, wanting her to know how special she was.

He'd messed up. There was no denying the facts. All he could do now was try to prove to her, to Marley that he was the man they needed him to be. No matter how long it took.

"I'm a patient man," he told her, fisting his hands at his sides because he wanted to reach out and touch her. He wanted to brush her hair back from her face and feel the silkiness of her skin once more. "I know I hurt you. I know I hurt Marley. But you know me, babe. I'm going to make this right."

"It's over," she whispered. "I don't want to keep dragging this out. What happened is in the past and we both need to move forward. It's not healthy, Sam."

"No, it's not," he agreed. "I'm starting over, Tara. I'm trying one day at a time."

"Maybe you should just sign the papers," she whispered through her emotion as she went back inside.

The door closed. The click of the lock seemed to echo in the dark of the night. But Sam couldn't give up. His family needed him.

He had every intention of proving to Tara that he could be a better man.

* * * * *

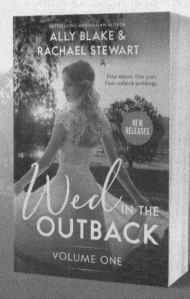 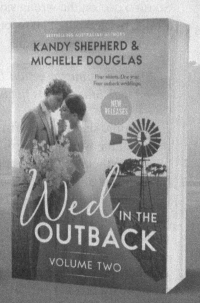

Keep reading for an excerpt of
Gift-Wrapped In Her Wedding Dress
by Kandy Shepherd.
Find it in the
Sydney Brides anthology,
out now!

CHAPTER ONE

SO HE'D GOT on the wrong side of the media. Again. Dominic's words, twisted out of all recognition, were all over newspapers, television and social media.

Billionaire businessman Dominic Hunt refuses to sleep out with other CEOs in charity event for homeless.

Dominic slammed his fist on his desk so hard the pain juddered all the way up his arm. He hadn't *refused* to support the charity in their Christmas appeal, just refused the invitation to publicly bed down for the night in a cardboard box on the forecourt of the Sydney Opera House. His donation to the worthy cause had been significant—but anonymous. *Why wasn't that enough?*

He buried his head in his hands. For a harrowing time in his life there had been no choice for him but to sleep rough for real, a cardboard box his only bed. He couldn't go there again—not even for a charity stunt, no matter how worthy. There could be no explanation—he would not share the secrets of his past. *Ever.*

With a sick feeling of dread he continued to read onscreen the highlights of the recent flurry of negative press about him and his company, thoughtfully compiled in a report by his Director of Marketing.

Predictably, the reporters had then gone on to rehash his well-known aversion to Christmas. Again he'd been misquoted. It was true he loathed the whole idea of celebrating Christmas. But not for the reasons the media had so fancifully contrived. Not because he was a *Scrooge*. How he hated that label and the erroneous aspersions that he didn't ever give to charity. Despaired that he was included in a round-up of Australia's Multi-Million-Dollar Misers. *It couldn't be further from the truth.*

He strongly believed that giving money to worthy causes should be conducted in private—not for public acclaim. But this time he couldn't ignore the name-calling and innuendo. He was near to closing a game-changing deal on a joint venture with a family-owned American corporation run by a man with a strict moral code that included obvious displays of philanthropy.

Dominic could not be seen to be a Scrooge. He had to publicly prove that he was not a miser. But he did not want to reveal the extent of his charitable support because to do so would blow away the smokescreen he had carefully constructed over his past.

He'd been in a bind. Until his marketing director had suggested he would attract positive press if he opened his harbourside home for a lavish fund-raising event for charity. 'Get your name in the newspaper for the right reasons,' he had been advised.

Dominic hated the idea of his privacy being invaded but he had reluctantly agreed. He wanted the joint venture to happen. If a party was what it took, he was prepared to put his qualms aside and commit to it.

The party would be too big an event for it to be organised in-house. His marketing people had got outside companies involved. Trouble was the three so-called 'party planners' he'd been sent so far had been incompetent and he'd shown them the door within minutes of meeting. Now there was a fourth. He glanced down at the eye-catching card on the desk in front of

him. Andrea Newman from a company called Party Queens—
No party too big or too small the card boasted.

Party Queens. It was an interesting choice for a business
name. Not nearly as stitched up as the other companies that had
pitched for this business. But did it have the gravitas required?
After all, this event could be the deciding factor in a deal that
would extend his business interests internationally.

He glanced at his watch. This morning he was working from
his home office. Ms Newman was due to meet with him right
now, here at his house where the party was to take place. Despite
the attention-grabbing name of the business, he had no reason
to expect Party Planner Number Four to be any more impressive than the other three he'd sent packing. But he would give
her twenty minutes—that was only fair and he made a point
of always being fair.

On cue, the doorbell rang. Punctuality, at least, was a point
in Andrea Newman's favour. He headed down the wide marble
stairs to the front door.

His first impression of the woman who stood on his porch
was that she was attractive, not in a conventionally pretty way
but something rather more interesting—an angular face framed
by a tangle of streaked blonde hair, a wide generous mouth, unusual green eyes. So attractive he found himself looking at her
for a moment longer than was required to sum up a possible
contractor. And the almost imperceptible curve of her mouth
let him know she'd noticed.

'Good morning, Mr Hunt—Andie Newman from Party
Queens,' she said. 'Thank you for the pass code that got me
through the gate. Your security is formidable, like an eastern
suburbs fortress.' Was that a hint of challenge underscoring her
warm, husky voice? If so, he wasn't going to bite.

'The pass code expires after one use, Ms Newman,' he said,
not attempting to hide a note of warning. The three party planners before her were never going to get a new pass code. But
none of them had been remotely like her—in looks or manner.

She was tall and wore a boldly patterned skirt of some silky fine fabric that fell below her knees in uneven layers, topped by a snug-fitting rust-coloured jacket and high heeled shoes that laced all the way up her calf. A soft leather satchel was slung casually across her shoulder. She presented as smart but more unconventional than the corporate dark suits and rigid brief-cases of the other three—whose ideas had been as pedestrian as their appearances.

'Andie,' she replied and started to say something else about his security system. But, as she did, a sudden gust of balmy spring breeze whipped up her skirt, revealing long slender legs and a tantalising hint of red underwear. Dominic tried to do the gentlemanly thing and look elsewhere—difficult when she was standing so near to him and her legs were so attention-worthy.

'Oh,' she gasped, and fought with the skirt to hold it down, but no sooner did she get the front of the skirt in place, the back whipped upwards and she had to twist around to hold it down. The back view of her legs was equally as impressive as the front. He balled his hands into fists by his sides so he did not give into the temptation to help her with the flyaway fabric.

She flushed high on elegant cheekbones, blonde hair tou-sled around her face, and laughed a husky, uninhibited laugh as she battled to preserve her modesty. The breeze died down as quickly as it had sprung up and her skirt floated back into place. Still, he noticed she continued to keep it in check with a hand on her thigh.

'That's made a wonderful first impression, hasn't it?' she said, looking up at him with a rueful smile. For a long mo-ment their eyes connected and he was the first to look away. *She was beautiful.*

As she spoke, the breeze gave a final last sigh that ruffled her hair across her face. Dominic wasn't a fanciful man, but it seemed as though the wind was ushering her into his house.

'There are worse ways of making an impression,' he said gruffly. 'I'm interested to see what you follow up with.'

* * *

Andie wasn't sure what to reply. She stood at the threshold of Dominic Hunt's multi-million-dollar mansion and knew for the first time in her career she was in serious danger of losing the professional cool in which she took such pride.

Not because of the incident with the wind and her skirt. Or because she was awestruck by the magnificence of the house and the postcard-worthy panorama of Sydney Harbour that stretched out in front of it. No. It was the man who towered above her who was making her feel so inordinately flustered. Too tongue-tied to come back with a quick quip or clever retort.

'Th...thank you,' she managed to stutter as she pushed the breeze-swept hair back from across her face.

During her career as a stylist for both magazines and advertising agencies, and now as a party planner, she had acquired the reputation of being able to manage difficult people. Which was why her two partners in their fledgling business had voted for her to be the one to deal with Dominic Hunt. Party Queens desperately needed a high-profile booking like this to help them get established. Winning it was now on her shoulders.

She had come to his mansion forewarned that he could be a demanding client. The gossip was that he had been scathing to three other planners from other companies much bigger than theirs before giving them the boot. Then there was his wider reputation as a Scrooge—a man who did not share his multitude of money with others less fortunate. He was everything she did not admire in a person.

Despite that, she been blithely confident Dominic Hunt wouldn't be more than she could handle. Until he had answered that door. Her reaction to him had her stupefied.

She had seen the photos, watched the interviews of the billionaire businessman, had recognised he was good-looking in a dark, brooding way. But no amount of research had prepared her for the pulse-raising reality of this man—tall, broad-shouldered, powerful muscles apparent even in his sleek tailored grey suit. He wasn't pretty-boy handsome. Not with that strong jaw, the crooked nose that looked as though it had been broken by a viciously aimed punch, the full, sensual mouth with the faded white scar on the corner, the spiky black hair. And then there was the almost palpable emanation of power.

She had to call on every bit of her professional savvy to ignore the warm flush that rose up her neck and onto her cheeks, the way her heart thudded into unwilling awareness of Dominic Hunt, not as a client but as a man.

She could not allow that to happen. This job was too important to her and her friends in their new business. *Anyway, dark and brooding wasn't her type.* Her ideal man was sensitive and sunny-natured, like her first lost love, for whom she felt she would always grieve.

She extended her hand, willing it to stay steady, and forced a smile. 'Mr Hunt, let's start again. Andie Newman from Party Queens.'

His grip in return was firm and warm and he nodded acknowledgement of her greeting. If a mere handshake could send shivers of awareness through her, she could be in trouble here.

Keep it businesslike. She took a deep breath, tilted back her head to meet his gaze full-on. 'I believe I'm the fourth party planner you've seen and I don't want there to be a fifth. I should be the person to plan your event.'

If he was surprised at her boldness, it didn't show in his scrutiny; his grey eyes remained cool and assessing.

'You'd better come inside and convince me why that should be the case,' he said. Even his voice was attractive—deep and measured and utterly masculine.

'I welcome the opportunity,' she said in the most confident voice she could muster.

She followed him into the entrance hall of the restored nineteen-twenties house, all dark stained wood floors and cream marble. A grand central marble staircase with wrought-iron balustrades split into two sides to climb to the next floor. This wasn't the first grand home she'd been in during the course of her work but it was so impressive she had to suppress an impulse to gawk.

'Wow,' she said, looking around her, forgetting all about how disconcerted Dominic Hunt made her feel. 'The staircase. It's amazing. I can just see a choir there, with a chorister on each step greeting your guests with Christmas carols as they step into the house.' Her thoughts raced ahead of her. Choristers' robes in red and white? Each chorister holding a scrolled parchment printed with the words to the carol? What about the music? A string quartet? A harpsichord?

'What do you mean?' he said, breaking into her reverie.

Andie blinked to bring herself back to earth and turned to look up at him. She smiled. 'Sorry. I'm getting ahead of myself. It was just an idea. Of course I realise I still need to convince you I'm the right person for your job.'

'I meant about the Christmas carols.'

So he would be that kind of pernickety client, pressing her for details before they'd even decided on the bigger picture. Did she need to spell out the message of 'Deck the Halls with Boughs of Holly'?

She shook her head in a don't-worry-about-it way. 'It was just a top-of-mind thought. But a choir would be an amazing use of the staircase. Maybe a children's choir. Get your guests into the Christmas spirit straight away, without being too cheesy about it.'

'It isn't going to be a Christmas party.' He virtually spat the word *Christmas*.

'But a party in December? I thought—'

He frowned and she could see where his reputation came from as his thick brows drew together and his eyes darkened. 'Truth be told, I don't want a party here at all. But it's a necessary evil—necessary to my business, that is.'

'Really?' she said, struggling not to jump in and say the wrong thing. A client who didn't actually want a party? This she hadn't anticipated. Her certainty that she knew how to handle this situation—this man—started to seep away.

She gritted her teeth, forced her voice to sound as conciliatory as possible. 'I understood from your brief that you wanted a big event benefiting a charity in the weeks leading up to Christmas on a date that will give you maximum publicity.'

'All that,' he said. 'Except it's not to be a Christmas party. Just a party that happens to be held around that time.'

Difficult and demanding didn't begin to describe this. But had she been guilty of assuming December translated into Christmas? Had it actually stated that in the brief? She didn't think she'd misread it.

She drew in a calming breath. 'There seems to have been a misunderstanding and I apologise for that,' she said. 'I have the official briefing from your marketing department here.' She patted her satchel. 'But I'd rather hear your thoughts, your ideas for the event in your own words. A successful party plan comes from the heart. Can we sit down and discuss this?'

He looked pointedly at his watch. Her heart sank to the level of the first lacing on her shoes. She did not want to be the fourth party planner he fired before she'd even started her pitch. 'I'll give you ten minutes,' he said.

He led her into a living room that ran across the entire front of the house and looked out to the blue waters of the harbour and its icons of the Sydney Harbour Bridge and the Opera House. Glass doors opened out to a large terrace. *A perfect summer party terrace.*

Immediately she recognised the work of one of Sydney's most fashionable high-end interior designers—a guy who only worked with budgets that started with six zeros after them. The room worked neutral tones and metallics in a nod to the art deco era of the original house. The result was masculine but very, very stylish.

What an awesome space for a party. But she forced thoughts of the party out of her head. She had ten minutes to win this business. Ten minutes to convince Dominic Hunt she was the one he needed.

Subscribe and fall in love with a Mills & Boon series today!

You'll be among the first to read stories delivered to your door monthly and enjoy great savings.

WE SIMPLY LOVE ROMANCE